FAMILY MONEY

FAMILY MONEY

Doris Shannon

St. Martin's Press
New York

Design by Manny Paul

Library of Congress Cataloging in Publication Data
Shannon, Doris.
    Family money.
    I. Title.   ○
PR9199.3.S49F3   1984   813'.54   83-26880
ISBN 0-312-28145-5

First Edition
10 9 8 7 6 5 4 3 2 1

This book is for Thomas L. Dunne

FAMILY MONEY

PART I
Poor Relations

— 1 —

Elizabeth paused beside the marble-topped table and flipped through a stack of mail on the silver salver. Glancing around the hall, she lifted an envelope and studied it. Heavy, good quality paper, William's name and address in a dainty feminine hand, a Boston postmark. She sniffed, detected a faint scent, and frowned. Boston? Who did William know in Boston?

Sliding it under a manila envelope, she glanced at the edition of *The New York Times* that was propped beside the telephone. Black headlines screamed HEIR TO THRONE OF AUSTRIA-HUNGARY SLAIN BY SERB NATIONALIST AT SARAJEVO! Just where was Sarajevo? Probably somewhere in the Balkans. Some Austrian archduke killed in a tinpot Balkan city meant nothing to her. On this June afternoon she was concerned with more personal worries. Why had William summoned her to his study? Her cousin was a man of rigid habits. On his return from the office he closeted himself before dinner, looked over his mail, and read the paper. In the three years Elizabeth had managed his home William had seldom broken this routine. And how long would he delay her? He was aware of her fear in going back to her rooming house in the dark.

She smiled grimly, the quick twitching movement of her lips designed to conceal her bad teeth. He would never consider having Briggs drive her home. Let Elizabeth take her chances on the dark streets.

Picking up the salver and the newspaper, she walked down the hall. She must speak to Hannah. This was the second time in a week the maid had been late in taking the mail to her master. William couldn't abide slackness and if Hannah wasn't careful she'd be out of a job. And New York in 1914 was no place to be unemployed.

Elizabeth tapped on the door, heard William's voice, and swung it open. He was a courteous man and rose as she entered the study. He took the salver and paper from her, glanced at the headline, and set both down at his elbow. Echoing her own thoughts, he said, "That maid Hannah, you must ginger her up. I've been waiting twenty minutes for my mail and then you have to bring it. Good positions aren't easy to find and there'll be no problem replacing her."

"Cookie is probably keeping her busy laying the table." She took a chair and continued, "As I've told you, there isn't an adequate staff to look after a house this size."

Pushing back his chair, he busied himself with a decanter and glass. Carefully he measured out a small amount of whiskey and added a large amount of soda. Elizabeth wistfully eyed another decanter. A fine dry sherry, and she would love a drop of sherry. But, courteous as he was, William would no more dream of offering her a drink that he would of having Briggs drive her home. Gingerly, she allowed her tongue to explore a back tooth. A twinge of pain lanced through her jaw and she withdrew the tip of her tongue. She should bring up her teeth again. These constant aches were driving her mad. Now, a drop of sherry might deaden that pain.

William took a sip of his drink, set the glass down, and reached for the silver humidor. While he clipped the cigar, sniffed it, rolled it between his palms, and finally scratched a match and applied flame to its tip, he gave her a lecture. "A well-run household does not require a large staff. Too many servants lead to sloth. Granted this house is large, but you must keep in mind that with only the boys and myself to look after, the work isn't all that arduous. You simply don't get enough work out of either Hannah or Sally. Cookie I can't complain about. She does her work well and manages with only one kitchen maid." He took a puff of his cigar, another sip from his glass. "I'm not unreasonable and certainly not stingy. But I do believe in full value for my dollar."

That certainly was the truth. William couldn't be called mean but he couldn't be called openhanded either. Hiding her resentment, Elizabeth glanced at the painted face framed in gilt and plush that hung on the wall behind his chair. It was a portrait of their grandfather and except for the old-fashioned clothes and the luxuriant side whiskers it could have been a likeness of William. The same strong bone structure, the same facial planes, gray eyes like chips of ice, a high bald dome, a fringe of light brown hair and, at the time the portrait was painted, about the same age—the early fifties. They had even both fathered two male children. Oliver Pendrell Meredith had sired her father Leon and William's father Peter. Elizabeth felt a surge of hate. Her grandfather, on a whim, had cut his older son off with a pittance and left everything, including this house, to his younger son and thence, of course, to this man facing her.

William noticed the direction of her eyes and swung around to look fondly up at the oil painting. "Grandfather never allowed this house to be mismanaged. I fear you take after your father, Elizabeth, and don't control your tendency toward extravagance."

Elizabeth nearly laughed aloud. Extravagance! Her face didn't betray her thoughts. She'd learned to hide her feelings. As her mother had told her, poor relatives must be meek. Meekness is the only defense they have. So meekly she bent her dark head and agreed, "Yes, William."

William was reaching for a ledger, the one with the blue cover. Oh God, Elizabeth thought, one of the household account books. Opening it, he found the page he was looking for and ran a finger down it. William's hands were beautiful, wide and powerful across the palms, long slender fingers, narrow tapering nails. He wore a heavy gold signet ring, their grandfather's. She'd often wondered if he was vain about those hands and decided he must be.

A narrow nail stopped and dug into the offending entry. "Lunches!"

"Lunches?"

"Extravagant lunches. For the last two months I've neglected to check the menus and look what I find when I do."

Bewildered, she stared at the page as he swung the ledger around. "They're the same lunches we've always served."

"'This is exactly the point I'm trying to make." Leaning

back, he lifted his glass. "Two months ago the boys transferred to their present school where lunch is provided. As they weren't home I've been taking my own meal either at my club or my office. These lunches were designed for the boys' hearty young appetites and for my own. You now have lunch by yourself. Look at the menu for today. Cold cuts—"

"From last night's roast . . ."

"Which might have been used as a casserole for dinner."

"You don't care for casseroles."

"No matter." Slender fingers beat out an impatient tattoo. "Thick soup, rolls, cheese. And dessert! Two kinds of dessert. Caramel pudding *and* pound cake. I've drawn up a sensible menu for your lunch. Before you leave take it to Cookie and inform her that, starting tomorrow, this will comprise your noonday meal. As you can see, it is more than adequate."

Elizabeth stared at the sheet of paper he handed her but she didn't see it. She told herself, I should stand up to him, I should tell him the servants are treated better than I am. Every morning I start work at seven and slave until six. I'm not allowed breakfast or dinner in this house. All I get is lunch and I have to sneak part of that home with me or I wouldn't have a decent dinner. She checked a sigh. William would only remind her of her *generous* salary. Hardly enough to pay for that miserable room and a little food. Nothing for clothes, not a spare cent to go to a dentist and have her teeth looked after.

"Adequate," he repeated firmly, "and nourishing. A clear soup, possibly beef broth, two rolls, and for a sweet a nice bowl of stewed fruit. After all, women are light eaters. Mother ate like a bird and my late wife also ate sparingly."

Neither of them, Elizabeth thought wrathfully, acted as glorified servants, running up and down five flights of stairs all day. But her mother had been right and Elizabeth said meekly, "As you wish, William."

For the first time since she'd entered the room he smiled. No tight grimace was necessary to conceal William's teeth. His teeth, like his sons', were white and even and beautifully cared for. Rebellion stirred in her breast. "There has been something that's disturbing me."

"Oh? By all means tell me."

"The boys have been—disrespectful to me."

His heavy brows arched and he knocked ash from his cigar. "George and Alan?"

"Not so much George. Mainly Alan."

"In what way has Alan showed disrespect?" William's lips set grimly. Gentlemanly behavior was strictly enforced in this house. Even from his younger and favorite son.

Elizabeth's hands twisted together. Absently, she noted their lack of beauty. They were the same shape as her cousin's but work and neglect had enlarged the knuckles, reddened and coarsened the skin. "Alan keeps calling me Tin Lizzie," she blurted, "and he makes sounds like a car horn at me."

He leaned forward and as he did his elbow touched the pile of mail and toppled it from the salver. He picked it up and stared down at the scented envelope with the feminine writing and the Boston postmark. Suddenly and astonishingly he blushed. Elizabeth stared from the envelope to him. Why the blush, the look of guilt? Hastily, he replaced the mail on the salver. "This, ah, behavior of Alan's doesn't sound so terrible, Elizabeth. After all, your name and . . ." He stopped, apparently to collect his thoughts, and glanced at the mail again. "Alan is wild about cars. He simply can't wait to learn to drive. You know he's always pestering me to allow Briggs to train him."

Not at the wheel of a Tin Lizzie, Elizabeth thought. With others William might be a careful man but with his sons and himself he was more than openhanded. His car was an imported one, a Panhard Levassor, with an open driver's seat and a luxurious *coupe de ville* body. It was a car unusual and expensive enough to incur envious stares. Aloud she said, "Alan does this in front of the servants and they giggle. William, I'm his cousin and a lady."

The word "lady" worked its usual magic. To William a lady was sacrosanct and Elizabeth, poor relative that she was, was a Meredith, which automatically made her a lady. "Be assured I'll speak to the young scamp. Alan means no harm, this is simply high spirits, but you're quite right. It is bordering on disrespect. Now, you'd better see Cookie about that menu change and then you're free to leave."

Politely dismissed, she rose. "It's late."

He consulted his heavy gold watch, digging it from his waistcoat. The coat bulged over a melon-shaped paunch. William was not a light eater. "So it is, barely time for me to change before dinner."

"It's getting dark, William."

"Nonsense. Barely dusk. However, you'd better scamper. The streets at night are scarcely the place for a lady alone."

Elizabeth bade him goodnight and he absently replied, but he was already reaching for the scented envelope. Crossing the hall, she checked the dining room. The table, which could easily seat twenty, had only three places laid at one end. She could find no fault with the array of crystal, china, and silver, and gave a small nod of approval at the centerpiece of pink roses and daisies she had arranged earlier. Behind the green baize door she found Cookie stirring a sauce. Cookie had been with William's family for years and she managed to fill all his qualifications for a perfect cook. Never pick a thin cook, he had confided in his cousin, and Cookie was far from thin. Her buxom figure was garbed in starched white and her graying hair neatly netted. At the sink her helper, a timid child of fifteen, was scraping vegetables. The errant Hannah scurried from the pantry and Elizabeth stopped her.

"Straighten your cap and change that apron before you serve. There's a stain on it. Mr. Meredith is displeased with you. You forgot to take the mail and paper to him at the proper time."

Hannah clapped a hand over her mouth, nearly dropping the plate she was carrying. "Oh Lawd! I'm sorry, Miss Elizabeth, but there was so much to do. The sideboard had to be turned out and trying to handle the china proper took so long. And 'fore that I—"

"No excuses," Cookie snapped. More kindly she added, "Good jobs aren't growing on trees, my girl. A lot of women walking the streets looking for work."

Hannah's face grayed, and as she set down the plate her hand trembled. Ships carrying immigrants crowded the docks of New York and each day streams of men, women, and children were unleashed on the city searching for work, any kind of work. Jobs as good as Hannah's were at a premium. The poor girl was thin, Elizabeth thought, and not strong. She always made a point of being kind to servants. In her own precarious position it was helpful at times. So she patted Hannah's trembling hand. "No matter how busy you are, do take time to see Mr. Meredith has no complaints."

She checked the food in the warming oven. The loin of pork was done to a turn, the potatoes roasted in meat drippings were brown and crisp. The odors made her mouth water. With a sigh she handed the menu change to the cook. "Mr. Meredith has decided on a new menu for lunch. Follow it exactly."

"Not enough here to keep a bird alive, Miss Elizabeth. And what about the leftover meat? The boys and master eat good but they never clean up a roast."

"Casseroles. I know Mr. Meredith doesn't care for them but the boys do and you can serve them for Saturday lunch and perhaps for supper on Sundays. Now, I'd better say goodnight and be on my way."

Leaving the cook scowling over the menu, Elizabeth went to the small room, once a butler's pantry, that William had set aside as her office. She closed the account book she'd been working on and picked up her covered wicker basket. The weight of it was comforting. Under the needlework were the remains of her last generous lunch—two thick slices of ham, a roll, a good sized chunk of cheese. A Spartan dinner but better than she'd have from now on.

In the hall she placed the basket on the marble-topped table and put on a hip length jacket as old and worn as her serge skirt. As she pinned on a shabby felt hat she gazed at her reflection in the oval mirror over the table. Elizabeth had the Meredith height and spare build. She also had the strong features and striking facial planes of the family. From her father's French mother she had inherited fine dark eyes, heavy dark eyebrows, and a thick head of hair so dark brown it looked black. She should have been handsome but wasn't. Her skin was sallow and inclined to be oily, and it was marred by small pocks from an adolescent skin problem. Her lips were tightly set to conceal the unsightly teeth, her smile merely a grimace, and when she spoke she moved her lips as little as possible. The thick hair was glossy but she had no time to style it fashionably, and pulled it from a center parting into a tight bun at the nape of her neck. Truly a spinster, Elizabeth thought, and the clothes helped not at all. Serge was too heavy for this time of year but she had only two decent summer dresses and they must be saved for good. Her shirtwaist was starched and immaculate, tiny ruffles painstakingly touched with an iron, but it was as old and worn as her suit. William was sixteen years her senior but right now she looked older than he did.

   · Then the dark eyes moved from her mirrored image to the mirror itself. An old mirror, encircled with gilt cherubs, as gay and lovely as the rest of this house. Taking a few steps, she gazed into the front drawing room. The beauty of the room, softly illuminated by table lamps, soothed her. Her grandfather, Oliver Pendrell Meredith, had taken his French wife mainly for the shipping line she eventually brought him, but Mariette Lafroux had brought more than that to her marriage. She'd had exquisite taste. Overriding her husband's desire for the dark clumsy furnishings of that era, she'd furnished her house with the dancing grace of cherry and rosewood and walnut. No heavy velvet gathered dust at her windows or shrouded the Adam mantel. Instead Mariette had hung silk, gossamer fine, over delicate lace. Silky Oriental rugs were spread on polished oak flooring. In only one room had Oliver Pendrell had his own way and that was in his bedroom. This room, now William's, was cluttered with the gloomy furniture of the mid-nineteenth century. When William's wife Ruth became mistress she had, either through wisdom or indifference, made few changes. As materials wore out she had simply replaced them as closely as possible. All she had added was a Louis Quinze chiffonier in her own room and hung on its wall a Greuze. In the dining room she had taken down a still life and replaced it with a charming tapestry.

   Of course, Elizabeth mused, changes had occurred through the years. William had had a good heating system installed, gas lights had given way to electricity, the bathrooms had been modernized, and for his wife, during her last illness, a small lift had been put in. The lift, which could have proved to be a godsend, was seldom used. William firmly believed such indulgences were only for the aged, the ill, or the infirm. Occasionally, when William was at his office, Elizabeth used it, but she didn't dare ride in it too often. Her cousin had an uncanny way of sensing what happened even if he was absent at the time.

Elizabeth was rudely jerked from her reverie. Behind her a sound, much like that of a car's horn, shrilled. She turned slowly, her features carefully expressionless. Her two young cousins, Alan in the lead, were trotting down the stairs. She regarded them with no affection. They'd changed their school clothes— duck trousers and blazers—and were dressed in dark suits for dinner. At eighteen George was as tall as his father, but slimmer, and he wore his brown hair parted in the middle and sleeked back with brilliantine. Elizabeth neither liked nor disliked the lad. His brother, two years younger, was a good-looking boy, pretty rather than handsome. Alan took after his mother. He was short and plump with a round face and a small full mouth. He had masses of light wavy hair, a lock of which fell over his rounded brow. Giving one more honk, he directed light blue eyes gleaming with malice at Elizabeth.

"There she is," he said to George in a singsong voice, "Tin Lizzie all ready to go home complete with her basket. Want a crank to get you started, Tin Lizzie?" He nudged her basket. "Bet you got it chock full of goodies for your pussy. Cousin Elizabeth has a nice ginger cat called Sussie she smuggles our food home for. How is Sussie? In good health I hope."

Elizabeth winced. Sussie had been dead for three years and Alan knew it. Only two creatures she'd ever loved and she'd lost both of them to the Merediths. Her father had died because of them and her cat had had to be destroyed because William refused to let her bring it into his house. My new landlady won't let me keep Sussie, she'd told William. She was the last present my father gave me and I love her. Well, he'd replied, you can't bring her here. Find a good home for the animal. No one will want her, Elizabeth pleaded, she's too old. No one had and that was the end of Sussie.

A gust of fury seized Elizabeth as she thought of her cat. She wished William and all his household dead. No, she wished something worse. She wanted William and his sons penniless and sick, wandering the streets as her own father had. She wanted him broken. But she hid her hatred under a composed smile, a twitch of a smile, an outward show of gratitude.

"Honk!" Alan called right in her face. "How's your cat, Cousin Elizabeth?"

A harmless fiction, she thought stonily, and I'm not even allowed that. Occasionally Cookie put some food in her basket, pretending, as all the servants did, that it was for Sussie. Saving her pride, but pride was a luxury not allowed Cousin Elizabeth. She regarded Alan's grinning face, wondering viciously how cocky he'd be when his father gave him the promised reprimand. William could be stern even with his favorite son and Alan was terrified of William's displeasure. So she merely twitched her smile at him and turned to leave. He gave a last honk but George wished her goodnight and mentioned she was late.

She shut the door behind her and hurried down the seven steps. It was dusk and the streetlights were glowing, little islands of light in the encroaching darkness. Soon it would be full dark and she knew she shouldn't linger but she couldn't resist pausing to look up at the house. With pride and yearning she drank it in. Oliver Meredith had not built this house of the brownstone used so extensively in the city but had imported Appalachian silver gray stone and in the twilight the facade glimmered more silver than gray. At the top of the steps a massive black door ornamented with a huge brass knocker that glinted like gold led into paradise for Elizabeth. Black and gold and silver, she thought dreamily, lamplight glowing through lace and silk, dinner about to be served on a gleaming table amid the scents of flowers, gracious bedrooms where Sally would be turning crisp sheets down over soft comforters. My home, Elizabeth thought, as much mine as William's, as much my father's as his.

Wrenching her eyes away, she hurried down the street. At least the room waiting was shelter and it did have the advantage of being within walking distance. The evening was warm and her jacket too heavy. She felt sweat between her shoulder blades, trickling down her armpits. Her feet in patched shoes were tired and swollen and her tooth ached. She thought of the loin of pork and her stomach rumbled audibly for food.

The district she was scurrying through was prosperous. Grandfather had built in an area that was fashionable in his time and fortunately had remained that way. Streetlights shone on substantial houses carefully maintained by armies of immigrant girls, clean streets and walks, a look of subdued luxury. But even here muggings and robberies occurred and danger to an unescorted woman could crouch behind a tree, lurk in the shadowed areaways. Behind her she heard the heavy thud of footsteps and her heart lurched as she quickened her steps.

"Miss Elizabeth, wait up," a voice called.

She darted a look over her shoulder and saw the gleam of brass buttons marching down a blue tunic. "Out late tonight, aren't you?" the policeman called.

Can't anyone say anything but that? she wondered. First William, then George, now this man. She played her assigned role. Meek and pleasant. "I was delayed, Officer Perkins."

"I'll walk a ways with you. Mr. Meredith should have sent you home in that grand car. The Stones' parlor maid had a bad time here t'other night. Some thug jumped her and threw her down and made off with her purse. Pretty badly bruised she was too." Elizabeth gasped and he said reassuringly, "'Course this area is a lot different from some. Safer. Take my last beat— Hell's Kitchen! Could tell things to make hair curl. Not fit for a lady's ears. The wife was sure pleased when I got this beat. Couldn't sleep nights for worrying I might get the Tenderloin next."

"How are your wife and daughters?"

His broad face split in a pleased smile. "Fine. Oldest girl going to be married soon. Nice young fellow. Policeman too."

As he majestically strode along with her she pretended interest in his offspring's doings. She remembered William's reaction when he found Perkins was dropping into the kitchen on his nightly rounds. "No harm in that," her cousin had said jovially. "There are worse things than having one of New York's Finest in the house, in the kitchen only of course. Tell Cookie to let the officer have a good warm and some refreshment."

That was the way it had been. Through the winter months Perkins could generally be found about nine each evening with his big feet stuck under the kitchen table sipping a mug of tea and munching on a sandwich. So she caught snatches of news about his family and made appropriate comments. At a corner he stopped, touched the rim of his hat, and told her, "Far as I can go with you, Miss Elizabeth. Keep close to the curb and I'll wait here until you're safely home."

As she turned down her own street she was comforted by the

thought that he would be watching. The few blocks that separated this street and the one where she worked were two different worlds. Opulence gave way to grubbiness, wealth to less than genteel poverty. The brownstones didn't look too bad under the streetlamps but daylight exposed flaking paint, grimy windows, areaways littered with trash cans and rubbish. The next block was even worse. Here the brownstones had been converted into businesses and an occasional lower floor into a saloon.

It was raining, a fine warm mist that clung to Elizabeth's hat and shoulders, dampened the knot of hair on her neck. With a sense of relief she turned into her walk. She sped up her steps, hoping Perkins was still stationed on the corner. As she closed the door behind her she glimpsed her landlady peering through the crack of the door leading to her own quarters.

"Ah, Miss Meredith. Home late tonight." Glacial eyes flicked at the wicker basket as though trying to see its contents. "Raining, is it?"

Elizabeth told her it was, forcing into her voice the same note she had used with the policeman. Ingratiating. She disliked Mrs. Clyde but couldn't afford to offend the old lady. The house was fairly clean, the rent cheap, and she didn't have to pay carfare to reach it.

"Care for a cup of tea?" Mrs. Clyde asked.

Elizabeth repressed a shudder. Mrs. Clyde's camomile tea was dreadful. She made a courteous refusal and partway up the stairs the shrill voice stopped her again. "Had to give third floor back his notice. Using too much gas. Cook, cook! That's all that man does. Told him how can a poor widow woman pay those bills."

"Generally," Elizabeth told her, "I have a cold dinner."

"Me too. Saves gas and just as nourishing."

Liar! Elizabeth thought. Smells of cooking wafted from Mrs. Clyde's room. Tonight she was cooking corned beef and cabbage. She wouldn't put it past that woman to snoop through the roomers' possessions. Stepping into her own room, she closed the door and leaned wearily against it. A center light glared down on the room. William persisted in calling this dump her 'flat.' Of course, he'd never deigned to set foot in it. When he'd asked her to manage his home she had eagerly offered to live in but he told her, "I'm sure you enjoy the privacy of your flat."

She clicked off the harsh ceiling light and turned on a table lamp. As night was kind to this street so dimmer light was kind to the room. It was square, the walls painted a dingy green, one window overlooking the street. It was clean with that barren cleanliness that shrieks poverty. She'd managed to hold on to a few of her parents' possessions and they looked out of place in the room. Leon Meredith's leather-covered armchair was flanked by a tiny malachite table bearing a green shaded lamp. Elizabeth's grandmother's desk sat in a corner. Tenderly, she ran a fingertip over the black and scarlet lacquer. This was valuable, a striking little piece that opened out into a writing desk. A bright Chinese screen concealed the work table, a hotplate, and a few cooking utensils. The low bed was covered with a gay afghan her mother had crocheted. Her clothes hung from pegs behind a curtain. The rest of her worldly possessions were kept in an old wicker trunk.

Welcome home, Elizabeth thought drearily. This room was bad enough but the bathroom was worse. It was at the end of the long corridor and she had to share with other roomers. Soap caked the basin, the tub was ringed with brown stains, hair littered the cracked counter. Once she'd left her towel and sponge there and someone had used them.

She peeled off her damp clothes, carefully hung them, slipped on a flannel wrapper, loosened her hair, and gratefully eased off the patched boots. Taking a kettle she went to the bathroom to fill it and turned on the hotplate. She sank on her father's chair and had her daily moment of peace. Lined up on the wall were three of her father's paintings, the only ones to survive. One was a seascape of a freighter, nose down, beating its way against a storm. Another depicted a country garden, the flowers so real one felt to touch them would bring the same sensation as to caress a living petal. Elizabeth's eyes lingered on both oils and then moved to her favorite. Elizabeth at five, a misty background, a wide-brimmed hat, a rose clutched in a chubby hand. Round face, solemn dark eyes, smooth olive skin, ringlets cascading, lips drawn back in a smile showing white baby teeth. The joy father had painted in that face, the happiness in the smile, the love in the dark eyes. She could barely remember sitting for it but she knew the emotions were genuine. How she had loved him, how she still loved him. When he'd died she hadn't cried. A few years ago when her mother had passed on Elizabeth *had* cried, dutiful tears from a dutiful daughter.

To Elizabeth, mother had always been security and stability but father was pure magic. A painter, a musician, a poet. A man unfit to make his own living and totally unable to support a wife and child. Turning through the cold hopeless years to the solace of drink. Devoted to his wife, worshipping his only child. Mother had provided the living from her scant wages as a milliner but father had provided the color, the joy. When Elizabeth had been very young and drink had not yet gained supremacy over him he had taken her to parks, to museums, on one memorable boat trip up the Hudson. Through his eyes she had discovered beauty. A gentle man who had kissed her bruises better, bound up cuts and scratches, read classics to her by the hour. Even at the end, when most of his days and nights were spent soddenly drunk, there were flashes of his wit, his humor, his compassion.

She clearly remembered the day two laborers had carried her father home and dumped him on his bed like a piece of refuse. The men had been rough but not unkind. Many would have left him where he lay in an alley on icy cobblestones sunk in a drunken stupor. She remembered his face on the pillow after mother washed him and put hot bottles around him. His fine features were bluish, his chin stubbled with beard, a thread of spittle oozed from the corner of his mouth. The eyelids, closed over eyes like his daughter's, looked transparent. His wife tried to spoon medicines and broth into the slack mouth while Elizabeth wiped the fluids away as fast as they dribbled down his bristly chin. Later, after a doctor had looked at him, shaken his head, and left, father's breathing rasped even more, blue lips blew bubbles, the thin chest heaved with the effort of getting breath to tortured lungs. Before he died his eyes opened and he gazed at the faces bending over him. He looked at his wife and perhaps he mutely pleaded for understanding and forgiveness. For his daughter there was only tenderness. "My lovely Elizabeth," he whispered.

The Meredith family, who for years had ignored his existence, arranged the funeral. Father's brother, Peter, was unwell but his son William took charge. It was December and the ground was packed hard. When the gravediggers started to fill the hole where father lay, clods of earth resounded against the cheap coffin lid like bullets. Elizabeth didn't weep but when mother tried to lead her away the child screamed and fought. After the service William came to see them. He sat stiffly in the parlor of their little flat, a thin young man not quite thirty, correct and well dressed, his clothes and manner emphasizing the poverty around him.

"Aunt Ethel," he said, "you are an industrious woman and I am grieved that Uncle Leon gave you such a hard life. Through his lifetime my father and I were powerless to assist you. We had to respect my grandfather's wishes. And he was right. Uncle Leon was a wastrel, a dabbler, lazy, and finally he perished because of his excesses."

Elizabeth made a choked sound but mother bent her head, meekly accepting William's censure. The young man looked not at her but at her daughter, saw and accepted the outrage in the child's face, and said soberly, "But my uncle is dead and Elizabeth is a Meredith and my cousin. You must set aside your pride and perhaps resentment and allow us to assist you."

Mother had little pride or resentment. She was only too willing to accept help from her husband's family. A glimmer of hope crossed her face and she sent a cautioning look at Elizabeth's rebellious facce. "We would be grateful," mother murmured.

He told them they would discuss the matter later and left. Turning on her mother, Elizabeth screamed, "They're murderers! They *killed* father! How can you act like this?"

In a flat voice her mother told her, "We are poor relatives of a wealthy family. They alone can help us. If I display pride what is our future? This flat is bad enough but at least it's clean. Would you like to live out your life in a filthy tenement?"

What was father's sin? Elizabeth demanded. His mother preferred Leon, mother answered drily, perhaps that was sin enough in the eyes of Oliver Pendrell. She named the boy herself— Napoleon Bonaparte Meredith. Perhaps that name alone was enough to make his father loathe him. Leon's father wanted a son to follow his own footsteps, to enter his shipping line. But Leon was an artist, a man who had no interest in commerce. The younger son, Peter, was like his father. So Peter had the business, the home, the family money. Leon was cut off with as little

as legally possible. And he spent that quickly. "Without me he'd
have died years ago," she sighed.

Mother put out a hand as thought to comfort the child and
then withdrew it. Harshly she said, "Elizabeth, know your place.
Poor relatives can't afford the luxuries of pride or anger. Be
meek, bend your head, say thank you, take what they offer."

Mother hoped what the Merediths would offer would be a
living allowance that would allow her to leave the milliner's shop
where she drudged, but she was to be disappointed. When William returned he perched on the edge of a chair as though he
feared to soil his broadcloth suit and offered an education for
Elizabeth and a clothing allowance while she attended the school.
Mother bent her head and tendered her gratitude.

Elizabeth was enrolled in Miss Penelope's Academy for
Young Ladies and proceeded to receive a totally useless education. She was taught to write a neat hand, tinkle a piano, converse in French, and paint on china. The allowance for clothing
was so tiny that if mother hadn't worked miracles by slaving long
hours at night on bargain fabrics Elizabeth would have looked
dreadfully out of place at the school. But she was out of place,
surrounded by bright young butterflies from wealthy families who
had pocket money, underclothes trimmed with lace, and who
chattered gaily about holidays in Europe and their coming-out
parties.

Elizabeth's coming-out party consisted of a diploma proving
she was qualified to do nothing, two embroidered handkerchiefs
from mother, a pen set from William, and a note telling her that
the Merediths had discharged their duties. While her classmates
whirled through balls, garden parties, and theaters, Elizabeth located a dressmaker who took her on as apprentice. With her tiny
earnings and her mother's they managed to eke out a living.

Years passed and Elizabeth was in her twenties. She was
becoming a spinster. She did get one offer of marriage from a
young man who worked on the elevated. He came, sat in the
parlor, sipped a glass of elderberry wine, and tried to court her.
His clothes were shabby and his nails were rimmed with black.
Mother pressed his suit. He's a hard worker, she told Elizabeth. I
can't abide him, her daughter said, and sent him on his way.

On her twenty-eighth birthday she was invited to dine with

William and his wife. This was the first time she had set foot in her grandfather's house and she accepted eagerly. Mother encouraged her. Perhaps, she said hopefully, now that Peter is dead William will offer us a little money. He may know I am not well and can't continue working much longer. Elizabeth had no such hopes. When she arrived she found there was another guest, a captain of one of the Meredith freighters. He had a bluff red face and a short white beard. He was fat and his breath was foul. He was old enough to be her grandfather.

Elizabeth paid no attention to the old sea dog. She was too busy looking around the dining room, watching maids in gray uniforms with crisp white caps and aprons serving a dinner of seven courses. When they had dined her cousin's wife Ruth and Elizabeth withdrew to the drawing room while the men applied themselves to port and cigars. Elizabeth's eyes devoured silk hangings, graceful furniture, vases of hothouse flowers. She compared Ruth's modish gown with her own pleated skirt and shirt-waist, Ruth's high piled coiffure with the simple styling of her own dark brown hair. They tried to make conversation but they had no interests in common. When the men finally joined them Elizabeth was relieved.

The captain was the worse for wear. He stumbled over a chair and when he gallantly bent over Elizabeth's hand in farewell he noisily broke wind. She was glad to see him ushered on his homeward way. Later William solemnly listed the man's assets. He is about to retire, Elizabeth was informed, he'll have a pension and has savings put by. I will provide you with a modest dowry. Elizabeth looked to her cousin's wife for assistance but Ruth merely looked bored. Do you expect me to marry this man? she demanded. He'd be a good catch, William told her, you aren't getting any younger and you need someone to look after you and your mother. Momentarily, Elizabeth lost her meekness. He smells, she cried, and he's ancient. Do you want to be an old maid? William asked. I *am* an old maid, she told him. I wash my hands of you, William declared icily, you are just like your father.

For five years it looked as though William had indeed dismissed her from his life. Then, within weeks of each other, Ruth Meredith and Elizabeth's mother died. After her mother's fu-

neral William took her to his house. We need each other, he
said, you are alone and my boys are motherless. This house must
be managed. Do you think you could handle it? He offered her a
small salary and a midday meal. Financially she would have been
better off staying with the dressmaking trade but she agreed immediately. She longed to be in that house, walking those gleaming floors, touching that lustrous furniture, acting, in a sense, as
its mistress. She was under no illusions about her cousin's
motives. William was a frugal man and for a pittance of a salary
he was obtaining a housekeeper. But she went, taking with her
efficiency, meekness, ingratiation. What she also brought to the
Meredith house was a steely determination to make it her own.

The whistling of the kettle on the hot plate interrupted her
memories. With a sigh she pulled herself from the leather chair.
Gazing at the wide joyous smile of the child her father had
painted, she said aloud, "I'm thirty-six, my teeth are rotting in
my jaw, I don't get enough to eat. Father, what ever happened to
your lovely Elizabeth?"

— 2 —

Elizabeth was working in the stuffy sewing room on the
fifth floor when Hannah, panting from the long climb, interrupted. The master was home and wanted her in the study. Setting aside the shirt she was mending, Elizabeth pulled the cover
over the machine, stood up, and stretched. Hannah's eyes fur-
tively avoided her own. "Is something wrong?" she asked the
maid.

"I broke a cup, miss." Hannah started to cry. "When I was
serving dinner last night it slipped outta my hands. Master was so
mad."

"One from the Spode set?" Hannah bobbed her head and
Elizabeth snapped, "That belonged to his mother."

"That's what he told me, miss. He's ever so mad."

Clapping her hands over her face, the maid bolted from the room. This, then, was the reason for the second summons in two days to William's study. Elizabeth shrugged. Hannah had been warned repeatedly. She wondered if she should mention to William that the girl had only been in the city for a few months, that she had no relatives here. Probably a waste of time.

She stepped out of the sewing room. This floor consisted mainly of storage rooms. On the next landing she stopped and gazed at the door of the lift but decided against using it. The fourth floor was given over to servants' rooms. Some of them were larger and nicer than her own. On the third floor were six bedrooms, two baths, and the unused nursery. None of the bedrooms were occupied. Here the hall was carpeted and paintings hung on the walls. The staircase to the second floor was wide and gracious. William's enormous room and his late wife's, separated by a dressing room and a bath, were at the front of the house. At the back, identical in size and comfort to the front ones, were George and Alan's rooms. A huge pottery vase held a mass of purple and white lilacs that perfumed the hall. At the head of the stairs a wicker stand contained an enormous Boston fern, its fronds sweeping to the carpet.

From Alan's room strains of music floated. He had a Victrola and stacks of disks. The classical ones, gifts from his father, were never played. Alan was mad about something called ragtime, by someone called Scott Joplin. Pausing, Elizabeth listened to the piano tinkling. She liked it. Twice she had sneaked into the boy's room and put a disk on. Standing beside the horn, she touched it, feeling vibrations through her body. For some reason the music reminded her of her father . . . William! She'd better not loiter here listening to ragtime.

When he admitted her to the study her cousin showed no trace of anger. His mail and paper sat untouched on a corner of his desk, his whiskey and soda were poured, and he was puffing on a cigar. There weren't any ledgers on the desk but the letter from Boston, flanked by a pile of small brown envelopes, sat in the middle of the green blotter. The weekly wages, Elizabeth thought, and none too soon. In her handbag was only a dime and three pennies and Mrs. Clyde would be stationed in the hall with her hand stretched out for the rent. Elizabeth's tooth throbbed.

and she resisted the impulse to touch it with her tongue.

William was giving her a beaming smile. She twitched her lips in response and unaccountably he blushed deeply. She stared. Even his bald pate was a dusky red. He certainly didn't have his mother's Spode cup on his mind. He cleared his throat. "How are you, Elizabeth?"

She stifled an impulse to tell him the truth. He wasn't interested anyway. He spoke much more rapidly than usual. "I have something of importance to tell you. Something that will make a great change in my life. Perhaps yours, certainly the boys'. You are the first to know . . . in New York, that is." Shifting in his chair, he took a long drink of whiskey. "Ruth has been dead for over three years and . . ." He threw down the rest of the drink and poured another generous one.

Elizabeth had a feeling one of her fears was to be realized. "You are considering marrying again?"

He gave a sigh of relief. "I can always count on you, Cousin Elizabeth. That's what I told Aunt Van a while ago. One of the nice things about Elizabeth is that she's so quick. No need to spell anything out for her. Yes, marrying, and not considering, it's decided." He tapped the envelope. "This is a letter from her mother. She has agreed to our marriage. I met Judith when I was in Boston last March. You remember when I made that business trip? At that time I spoke with her mother of the possibility . . ." His voice trailed off and he blushed again.

Mother? Elizabeth had immediately assumed that William's future wife would be around his own age, a spinster or perhaps a widow. "Yes?" she prompted.

"I'll be frank. Mrs. Arnold—she's asked me to call her Emma but I find that difficult—her only reservation to our engagement was the age difference. Judith is considerably younger than I. But—" He jumped from his chair and for an instant Elizabeth thought he might break into a jig. "She's agreed!"

While Elizabeth was wondering how to elicit the age of his bride he told her. "Judith's birthday was last week. She's twenty-one and Mrs. Arnold, Emma, has decided to give her consent."

Only three years older than his son George, Elizabeth thought, a mere child. "You haven't told Aunt Van?"

The name of that formidable woman quenched his high spirits. Sinking back into his chair he applied himself to his whiskey. "Not yet, Elizabeth."

Aunt Van was going to be displeased and they both knew it. And it wasn't wise to displease Aunt Van. Although she allowed Elizabeth to address her as aunt the woman was no relative. Georgia Vandercourt was William's aunt by marriage, the widow of his mother's only brother. She ruled the society William moved in with a pudgy but strong hand. In many ways she was a ridiculous figure but she seemed to be related either by blood or marriage to many wealthy New York families. Not Vanderbilts or Astors or Rockefellers, but the second echelon, the quite comfortably affluent like the Meredith family.

"You'd better tell her soon," Elizabeth advised.

"She'll be disappointed. Since my mourning period for Ruth passed Aunt Van has been pushing her own candidates. The latest is that widowed cousin of hers—what's her name?"

"Mrs. Nesbitt."

"Right. Agatha Nesbitt." He chuckled. "Years older than I and she must hit the scales at over two hundred."

Mrs. Nesbitt was actually younger than William and while plump certainly wasn't fat. Briefly Elizabeth had a fleeting memory of the old, smelly seaman William had offered as husband to her. "Aunt Van is dining with you tomorrow."

"I'll tell her then."

"And the boys?"

"Certainly."

"Have you set a wedding date?"

"Not as yet. Mrs. Arnold will be bringing her daughter to New York next month and we'll decide at that time. Which is the reason I must consult with you. They can't stay here. Even with her mother acting as chaperon it would be unseemly. I thought of asking Aunt Van to take them in but her temper is so uncertain."

"Nina Flanders would certainly do it and she's a nice person."

"Yes. I considered Nina and Albert but Aunt Van might feel passed over. So I decided to take a hotel suite for them. But I do want you to arrange a soiree so Judith can meet her new family and some friends. Not too many as she's inclined to be shy. I'll go over the guest list with you. I want the house in tiptop shape.

Spare no expense. I'll leave the details to you. One point—Judith loves fresh flowers. Make sure you order enough to make a good showing. They'll arrive on the ninth of July . . . Judith and Mrs. Arnold I mean. Plan the reception for the tenth."

Elizabeth was making notes in the small book she carried in her skirt pocket. "Anything else?"

"Not at this moment. We'll discuss details later. Oh, one more thing." Picking up the brown envelopes he slid them across the desk. "This will be Hannah's last week. Tell her I'm sorry she didn't work out and I hope when she finds another position she'll apply herself more assiduously to it."

"She's not strong and has no relatives to take her in."

"I can't be responsible for a girl clumsy enough to break one of my mother's finest pieces of china. She broke a cup, you know."

"She told me, but it will be difficult to break another maid in before the Arnolds' visit. You know how they are. Completely untrained."

William the lover was definitely gone. "You'll manage. You can't expect me to oversee every detail in this house. After all, that's your job." Rather ominously, he added, "For the present."

She tucked the book away and stood up. As she did a stab of pain lanced from the decaying tooth and she winced and rubbed her jaw. William noticed. "You have a toothache again. I've told you repeatedly it does no good to neglect proper dental care. Better see the dentist right away. We wouldn't want you out of sorts with so much to arrange."

The time has come, she thought. "I haven't money to go to a dentist. I can barely cover the rent for my room and . . ."

"Nonsense. Elizabeth, you are a poor manager. Like your father you throw your wages around on frivolities and don't provide for necessities." Plucking out his handsome watch he consulted it. "I must really dress for dinner. Goodnight, Elizabeth."

Her mouth opened and then she bent her head and left the study. Meek, her mother had said, a poor relative couldn't stand and argue. She went to the kitchen and handed an envelope to Cookie and a thinner one to the kitchen maid. Hannah swung open the door to the dining room, carrying a platter in one hand, a vegetable bowl in the other. They were Spode. Carefully Elizabeth took both from the girl and set them on the table. Then she handed her the envelope. "Mr. Meredith is discharging you. Your time is up next Friday." She put two envelopes on the table. "See Sally and Briggs get these, Cookie."

Hannah's face was the color of veal. "What'll I do, miss?"

"I'll tell you what *not* to do. Don't break any more china or your last pay will be docked."

Hannah let out a wail and tenderhearted Cookie put down a wooden spoon and enveloped the girl in comforting arms. "There, there," she murmured. Over Hannah's head she looked appealingly at Elizabeth. "Can nothing be done?"

Having no desire to alienate the cook, Elizabeth told her truthfully, "I did my best but it was a waste of time."

Leaving Cookie to comfort the distraught maid, Elizabeth went to the butler's pantry for her wicker basket. In it were only a few odds and ends and a blouse she had mended. It should have been light but it wasn't. She sniffed the aroma from the kitchen. Lamb chops. The cook must have put food into her basket. Elizabeth's mouth watered.

On the clothes rack in the hall two straw boaters with hatbands in school colors hung but there was no sign of Alan. As she hurried down the steps she thought it would be a long time before that young man honked at Tin Lizzie again.

In George's room Alan was putting much the same thought into disgruntled words. He sprawled on his brother's bed, his hands under his head, glaring at the ceiling. "That dried up old crabapple ratted on me. Some nerve!"

George didn't look up from the pile of books on his desk. "The punishment isn't all that bad."

"No band concert tomorrow. And the old man knows how much I like those concerts in Central Park. Blast her!"

"I'd no idea you were such a music lover. Except for ragtime, of course."

"Isn't the stupid old band, Georgie Porgie, it's those Italian and Irish girls who hang around there. Some of them aren't bad." Alan pushed himself up on his elbow and looked at his brother's back. "Don't you like girls?"

"Not the kind you do. I prefer mine smelling of lilac water, not tenements."

Alan fondled his crotch. Just thinking of those girls in their ragged shawls and revealing clothes got him hot. The way their bodies pushed against thin dresses, budding breasts jiggling under blouses . . . bet they weren't all trussed up with stays. His erection was painfully full and he wondered whether to go to his room and masturbate. Hell with it! He wanted the real thing. Last night as Sally bent over his bed turning down the sheet he'd caught a glimpse of her round bottom outlined against her skirt. He couldn't stop himself. Weak with desire he drove his hands up into the warmth of her crotch. Sally had slapped his face and threatened to tell the old man. Alan licked his lips. Sally was sure a pretty thing and that starched apron couldn't hide her surging breasts. If it wasn't for that hag of an Elizabeth he might have been able to find a willing girl tomorrow and . . . His full lips curved into a smile. "Anyway, I got Tin Lizzie good, Georgie Porgie."

His brother swung around, his gray eyes serious. "That's not bright. If she tells father, you're really in for it."

"The old man will never hear about this one. Foolproof. She wouldn't dare blab to him."

Fear of the dark streets hadn't dulled Elizabeth's anticipation for the food Cookie had slipped into her basket. As she mounted the steps to the stoop her knees felt weak from hunger. She could even force a smile at her landlady, who was stationed in the hall. Elizabeth waited for the usual offer of tea but it wasn't forthcoming. After counting the money carefully and as carefully putting it into a leather purse with steel clasps, Mrs. Clyde told her, "Telephone call for you from Mr. Meredith. Wants you to phone him right away. That'll be five cents for the use of the phone."

Digging out the nickel, a puzzled Elizabeth picked up the telephone. She gave the operator the number and tried to remember to keep her voice down. She wasn't accustomed to using a telephone and she hung onto the black shaft with an iron grip, jammed the receiver too tightly to her ear, and had a tendency to shout. The conversation, to the landlady's frustration, was brief. "Something wrong?"

"My cousin wants me to dine with him tomorrow evening. That's all."

"Not often he has you for dinner, is it?"

"My aunt will be there," Elizabeth told her and started up to her room. She was no longer puzzled. William was afraid of facing Aunt Van's wrath alone. Well, at least it would be a good dinner. An extra effort was made when Aunt Van was entertained.

Setting down the basket on the table, Elizabeth stood over it, playing a game, guessing what Cookie had put in it. Chops . . . maybe buns and cheese. Devil's food was being served for dessert, perhaps a large slice of that dark succulent cake. Eagerly she flipped up the lid, took out the needlework and blouse, and found a package wrapped in newspaper. She lifted it, weighing it in her hands. It was heavy and there were dark stains on the paper. Could Cookie have given her a roast?

With hands trembling with hunger she unwrapped it. Then she dropped it, stifling a scream. Oh God! The mangled body of a ginger cat. Blood stained the matted fur. Around the poor creature's neck was a blue ribbon and a piece of cardboard. In block printing were words. SOMETHING FOR SUSSIE.

Alan! He'd killed a poor stray and put it into her basket. Rage overcame shock and she started toward the door. She'd spend another nickel and tell his father! Then she stopped and her shoulders drooped. She couldn't. If she did that she'd have to admit to William that she stole food from his kitchen, that Cookie stole food for her.

Wild with impotent rage, she rewrapped the body, stuck it in the basket, and headed downstairs. From Mrs. Clyde's room the strains of ragtime drifted, and the smell of cooking meat. She found an ashcan in an areaway down the street and gently deposited the body of the cat who had looked so much like her own. Then she went into the market and defiantly spent most of her wages. She bought bread, half a pound of butter, two lamb chops, and some small rich cakes. On her way home she stopped at a tobacco store and bought a package of cigarettes. Forbidden fruit but she liked them and tonight she just didn't care.

While the chops cooked she laid out her purchases, brewed tea, and smoked two cigarettes. But when the chops were done to a turn, pink and crisp with fat, she was so famished she forgot the decaying tooth, bringing it directly down on a chunk of lamb. Fire lanced through her head and she stumbled blindly back from the dinner she couldn't eat and collapsed across the bed.

Burying her face in her mother's afghan she wept for the first time in many years.

— 3 —

Aunt Van had three passions in life—food, gossip, and bridge. This balmy July evening she was indulging in two—food and gossip—and anticipating the third. Food took precedence over gossip and tales about relatives and friends were relegated to the interludes between courses. While the bowls that had contained terrapin soup were removed she gave her attentive audience the lurid details on the Standford's daughter Maud who had left school and eloped with a young Italian. Handsome boy, Aunt Van admitted, but really! His family ran a cafe in the Village, one of those squalid places serving greasy spaghetti and cheap wine. Poor dear Horace and Estelle, they were shattered! Salad arrived and Aunt Van fell on it.

As the older woman devoured the salad, Elizabeth surreptitiously watched her. Aunt Van not only had the appetite of a hog but she resembled one. Short and nearly as broad as she was high, her corseted figure draped in peach chiffon over taffeta, three strands of pearls cascading over her bulging chest, no-color hair elaborately coiffed, rings sparkling on tiny hands. But her small eyes, ah, they were the key to Aunt Van. They were shrewd and missed nothing.

Enviously, the poor relation eyed the lavish dress and jewels. Elizabeth had taken trouble with her own hair, her cotton dress was starched and she'd freshened it with an edging of lace at the throat and sleeves but, compared to the porcine woman opposite her, she felt like a scarecrow.

Scooping up the last scrap on her plate, Aunt Van leaned back and drained her glass. Immediately the bottle of wine was tilted over it. Having exhausted the Standford scandal, she turned her attention to the boys, inquiring how school was going. George answered politely but Alan, still sulking because of the loss of his weekly treat at the band concert, merely mumbled. It didn't matter. Aunt Van seldom listened to anyone. Cutting in on Alan's mumble, she asked, "How are you, Elizabeth?" Without waiting for a reply she raced on, "That yellow dress makes you look jaundiced. Blue and green are your colors. William, you have no appetite. Are you ailing?"

William, who was playing with his food, gave a guilty start. But Hannah was carrying in the fish and for the moment he was saved. While waiting for the roast Aunt Van told them about her own children. Or child. The older daughter, Sophie, a spinster slightly younger than Elizabeth, she brushed over. Sixteen-year-old Earl, the namesake and image of his late father, she didn't mention. Charity she raved on about—the child's cleverness, her charming ways, how at barely fourteen the little imp was demanding her hair be put up and her hems down. So carried away was Aunt Van that the monologue extended beyond the heaping of her plate. "I wish," she said mournfully, "the dear departed could have lived to see Charity growing up."

"A tragedy," William agreed. "Uncle Earl died only two weeks after her birth, didn't he?"

"Less. Ten days. He did see the little darling. Nurse took the baby in to him and he said, 'She's another Georgia!' He died that night."

Hastily, Elizabeth bent her head and cut a slice of beef into small pieces. She'd heard rumors about the dear departed's actual words. His last remark was supposed to have been, "She looks just like Georgia. Thank God I'm not going to have to put up with two of them!" Which was the true account she didn't know, but there was no doubt Charity was her mother's daughter. She was the apple of the maternal eye, and apple was an appropriate term because if an apple were jammed in her mouth the child would look remarkably like a suckling pig.

William was urging a second helping of beef on Aunt Van and she accepted readily. But plying his aunt with food didn't deter her for long. She cleaned her place and shrewd eyes again fastened on his face. "You have absolutely no appetite tonight, William. Perhaps you should dose with molasses and sulphur. The turn of the season can be hard on us older people."

Elizabeth came to his rescue. "Cookie baked your favorite cake, Aunt Van."

She beamed, showing excellent teeth. "Your cook is a jewel. Much better than Aggie. I warn you, William, I'm going to kidnap Cookie. Ah, seedcake and sherbet and *two* flavors of ice cream. I'll have a little of each, Hannah. No, more than that. Don't be stingy, girl." As Hannah left the room, Aunt Van lowered her voice. "Girl's eyes are swollen. Something wrong with her?"

"She has her notice," William told her. "She's been lax and clumsy. The other night she broke a piece of Spode."

"Quite right too. Have you found a replacement for her?"

William glanced at Elizabeth and she said, "She was only discharged last night."

"Look for a bigger girl, stronger. Not plump but bigboned." Leaning back, Aunt Van massaged her midriff and stifled a burp. "I swear my appetite's a little off these days. I simply can't eat a bite more."

"Surely a morsel of cheese," William coaxed, "with some fruit."

"If you have Brie I might be tempted. And some grapes. William, I'd like a brandy. It settles my stomach."

Her nephew went to get the decanter himself. Hopefully Elizabeth waited for an offer of brandy but William poured only for himself and Aunt Van. When William mentioned bridge Elizabeth heard George sigh. He was to be Aunt Van's partner and was dreading it. So was Elizabeth. She didn't play well and William would be critical. She was wondering when William would work up courage enough to tell his aunt about his marriage.

Waving away the mention of her favorite game, Aunt Van's small eyes probed her nephew's. Immediately he blushed and she leaned forward. "Out with it."

"You're most astute, Aunt Van. As a matter of fact I have good news and I'm certain you and the boys will be delighted."

"About what?"

In halting words he told her he intended to marry. George

raised his brows, Alan shook off his sulkiness and looked interested, and their aunt beamed. "You sly boots! And Agatha too.
Why I played bridge with her last evening and she didn't let on
by a—"

"It's not Mrs. Nesbitt."

The wide smile faltered and then reformed. "So it's Jessie!
An excellent choice. Jessie is an able manager and has a nice
inheritance from her late husband."

"No, not Mrs. Cantrell either."

The loose mouth lost its delighted curve. "Then *who* in tar-
nation is it?"

He stumbled into an explanation. Aunt Van caught a name
and was off. "I know Emma Arnold. In fact we're related. Let's
see, her Aunt Clara was the second wife of my cousin . . . Surely
not Emma Arnold? A flibbertigibbet if there ever was one. Why
that woman drove her poor husband into an early grave with her
extravagances."

William's mouth hardened and he said coldly, "You're in-
sulting my future mother-in-law. I'm engaged to her daughter Judith."

"Judith? You can't be serious. The last time I saw the girl
she was in pigtails. She can't be any older than—" Aunt Van
broke off but her eyes strayed to George.

"Judith is twenty-one and quite old enough to marry. Mrs.
Arnold has given her consent and—" A lesser man would have
hit the table with his fist. William merely snapped his thumb and
third finger but Aunt Van looked as outraged as though he had
hit her. He continued more quietly, "As far as I'm concerned the
matter is settled."

Elizabeth waited hopefully. This should produce a flaming
row with his aunt. Foolish, she thought gleefully; if Aunt Van
decided not to receive his bride Judith would be ostracized by
William's relations and friends. But Aunt Van was looking
thoughtful. "Well, William, if it's settled there's no more to say.
Apparently you wouldn't heed my advice anyway. I spent a lot of
time and trouble introducing you to suitable wives but . . . Will I
have a chance to see your fiancée before the wedding?"

"Of course!" William relaxed and reached for the decanter.
Imperiously his aunt waved it away. "Next week Judith and her

mother will be in New York and Elizabeth is arranging a little party for Judith. You will be there?"

"Dear boy, I wouldn't miss it for the world. You must invite Doctor John and Lavinia and Albert and Nina. Don't forget Uncle Herman. He's the oldest in the family."

"I most certainly will. You'll be pleasantly surprised. Judith is much older than her years."

She paid no attention. Busily she ticked names off on tiny, ring-heavy fingers. "And the Standfords and the Grants—"

"Whoa! We plan only a small gathering. Judith is a bit shy."

"Shy is she? And older than her years? Quite a combination." Aunt Van heaved her bulk up. "I always say the proof of the pudding is in the eating."

William sprang to pull back her chair. "Now for a game of bridge."

"Not tonight."

"Are you angry?"

"Of course not, dear boy. If you choose to disregard my advice, that's your affair. I'm having a little heartburn and I'd better get home." Abruptly she jerked her head at Elizabeth. "Get your coat. I'll take you home."

Elizabeth scurried to do as she was told and as they were milling around in the hall, saying goodnight while William and George helped their aunt into her cape, Alan edged close to his cousin. In a whisper, he asked, "How did you enjoy your nice dinner *last* night, Cousin Elizabeth?"

She was unprepared and a vision of the mutilated cat on blood-soaked paper flashed across her mind. She must have shown her revulsion because Alan grinned and George sent his brother a questioning look. William and his aunt's long-suffering chauffeur escorted the ladies to the car. George turned on his brother. "What did you say to Elizabeth?"

Alan managed to look both innocent and righteous. "The old man ordered me to be polite to the crabapple so I politely asked how her dinner was last night."

George's eyes narrowed. "What was the trick you played on her?"

With a shrug Alan turned away but George grasped his arm. "Don't play games with me. What did you do?"

"Put a present into her basket." Alan giggled. "An alley cat

I caught raiding the garbage and finished off. Cookie said the
crabapple's Sussie was ginger and so was this one. Ouch! Cut it
out. You're hurting!"

"You torment her anymore and I'll hurt more than your
arm. You're disgusting! No wonder she looked sick."

"What do you care? She's nothing but a snitch and I hate—"
Breaking off, Alan yanked his arm loose and asked brightly,
"Aunt Van on her way, father?"

William nodded and put an affectionate arm around Alan's
plump shoulders. "Come into the study, boys. We'll talk about
your new mother." He beamed from one boy to the other. "That
went rather well, didn't it? Aunt Van didn't make the fuss I was
expecting."

William was mistaken. Aunt Van wasn't taking it well. As
soon as her sleek Packard pulled away from the curb she proceeded to tell Elizabeth exactly what she thought. Secretly
pleased, Elizabeth listened to her rave.

"No fool like an old fool! William is close to my age and that
snip of a girl has him wrapped right around her finger." Completely forgetting the age similarity she'd just mentioned she said
tearfully, "I've always been like a mother to that boy. Trying to
steer him right, keep him away from designing women. Henry,
you're driving much too fast! How many times must you be told?
As I was saying, I know Emma Arnold and she's a cunning one.
Spent her husband's money faster than he could make it and
killed him by extravagance. Got a big house on Beacon Hill and
not a bean to look after it. Why are we stopping? Henry? Oh,
we're here."

She peered at the street. "Dreadful neighborhood, Elizabeth. Is that a saloon down there? You should live in William's
house. No sense in false pride. No, don't get out. I'm not
through. What was I saying?"

"Mrs. Arnold."

"I'll lay you a wager that dreadful woman made a dead set
for William herself and when she couldn't catch him pressed that
daughter of hers on him. Mark my words, between them they'll
drain the boy. Why are you so quiet, Elizabeth? Cat got your
tongue?"

"I don't—"

"You're going to be hurt too. New brooms sweep clean. Mark my words, that little thing will have you out of the house before you can say . . . What's that?"

"I said I could always go back to dressmaking, Aunt Van."

"That's true. You're an excellent seamstress. That outfit you made me for Easter was better than anything my dressmaker's ever made. Charity loved that little voile you ran up for her too. But you must feel terrible. Devoting years to William and his sons and then to be thrown aside like an old shoe. Mark my words, William will rue the day he set eyes on Judith and Emma Arnold. Well, what are you waiting for? I can't sit here all night." Aunt Van rubbed her stomach and made no effort to hide a belch. "Got the heartburn something awful. Better get home and take some fruit salts." Henry assisted Elizabeth out of the car but before he could close the door Aunt Van stuck her head out for a last word. "Easier to get a young wife than keep her. Watch out, Elizabeth! New brooms sweep clean."

Elizabeth stood on the curb, watching the taillights of the Packard as the car moved smoothly and sedately away. She didn't see her landlady peering out from between net curtains. All she could see was a huge broom with the head of a young girl ruthlessly sweeping graceful old furniture, mellow carpets, and silk hangings down the steps of the Meredith house. The doors of a saloon swung open and a couple of drunks staggered toward her. Feeling ill she hurried up the steps to her bleak room.

— 4 —

The first guest to arrive at the soiree for Judith Arnold was Aunt Van. She was elaborately gowned in beige silk. Set squarely on her head was a cartwheel hat that made her look not unlike a fat mushroom. She appeared to be hung with every diamond she possessed—a choker half-buried in the folds of her short neck, bracelets at both wrists, a starburst on her bosom.

Tiny jeweled hands wafted a painted fan briskly to and fro. "Hot," she grumbled. "Much too hot to be in the city. If it wasn't for this foolishness the children and I would be out at the Long Island house."

The city was reeling under a heat wave. Elizabeth had had awnings lowered over the windows and had opened the double doors leading to the back drawing room hoping to get a through draft, but the rooms were still stifling. But she looked around with approval. Elizabeth had driven both herself and the servants to prepare for this party. The furniture and floors gleamed with polish and the rugs had been cleaned and beaten by two husky men hired for the heavy work. The hearth of the Adam fireplace was banked with a spray of vivid gladioli, mauve iris in silver bowls sat on end tables, and an enormous bouquet of pink roses decorated the marble-topped table in the hall. On impulse she'd placed a cluster of tiny yellow rosebuds on the mantel. Thank God the new downstairs maid was working out well.

Over her fan Aunt Van was also critically eyeing the room. "Looks like your new girl is worth two of Hannah. Noticed how smart she moved when she let me in. Irish or Italian?"

"German. From upstate New York. Her name's Gerda. She's efficient and catches on quickly."

"Got a good build there. Big-boned but not an ounce of fat. Looks pretty young."

"She says she's eighteen but I think she's a couple of years younger."

"As long as she works hard age doesn't matter." Impatiently, Aunt Van pulled out her bodice and consulted the watch pinned to it. "What can be keeping the others? I told them four at the latest and it's ten minutes past this minute."

"William and the Arnold ladies aren't due until five."

"Must be Uncle Herman holding them up. Doctor John and Lavinia are picking up Albert and Nina and then Uncle Herman. Don't know why he doesn't maintain a car and driver. Always after someone to run him here, pick him up there."

"Perhaps he can't afford a car."

"Don't you believe that poor act of his for a minute, Elizabeth. Certainly he cries poor but he's well off. Told my dear departed oldest sister when she married him that he was a miser. Do I hear a car?"

Elizabeth rose, smoothing down the skirt of her best dress, a white organdy sashed with black velvet. It had been her mother's but she'd made it over and it looked quite nice. However her shabby shoes ruined the effect. How she longed for a dainty pair of slippers. She glanced enviously at Aunt Van's silken slippers. "Yes, they're arriving, Aunt Van."

Without waiting for the knocker or the maid, Aunt Van sailed into the hall and flung the door wide. "What kept you?"

Behind the broad back, Elizabeth consulted the mirror. Her hair was gleaming and was styled quite attractively, swept back from her brow in a pompadour and dressed high on her head. She pinched color into her cheeks and turned to look over Aunt Van's hat.

Doctor John and Lavinia Stokes, supporting Uncle Herman, were leading the way. Behind them were the Flanderses, Albert and his wife Nina. The men were dressed in blue blazers, white pants, and two-toned shoes, the women wore filmy gowns and wide hats. Even Uncle Herman, leaning heavily on his cane with his brass ear trumpet at the ready, was nattily attired in what looked like new clothes. The men doffed straw boaters and the doctor smiled genially at Aunt Van and nodded pleasantly at Elizabeth. "Calm down, Aunt Van. Lots of time."

"What's that?" Uncle Herman shouted.

Lavinia shouted into the ear trumpet. "John says there's lots of time."

"Yes. Fine weather but a little warm. Hullo, Cousin Elizabeth."

Taking his hat, she shouted a greeting into the trumpet. With the exception of the doctor and Nina Flanders, who smiled kindly at her, Uncle Herman was the only one to acknowledge she was there. So much for her efforts to look nice, she thought dismally as Lavinia and Albert swept by her. She'd get about as much attention as a piece of furniture. Aunt Van was taking charge. "Into the drawing room. Do you want William to arrive with the ladies and find you all standing around gawking?"

She shooed them in as though they were a flock of chickens and pointed out seats. Perching on the chair near the archway, Elizabeth looked them over. Lavinia and Albert were brother and sister and they were both handsome, short and fine-boned, curly dark hair, lushly lashed dark blue eyes. They had noses like delicate scimitars and discontented mouths. Despite their good looks they'd both chosen large, plain mates. Doctor John towered over his dainty wife and Nina was half a head taller than Albert. Elizabeth could never figure out what relation the brother and sister were to Aunt Van. Perhaps they were distant cousins.

Conversation was general. The weather was worked over and the fact that at this time of year they'd ordinarily be at their summer homes and away from the heat of the city. Then they got down to the business of the day, speculating about William's fiancée and deferring to Aunt Van as the authority on the Arnold family.

Lavinia Stokes's discontented lips curled. "I call it disgraceful. Imagine a man William's age taking a bride no older than his own children!"

"Oh, I don't know," Doctor John said mildly. "Must remember, my dear, you were a child bride yourself."

She turned on him, her eyes blazing. "Not *thirty* years younger than you, John."

As usual Nina Flanders spread oil on the troubled waters. "It may work out well. William is quite youthful for his age."

"Mark my words, he'll age fast." Aunt Van plied her fan vigorously. "And what a mother-in-law he's getting."

Albert stroked his dashing black mustache. "What's this Mrs. Arnold like?"

"Pretty little thing and does she know it. Puts on a southern accent and pretends her family came from Georgia. I happen to know for a fact they hail from Pennsylvania. She's a flirt too. Lets on she's a delicate clinging vine and underneath I'd swear Emma Arnold is pure steel."

Leaning forward, Uncle Herman thrust the ear trumpet at Aunt Van. "What's that?"

"Steel!" she bellowed. Lowering her voice she said irascibly, "Dratted man! I wear my lungs out on that trumpet."

Doctor John winked at Albert Flanders. "Mrs. Arnold sounds like quite a little lady. But don't try and fool us about how gentle *any* of you ladies are. Look at what the suffragettes are up to. To say nothing about that revolutionary Emma Goldman."

The women all started talking at once. Lavinia claimed that
women now had the vote in many states, Nevada and Montana
had recently granted suffrage, and yet in New York ladies had no
right to cast a vote.

Brushing at his mustache to conceal a smile, Albert asked,
"If you *did* have the vote how would you know which candidate
to elect?"

His sister aimed her scimitar nose at him but it was his placid
wife who drawled, "One of these days, Albert, you may be
amazed at what women can do."

Aunt Van swept aside the suffrage movement with a pudgy
hand and fastened on the other name that Doctor John had mentioned. "That outrageous Emma Goldman! My young nephew
was foolish enough to attend a meeting the other night to hear
her speak and the police raided it. He nearly went to jail and I
told him it would have served him right if he had been put behind
bars. As usual that Emma Goldman managed to slip out a back
way. Takes good care of her skin, she does."

Poking a sly elbow in Doctor John's ribs, Albert asked Aunt
Van, "What do you think of Margaret Sanger and her work?"

Aunt Van went crimson and rapped his wrist sharply with
her fan. "Really," his sister gasped. "That's no subject to mention before ladies."

"Why not, Lavinia? Ladies claim their minds should be their
own and they should have the vote. Margaret Sanger only goes a
step further and advocates that their bodies should be their
own." Albert appealed to the doctor. "What are your ideas on
birth control?"

"Have you no delicacy?" Aunt Van demanded.

"Come now. You're all married ladies."

"Have you forgotten Cousin Elizabeth?"

Elizabeth felt all eyes turning in her direction. She sat
quietly, her head modestly lowered, inwardly seething. Of course
they had forgotten she was here. She bore no more importance
than if she had been one of the flowers in the silver bowls. Probably less, at least flowers were eye-appealing and fragrant. As for
Margaret Sanger's preaching of birth control—how dare these
people feel because she was unwed she had no knowledge of life.
Celibacy certainly hadn't stultified her mind and made her an
imbecile. I'm more intelligent than most of you, she silently

cried. Take away your wealth, your secure little social group, and what are you? Coldly she tabulated them. Portly Doctor John Stokes, fortunate in finding his patients among relatives and friends. Fortunate in marrying well and taking a wife with both looks and money. Lavinia, handsome and discontented and spiteful. Albert Flanders, wealthy attorney (again for relatives and friends), as handsome as his sister and, from the rumors, a lecher. Elizabeth hesitated over Albert's wife. She had a feeling Nina Flanders, outwardly placid and uxorious, was much like the tip of an iceberg. In Nina's eyes were kindness, understanding, an occasional flash of mockery.

It was Nina who came to the rescue and changed the subject. "It's unfortunate our young people weren't invited today. Susan and little Marilou were so disappointed.

There were immediate outcries about the injustice of William's decision. Aunt Van explained at length how distraught her Charity was at being excluded. So sensitive that child is, just like me, she cried. How her daughter Sophie or Earl felt she didn't mention. John and Lavinia, speaking at the same time and paying not the slightest attention to each other, echoed Aunt Van's words, but the objects of their solicitude was their only son and his fiancée.

Aunt Van had no interest in the Stokeses' son and heir. Shifting impatiently and snapping her fan closed, she broke into the spate of complaints. "What time is it?"

Doctor John looked pointedly at the watch on her bodice but fished across his paunch and pulled out a heavy gold hunter. "Twenty after five."

"So thoughtless of William. The boy knows the state of my stomach. We shall be late at table and that always upsets my digestion. Gives me the heartburn."

Albert cocked his head, "Your stomach is safe, Aunt Van. Methinks I hear the lovers' chariot."

She waved the fan at them. "Now, all of you stay right where you are. Won't do to look curious."

Uncle Herman's trumpet came to the ready. "What's that?"

"Sit!" she screamed into it.

He looked injured. "What do you think I'm doing?" He mumbled into his beard, "Stupid woman."

Ignoring her own order, Aunt Van bounced up and nimbly

made her way to a window. She looked through the lace and muttered, "Yes, it is they. Good Lord! What is the boy wearing? Elizabeth, how could you?"

Elizabeth made no effort to defend herself. William certainly hadn't consulted her about his clothes. Unable to contain her curiosity, Lavinia joined Aunt Van. "What are you talking about? That's a perfectly suitable broadcloth."

"Wait until he turns around. There! Red piping on the waistcoat and . . . yes, on his spats. And that tie. Red! Has the boy lost his mind? Trying to look a mere lad. Mark my words, that's what comes of taking a bride young enough to be a daughter. And Emma! I do believe her hat's trimmed with fresh roses. Ladies, better watch your husbands. She's a vamp."

Albert and the doctor exchanged interested glances while Aunt Van rushed on. "Who should be at the door to welcome them?"

Albert brushed his mustache. "I'll go."

"No, dear boy, it wouldn't do. A woman. No, Lavinia, not you. I'd go myself but it wouldn't be dignified."

Nina was smiling and Elizabeth sharply regarded that smile. There was mockery in the twist of her lips. She suggested demurely, "Perhaps Cousin Elizabeth?"

"The very one. Elizabeth, you get to the door." Tugging Lavinia with her, Aunt Van steered a course for her chair. As Elizabeth obediently took up her post she could hear Aunt Van issuing orders. "Everyone converse normally. Wouldn't do for Emma to think we were discussing her."

They obeyed, all talking at once. John and Albert were feverishly discussing investments, Lavinia was working on her son's recent engagement, Aunt Van easily overriding their voices with an account of the cutest remark her Charity had made just that morning. A baffled Uncle Herman was turning his trumpet from one to another and crying, "What's that?" at intervals. Only Nina was silent. It sounded, Elizabeth decided, not unlike the Tower of Babel.

She opened the door. William, jaunty in his new suit, was escorting the ladies up the steps. George and Alan were tagging along behind. Alan whispered to his brother and giggled but George shook his head. Both ladies were dressed in shantung suits, one in rose, the other in a misty blue. The taller woman wore a turban of draped blue chiffon, the shorter woman balanced an enormous hat strewn with fresh roses. They were both fair and, at first glance, looked about the same age.

Gallantly, William handed them into the hall. "Cousin Elizabeth, may I present Mrs. and Miss Arnold. Emma, Judith, my cousin."

As Elizabeth greeted the ladies the tempo of conversation from the drawing room picked up and Alan whispered audibly to his brother, "Sounds like they're all hitting the bottle."

His father glared at him and the boy fell silent. Then William steered his ladies like porcelain figurines to the archway of the drawing room and the blessed silence reigned. Elizabeth slid into the chair against the wall and watched while William attempted to make introductions. Paying no attention to her nephew, Aunt Van sprang from her chair and in mincing steps ran to greet Emma Arnold. "No need to introduce me, dear William. Emma and I are old friends and relatives. Darling Emma, how are you? Let me look at you. Still so pretty. I do declare you never grow older. You look younger than Judith."

Emma and Aunt Van embraced, pecking kisses at each other's cheeks, careful not to bump their broad hats. Emma was as effusive as the older woman. "Dear Aunt Van. I told Judith one of the wonderful things about her marriage is in having Aunt Van so close to her now. I declare she's a lucky girl. Judith, you come right here and give your aunt a kiss."

Emma's voice was as sweet as the one Aunt Van had adopted, and dripped honeysuckle. Confusion continued to reign as the ladies embraced, the gentlemen gallantly bent over dainty hands, and seats were selected. When they sorted themselves out Aunt Van had managed to squeeze her bulk between Judith and William on a sofa and Emma was flanked by an admiring Albert and Doctor John. She turned a rosy face from one to the other, extravagantly long lashes fluttering. "Such handsome gentlemen!" Lavinia's scimitar nose swung dangerously in Emma's direction but Nina merely looked amused. "I do hope you ladies don't mind my admiring your husbands but I must confess even at my age I find handsome men so . . . so stimulating."

Doctor John looked properly stimulated and Albert, with

lashes fully as lush as Emma's, used them to much advantage.
"Mrs. Arnold," the lawyer said gallantly, "your age, as Aunt
Van just mentioned, appears to be close to your charming daugh-
ter's."

He wasn't far wrong. Emma Arnold doubtless had to work
for the effect but she certainly didn't look like Judith's mother.
She was tiny, with fair curls peeking from under the brim of her
hat framing a pointed face with guileless blue eyes and a rosebud
mouth. Although she appeared to be the center of attention, actually it was her daughter who was receiving a more covert exam-
ination. Unlike her mother, Judith was not pretty. She was
lovely. She was tall with sloping shoulders and a swelling bosom,
a narrow waist and generous hips. Well-turned ankles were displayed in embroidered hose above dainty silk slippers.

Elizabeth stifled a sigh. She could see the reason for William's infatuation. Forgetting his duties as host, he bent forward
so he could see past his aunt's bulk and gazed soulfully at his
fiancée. Under sleekly arranged blond hair was a face worth staring at. Judith had a rounded brow, a slender uptilted nose, a
charming line of chin. Her short upper lip was drawn up in the
middle, exposing perfect teeth. Her skin was superb, white and
translucent, tiny blue lines veining the brow, warm color man-
tling the cheeks. Judith Arnold's eyes were her most arresting
feature. Elizabeth had read of violet eyes but never before had
she seen them. And Judith's large eyes were violet, the purplish
blue of the cluster of fragrant flowers that nestled against Lavinia
Stokes's shapely breast.

If, as William had claimed, Judith was shy, she didn't show
it. She was poised and completely charming. Her voice was lower
than her mother's, had no trace of honeysuckle, and was clear
but husky. There was a quality about the girl that Elizabeth
couldn't pin down. She searched the faces of the guests for a
clue. Alan was staring at his future stepmother, George was obviously avoiding looking at her, both Doctor John and Albert
were carrying on mild flirtations with her mother and managing
to ogle the daughter. It was in Nina Flanders's placid face that
Elizabeth found the answer. Her mild eyes flickered toward Judith and then toward her husband, Albert. In those eyes was a
hint of alarm. Surrounding Judith was an aura that had no connection to either her looks or her youth. It was dusted over the

perfect skin, the fine features, the slender body, like a layer of perfume. Sexuality, delicate but beckoning, sending out tendrils to every male in the room. Filing this away for further reference, Elizabeth returned her attention to the conversation.

William tore his eyes away from Judith and raised a beautiful hand. "Elizabeth," he said, "Would you ring for the champagne?" He beamed at his guests. "Dear friends, all of you are aware of the reason for this gathering. Mrs. Arnold—Emma—has graciously consented to the marriage of her daughter Judith and—ah, here is the champagne."

As Elizabeth had instructed, the drink tray was indeed ready. Gerda carried a huge ice bucket filled with bottles and she was followed by Sally balancing a tray of the best cut crystal glasses. They placed them on the table, were waved away by William who uncorked the bottles. George and Alan handed round the glasses and when all the guests were served William raised his own glass. "Shall we toast my bride?"

Judith bent her sleek head and Doctor John stood and raised his own glass. "A toast to the betrothed. To Judith and William! I will add I consider William to be a most fortunate man."

Glasses were drained and refilled. Making his way to Judith's side, William tenderly clasped her hand. Aunt Van was greedily downing champagne but she paused long enough to ask, "Has the wedding date been set?"

Emma Arnold took a dainty sip and told her brightly, "Indeed it has, dear aunt. We've decided on the eighth of August."

Aunt Van choked, set her glass down, and sputtered, "Isn't that rather hasty? I mean, surely you can't arrange a wedding that quickly."

"Judith and I have been as busy as bees. The trousseau is nearly ready, I've arranged for the church and the reception. Of course, there are a number of last minute details but they'll be no bother."

Aunt Van's sweetness was slipping. Her lips curled as she asked bleakly, "The ceremony will be held in Boston?"

"Of course. Judith was born and raised there. It's expected."

William said hastily, "You'll all be guests. The invitations will be arriving within the week."

"For the Standfords and the Grants?"

"No one will be overlooked, Aunt Van."

Elizabeth felt a stirring of hope. William had promised they'd all be guests. Surely he meant her too. He'd have to buy her a new outfit. A dress, shoes, certainly a hat. Covetously she pictured a watered silk gown, slippers to match, a large hat with ostrich plumes.

Lavinia Stokes, her eyes arch, was asking another question. "And your wedding trip?"

William blushed a dusty pink and it was Emma who said sweetly, "Judith has her heart set on Atlantic City. I suggested Saratoga but if this is what she wants . . ."

"Atlantic City," her daughter said firmly. "I've always wanted to visit it." The violet eyes restlessly wandered around the room until they settled on the vase of tiny yellow roses. She jumped up and touched a petal. "How charming! William, how did you guess these are my favorite flowers?"

Looking pleased, he went to her side. For a moment Elizabeth thought he was about to take the credit himself but he said, "This you owe to Cousin Elizabeth. She selected all the flowers."

Carefully, the girl removed a bud and taking the carnation from his buttonhole, she replaced it with the rose. Then she went to Elizabeth, who stood at the girl's approach. Judith took one of the spinster's hands in both of hers and Elizabeth noticed the coolness and softness of those hands. In a low voice Judith told her, "I've been looking forward to meeting you, Elizabeth."

Her mother rose regally, smoothed down the rose colored skirt, straightened the huge hat, and joined her daughter. "You are William's housekeeper?" Emma asked and honeysuckle no longer dripped from her voice.

"Mama! You know very well Elizabeth is William's cousin. He told us all about her, how she kindly left her own work and took charge of his house and his sons and how much he relies on her."

Emma's rosebud lips thinned. "No doubt, Elizabeth, you'll be happy to know you are free now to live your own life. William will no longer be in need of assistance. I've trained my daughter in the management of a home and soon this will be her house."

The new broom, Elizabeth thought drearily, and Emma Arnold was going to see that the first thing to be swept out was her son-in-law's cousin. Aloud she said, "I'm sure Judith will handle it beautifully."

"And I'm certain I won't!" Judith frowned at her mother and called, "William!" She looked up at his adoring face. "You must tell Elizabeth I simply can't cope without her. Mama feels I should take over her duties right after our wedding trip. And I can't. I know I can't."

He slipped an arm around her waist. "Anything you wish, my dear. Elizabeth will be happy to stay on and see you understand everything thoroughly. Won't you, Elizabeth?"

"Very happy," Elizabeth said truthfully. Over William's shoulder she saw Gerda trying to catch her attention. She raised her brows and the maid nodded. "Dinner is ready," she told her cousin.

At the magic words Aunt Van stirred and her face lightened. She waited for William to offer his arm but instead he extended one arm to Judith, the other to Emma. Aunt Van looked murderous. In any house she was traditionally the first lady to be escorted to table. It was clear she was affronted. She glared at William's back and as Doctor John hastened to help her up she growled, "Rude! Positively rude! I'm the oldest woman here."

Doctor John made soothing sounds and the other gentlemen helped the ladies up. Lavinia Stokes was taken in on her brother's arm, young George escorted Nina Flanders, and the only people left in the drawing room were Uncle Herman, fast asleep in his deep chair, Elizabeth, and Alan. The boy made a face at her, brushed by her so close he touched her skirt, and hissed something that wasn't a honk but could have been a meow. Ignoring him, she picked up the brass trumpet that had fallen from Uncle Herman's limp hand and touched his shoulder.

"Huh, what's that?" His eyes opened and he regarded her blearily. "Oh, Elizabeth." Then, his memory as faulty as his hearing, he asked, "And how is your father?"

Holding the trumpet to his ear, she shouted, "Dead."

She pulled him up, handed him the cane and trumpet, and guided him toward the hall. "Is that right? Always said the boy would come to a bad end. How'd Leon die, eh?"

Elizabeth winced but Uncle Herman had already forgotten

the question and was moving his withered lips in and out as though already savoring his dinner.

As they made their slow way to the dining room, her mind busily tabulated her impressions. Aunt Van, no matter how sweet her outward demeanor, was an enemy of Judith and Emma Arnold. George's sideways glances at his lovely new stepmother betrayed feeling for her that was hardly that of a son, and Judith had been the one to offer a reprieve to Cousin Elizabeth.

I'll make myself indispensable to Judith, Elizabeth vowed, she is my only hope of remaining in this house. And no matter what I have to do, I'm staying here, for this is my house as much as hers.

— 5 —

Judith and Emma had a brief stay in the city. Two days after the soiree, arrangements were made for their return to Boston and the duties connected with the August wedding. On the morning of their departure, while William was attanding to their tickets and their luggage, Emma and her daughter closeted themselves in the library. This room was across the wide hall from the drawing room and was much admired by Elizabeth. She had no idea why the Meredith males had always used the small room toward the rear of the house as a study instead of using the spacious library. It was paneled with white painted wood and what wall space was free of paintings was given over to glass fronted bookcases. It contained deep chairs and a long divan covered in glove leather, an Empire desk, and a fine refectory table.

Next to the library was a cloakroom. She had found that if a glass was placed in a spot above the marble washbasin, all that was said in the library was audible.

As soon as the door closed behind the Arnold women Elizabeth tiptoed into the cloakroom and applied her ear to the glass she kept there. As she listened, she smiled. Emma's high pitched voice and Judith's husky one were quite clear.

"—and I don't know," Emma was saying, "why you are insisting on keeping that old maid in this house. She's bound to resent you and make things difficult, and besides she may act as spy for that horrible old woman."

"Don't fret, mama. I'm sure Elizabeth will prove loyal and I can't see her carrying tales to Aunt Van. Besides, as you've repeatedly pointed out, this is *my* house and I can do as I wish."

"I'm only trying to give you good advice. Judith, you've always been stubborn as a mule."

"If I'd been truly stubborn you'd never have got your way and we wouldn't be here right now."

"Yes. You did see sense in the end, but what a fight to get it through your head this is the only course possible."

Elizabeth noticed that Emma's voice had lost its sugary sweetness and was as crisp as her daughter's. There was an edge to Judith's voice as she told her mother, "Best course for you too, dear mama. Was William generous in his settlement?"

"Not as free-handed as I'd hoped. You'll have to handle him, Judith. If he proves stingy cut off his husbandly privileges."

"You mean bar him from my bed?"

"That's my clever girl. But don't stand for it! I never did with your father."

"Which is why I'm being forced into marriage with a man five years older than daddy would have been now."

"Don't take that tone with me, my girl! Your mama has sacrificed for you, done without so you could have the clothes and education suitable to make a good marriage. And this is the gratitude I get."

It sounded as though Emma was weeping but her daughter's voice didn't warm in the slightest. "How much?"

"If you must know, William gave me an allowance. To be paid quarterly. If I marry again it will be cut off."

Elizabeth's lips twitched in her peculiar smile. William hadn't been foolish. The allowance could also be cut off if anything happened with his marriage. Through the wall she could hear her amusement echoed. Judith was laughing. She also heard

the rustle of skirts and hastily scuttled out of the cloakroom. By
the time the ladies came out of the library her head was bent
studiously over the account books in the butler's pantry.

For the next three weeks the Meredith house was in turmoil.
As Elizabeth scurried around she thought anyone would think
the service was to be conducted right there. The house was thoroughly turned out, new silk was ordered for curtains, linens were
bought, towels were selected, silver was polished, and crystal and
china washed. William drove himself as hard. He visited his attorney, Albert Flanders, he took his sons to his tailor for numerous fittings for wedding clothes, he made arrangements at the
best hotel in Atlantic City, and he put through expensive calls to
Boston consulting with Emma on floral arrangements.
    Elizabeth labored willingly, sustained by the thought that
she too would be going to Boston and that she would have a new
wardrobe. When no invitation arrived for her she timidly approached her cousin in his study.
    William raised puzzled brows. "I never thought that you
would . . . no, Elizabeth, your place is here with the house, preparing for our return from our wedding trip."
    She felt like a child denied a treat. At that moment her tooth
throbbed and the pain added to her rebellion. "There'll be nothing to look after. After the wedding the boys will be going to
camp and what more can be done with the house?"
    "I'll admit there's not much left to do but the servants can't
be left without supervision. They'll be shiftless and heavens
knows what mischief they might get up to. Also, provisions have
to be ordered. Here is a list that Emma kindly gave me of Judith's favorite foods. And flowers. I do want the house to be
perfect. Be sure you get those flowers Judith admires. Now, what
kind . . ."
    "Miniature yellow roses."
    "See what a head you have for details! I don't know what I'd
have done without you this last while."
    Elizabeth refused to be appeased by faint praise. Deter-
mined something was to come out of this for herself, she said
boldly, "Then you will want me to live in while you're gone. So I
can keep an eye on the staff."

He hadn't wanted that at all but he nodded reluctantly. "I
suppose that would be best. Only until we return, of course. You
may air and make up one of the rooms on the third floor."

At least he hadn't consigned her to the servants' quarters.
She pressed him further. She coveted one of the front bedrooms,
a charming room with two long windows and a marvelous canopied bed. When she mentioned it, he shook his head. "That
back room beside the staircase will serve."

He bent his head over his book in dismissal. The room he
had chosen for her was the smallest and darkest of the lot. As she
made her way back to her tiny office she glanced at the list of
Judith's favorite foods. It would appear his bride was not a light
eater. Grimly Elizabeth decided that during the master's absence
her meals would be substantial. Ignoring the ache in her jaw, she
began to prepare lavish menus for herself. As one other small
revenge she determined to use the lift any time she wished. In
the end she probably enjoyed the honeymoon as much as William did. For a brief time Elizabeth was allowed to act as mistress
of the house she coveted.

The return of the bride and groom was an involved ritual
that wouldn't have shamed a royal couple. In the hall were Elizabeth, Cookie, Gerda, Sally, and the scullery maid, standing
stiffly in a line as though drawn up for inspection. Cookie was in
immaculate white and the maids, even the scullery maid, wore
new uniforms and lace-trimmed aprons and caps. Briggs, who
had brought William and his wife from the station, hastily ran
around the house and through the rear entrance and took his
place in the line. He was resplendent in a new uniform, his boots
were gleaming, his face was the same color as his carroty hair.
He'd forgotten to remove his cap and Elizabeth caught his eye
and gestured. Whipping it off his head, he twisted it in large
hands. Then and only then did the spinster open the door.

William was glowing and Judith wore a pleasant smile. To
Elizabeth's surprise the girl embraced her and warmly kissed her
cheek. "How marvelous everything looks! You really are too
good to me, Elizabeth."

Then, although Judith had already met the staff, William insisted on introducing each of them again. She had a gracious

word for each of the women, gravely shook the chauffeur's hand,
and then rather ruined the effect by exclaiming, "How small the
staff is, William. It's amazing how well they do in this size
house."

"Quite large enough, darling. Elizabeth, is dinner ready?"
He touched his wife's wrist and managed to look coy. "Dinner
for two. We must enjoy it. The boys will be home from camp
soon."

Hastily, Elizabeth drew Gerda aside. "Take off the third
place setting," she hissed. She should have known it was too
good to last. Elizabeth was not to share the first dinner in Judith's home. All afternoon she had worked over the flowers that
banked the hall, the drawing room, Judith's bedroom. She'd
carefully arranged a centerpiece of freesia and yellow roses for
the dining table and had gone over and over the dinner menu
with Cookie. Surely not even William would force her to leave
without dinner. It had been a forlorn hope and was immediately
dashed.

William not only could but did. "We mustn't keep you, Elizabeth. You'll be anxious to return to your cosy flat."

She bent her head to hide the expression in her eyes. Unpinning her lacy hat, Judith tried to intercede. "Surely morning
would be better, William. Elizabeth's worked so hard I know
she'd enjoy having dinner with us."

"We mustn't be selfish, darling. Run along, Elizabeth, and
gather your things together."

Meekly, Elizabeth climbed the stairs toward the room she no
longer could call her own. At the bend of the staircase she
paused and listened. In the hall below there was silence and she
guessed William was embracing his bride. After a time he said
huskily, "Judith, my love, how I adore you. You . . . you light
up this house. Do anything you wish with it. If the furniture
doesn't please you or—"

His voice cut off so quickly Elizabeth guessed a soft palm
had been laid across his lips. Holding her breath she saw again an
image of a huge broom bearing Judith's blond head sweeping all
the treasured possessions down the front steps.

Then Judith said softly, "No changes will be made. This
house is perfect."

There was another silence, evidently the passionate bridegroom was again embracing his young wife, then the rustle of skirts and Elizabeth knew they were walking down the hall toward the dining room. She made her way up to the tiny room beside the servants' stairs. As she packed her carpetbag she found her mind wasn't brooding on dispossession or the loss of the dinner she'd slaved over. Instead she was conscious of a warmth she hadn't felt since her father's death. Elizabeth Meredith had never had a friend. She had only one acquaintance, a pallid old maid who had also attended Miss Penelope's Academy for Young Ladies and had also been a pauper among the wealthy students. Nettie Towers lived in Westchester and Elizabeth and the other old maid corresponded but they weren't close. Elizabeth stuck her nightgown into the shabby carpetbag and put a hand to her cheek. She still felt the soft touch of Judith's lips against her skin, the warmth of the girl's embrace. Judith had even tried to intercede with William for her sake.

As Elizabeth trudged back to her boarding house through the dark streets a feeling of happiness persisted. Perhaps, at last, she had found a friend.

Judith kept her word. Not a piece of furniture, an ornament, a vase, or a painting was moved in the Meredith house. Elizabeth came as usual and did her best to instruct Judith on her duties as mistress. But the girl had little interest in household affairs and to Elizabeth's surprise William didn't chide his bride. Judith liked to sleep late, breakfast in bed, and spend the remainder of the day amusing herself. She did accede to her husband's desire that she should visit and issue invitations to the ladies connected with the family. Many of her afternoons were spent with Aunt Van, Lavinia Stokes, and Nina Flanders. Judith was polite to all of them but Elizabeth knew the girl didn't care for any of the women. The one person she did take a fancy to proved to be Aunt Van's older daughter Sophie, though Elizabeth failed to see the reason for the attraction. At twenty-nine Sophie was a spinster, a string bean with stooping shoulders and mousy hair that always seemed to be falling loose from its coils. Judith confided she felt sorry for the woman. "Aunt Van devours her," she said.

"Sophie has had no life of her own and she's a slave to that woman."

"That's what I've heard. I don't know Sophie well but Nina Flanders told me all about her."

"What ever happened to the poor creature?"

"Her mother. Nina said when Sophie was quite young, around eighteen, she was in love with a young man who worked in her father's bank. He adored Sophie and they were planning to marry when Aunt Van stepped in, had the chap fired, and wouldn't allow Sophie even to see him. Nina said he moved to Chicago and married a girl there. Sophie was heartbroken."

Judith raised her brows. "Did Aunt Van find him unsuitable for some reason?"

"Any man would have been unsuitable. Aunt Van simply had no intention of allowing Sophie to marry."

"So she could have an unpaid companion, a slave to wait on her." The girl flushed with anger. "How Sophie must hate her mother!"

"If she does she certainly conceals it. But I suppose she'd be forced to. How do you like Sophie's young brother and Charity?"

"The boy seems all right. He looks like Sophie and Aunt Van orders him around the same way. The other day—what's his name?"

"Earl."

"I asked Earl what he intended to do when his education was finished and he wasn't allowed to answer. Aunt Van took right over and told me Earl is going to be a banker like his father—" Breaking off, Judith giggled. "Pardon me, like the *dear departed* was. Then Earl did speak up and said he didn't want to enter a bank but Aunt Van brushed him aside. She's a . . . a perfect harridan!"

To Elizabeth's amazement she found she was warning Judith. "No matter what you think of Aunt Van, do try to stay on her good side."

"Why should I? What's she to me?"

"She could be a menace. She has influence with William and all his friends. She may look and act rather silly but she'd make a terrible enemy."

"Very well. I'll be nice to the old bat if I have to bite my tongue. But there's another Aunt Van coming along." Judith rolled violet eyes. "Charity! That child reminds me of a piglet."

Elizabeth found she was laughing. How long was it since she'd genuinely laughed? Day by day her affection for William's young wife was growing. The new broom was sweeping clean but not in the manner that she had feared. Changes were being made in Elizabeth's life. The first change was the luncheon menu. Without consulting her husband, Judith took the lunch sheet and tore it up. From then on the meals were large and rich enough that Elizabeth was delighted. The second change came as a shock not only to Elizabeth but to William. His bride forced him to raise his cousin's salary. William grumbled but the next envelope he handed Elizabeth was thicker. With it went a long lecture on restraining her tendency toward extravagance.

Elizabeth had hardly digested this piece of luck when Judith invited her on a shopping expedition. Again William protested, but his bride told him frostily that even if he didn't mind his cousin looking like a scarecrow, she did. Elizabeth came home with lengths for two woolen suits, thin cotton for underwear, heavier cotton for shirtwaists, a length of fine lace for trim, and two pairs of shoes. A week later they shopped again and a winter coat with a small fur collar and a hat with a jaunty bunch of cherries were added to her wardrobe.

Elizabeth's devotion to her young protector was growing. Thanks to Judith's generosity she now enjoyed sufficient food, a little extra money, and respectable clothes.

George was now in his first year at Harvard and Alan, still in day school, had become meek and respectful toward Elizabeth. The boy had little intelligence but he was cunning and he realized he'd better be careful. His favorite object of ridicule now was under his stepmother's protection, and he knew he was no match for Judith. If it came to friction his infatuated father would take his new wife's side.

The second week in September brought down the last barrier around Elizabeth's emotion. She was in the butler's pantry working on the account books when agony lanced through her jaw. This time it wasn't one tooth aching but several. She buried her face in her hands. Judith found her there in that position.

Pausing beside the desk, Judith asked, "What's wrong? Have you had bad news?"

Behind her mistress Cookie stood with her arms akimbo. "I'll tell you what it is, Mrs. Meredith. It's her teeth, that's what. Ever since I knew her she's been suffering from bad teeth. And the poor lamb without a cent to have them fixed. I call it a disgrace!"

"I'll take care of it, Cookie. You get back to work."

Hands touched Elizabeth's head and forced it back. Reluctantly, at Judith's urging, she opened her mouth. The younger woman gasped. "My dear Lord! I'm phoning my dentist right now!"

Tears flooded Elizabeth's eyes. "No. I've no money."

"Money be damned! I'll have Briggs bring around the car."

"William."

"I'll handle William."

And handle William she did. Elizabeth's teeth were extracted and it was two months before the gums were healed enough to wear dentures. Elizabeth suffered the agony of the damned but there was now hope her suffering would soon be over. And the miracle occurred. When the dentures were placed in her mouth the dentist held up a hand mirror and Elizabeth allowed her lips to relax in a wide smile reminiscent of the child in her father's painting. Turning from the mirrored reflection of that smile she lifted her dark eyes to Judith's smiling violet ones.

The last defense was breeched and Elizabeth gave to William's wife the devotion she might have felt for a younger and beloved sister.

— 6 —

The assassination of the heir to the throne of Austria-Hungary produced reverberations that led the world into the Great War. Shortly before the wedding of Judith and William Meredith Germany declared war on Russia. Two days later war was declared between France and Germany. The following day Great Britain was drawn into the conflict. The *New York Times* headlines gave the fateful news that was to affect all the nations of the world. In the United States the news was received with mixed reactions. Sympathy lay with the great three—France, Britain, Russia—but the Americans had no desire to be drawn into the conflict. President Wilson leaned toward neutrality and most Americans settled comfortably into that role.

In the autumn of 1914 the war in Europe was a chief source of conversation. In the Merediths' circle on every occasion they met the men discussed the possibility that their country might be forced to enter the war. With the exception of Doctor John Stokes and to a lesser extent William Meredith, most opinions were that the United States would never become involved. As Albert Flanders succinctly put it, "Why should we? The Europeans started the whole mess. Let them finish it. What business is it of ours?"

Doctor John glowered at his handsome brother-in-law. "You're hiding your head in the sand. Sooner or later we'll be drawn into it. I like the thought no more than you do but we have to face it. Before long our sons will be fighting."

Albert smoothed his mustache, smiling complacently. Even if war did come he had no reason for personal unease. Nina had given him two daughters. But John Stokes was thinking of his son who had just finished medical school and had recently married. William, half-swayed by the doctor's words, didn't know what to think. His thoughts were with his own sons. Alan was not yet seventeen but George was nearly nineteen and in his letters constantly mentioned the European conflict. George spoke of the talk at Harvard, the glamor of the British R.A.F., the training of troops in Canada. William wrote the boy long letters stressing the neutrality of their own country, urging caution.

So distressed was William that more and more he turned to his young wife for relief. He catered to her every whim. She played the piano, and so the piano in the back drawing room, untouched since his grandmother's death, was tuned. She played for him in the evening when they were alone or for their guests when they entertained. Judith tinkled pretty snatches of popular songs, bits of Strauss and Brahms. In the afternoons she sometimes played music that might have disturbed her husband if he had heard it. As Elizabeth went about her duties she often paused, listening to the passionate strains that filled the drawing rooms. In that music were hints of despair, of grief and frustration, at other times frenetic sounds of hope.

It was the middle of November before William showed the first sign of opposing Judith's wishes and at the time it certainly didn't seem serious. As was his custom, he entered his wife's room soon after he had breakfasted. He sat beside the bed while she consumed a hearty breakfast, feasting his eyes on her loveliness. Bright hair fell around her face and over silk pillows, her nightgown had slipped off one rounded shoulder and displayed the curves of a breast. Judith was as fresh and beautiful as the single yellow rose Elizabeth always placed on the tray.

Touching the rose, William told her his thoughts. One of her hands moved to caress his and his face glowed. The finger slid down over the curve of her naked breast and she jerked away and adjusted her gown. "Really, William!"

"I know, but I can't seem to keep my hands off you. I feel as though I've never loved before." He thought this over and then said softly, "I haven't, you know. My first marriage was arranged and although Ruth was a good wife we—"

Her hand covered his lips. "You told me on our honeymoon."

He kissed her palm. "What are your plans for today, darling?"

"I thought I'd do a little Christmas shopping, perhaps have lunch out."

"I'll leave the car for you. I hope you aren't going alone.
You know how I worry."

"I never go out alone."

"Aunt Van, I'll bet, or is it Sophie?"

"I've asked Elizabeth."

He watched her pour coffee into a china cup. "Aren't you
making too much of a fuss over Elizabeth? Her teeth and all
those clothes. You must tread carefully. Her father. Dreadfully
unstable."

"What is the mystery about your uncle? Was he a criminal?"

"Of course he wasn't! Leon was a Meredith. But he was a
dreamer, dabbled with painting and music and that sort of thing.
Wasted his inheritance on high living. We mustn't give his daughter ideas above her station."

"And what *is* her station?"

"Well . . . Elizabeth's a . . . she's a—"

"Poor relative?"

"To be blunt—yes. Her father drank himself to death and
her mother . . . Aunt Ethel was a good sort, a respectable
woman, but she was a milliner. We, father and I, had to educate
Elizabeth and more or less look after her. With her background
one must exercise caution. That type *always* tries to move in, to
get everything they can. You've spoilt her, Judith. Before we
were married I handled Elizabeth quite well."

Violet eyes flashed with rage. "I noticed. Half-starved, practically in rags, her teeth rotting in her mouth."

"She was adequately paid." William drew himself up and his
voice was icy as he said, "It certainly was not my fault she chose
to squander her salary rather than buy food and clothes."

"And her teeth?"

"Perhaps I was remiss there but I had my own life, the boys
to consider. Motherless boys—" His voice broke and his eyes
looked moist. "Judith, darling, let's not quarrel. I can't bear to
quarrel with you!" Pushing the tray aside, he buried his head in
her lap.

"I have your permission to take Elizabeth with me?"

"Of course. Anything you wish. And she has been good to
you, hasn't she?"

She patted the bald head burrowing into the warmth of her

body. "I don't know what I'd do without Cousin Elizabeth," she murmured, and smiled.

Pushing aside the stack of parcels, Judith allowed Briggs to help her from the tonneau of the Panhard Levassor. She joined Elizabeth, who was huddling closer into the warmth of her new coat and tugging up the fur collar against the chill of the wind. Rather dubiously, Elizabeth looked at the sign above the door. "The Oasis. Are you sure you want to lunch here? There's a nice little tearoom a few blocks uptown where Aunt Van took me once. Quite respectable for ladies lunching alone."

Judith smiled and told the chauffeur, "You may pick us up . . . oh, better make it about two. I don't want to rush lunch." To Elizabeth she said, "What's wrong with this cafe?"

"It *is* in the Village. Oh, only on the outskirts, I know, but I don't think William would approve. And it looks a bit like a saloon."

"We'll have a look inside and if you don't care for it we'll try that tearoom you mentioned."

The interior was reassuring. Small oak tables and basket chairs cushioned in red and white stood against white painted walls. Waitresses in neat uniforms moved among the tables and one of them, a welcoming smile on her face, approached them. Elizabeth was relieved to see that at some of the tables well-dressed women were seated. Quite respectable, she thought, as she followed Judith's slender back toward a corner table. Hardly a glance was directed at Elizabeth. All eyes, certainly all masculine eyes, were fastened on her young companion. Elizabeth felt a thrill of vicarious pride. Judith wore a long mink coat, a scrap of fur fashioned as a hat, and her gloved hands were cradled in a mink muff. Against the dark fur her blond hair and lovely skin glowed.

Taking a chair, Judith shrugged off the mink, and plucked menus from a china holder made in the shape of a camel. "I breakfasted rather late ¿nd I'll have something light. But you order a hearty lunch."

Elizabeth accepted a menu and bent eagerly over it. She decided on chicken stew with dumplings and peach cobbler with cream. Judith asked for salad and smoked salmon. She added, "And please bring two sherries."

Quite daring, Elizabeth thought, but she was delighted. Sipping sherry she gazed around. A party of men were being seated at a nearby table. All of them were youngish and were dressed rather casually. She noticed three of them were taking good looks at Judith and then her eyes strayed to the fourth. He was the tallest and the most striking. His hair alone was enough to warrant attention, a flaming red gold, sweeping back in waves from a wide brow, worn rather long and tending to curl behind his ears. He had striking eyes too, a greenish color under shaggy russet brows. To her shock she realized those eyes were staring not at Judith but at her. Lowering her head, she pretended to study her glass of sherry.

Judith was chatting about their purchases. "I do hope Aunt Van will like the present I got for her. She's so hard to please."

"She'll love it. Aunt Van adores fine crystal. Have you made up your mind about William's Christmas present?"

"Not as yet. I'll have to speak with Doctor John or Albert. William is as hard to please as Aunt Van."

"Perhaps he'd like a smoking jacket. That claret colored velvet one was nice."

Elizabeth continued to chat but her eyes kept straying to the red-haired man. She catalogued him thoroughly. About her age, well over six feet, good looking in a rugged way, a warm smile. She liked the way he dressed, the shabby tweed jacket with leather patches, the turtleneck sweater, the look of his clothes being perfectly at home on his rangy frame. She also liked the way he kept giving her sidelong glances. Of course, Elizabeth assured herself, in the garnet suit with a flood of snowy lace at the throat, she didn't look that bad. Judith had lent her lotions for her skin and taught her to rub her face with lemon rind to remove the oiliness. Her color was high and she did have nice hair and eyes. A man might well want to look at her now. Her only problem was the habit of that twitching smile. Hard as she tried she still found it necessary to remind herself to relax her lips. She relaxed her lips and gave Judith a beaming smile.

Judith hadn't said anything to deserve that smile and she gave the older woman a puzzled look. Elizabeth darted another look at the men's table and was disappointed to see they were leaving. At the same moment she realized she'd finished her lunch and the waitress was setting down pots of tea. She busied

herself pouring, squeezing lemon, stirring unnecessarily hard.
"Elizabeth!" Judith bent over the table. "Do you know that
man? He's been staring at you and—"

Elizabeth turned and saw that only three of the men had
left. The other one was standing beside his table, looking intently
at her. "No! Judith, I do believe he's coming over. What will I
do?"

"Let me handle it. I'll make short shrift of him."

He towered over them. He's much taller than I thought,
Elizabeth thought wildly. He bent over and she felt hot color
flooding her cheeks. "Don't be alarmed," he told her. His voice
wasn't as deep as she'd imagined it would be. "I'm not a masher
though I may have been acting like one. Haven't we met before?
Aren't you Elizabeth, daughter of Leon Meredith?"

Elizabeth looked at Judith for guidance but she was staring
in quite an interested way at the man. "Yes," Elizabeth admitted, realized she was whispering, and raised her voice. "Leon
Meredith was my father."

"Allow me to introduce myself. I'm Lafcadio Norton. Lafe
for short. Ah, you don't remember me. I'm not surprised. We
met only once and I was about nine at the time. Your parents
were living on East 24th and—"

"Oh! Give me a minute." Elizabeth said slowly, "You were
with an older man, a man about my father's age . . ."

"My father, Thomas Norton. Your father and mine went to
college together. That afternoon your father drew a sketch of
me. Father was so pleased with it he had it framed and it hung
above his desk until his death. I still have it and I've always remembered Leon Meredith and you. You were such a pretty little
girl. How is your father?"

"He died many years ago, Mr. Norton."

"Lafe, please. I'm sorry, Elizabeth. I never heard. I've been
out of the country a great deal. Such a waste. Your father was so
talented."

There was an awkward pause and Elizabeth was at a loss to
know what to do or say next. Judith solved the problem. "Won't
you join us, Mr. Norton?"

"Thank you." He gave her a courteous nod and sank into
the chair facing Elizabeth. "May I offer you fresh tea? Waitress."

With a start Elizabeth remembered her manners. "Mr. Norton . . . Lafe, may I introduce my companion. Mrs. William Meredith."

Graciously, Judith inclined her bright head and Lafe snapped his fingers. "William. Leon's younger brother's son. I believe my father was an acquaintance of your husband. I think they belonged to the same club. It's an honor to meet you, Mrs. Meredith." His eyes snapped back to Elizabeth. "Now I can truly say it's a small world. To drop into a cafe and meet an old friend like this. What are you doing with yourself, Elizabeth?"

She noticed wryly he didn't ask if she had married. Of course, he had glanced at her hand perhaps to see of there was a wedding ring. She gave him the meager details with Judith chiming in to tell Lafe she had no idea what she should do without Cousin Elizabeth. Then Elizabeth asked him, "And you, Lafe?"

"You might say following in my father's steps. He was a writer. Highly regarded by many critics but, using a financial yardstick, completely unsuccessful. I do manage to make a living. I work for the *Tribune.*"

"A journalist! How exciting. That's why you travel a great deal."

"Far too much. And I have a hunch I'll soon be sent to England to cover the war. But we can't hope to catch up with all the years in a few minutes." He consulted his watch. "I'm late in getting back to the office but I mustn't lose track of you again. Could you . . . would you dine with me soon?"

She blushed, wondering how to tell him William would be highly incensed at the idea. Adjusting her little mink hat, Judith gave Elizabeth a reassuring smile and made another suggestion. "I'm sure William would be pleased to meet you, Mr. Norton. After all, your father and he were friends."

"Only acquaintances, and Mr. Meredith may not even remember him."

"What was his first name?"

"Thomas."

"William's memory is exceptional. Would you care to dine with us? Friday, about eight. Elizabeth, that night is free, isn't it?"

At that point, Elizabeth couldn't even remember what day it

was but she murmured that she believed they were free. Lafe Norton was hesitant but finally agreed he would be delighted. "If you do remember a previous engagement, Mrs. Meredith, you can reach me at the *Tribune*. If I'm not in, leave a message."

He rose, picked up his shabby topcoat, shook both their hands, and made his way out of the cafe. Elizabeth watched his broad back until the door closed. She turned to her companion, her face flushed, close to tears. "It's all too much. So much has happened lately, now *this*. I feel as though I'm dreaming!"

Judith slipped on her coat, the fur collar framing her vivid face. "You're wide awake but I can't say I blame you. Mr. Norton definitely seems interested in you."

"Why? A spinster no man looks at twice. And he's so handsome, so vital."

"Come along, Briggs will be waiting. And you're not a spinster. You're an attractive woman."

Elizabeth followed her, too distraught to button up her coat. In the comfortable tonneau of William's car she sat bolt upright, staring through the glass at Briggs's thick neck. "William will never agree to receive Lafe. He'll say—"

"I know what he'll say. I'll do my best, Elizabeth."

That evening it appeared even Judith's best wasn't enough to sway her husband. She waited until dinner was over and William was comfortable in his favorite chair, puffing at a cigar, sipping a brandy. She played two Strauss waltzes for him and then her hands fell into her lap and she swung around on the stool. How old he looks, she thought as the recent memory of Lafe Norton brushed across her mind. The melon-shaped paunch bulged his waistcoat and his bald head gleamed in the lamplight. How well she knew that body, the narrow chest, the spindly arms and hairy legs. The body of an aging man with the lust of one much younger. Night after night her door creaked open and William, attired in a flannel nightshirt, slid that body into her bed. How sad that only old men like him had money. Sighing, Judith wondered how best to broach the subject.

"Darling," William said fondly. "You've been quiet all evening. Is something troubling you?"

She went to sit on his knee. Putting the cigar down, he eagerly cradled her in his arms. "What is it? A new gown, a fur?"

"It's not for me. William, it's a favor for Elizabeth." His body stiffened and she hurried on, "This is important for her. While we were lunching she met an old friend and—"

"A man?"

"Yes. His name is Lafcadio Norton and his father and hers were friends. Mr. Norton and Elizabeth met when they were children and he recognized—"

He straightened so suddenly she nearly tumbled from his knees. "You allowed a strange man to approach you? Judith, how indiscreet! That simply isn't done."

"Not a stranger. I told you his father and Elizabeth's were friends."

"Uncle Leon!" William snorted. "Now, what sort of friend would that ne'er-do-well have?"

Stroking his cheek, she wheedled, "Mr. Norton said his father and you were acquainted at one time."

"Norton? No, I remember no one of that name."

"Thomas Norton. You belonged to the same club."

"I remember no one of that name. What is all this leading up to?"

"He wanted to take Elizabeth out to dine and I knew you'd never agree so . . . so I invited him to dine with us on Friday night."

Clasping her narrow waist, he lifted her from his lap. "You had the effrontery to issue an invitation to a strange man without consulting me? You will cancel it. Do you understand?"

"William, please. Think of Elizabeth."

"I'm sorry but I'm adamant. The subject is closed."

For a moment she stared down at his austere face. Then she tossed her head and bolted from the room. She mounted the stairs, her eyes blazing, her cheeks hot. In her room she slid the bolts on both doors. Later that night she heard William at the door that connected their rooms. He rattled the knob but she didn't move. After a time he went away. When he tried the door the following morning it was still barred.

William spent miserable hours at his office that day giving scant attention to the work piled up on his desk. Early in the afternoon he gave up, told his secretary he was going home, and left. Miss Patterson, who had been with him for years, was amazed. This was the first time her employer had ever left early. He looked dreadful, she thought, might he be ill?

When William reached the Vandercourt house, Aunt Van wondered the same thing. As he was admitted to her drawing room she glanced up, not bothering to raise her bulk from the soft cushions on the sofa. On the table before her was an open box of chocolates and she held a romance with a lurid cover. "Well, William. How unusual to see you at this time. Are you sickening for something? You looked quite gray."

"No, no, Aunt Van. I feel fine. Thought I'd drop in and have a chat."

William eyed a chair before he sank onto it and repressed a shudder. Aunt Van had succumbed to the current fashion and had done her drawing room over in fake Egyptian. The chairs were not only hideous but uncomfortable, huge thronelike monsters with carved serpent arms. Bronze scarabs were scattered over the tables, and in a corner of the room was a lacquered screen covered with sloe-eyed figures, palms, and sheaves of wheat. The only decent piece was the long sofa where his aunt sprawled.

She glanced complacently around. "How do you like the new decor?"

"Completely fascinating and highly unusual."

"What shall we chat about, dear boy?" Silently she exulted. I know what we'll chat about, she thought, that hussy you married against my advice. Sooner or later I knew she'd be giving you hell.

"Aunt Van, do you know a family named Norton?"

"Norton?"

"Thomas or Lafcadio?"

"Lafcadio? An unusual name. Sounds foreign. Thomas Norton? Give me a moment. I should know *that* name. Of course! Dear boy, my memory must be slipping. They're in the way of being related to me, distantly, and I haven't seen any of them for years."

"Related?"

"Not the Nortons. Thomas's wife. She was an Allenby. Her

second cousin—or was it first? Anyway a cousin of Hazel Allenby's is the stepson of my Aunt Minnie."

"Are they a good family?"

"The Allenbys certainly are. And the Nortons are decent enough people although Hazel's husband Thomas was an artist of some kind. Writer, if I remember correctly. Hazel brought him quite a nice dowry but Thomas managed to waste it while he wrote those silly books no one could make head or tail of. Dreadfully poor, Thomas and Hazel were. I went to her funeral twenty . . . no, it must have been nearly twenty-five years ago. She died quite young, poor dear, and no wonder. It was very small, that funeral, and the coffin, my dear boy, the cheapest that could be bought. Simply a wood box! There was a son. Ah, yes, Lafcadio. Such a silly name but with a father like that who can wonder."

"Were they respectable?"

"Of course. Nothing wrong with them except the way Thomas lazed around writing instead of taking an honest job. I always said Hazel would have lived longer if he'd looked after her better." Aunt Van tilted her head, pinning her nephew with sharp eyes. "What is your interest in Hazel and Thomas?"

He told her and she was so intrigued she neglected the chocolates. "And Judith picked up this man, a stranger in a restaurant, and invited him to dine? Really, William!"

"He *is* the son of a man who was a close friend of Uncle Leon's."

"Leon. About what you would expect. A writer and a painter! But, a minute, William. You say this young man is interested in Cousin Elizabeth?"

"It would appear he is. Apparently they met when they were children . . . but he could be a fortune hunter, couldn't he? The Meredith name, you know."

"He might be but you can easily disabuse him of any idea Elizabeth is an heiress."

William looked baffled. "Why else would a man be interested in Elizabeth?"

"Have you looked at your cousin lately? I must admit Judith has worked a miracle. Elizabeth is quite a handsome woman now. Takes after her father in looks. As I said to Charity only the other day—that child is so wise for her years, William—I said to her, I knew Elizabeth could be quite decent looking if she bothered to take care of herself. If you play your cards right you might marry her off."

William showed interest in this remark. More and more he was finding Elizabeth a trial. The way Judith coddled her and fussed over her . . . abruptly he realized he was jealous of an old maid cousin. His aunt was following his thoughts. If he could, Aunt Van thought disgustedly, he'd lock that hussy of a wife away all for himself. No fool like an old fool. Infatuated and moonstruck as a boy!

He rubbed his chin with a tapered finger. "You always help me reason a problem through, Aunt Van. In all fairness to Elizabeth it would be sensible to have this chap in and look him over. If there is a chance he's interested in her I certainly can't stand in the way."

"You've always had her welfare at heart. By all means receive the young fellow. Make it clear to him Cousin Elizabeth is a poor relative and as such will not be inheriting." Aunt Van laid a finger along her nose. "But it wouldn't hurt to hint you might consider giving her a small dowry."

"I've spent enough on that woman now! The dentist's bill and then all those clothes and a raise in salary. No!"

"Don't be headstrong, dear boy. Only a *small* dowry. If Elizabeth continues to be in your house and with the presents Judith—who is well intentioned but young and heedless—lavishes on her, it could cost you a great deal more."

Pulling himself from the hideous chair, he stretched his long frame. "You're a wonder, Aunt Van. I'll think about the dowry but we'll definitely have this Norton to dinner. If I don't like his looks or his manner I'll have a quiet word with him and warn him off."

"That's my good boy," she told him. After he left Aunt Van lay back among the cushions, her hand fumbling for a candy from time to time, her fat body quaking with silent laughter.

— 7 —

Friday night on the dot of eight Lafe Norton arrived at the Meredith house. He was freshly barbered, clad in a sober dark suit, and clutching nosegays of violets for Judith and Elizabeth. William subjected the younger man to a covert but thorough inspection. He could find no fault with Elizabeth's friend. Lafe's manners were impeccable—he was personable, articulate, relaxed, and yet properly deferential to William's age and position. At table he was amusing, regaling his audience with anecdotes about Teddy Roosevelt, the militant Emma Goldman, and even the Coronation Durbar for Edward VII at Delhi. As Lafe explained modestly, he had been only a lowly cub reporter at the time of the coronation but because an outbreak of grippe had afflicted the experienced reporters, he had represented his paper there.

Judith, William, and an awestruck Alan hung on the young man's tales. Elizabeth heard only the cadence of his rather light voice and she understood nothing of the meaning. She was too preoccupied with Lafe's presence, his hand brushing hers as they bent at the same moment for a napkin that had fallen from her lap.

Elizabeth fairly glowed and when William could tear his eyes away from his entertaining guest he regarded his cousin with amazement. Elizabeth had worked over her toilette. She wore her new blue suit, a pair of Judith's embroidered hose displaying surprisingly shapely ankles, her hair was waved back and caught in a huge chignon on her neck. At her ears Judith's pearl studs glowed and her dark eyes were brilliant with excitement.

When Judith and Elizabeth retired to the drawing room and Alan was sent upstairs William kept his guest for nearly an hour over cigars and brandy. Lafe told him bits and pieces about the Spanish American War and the Boer War that were considered unfit for delicate ladies' ears. From that they moved to the present conflict and William regarded the younger man admiringly when Lafe mentioned he hoped to be sent to London early in the new year. So impressed was William that at the end of the evening he offered his car and chauffeur for Lafe's use in escorting Elizabeth home. Lafe smilingly declined and as the door closed behind them William turned to his wife.

Judith, deliciously lovely in ivory taffeta and garnets set in heavy gold, asked with a smile, "Well?"

"A splendid young man." He hugged her. "You did quite right to invite him."

"You approve of him?"

"Most certainly. I'm going to ask Aunt Van to invite him to dine."

Aunt Van was happy to oblige. Lafe had been told it would only be a small affair but when he arrived at the Vandercourt house he found the guests included not only Elizabeth and the Merediths but also the Stokeses, the Flanderses, and the Standfords. Uncle Herman hadn't been forgotten, and he occupied the position of honor at the foot of the table, linked to the hostess's place by a procession of china Nubian slaves each with a candle twisting from the top of its skull.

Ancient Egypt had not only taken over the Vandercourt living room but was also reaching sinister fingers into the dining room. Against the wall a sarcophagus in shades of red ochre, blue, and tan rested against the wall. The gilded face and ornate headdress of the fictional occupant leered over the dining table. Papier-mâché, Lafe thought, and not well done at that. But taking his cue, he cunningly led the conversation to the British and American archeologists working in the ancient tombs. The ladies, led by an eager Aunt Van, were soon in full cry, tripping over each other's words to ask questions about the Valley of the Kings, the Temple of Karnak, the Great Pyramid at Giza. Trembling with delicious fear they accepted Lafe as an authority on their favorite subject and listened to his accounts of the curses laid on violators of those tombs.

Lafe, conscious of the men's skeptical expressions, modestly explained he had no firsthand knowledge, he was only repeating conversations of other reporters. In the end he charmed them all, both women and men. Even Aunt Van, suspicious by nature, succumbed, and as she watched Elizabeth and Lafe Norton leave her house she announced to her guests it was high time they did admit a new person to their group.

The reason for Lafe's impact was simple. Only a handful of families comprised their tight little circle. They fed on each other for company, for social events, for gossip. They didn't realize it but they were tired of each other's faces, children, homes, conversation. Lafe Norton, with his good looks and charm, was a fresh breeze through their lives. He brought exotic adventure into secure havens, a whiff of faraway places and events that blew through old drawing rooms. Some of the ladies, particularly Lavinia Stokes, also welcomed a chance for harmless flirtation with a handsome stranger.

If they had been outside the Vandercourt house that evening they would have seen quite a different stranger. In front of the line of shining card Lafe paused and enviously kicked the tires of the Standfords' Cadillac. None of the chauffeurs remained with the vehicles. A light snow was falling and they'd sought refuge in Aunt Van's kitchen, sitting around the stove, mugs of coffee in their hands, telling jokes and lies to each other.

"It's a long walk," Lafe said morosely. "Sorry I can't afford a taxi."

Elizabeth didn't mention he'd turned down the use of Aunt Van's Packard and its driver. "I don't mind. I'm used to walking."

He turned up the collar of his threadbare overcoat. A coat much too light for December, Elizabeth thought. She studied his face. He looked entirely different than he had at dinner. His expression was remote and withdrawn. "It's not easy," she told him gently, "being on display."

"People like me get used to singing for their supper." Glancing down at her, he grinned. "Though I must admit that meal was worth singing for. What a spread!"

"Aunt Van likes good food."

"And shows it."

With her arm tucked in the crook of his elbow, they strode down the sidewalk. Elizabeth didn't notice the icy wind or the snowflakes brushing against her face. She was lost in the feeling of Lafe's thick arm, the solid body pressed against her. She kept darting looks at his face, her eyes tracing the line of his brow, his nose, his lips. All evening she'd taken pride in him, conscious of the envy felt by the women. She'd basked in a glow of vicarious triumph as Lafe effortlessly held the center of attention. Could this actually be happening to Cousin Elizabeth, she wondered, or was it a dream from which she soon would wake? But Lafe's arm was real and so was his voice.

"I've sung for everything I've ever had, Elizabeth. God knows that hasn't been much."

"I suppose your family wasn't much better off than mine was."

"If it hadn't been for mother's family we'd have starved. Once in a while they came through. Crumbs from their table. But after mother's death all they'd do was see I had an education. Then they washed their hands of dad and me."

"That's all the Merediths did for mother and me. But it's easier for a man to make his way than for a woman."

With his free hand he brushed a snowflake from the tip of her nose. "I keep forgetting you're a poor relative too. You're well dressed and the bits of jewelry . . ."

"Judith's. Until she married William I had neither clothes nor even enough to eat."

"You really like Mrs. Meredith, don't you?"

"More than like. She's the only one, except my father, to show me kindness. She's been like a young and lovely fairy god-mother."

"Or a Lady Bountiful."

"No! She doesn't condescend. She's . . . she's wonderful."

He squeezed her arm against his side. "If you could have anything you wanted, what would you ask?"

A few weeks earlier the old Elizabeth would have said, "The family house and the family money." But the new Elizabeth felt like shouting, "You! Only you." I love this man, she thought fiercely, he's all I want. Aloud she said carefully, "I suppose what everyone would like—a house, even a tiny one, enough money to live on."

"Not very ambitious. What about furs, jewelry, traveling, cars?"

"Is that what you want?"

"Yes. I'm sick of being poor. Sure I'd like a car like one of those back there. And a house like William's. Sure I'd like to travel first class, have servants to do the work. There's nothing wrong with dreams."

"Nothing," she agreed but suddenly she felt the cold, the biting wind. I can't give him those things, she thought forlornly, all I can give is myself. Does he want that?

Lafe seemed in better spirits and started to hum a catchy tune. Elizabeth had heard it before. "What's that?" she asked.

" 'Wall Street Rag.' Scott Joplin."

"Alan plays it on his Victrola. I like it."

She hummed along with him and the blocks went by like magic. Much too soon she was standing with Lafe on the steps of her rooming house. He took the key from her, unlocked the door, bid her good night, and then he suddenly bent, cupped her face in cold hands, and dropped a kiss on her brow. Long after he'd vanished in the snow she stood on the doorstep, her heart singing a paean of joy, her skin tingling where his lips had pressed. I love him, she thought, I've never loved before but oh, how I love Lafcadio Norton!

On the way down the block Lafe looked longingly at warm lights falling from the windows of saloons. But he passed them by and continued to the one he frequented. Thankfully he brushed snow from his coat, kicked his overshoes clean, and swung open the doors. A blast of heat, the rank smells of beer, food, and sawdust rushed out in greeting.

As he wended his way among the tables, men called ribald greetings and shoved out chairs for him. He waved and called back but ignored the chairs and leaned against the wide oak bar, one foot braced on the brass rail. The grinning barman skidded a foaming stein down to him and Lafe took a long drink. In this atmosphere, redolent with smoke and beer fumes, amid the jostling, good-natured men he felt more at ease than in the Vandercourts' dining room.

Glancing down the bar he spotted a man in a loud checkered suit loading up a saucer at the free lunch counter and called a greeting. The man finished his selection and shouldered in beside

Lafe. "Set 'em up, Tony," he yelled at the barman, slapped down the saucer, and turned to face Lafe. "Where'd you get that outfit? Rob an undertaker?"

Lafe patted the lapel of the neatly pressed dark suit and grinned. "All my own, Alfie. Oafs like you don't know class when you see it."

Alfie pushed his battered hat further back from his sweating face and removed the stump of a rank black cigar from his mouth. He aimed it at a cuspidor and missed by inches. "Where you been keeping yourself lately? Haven't seen you for days."

"Liar! Saw you this afternoon in the pressroom."

"Wasn't talking about work." Alfie was wolfing down a dripping pickled pig's foot and he spoke thickly around it. "You haven't turned up for a poker game in weeks." He tossed the remains of the meat at the cuspidor and missed again. "Better get your ass moving and fill up a plate before the platter's clean."

The free lunch was fast disappearing but Lafe shrugged and picked up the stein of beer. He blew foam from its top. "Such plebeian fare holds no interest for me."

Snorting, Alfie speared a hardboiled egg and peered at it. "Don't see any mold on this one." He shouted at the barman, "Hey, Tony! Musta made a mistake. Got a fresh egg here." Tony promptly thumbed his nose and Alfie turned back to his companion. "All dressed up and not fighting for your share of food. What's up? You can level with me. I'm like a tomb."

Alfie *was* close-mouthed. Lafe took a long swallow and held up the stein, looking through the amber beer at the ceiling light. Tossing the egg in his mouth, Alfie chewed vigorously, took a gulp of his own beer, and said, "C'mon. What you been up to?"

"I am fresh from the lair of the filthy rich." Lafe struck a pose. "This evening I was guest of honor at the palatial home of Mrs. Georgia Vandercourt, widow of the distinguished bank president Earl P. Vandercourt. Among the other guests—"

"Holy cow!"

"—among the other guests were Mr. and Mr. H. T. Standford of the Standford Textile Company, Mr. and Mrs. William Meredith of the Meredith Lafroux Shipping Line and—"

"Are you pulling my leg?"

"Would I lie to you, Alfie?"

"Meredith? Remember seeing a picture of his new wife in

the society page. Looks like a beauty and young enough to be his granddaughter."

"A gross exaggeration. More like his daughter."

"But a beauty?"

"Her pictures don't do her justice. She's a veritable Venus."

"How come old duffers like Meredith end up with the gorgeous gals?"

"Because they own companies and you and I don't own the clothes on our backs."

"True." Pushing at his hat until it wobbled precariously on the back of his head, Alfie scratched at his thinning hair. "Lafe, you're moving in an illustrious circle and that circle is a tight one. Hear it's harder to break into than a bank vault. How'd you manage?"

"Through the back door. I happen to be a childhood friend of Miss Elizabeth Meredith, cousin of the wealthy William."

"I suppose she's young, a beauty, and rich."

"Not so. Miss Meredith is poor as a church mouse, about my age, not bad looking but no beauty."

Alfie darted a shrewd look at the younger man. "Figure some of her cousin's dough might rub off on you if you marry the lady?"

"William's already let me know Elizabeth won't be mentioned in his will."

"Maybe a little marriage settlement?"

"He's so tight he squeaks."

"Tony, get off your ass and draw a couple." No sooner were the words out of Alfie's mouth than two steins came skidding down the counter. Alfie grabbed one, stuck his mouth into it, and when he lifted his head he wore a mustache of white foam over his ginger one. Swabbing the foam off with a none too clean handkerchief, he growled, "So what's your game, buddy?"

"Game? Have you ever considered it could be love?"

"That's a good one!" Picking up the last morsel of food, a chunk of hard cheese, Alfie crammed it into his mouth. "You're talking to an expert on love. Let me tell you a little story. Once upon a time, twelve long years ago, this guy was full of dreams and ambitions too. Then I fell head over heels for a sweet little gal. Even wrote poems about her eyes and hair. But, alas, I was a loser at the love game."

"You lost your love?"

"No such luck." Alfie shook his head so violently the hat tumbled off and fell in the sawdust. He ignored it. "I got her and lost everything else. I got her, two sniveling brats, a cold water walk-up, a darling wifie who weighs more than I do and wanders around in a dirty housecoat and curl papers and whines about how *I* ruined *her* life. Honest to God! That woman! Waiting right now to give me hell for having a couple of lousy beers." Abruptly he swung on his companion. "How old are you?"

"Thirty-seven."

"And you won't get any younger, buddy. Take my advice. You're a good looking guy and you'd like to write. I mean really write, not hack out articles for a newspaper."

"Yes, I want to write." Lafe frowned. "But not like my dad did. I loved him and admired him but what a life he gave my mother and me. Sure I want to write, Alfie, in a nice house with lots of food on the table and servants to look after me."

"Okay." Alfie bent and picked up his hat. He stuck it on his head, upended his stein, and slammed it on the counter. "So steer clear of penniless dames. Keep clear of this love stuff. For God's sake don't let anyone drag you to the altar. If you do I'll tell you what you're going to be like. Just like me, old buddy, just like Alfie." He pushed himself away from the bar. "Better get home and let the little woman exercise her jaw on me. Only muscle she ever uses. Wonder why she wears those curl papers. Hair always looks like a mop." He dug an elbow into Lafe's ribs. "Don't take any wooden nickels."

Swinging around, Lafe watched the other man steering a slightly listing course toward the swinging doors. As he reached them Alfie turned, jammed the sawdust speckled hat over his eyes, and bellowed, "Remember, Lafe, just like old Alfie!"

Lafe signaled to Tony for another beer. With hard eyes he stared at his reflection in the fly-specked mirror. "Not like you," he whispered. "Never like you, Alfie."

— 8 —

The days of December flew by for Elizabeth. She supervised the erection of a tall tree in the drawing room and helped Alan, Judith, and George, who was home for the holidays, hang it with glass baubles, glittering strands of silver tinsel, and candles. Mistletoe was hung in archways, pine boughs spread on walls, lavish provisions ordered.

As she worked only part of her mind was on that task. The other part lived in a dream world, peopled by herself and Lafe Norton. She pictured a cosy home she would keep neat and welcoming for Lafe. She could see him sitting on her father's leather chair holding a small boy with his hair and eyes. She would be close to them, cradling a tiny baby girl with her own eyes and hair. She named the children, the boy was Lafe and the girl Judith. She wondered if journalists were allowed to take their families with them when they traveled and promptly added other pictures to the fantasy. Lafe, tall and handsome, at her side in London, Paris, Rome.

Her dreams were fed by Lafe's telephone calls and a dinner given by Lavinia Stokes that they attended. She wondered whether Lafe would be invited to spend Christmas in the Meredith house. William always gave the Christmas dinner for his closest friends and Aunt Van always had the same group on New Year's Day. Not daring to ask her cousin, Elizabeth went to Judith. Judith was working at a long table in the larder, concocting from ribbons and holly and pine cones decorations for the mantelpieces. Her dainty hands were moving briskly among the bright objects but at Elizabeth's question they stilled.

"Christmas dinner? I doubt it. I did mention it to William but he said only the usual guests would be invited."

"Surely one other guest wouldn't matter. Everyone likes Lafe."

"That's what I told William but you know him. At times he can't be budged."

Elizabeth did know William but she couldn't hide her disappointment. Judith spoke to her husband again but William wouldn't reverse his decision. He did make one concession. "I suppose we should do something for Elizabeth's young man. I have a thought but I'm not sure . . ."

"What are you thinking?"

"Aunt Van always takes us to the opera a week before Christmas. Usually the boys are invited too, but this year neither George nor Alan is interested. Perhaps I could arrange she invite Lafe and Elizabeth." He rubbed at his chin. "But . . ."

"But what?"

"Formal clothes, darling. I don't want to embarrass the young chap."

"You're thinking Mr. Norton may not dress properly. I'm certain he can arrange to rent or borrow a tuxedo. Who knows? He might have one himself."

"In that case I'll speak to Aunt Van and you may extend invitations to the young people." William smiled widely. "Now, does that make you happy, my little matchmaker?"

It not only made Judith happy, it made Elizabeth delirious. She had never attended an opera. To her the opera house was a magical place for men in evening clothes and ladies in exquisite gowns. It wasn't the place for a dowdy spinster. "I can't believe it," she told Judith. "*Der Rosenkavalier!*" Then her face darkened. "I won't be able to go."

"Why on earth not?" Judith asked impatiently.

"My suits are nice but they won't do."

Judith took her hand. "Come with me, Cinderella." In her room, the younger woman said, "Turn your back."

Elizabeth turned her back. Enviously she stared around Judith's room. The tester bed, tiny tables, elegant chairs chosen long before by Mariette Lafroux Meredith, were still in place. Ruth Meredith's Greuze and chiffonier were still there. The only piece of furniture brought by Judith was an ornate dressing table, once owned by her grandmother. It was so lovely it fitted in perfectly.

Behind her she heard the rustle of paper and then Judith said in her ear, "Shut your eyes."

Squeezing her eyes shut, Elizabeth felt the girl turning her
and then draping something over her body. "You can look now."
Speechless, Elizabeth stared at the cheval mirror. Pale blue
velvet cascaded down her body. The gown had a scooped neck-
line, tiny puffed sleeves, and a flowing skirt. The color was kind
to her dark eyes and hair, to her olive skin.

"I had it made for your Christmas present," Judith told her.
"But Christmas is going to come early. Now, do you think you
can go to the opera?"

"It's perfect, but . . ."

Judith's eyes followed the older woman's. Elizabeth was
staring at the toes of her heavy black shoes peeking from under
the folds of velvet. Without a word Judith went to the wardrobe
and handed Elizabeth a pair of dainty matching slippers. "The
rest of your Christmas present. Slippers for Cinderella."

Crushing the slippers to her breast, Elizabeth embraced her
friend. "You *are* my fairy godmother. How can I ever repay—"

Judith put a hand over Elizabeth's lips. "Be happy dear,
that's all I ask."

Elizabeth's happiness permeated the Meredith house.
Through the days and nights before the momentous performance
Elizabeth dreamed and hummed and sang snatches of ballads and
ragtime. Alan eyed her with disgust and George with amazement. This Elizabeth they'd never seen before. "It's that guy,"
Alan told his brother disgustedly. "Can't see what a smart good-
looking chap like Lafe sees in the old crabapple."

"They're in love," George told him.

George knew all about love. God, he thought, I love my
father's wife. It was sheer agony, watching Judith, lusting for her,
knowing he could never have her. He loved with the desperation
of first love, careful not to betray his feelings, biting his pillow
with frustration each night picturing his father in Judith's bed.
Time rushed by for Elizabeth but the hours dragged for George.
He longed for the festive season to pass so he could escape the
daily hell and return to Harvard.

The night of the opera Lafe Norton arrived in impeccable
evening dress. Even Aunt Van gave a nod of approval. Lafe had
the build for tails and carried his borrowed clothes with more
distinction than William did. Above the gleaming white of his
shirt his ruddy face and flaming hair were spectacular. Elizabeth,

after hours of fussing in Judith's room, did her escort credit. Judith styled her hair, plaiting it and arranging it in large knots over her ears. Strands of seed pearls were interwoven with the braids and twined in milky color against the dark hair. The velvet gown fit her perfectly, baring her throat and shoulders, hugging her waist, and cascading to the velvet slippers. After dozens of buttons on white silk gloves had been done up she stood before the cheval glass, staring wonderingly at the handsome stranger.

Judith was rummaging through her jewel box. "You need something at your throat." She held up a string of pearls.

"No. Those were William's wedding present. He'd be furious."

"True, and he'd recognize anything else I have here." Dropping the pearls into the box, Judith sighed. She hadn't told Elizabeth about the fury her husband had flown into when he found out about the gown and slippers. Judith didn't dare provoke him further. Then her face cleared. "I know! The very thing." She darted over to the dressing table and touched one carved molding and then another. A slender drawer slid out. "This was grandmother's secret drawer. William knows nothing about this locket. Let's try it."

She held the locket up against Elizabeth's throat. It was oval with an engraved pattern of violets and was suspended by a fine gold chain. "It's perfect." Carefully she fastened the clasp. "This is my little secret, dear. Promise you won't open it and peek."

"I promise. I'll take great care of it and return it to you in the morning." She reached for her coat and Judith shook her bright head. "I've nothing else to wear," Elizabeth said.

"It would ruin the whole effect. Here, take my fox cape." Sliding the white fur over Elizabeth's shoulders, Judith stood back and looked her friend up and down.

"I can't do it," Elizabeth protested. "This goes with your gown."

Judith fingered the rich violet brocade. "I'll wear my mink jacket. The men are waiting and Aunt Van will be impatient. Come, Cinderella, we'll go to the ball."

And Cinderella, in velvet and white fur, went to the ball on the arm of her handsome prince. She sat in Aunt Van's box and felt Lafe's sleeve touching her arm, she felt the warmth from his body, she was aware that music swirled around them and figures moved on the stage below but to Elizabeth they were the dream, the reality was Lafe. She dropped her bag and as she bent to pick it up so did Lafe. His fingers touched hers and she thought his lips brushed her hair.

When the house lights went up their brilliance didn't waken Elizabeth. Like a sleepwalker she went with the others down the stairs. A glass was put in her hand and she sipped champagne without tasting it. Friends in rich clothes moved around them and stopped to chat. She didn't comprehend what they were saying but smiled and nodded. Afterward she remembered only Lavinia Stokes's look of bitter envy, and the shock she'd felt when she met Nina Flanders's eyes. In those placid eyes there was understanding and a hint of compassion. What does she see? Elizabeth wondered. An old maid masquerading as belle of the ball?

Chilled, she took Lafe's arm. "I'm out of place," she whispered. "Everyone's staring and I feel they're laughing at me."

"Not laughing," he said in her ear. "Admiring. We make a handsome couple."

A handsome couple, she thought, and the chill vanished. The opera ended, the cast took their bows, the applause died, and in front of the opera house Aunt Van took her leave. William and Lafe, with Briggs's help, lifted the ladies into the car, tucked in froths of velvet and brocade, and they drove home through gently falling snow.

In the Meredith drawing room there was warmth from the hearth, talk, laughter, more champagne. William monopolized the younger man, asking questions about the latest war news, questioning him about his posting to England. Lafe shook his flaming head and said, "I've had a disappointment. Jenkins is off to England. I'm bound for Canada—Montreal and Toronto—to report on the war effort there."

"That's a shame," William commiserated. "I know how eager you were to go overseas. What was the reason for the change of plan?"

"Willy Jenkins happens to be the publisher's son-in-law. The fact that he can hardly put a sentence together doesn't matter. So Willy will be right on the spot while I'm up in my hips in snow watching farm boys marching out of step."

"A shame," William echoed. "I have a book you might like

to take with you. Canadian history and quite interesting. You . . ."

"William," his young wife chided. "The time."

"Of course, darling. We'd better not keep the young people. I'll nip along to my study, Lafe, and get that book for you."

Elizabeth set her glass down. "I'll run up to your room, Judith, for my coat.

Directing a dark look at the white fox, William said coldly, "A good idea, Elizabeth." He followed her to the foot of the stairs and told her in a low voice, "Be sure to hang that properly. Judith shouldn't have lent it to you. You must stop taking advantage of her generosity."

She bent her head meekly but as she went upstairs her eyes were blazing. In Judith's room she recovered her joy as she stood before the mirror, gazing at the pearl-ornamented dark head framed in fluffy fur, the gleam of gold on her breast, the delicate slippers peeking from blue velvet. Then she carefully hung the fur, paused to apply the stopper from a crystal scent bottle to her throat and wrists, and opened the door.

Across the hall the door to Alan's room swung open and he looked disdainfully at her. "Watch it, Cinderella!" he hissed. "It's midnight and you're going to turn back into an ugly old pumpkin."

She ignored him and went down the stairs, her soft-soled slippers as noiseless as a cat's paws on the thick carpet. Silently she stopped in the archway and midnight arrived for Cinderella. Against the mantel Lafe's sober black and white and Judith's flowing violet gown were starkly outlined. Judith was in Lafe's arms, her slender throat thrown back, her hair gleaming gold. Their lips were pressed together and Lafe's hand was cupping her breast. In that moment Elizabeth knew this was no spontaneous first embrace. Their bodies fitted together, their lips met as though those bodies and lips had done this many times before. Lovers, Elizabeth thought wildly, and then she heard William's voice further down the hall.

"Got it," he called. "Elizabeth, you must really speak to that maid! Gerda never puts anything back where I keep it."

Elizabeth moved into the room and the lovers jumped apart, their faces turning, color draining from their features. Moments later William went past her and handed a book to Lafe, who nearly dropped it. She heard William's voice, something about her slippers and snow, something about the car and Briggs. She slipped into her coat, automatically buttoned it to the throat, automatically moved toward the front door.

She was aware of Lafe beside her, of Judith's eyes mutely pleading, of William speaking about Christmas and about seeing Lafe at the Standfords' party on New Year's Eve. Then, horribly, Judith brushed a Judas kiss on Elizabeth's cheek. Wrenching away from her, Elizabeth thrust past Lafe and ran down the steps into the snow.

William stood in the doorway, the snow drifting down on his bald pate, watching Briggs helping his cousin into the tonneau. He shook his head. "What on earth is wrong with that woman? She didn't say goodnight or thank you. After all we've done to make her—"

"She's tired," Judith said quickly. "Exhausted, and the evening may have been too much for her. She's never had one like it before."

"That must be it." Closing the door, he barred it, and turned to sweep her into his arms. He tried to kiss her lips but she turned her head and his mouth brushed her hair. "My darling," he murmured, and then he eagerly led her up the stairs to bed.

In the tonneau of the Panhard Levassor Elizabeth pulled herself into a corner as far away from Lafe as she could get. He pointed at the back of Briggs's head. "Can he hear us?"

Shaking her head, she touched the speaking tube. Lafe turned to face her. "Elizabeth—"

"Don't."

"Let me explain."

"One more word and I'll tell Briggs to take us back. I'll go to William."

He fell silent, his blunt fingers drumming against his knee. When the car stopped he stretched out an imploring hand. "Please, tell me this. Are you going to betray us?"

Briggs started to climb down and Elizabeth knocked on the glass and waved him back. "You have a way to get in touch with her?"

"Telephone. Between twelve and one in the afternoon. Sometimes I phone, more often she does."

Clever, she thought. William out of the house and the hour she always spent closeted in the butler's pantry working on the accounts. Opening the door, she slid out. "Call her tomorrow. You'll both know by then."

She marched up the steps without looking back. By the time she reached the hall her slippers were caked with snow and the hem of her gown was damp. Her landlady stuck her head, encased in a ruffled nightcap, out of the crack in her door. "My, my, but don't you look grand, Miss Meredith!"

Elizabeth couldn't say a word. Midnight had arrived and she still had both slippers. A handsome prince would never be able to find her now. The ball was over and Cousin Elizabeth, unloved and unwanted, returned to the cinders.

— 9 —

That night Elizabeth didn't close her eyes. Wrapped in her old dressing gown and the afghan from the bed, she huddled in her father's chair, a lamp burning at her elbow, her eyes gazing steadily at the paintings on the wall.

The trusting Elizabeth who had flowered under the warmth of Judith Meredith and Lafcadio Norton gradually died and a new Elizabeth, scheming and secretive and ruthless, was born. As the hours crawled past she closed from her mind the shock and grief that night had brought her and turned the events of the evening this way and that, seeking a course that would bring the greatest benefit to herself.

Dispassionately she weighed the alternatives. She could go directly to William and tell him what she had witnessed in his drawing room. For proof her cousin would only have her word and . . . She reached for Judith's locket and with no compunction separated the gold leaves. She stared down at tiny oval pictures. Around the pictured likeness of Judith were engraved the words "My Darling;" Lafe's smiling face was ringed with "Eternal Love."

Elizabeth frowned. Why on earth would Judith have lent this damning locket to her? Then her lips tightened. Judith must feel so secure, so disdainful of her, so certain she would meekly keep her promise and not open the locket, that she had carelessly handed it over. Of course, Judith hadn't dreamed she would witness the love scene in the drawing room. But this locket, brought into William's house and hidden from him, would surely be enough to convince him. But would it? He was in the grip of powerful infatuation, the calflike love of a boy in an aging man's body. William might refuse to believe even this evidence and would expel not Judith but her, condemning her as an interfering, bitter spinster. Judith, with her lissome body and winning ways, might somehow wheedle her way out of danger. In any event neither William nor Judith would allow Elizabeth to remain in her grandfather's house.

The locket clasped in her hand, the metal cold against her skin, she mulled over the possibility of enlisting Aunt Van as an ally. Instead of going to William she could take her story and the locket to the older woman. Aunt Van would be delighted at Judith's perfidy and her opinion would hold weight with her nephew. But, Elizabeth thought as she pictured Judith's beauty, perhaps even then William might choose his wife. Much as he respected and feared his aunt, his young wife was in the stronger position.

Exposing the lovers might give Elizabeth momentary satisfaction, but the only one to suffer lasting hurt would be Cousin Elizabeth. She couldn't face expulsion from that house.

When the feeble light of dawn seeped through the snow outside her windows she made her decision. Patience was the word, and patience she had in abundance. She looked down at the fine golden chain twisting between her fingers, and one of Aunt Van's axioms passed through her mind. Give them enough rope . . . She smiled, though there was no humor in her eyes.

William had scarcely left for his office when Gerda came seeking Elizabeth. She was polishing silver but dropped the chamois and exited the butler's pantry. Judith had set aside an untouched breakfast tray and was seated at a window. She adjusted a silk robe trimmed with fringe and turned a face as bleak as the snow brushing against the window panes. Without any preliminaries she asked Elizabeth, "Do you hate me?"

Careful, Elizabeth cautioned herself, it won't do to appear to take this lightly. "For a while I did. Last night . . ."

"I saw hate in your face when . . . when you found us." Again the girl came directly to the point. "Will you tell William?"

Reaching into her pocket, Elizabeth pulled the locket out and tossed it into Judith's lap. "I broke my promise. I opened it."

"Then you know."

"I know Lafe isn't a stranger to you. I think I deserve to know more."

"So you can run and tell William that too?"

"I don't intend to tell your husband or anyone else."

"Why not? You have good reason to."

Elizabeth sank into a chair opposite the girl. "You've been kind to me, much kinder than anyone else ever was. Yes, I'm terribly hurt. For a time I believed that Lafe . . . that he cared for me, but I should have known a man like him would never look twice at a woman like me."

Covering her eyes with both hands, the girl said faintly, "Don't, please don't. I know we were cruel."

"What hurts me most is that you didn't *trust* me. If you'd confided in me I would gladly have helped you. My loyalty isn't to William, it's to you."

Judith dropped her hands and displayed a distressed face. She was weeping and she even managed to do that beautifully. Two round tears fell from violet eyes and traced the lovely curves of cheekbones. "I don't deserve you, Elizabeth. You're so good, such a saint!"

The tears, Elizabeth told herself sardonically, were not for Saint Elizabeth—they were from sheer relief. Aloud she told the girl, "Confide in me now, dear. Tell me everything so I can help you. Trust me."

"I do. I do trust you." Leaning forward the girl grasped the older woman's hand as though it were a life line. "I don't know what to do, which way to turn. I *must* continue seeing Lafe. I can't give him up. But William . . . Elizabeth, help me!"

Elizabeth managed a reassuring smile and a gentle squeeze. "Tell me."

In words halting at first and then coming in a rush, Judith complied. Shortly before William Meredith made his fateful trip to Boston and met and coveted Judith, Lafcadio Norton had also come to the city to cover a news story. Judith and Lafe met at the home of friends. It was immediately a flaming love affair. "We fell in love, Elizabeth. Looked across a room and we were in love. We couldn't help ourselves."

"Did you become lovers in Boston?"

Judith made no effort at concealment. "Yes. We'd meet in Lafe's hotel room—"

"How did you hide this from your mother?"

"My best friend helped. Winnie didn't approve but she helped. I'd pretend I was visiting her and I'd go to Lafe. It was strange, sordid, but so exciting. His room was horrible. He had to stay at this cheap run-down hotel and it was dingy and not clean but it was thrilling." Judith gave a tremulous little laugh. "Once Lafe smuggled me up by a fire escape and I nearly fell. He caught me and held me in his arms."

Making an effort to control her expression at the thought of Judith enfolded in the arms of the man she herself loved, Elizabeth said slowly, "You're fortunate you didn't get pregnant."

"Oh, Lafe knows all about that and he took care of it. Those things . . . you know."

Spinster though she was, Elizabeth did know. She'd heard whispers about the rubber sheaths some men used. She filed another thought away. Obviously Lafe was experienced and took no chances. "If you are so much in love why didn't you marry? Run away if you had to?"

"We couldn't. Mama!"

"Did she find out?"

"Eventually, and she nearly went out of her mind. By that time we'd met William and mama was determined I would marry him. She had debts and it looked as though she'd lose her house. Mama was desperate. I couldn't desert her."

You would have deserted dear mama in a moment, Elizabeth thought. "Was there another reason?"

"Yes . . . but I'm going to sound terrible. I didn't have a penny and all Lafe has is a salary hardly large enough to keep himself. After daddy died, mama and I didn't have much either but she was able to get loans and we lived well. Elizabeth, I've never had to do without. I don't even know how to make tea or take care of my clothes. Lafe said in time even love like ours couldn't survive poverty. He said we'd be like his parents; in time we'd hate each other. I didn't have any choice. I *had* to marry William."

"But you have no intention of giving Lafe up."

Judith pouted charmingly. "Of course not. Before my marriage Lafe and I went over and over the chances of seeing each other in New York. For a time we despaired of ever meeting again. But then I mentioned you and Lafe remembered his visit to your home when he was a child. Lafe said I couldn't introduce him as my own friend, William is so jealous and suspicious, but perhaps we could use you—"

"*Use.*"

"I'm *so* sorry, but we had to! You can see that, can't you?"

Elizabeth didn't trust her voice but she managed to nod.

"So we planned to meet at the Oasis. I was to bring you and Lafe would arrive and . . . you know the rest."

Now she did know it all. She understood why Judith, the day they met, had singled her out for kindness, insisted she stay on in the Meredith house. Judith had bought her for a few clothes, a skillful dentist, and worst of all, a deceitful appearance of love. For a small price Cousin Elizabeth had been delivered into the lovers' hands.

She hid her thoughts, cleared her throat, and said briskly, "I'm glad you think enough of me to confide, Judith. And it was high time. It was only a lucky chance that I reached the drawing room last night before William did. You must be more discreet or William *will* find out."

Like a chastened child, Judith asked, "What shall we do?"

"Start with the telephone calls. Don't you realize the servants aren't blind or deaf?"

"Would they tell William?"

"Cookie and Briggs have been with William since long before his first wife's death. I don't think Cookie would tattle but she might mention something to Briggs and I wouldn't put it past

him. He worships William. Then there's the problem of my relationship with Lafe."

"I don't understand."

"You've convinced not only William but all his friends, Aunt
Van in particular, that Lafe is my suitor. Time will pass and Lafe
won't declare himself. People will become suspicious of his intentions and that will be the end of Lafe."

"But how—"

"Leave it to me, my dear. Sooner or later William or Aunt
Van will ask me about my young man. I'll tell them we're merely
friends, that Lafe's interest isn't romantic, simply a matter of our
fathers' friendship. They like Lafe and will continue to receive
him on those terms. I'll explain to Aunt Van that even if Lafe did
want to marry me I would have to refuse as I don't want to wed
and lose my freedom."

"You might fool William but what about that horrid
woman? She is shrewd."

"She is, but Aunt Van has her weaknesses. As you know,
she deliberately prevented her older daughter from marrying."

"So she could make Sophie a slave, an unpaid companion!"

"Regardless of her reason, Aunt Van has thoroughly convinced herself that Sophie enjoys being a spinster. Yes, Aunt
Van can be hoodwinked."

Violet eyes beamed confidence. "You're so *clever.*"

Elizabeth simply grunted. "Those telephone calls must stop.
Let me be go-between. Either Lafe can come to me or I'll telephone him. The servants won't question that."

Clasping her hands together, the girl smiled with delight.
Then some of the radiance dimmed. "But how can we be together? I can't stand much more of this! The only time Lafe and I
have even managed to touch was last night. We've had to be so
careful. Mr. Norton. Mrs. Meredith. Pretending, always pretending!"

Ironically Elizabeth studied the girl. Lust stared from her
eyes, radiated from the curves of her body, lust dusted the fine
skin like talcum. She contented herself with saying drily, "Pretense is necessary for a clandestine affair, Judith."

"You will find some way for us to be together?"

"Oh, yes," Elizabeth said truthfully. "You can depend on
me. I'll find a way. Tell me, what are your long-range plans?"

The smooth skin between fair brows wrinkled. "Long-range?"

"If you can't stand being parted from Lafe for even a few months how will you handle the long years of your marriage?"

"Lafe said . . ." Judith had the grace to lower her eyes. "He said William might not live too long. William's an old man and he's so insistent on his husbandly rights. Nearly every night he comes to my bed and it's dreadful. Elizabeth, my skin crawls when he puts his hands on me. He's like a bull, just rams and rams. He knows nothing about lovemaking. He expects me to lie there and let him . . . and not even move. Not ladylike to enjoy. Not like Lafe." Her eyes lifted and dreams filled them. "Lafe knows how to make love. He's wonderful!"

Elizabeth fought for control and found it. "In other words, you're planning on being a young widow?"

"Yes."

"In the first place William is *not* old. He's only fifty-two and he takes good care of himself. Our grandfather lived to be over ninety."

"Perhaps he'll die accidentally. Fall down stairs or get in a car accident. I wish he *would* die."

Elizabeth raised dark brows. "You and Lafe aren't considering shortening your husband's life, are you?"

"Of course not!" Judith exclaimed virtuously, rather ruining the effect by adding, "We should probably be found out and have to go to prison."

So much for the young lovers' ethics, Elizabeth thought as she returned to her work. If Lafe and Judith figured they could get away with it they'd finish William off. The hint of a smile played around the corners of the old maid's lips—the balance of control had subtly shifted to her.

On Christmas Day Elizabeth's hopes were dashed.

Except that William had a wife to act as hostess the day was the same as the other Christmases she had spent in the Meredith house. Aunt Van, the Stokeses, and the Flanderses, accompanied by their children, arrived in the afternoon. On one sofa Doctor John and Lavinia relaxed with their son Edward and their new daughter-in-law between them. Edward was a stocky young man with a bluff face and his mother's long-lashed eyes. His bride Cynthia was pretty and demure and the daughter of a titled English family. Lavinia, who had never shown a trace of affection for her husband or son, appeared to dote on the English girl.

On the sofa opposite, Albert and Nina proudly displayed their two daughters. The younger, Marilou, leaned against her father's knee and he toyed with her gleaming ringlets. At ten it was obvious Marilou had inherited her father's and her Aunt Lavinia's striking looks. The older child, Susan, also looked like her father but her dark blue eyes mirrored her mother's intelligence. Beside the leaping fire Uncle Herman dozed, his head falling forward, the silky beard spread over his chest. Near him Aunt Van's three offspring perched on a loveseat.

For a time Aunt Van held the center of the stage, regaling her friends with the latest gossip. When that was exhausted she moved over beside Elizabeth, lowered her voice to a husky whisper, and proceeded unabashedly to cannibalize the other guests. It would appear handsome Albert had yet another mistress. "I don't know how Nina puts up with that man," Aunt Van muttered. "I have it on good authority that his latest flame is one of those Village girls. You know, the kind of hussy who shingles her hair and paints her face. I understand she poses nude for artists. Disgusting, isn't it?"

Without waiting for an answer she raced on. "And Marilou is nothing but a minx. Still in short dresses and already ogling the boys. See how she's looking at George and Alan."

Elizabeth had already noticed the precocious child. Marilou was playing the flirt, fluttering the lashes that ringed her bold eyes, darting smiles at the Meredith boys. George ignored her but Alan was returning the looks ardently.

"Mark my words," Aunt Van said, "Nina and Albert are going to have trouble with that one. Now her sister Susan is a different kettle of fish. Nice, quiet, modest girl. But she's a bit too clever for my liking. In my girlhood Susan would've been called a bluestocking. Nina tells me Susan is begging to take a business education. Outlandish! Albert won't hear of it and for once I agree with him. Susan is pretty and could make a dandy marriage."

Aunt Van stopped to get her breath and Elizabeth watched

Judith as she moved among her guests, pausing for a kind word with Sophie, a smile at Nina, stooping to retrieve Uncle Herman's ear trumpet. Judith was pale, with none of the usual fresh color in her cheeks or lips. Among the other ladies, who were dressed like peacocks, Judith stood out. She was wearing a simple gray silk gown, her only ornament William's Christmas gift, a single sapphire suspended on a long platinum chain. Pale and modestly attired as she was she still put every other woman to shame.

Aunt Van was also looking searchingly at her hostess. "Judith's looking peaked. Does she usually paint her face?"

"She uses a little powder, but all ladies do now."

"Not my Charity." Fondly, Aunt Van regarded her treasured daughter. The fat child sat stolidly between her sister Sophie and brother Earl, piggish eyes gazing vacantly into space. No doubt dreaming of dinner, Elizabeth thought wryly. "I shall never," Aunt Van was saying, "allow Charity to hide that lovely skin!"

Elizabeth failed to see anything lovely about Charity including her skin but she hastened to give a dutiful compliment. "That pink dress looks well on her."

"Indeed it does. Pink is her color. I told her this morning, Charity, I said, you look quite the grown up lady! See that jacket Cynthia Stokes is wearing?"

Elizabeth glanced toward the young English girl. "It's pretty. Brocade is such a rich fabric."

"Covering up something not quite as pretty, Cousin Elizabeth. Only been married to Edward for a little over four months and pregnant. See, when she moves. She's showing already. I wonder . . . well, we'll wait and see. I always say the first baby can come any time but the second takes a full nine months." Pleating her silk skirt with a tiny hand, Aunt Van darted Edward's bride a look of bright malice. "We may never know for sure. Lavinia tells me her daughter-in-law is hoping to return to London to visit her parents. Says Cynthia's homesick. I say they're sneaking the girl away to have a baby sooner than she should. And that Lavinia! All she thinks about and talks about is Cynthia. Couldn't stand her own son and goes gaga about that girl. Keeps mentioning her parents and Sir this and Lady that. Makes you sick, doesn't it?" Without waiting for an answer Aunt

Van changed the subject. "Look at William. Can't keep his eyes off that little snip he married. It's indecent, mooning around like that. Mark my words, Elizabeth, he's going to rue the day he set eyes on Judith."

I sincerely hope so, Elizabeth silently agreed. Aloud she murmured, "They seem to be getting along well."

"Early days yet. Still bride and groom. And how well are they getting along when that woman lazes in bed all morning and makes you handle all her duties? Oh yes, I know how Judith is acting. Lazy and shiftless and wanton—"

"Aunt Van!"

"Hasn't showed it openly yet but I can always spot a wanton. Knew the minute I set eyes on that hussy she was no good. Where are you going?"

Elizabeth had risen and was smoothing down her skirt. "I must look in on Cookie. Sally and Gerda are helping but Cookie always gets nervy on Christmas. She wants everything perfect."

"It always is. My Aggie could take lessons from Cookie." Aunt Van patted her stomach, her eyes bright with anticipation. "And William does insist on an English dinner at Christmas. Quite right too. You can't beat a hearty meal. Where's that young man of yours, eh?"

As good a time as any, Elizabeth thought. "Lafe wasn't invited, Aunt Van. You know William always keeps this day for family. And Lafe isn't my young man. At least not in that way."

"How do you mean?"

"He's only a friend. Nothing romantic. Our fathers were close friends. Even if Lafe does feel differently about me, it wouldn't be of any use." She gave the older woman a guileless smile. "I'm afraid not only am I a confirmed spinster but prefer it that way."

Patting Elizabeth's hand, Aunt Van said approvingly, "You're so sensible. Little late for you to marry. People get set in their ways. Take my Sophie. How she fought me to marry that ne'er-do-well years ago. And Sophie only eighteen and not even knowing her own mind. When I broke it up I told her, mark my words, my girl, someday you'll thank me. Proved I was right too. Sophie's never even looked at another man. Good for you, Elizabeth, you know your place in life."

Escaping from the older woman, Elizabeth went to the

kitchen. She'd told Aunt Van the truth about the cook. Cookie was sitting at the long table, her head in her hands, close to tears. Gerda, Sally, and the scullery maid were scurrying around and when Elizabeth appeared they looked relieved. She put a comforting hand on Cookie's plump shoulder. "One of the sauces?"

"The oysters, Miss Elizabeth. I'm beside myself. You know how Mrs. Vandercourt relishes her carpetbag steak. I think . . . they may be off!"

Elizabeth opened the door of the immense icebox and took out the dish of oysters. "They're fine, Cookie. You're overwrought."

Pushing her bulk up, the cook bent over the plate. "Guess I was wrong. They do smell fresh."

"Now," Elizabeth said briskly, "let's have a look."

It took time to look. As Aunt Van had mentioned, William did pride himself on an English Christmas. On the stove thick soup simmered and there were eight pots of vegetables. In the oven were a saddle of mutton, a sirloin of beef, a leg of pork. There were roast turkey, boiled turkey, two fat geese, enough squab to fill a large platter. On the sideboard were green salads and jellied salads. River trout in rich sauce and almonds were ready for the broiler and the desserts covered a table that had been moved in from the larder. Elizabeth checked them over. Mince pies, plum pudding, trifle, plates of iced cakes, platters of bonbons, bowls of fruit, six kinds of cheeses—

"Elizabeth!" She swung around. Aunt Van was so excited she didn't cast a look at the bounty of food around her. "Come quickly! Judith."

Elizabeth took the older woman's fat arm. "Calm down and tell me."

"She fainted dead away. William and she were lighting the candles on the tree and she fell as though she were dead. Her taper burnt the carpet and Albert had to stamp it out. William looks like he's going to collapse too."

"Get on with your work," Elizabeth snapped at Cookie and the openmouthed maids. She ran past Aunt Van down the hall.

She stopped at the foot of the stairs among a cluster of guests. Doctor John and George were carrying Judith's limp body up the staircase. George's thin face was as pallid as Judith's. Behind them was William, clinging to the bannister and piteously questioning the doctor. "What is it, John?"

"How do I know? Give me a chance to examine her. Get hold of yourself, man! It won't help if you go to pieces."

Sophie grasped at Elizabeth's wrist so hard she winced. "Has she been ill?" When Elizabeth shook her head Sophie sobbed, "I do hope it's nothing serious. Just a moment before she fell she was talking to me. Talking and laughing. Judith's so kind." Tears spurted from Sophie's eyes, misting the lenses of her glasses. "I couldn't bear it if she were to die."

"Judith is not going to die," Elizabeth said sternly. "Stop that, Sophie." She appealed to the other guests. "Please come and sit down. Judith's in good hands."

"Indeed she is," Lavinia said. "John will look after her. Edward, do you think you should go up and see if you can help your father?"

The younger Doctor Stokes appeared to be the only composed one in the group. He patted his mother's shoulder. "One doctor at a time, mother. If dad wants me, he'll call down. Now, I think Cousin Elizabeth is correct. All of you sit down. Elizabeth, a drop of sherry might be in order."

"I'll get it," she told him and gratefully watched him herd the agitated group back into the drawing room. When she passed around the tray of sherry she noticed that Uncle Herman had managed to sleep through the excitement. She also noticed the ugly burn on the carpet. Her lips tightened while she planned what piece of furniture could be moved to cover it. Aunt Van, her bosom heaving, massaged her stomach. "Such an upset. I do think it might ruin my dinner." Hastily she added, "I do hope dear Judith has only had a spell of the vapors."

The young doctor grinned and tightened his grip around his bride's waist. "If I were to hazard a diagnosis I'd say there's nothing to worry about."

Lavinia pointed her rapier nose at her son. "What do you think is the problem?"

"Mother dearest, what do *you* think is the problem?"

Comprehension flashed across Aunt Van's face. "Aha!" She held out her glass. "A little more, Cousin Elizabeth. A drop to settle my nerves."

Giving her more sherry, Elizabeth moved briskly around serving the others. Her mind was racing. God, this could ruin everything. Perhaps Edward was wrong. George came down but he could tell them nothing. The boy was still the color of paper and his hands were shaking. Finally Doctor John bounced into the room and both George and Sophie jumped up. "Judith?" Sophie cried.

"Judith is resting comfortably." Doctor John chuckled. "In fact I'd say at this moment she's in better shape than her husband is." He beamed at George and Alan. "In a few months you boys are going to have a little brother or sister."

George sat down so abruptly it looked as though his legs had given way. That makes two of us, George, Elizabeth thought. Judith must have been well aware of this when she pleaded for help to see her lover. Her name, spoken sharply, wrenched her from her thoughts. Doctor John was at her elbow. He took the decanter from her. "Elizabeth, I've spoken to you twice."

"I'm sorry. What . . ."

"William wants you to go up to him."

As she passed Aunt Van, the older woman tugged at her skirt. "I do hope dinner won't be delayed. My stomach, you know."

"Dinner will be served on time," Doctor John reassured her. "That's what William wants Elizabeth for. Judith insists he come down and be host."

At Judith's door Elizabeth hesitated and then tapped softly. William opened the door, stepped into the hall, and closed it behind him. His face was radiant. "You've heard our wonderful news?"

"Doctor John told us."

"Judith is upset. John says it's only natural. Her age and the first baby. But she's so thoughtful. I offered to stay up here with her and she wouldn't hear of it. She doesn't want our guests disappointed. There's dinner and the children have prepared a pantomime. We'll finish the evening with caroling . . ." His voice trailed off. "Judith won't be able to play for us."

"Sophie plays well."

"Not like Judith. But then there's no one else quite like Judith. Now, you will settle her down, won't you? She's so highstrung. John gave her something to make her rest but she's still unnerved."

Nodding, Elizabeth put her hand on the doorknob but he

stopped her. "One moment. I have a favor to ask of you. Judith
must have a woman near her from now on. I suggested we send
for her mother but she says Emma has a tendency to fuss and
Judith won't hear of it." William looked obscurely pleased that
his mother-in-law wouldn't be fussing around his house. "Judith
insists on having you, Cousin Elizabeth. I know it's asking a great
deal but would you be willing to give up your flat and move in
here? Only until the baby is born, of course."

Elizabeth was more than willing but she deliberately hesitated. Let him persuade her. He proceeded to. "I know you're
fond of Judith and grateful to her. Do say yes."

"I should be happy to be of assistance. But . . ."

"But what?"

"I have some of my parents' furniture I'm attached to. Not a
great deal but too much to squeeze into that bedroom I used
when I stayed here before. If I could use that big room at the
front of the house I would make out quite well."

For a moment she thought William would agree but then he
shook his head. "No, I'm afraid that wouldn't do. That room is
our best guest room. Surely you can squeeze a few pieces into the
smaller one and there's all sorts of room in the attic for the remainder."

Elizabeth bent her head in agreement. Let it be the small
room. At least she would be staying in this house. William rewarded her with a smile and proceeded to press his advantage.
"There will have to be an adjustment made on your salary. Your
expenses will be negligible. You'll no longer have rent to consider and you'll take all your meals here."

That was too much. She raised her dark eyes to his austere
face. "I'm afraid I can't consider a pay cut. As you say I'll be
giving up my flat and my privacy. I don't want to disappoint Judith but . . ."

He sighed heavily. "Very well. When can you move?"

"I'll pack my clothes tonight. Perhaps you can send Briggs to
pick me up tomorrow. I'll arrange for a carter to move my furniture."

"At your expense?"

"Yes."

"That's settled then. Now, go to Judith and reassure her."

She went to Judith with no intention of offering reassurance.

The huge room was softly lit by the pink shaded lamp beside the bed. The light cast a roseate glow over the girl. She lay against a pile of pillows, her hair loosened and falling in a bright flame around her face. Her eyes were closed but as Elizabeth stood over her they snapped open. The older woman glared down. "You knew about this when you begged me to help you see Lafe."

"I wasn't certain. My periods . . . they've always been irregular. I was hoping . . ." Judith started to cry, not a few artistic tears dropping from violet eyes but a storm of bitterness that splotched her face and reddened her eyelids and nose. "Don't scold me! I can't stand it. I can't stand having this baby. I don't *want* William's child."

"A little late for that," Elizabeth told her, and plumped down on a chair. "How far along are you?"

"John says I'm due about the middle of May."

"A fine kettle of fish!"

Balling her hands into small fists, Judith beat at her stomach. "I hate it and I hate *him*. Clumsy old fool! Didn't have sense enough to take precautions. Now Lafe . . ."

"William is certainly not Lafe, and even if you don't want this baby, he does. Stop that bleating and let me think."

Judith stopped punishing her stomach but tears continued to ooze from her eyes. "It's ruined everything. Lafe will be leaving for Canada in a couple of weeks and I won't be able to see him. He'll hate me."

She sounded, Elizabeth thought, as though Lafe was the husband with horns, William the illicit lover. "You'll see Lafe at the party on New Year's Eve. The Standfords invited him."

"No! I refuse to go." Judith wiped at her face with a lace-edged scrap of cambric. "I can't face him. Not this way. Everyone will be talking about the baby, making a fuss and . . . no, I don't want to see Lafe."

Slumping back in the chair, Elizabeth closed her eyes. Her hopes for using the affair to her own advantage seemed to be shattered. "Is there any chance this could be Lafe's child?"

"No, but I wish it were!" Judith lifted swollen eyes. "No, I take that back. If this were Lafe's baby it would be disastrous. William would know it wasn't his."

"Lafe's coloring?"

Judith shook her head. "Haven't you noticed his little finger?"

"On his right . . . no, his left hand. It's nearly as long as the next finger."

"Lafe says he inherited it from his mother's family. The Allenbys. Many of them had the same overlong finger."

Elizabeth glanced at Judith and noticed that the girl had calmed down. Thick eyelashes drifted down and she said drowsily, "At least I have an excuse to avoid William's lovemaking. I swear, Elizabeth, that old man is never going to climb into my bed again. And this won't last forever. The baby will be born, Lafe will come back, and . . ."

On that optimistic thought, Judith drifted peacefully off to sleep.

Elizabeth saw the new year in at Judith's bedside. William had urged his wife to go to the Standfords' party and when she continued to refuse he offered to stay with her. Judith, in her sweet, unselfish way, told him she wouldn't spoil his evening, Cousin Elizabeth would take care of her.

He finally agreed, directed that Cookie provide a tray of delicacies, carried up champagne in an ice bucket, and after an affectionate farewell left with his sons. The servants all had the evening off and Elizabeth sat in Judith's room, a chill glass in her hand and not a sound, except the girl's soft breathing, breaking the silence.

Happy 1915, Elizabeth thought morosely, eyeing the sleeping girl. Judith's face, cradled against silk pillows, was peaceful; her full breasts stirred the lace on her nightgown, and her lashes lay in crescents against cheeks like warm peaches. Only two thoughts gave Elizabeth any comfort. At last William was allowing her to stay in her grandfather's house, and though he thought it was only for a few months he was mistaken. Judith needed her and she was going to make certain Judith continued to need her. Cousin Elizabeth, like the camel in the fable, had her nose in the tent and in that tent she was going to remain.

The other consolation was the temperament of the lovers. This enforced separation would only whet their desire. By the time the baby was born Judith and Lafe would be wild to see each other and resume their relations. Elizabeth was determined to act as Cupid and make certain their desires were fulfilled.

She drained the rest of the champagne into her glass and lifted it for a solitary toast. "To poor Cousin Elizabeth," she whispered. "To 1915 and the fulfillment, for once, of *my* desires."

She was sitting between the pink shaded lamp and the bed. As she drank her shadow fell across the bed, darkening the face of Judith Meredith.

— 10 —

The new year gave little promise of fulfilling anyone's desires. In Russia the demoniac Gregory Rasputin became the power behind the tsarist throne and that country surged with internal unrest. Germany and Britain and her allies had dug in with battle lines extending from Switzerland to the North Sea, and trench warfare, a static type of war, came into being. At the second Battle of Ypres in April the Germans sent clouds of deadly chlorine gas swirling over the British and French lines and settling into their trenches.

In New York the war began to touch William Meredith and his friends. The Standfords' son Arnold and their daughter's unwelcome Italian husband Antonio Luciano slipped off to England and joined the British Expeditionary Force. A month later Ronnie Grant, the only child of Grace and Robert Grant, joined his friends. Arnold Standford had a brief war. At Ypres the raw recruit was gassed and was taken to a hospital in Paris.

William and John Stokes anxiously watched and listened. Lavinia and John were also concerned about their daughter-in-law Cynthia. Much against Lavinia's wishes the English girl was determined to return to London and her parents for her baby's birth. To Lavinia's rage Edward and Doctor John seemed to be taking the girl's side and encouraging her.

William had worries of his own. Judith wasn't taking pregnancy well. His lovely wife, as Aunt Van baldly put it, had blown up like a balloon. Even the gay maternity dresses that Elizabeth made couldn't disguise Judith's bulging abdomen and bloated arms. Her complexion suffered and became covered with unsightly blotches, and the bright hair lay lank and lifeless against her head. Her disposition matched her appearance. Judith was morose, pettish, given to temper tantrums. At the end of January she declared she would no longer receive guests or accept invitations. No matter how her husband coaxed, Judith couldn't be budged out of the house, and sought sanctuary in her own room. William did his best to reason with her but Judith either ignored him or burst into storms of tears that sent him scurrying for Elizabeth. He neglected his business while he catered to her, constantly bringing gifts. He offered her a gold link bracelet, sapphire earrings to match her Christmas present, a brooch made of the iridescent wings of butterflies. He came home laden with baskets of fruit, armloads of flowers, ribboned boxes of chocolates. His wife accepted the gifts with neither gratitude nor any change of attitude. Finally, one day in the spring, he sought out Elizabeth in the sewing room on the fifth floor.

Setting aside the baby dress she was stitching, his cousin looked up enquiringly. He was panting from the long climb. William might not allow anyone but Judith to use the lift but he was fair and seldom made use of it himself.

"It's Judith," he told his cousin. "I don't know where to turn. Nothing I do pleases her. Can't you do anything?"

"I've tried everything. I can't even interest her in the baby's clothes. I suppose we'll just have to be patient."

"I'm certain she's injuring her health, maybe the baby's. I'd better see John."

William went directly to Doctor John's office. In the waiting room he found there were a number of patients and he was forced to wait. Estelle Standford was there, and her daughter Maud. William sat down beside Estelle. He didn't really care for the woman. Estelle was a lean, lacquered blonde in her forties. A great deal of effort, time, and money had been used to make her look younger but they had been wasted. Today every line in her face seem to pull down. William was fond of Maud. She'd always reminded him of her father Horace, who was dark, stocky, and even-tempered. He couldn't help but compare Maud Luciano with his own wife. The girl was as heavily pregnant but above the swollen body her face was fresh and contented. And Maud had the added worry of a young husband somewhere on the Western Front.

Turning to Estelle, William asked, "Any more news on Arnold?"

"Horace has been in touch with the American consulate in Paris. We're hoping he will be sent home."

"Arnold may be too ill to move, Estelle."

"That's what they say. The mustard gas—" She broke off and averted her head. "Then there's Antonio, we don't even know where he is."

"I know how you feel. George is determined to go, too. So far I've held him back but from day to day I don't know what he'll do. I have no idea what's getting into these boys. It's not even our war."

A nurse bustled out, her starched skirt rustling. "Mrs. Standford and Mrs. Luciano. Doctor will see you now."

"You go ahead, William," Estelle told him. "We're in no hurry."

William raised his brows at the younger woman. "Are you sure, Maud?"

She smiled up at him. "Yes, Uncle William. Go along."

Doctor John met his friend at the door of his office. "Not ailing, are you?"

"It's Judith."

"I saw her yesterday. Better sit down, Williiam, you look exhausted."

"I'm at my wit's end. I'm—"

"Whoa." The doctor opened a cupboard, took out a bottle and two glasses, and poured generous amounts. "Some medicine for both of us. Tell you the truth, William, I'm more worried about you than I am about your wife. Good God, this isn't your first child. Ruth gave you the two boys and you never lost a night's sleep."

"It was different with Ruth. She was much stronger than Judith. John, I'm terrified she may . . . I may lose her."

"Nonsense! Judith is young and healthy as a horse. As well

able to bear a child as Ruth was. Possibly better able. As I said, I examined Judith yesterday and she's fine. The only thing I can advise is exercise. She sits around too much. Never moves out of the house, does she?"

"Seldom moves out of her bedroom."

"Put your foot down. Take her out for walks yourself. Most of the trouble is your attitude toward her. Judith's not made of glass. Treat her like the young healthy woman she is."

"She acts as if she hates me. And the way she looks. John, she's changed so much."

"Of course she's not too fond of you now." The doctor chuckled. "Blames you, as most women do, for the condition she's in. As for her looks, she'll snap back to normal after the baby is born. Harder for a beautiful woman to be pregnant than a plain one. My advice is to go home and assert yourself. Don't ask her, tell her." He glanced at his desk calendar. "Only a month to go. Think you'll make it?"

William managed a smile. "I'll make it." He changed the subject. "A shame about young Arnold. I was talking to Estelle in the waiting room and I gather he's in bad shape."

"He is. Lungs pretty well destroyed and he's blinded."

"What about Edward's wife?"

Doctor John's ruddy face glowed. "Got a wire yesterday from Cynthia's father." Pausing to give the proper emphasis to the exalted name, he continued, "Sir Andrew feels it's quite safe for her to return to London. Thank God for that. Cynthia really is impatient to go."

"How is Lavinia taking it?"

"Raising hell. Blames Edward and me for encouraging the girl. Lavinia doesn't want Cynthia out of her sight. You'd think this was the first baby ever born."

"When does she leave?"

"Soon. We've booked passage on one of the Cunards."

Doctor John watched his friend leave and shook his head. That evening he told Lavinia that Aunt Van's prediction was coming true. William's young wife was aging him. Lavinia nodded but her thoughts were elsewhere. She was thinking of Cynthia and making plans to redecorate the nursery for the grandchild her cherished daughter-in-law was soon to bear.

*   *   *

Elizabeth's thoughts were running along the same lines. After William left for his consultation with the doctor she put aside her work and went down to the third floor. She swung open the door of the nursery and nodded her head. It was close to ready. The walls were freshly painted, the cradle that had held generations of Meredith babies had been relined, behind a screen were the bed and the wardrobe for a nurse. On her way to the staircase she paused to look in at the spacious room and canopied bed she coveted.

When she reached Judith's room she found the girl reclining on the lounge covered with a silk throw that outlined the bulge of her abdomen, her head propped up on pillows. Sunlight poured through an open window, creating a puddle of darker gold on the pale gold silk across her body. Judith's eyes were vacantly fixed on the ceiling.

"How are you feeling?" Elizabeth asked.

Her answer was a shrug. Fishing in her sweater pocket, Elizabeth found a pack of cigarettes and lit one. She took a greedy puff. "William came up to see me this afternoon. He went to Doctor John; he's upset about you."

The violet eyes snapped to the cigarette in Elizabeth's hand. "If he knew you smoked he'd be even more upset."

"But he won't, will he? That's another of our little secrets."

Wandering over, Elizabeth pulled back a curtain and stared down at the street. A nursemaid in a blue cape and starched cap was maneuvering a high-wheeled pram around a pile of smoking horse dung. Elizabeth caught a glimpse of a chubby fist waving a rattle. She knocked ash out of the window and watched the breeze catch it. In the opposite house she caught sight of a lace curtain being pulled back on an upper window and she hastily backed away. It wouldn't do for the neighbors to know Cousin Elizabeth did something sinful like smoking.

She turned to Judith and saw her own image wavering in the cheval glass. In a new woolen dress with points of lace at her throat and wrists she looked quite handsome.

Judith's head turned. "What are you doing? Oh, staring at yourself in the mirror. Thinking you look better than I do, I'll bet."

Even Charity Vandercourt looks better than you do right

now, Elizabeth told the girl silently. Aloud she said, "Just wondering if I got the shoulders right on this dress. One looks a bit
puckered."

"It's perfect," Judith said bitterly. "Everything Cousin Elizabeth does is perfect."

Elizabeth returned to the window, checked the house opposite, and flicked out the cigarette butt. Then she drew up a
chair to the lounge and took one of the girl's hands in both of
hers. "What's wrong, dear?"

Wrenching her hand away, Judith threw back the silk throw.
She looked like a beached whale. "It's more than this," Elizabeth said flatly. "You know this will pass. In a few weeks you'll
be back to normal."

Judith's mouth quivered. "He hasn't written me, not once.
Elizabeth, when you telephoned, he did say he'd write, didn't
he?"

Elizabeth took the girl's hand again and this time Judith
didn't pull away. "I told you everything Lafe said. He said he'd
try to write but you must remember he knows William opens
every letter that comes to this house."

"William has no right! He even opens mama's letters to me.
I've had to warn her to watch what she says in them."

"I know. He opens the servants' mail and mine too. Not that
I ever get much. A few cards at Christmas and an occasional
letter from Nettie Towers." Elizabeth smiled. "Why he's interested in church news from an old maid librarian I fail to see."

"It's an invasion of privacy. He has no right."

"He feels he has every right. Like his father and his grandfather, William's a patriarch. They knew everything that went on
in their household and William must know all too."

Judith gave a sly little smirk. "Not all. Would you get my
locket?"

Opening the secret door in the dressing table, Elizabeth
found the locket and handed it to the girl. Judith snapped open
the case and looked down at Lafe's smiling face. "I miss him so
much! I haven't seen him since the night of the opera."

Neither have I, Elizabeth brooded. She didn't glance at
Lafe's picture, though she carried that face with her constantly.
The bright hair waving back from the wide brow, the large nose,
the mouth that could be as tender as a woman's or as hard as the

square chin. She checked a sigh. No matter how she tried she couldn't stop loving him. No matter what he'd done to her, that love lingered.

"You did tell him," Judith was saying, "that you could take the letters out of the mail before Gerda takes it to William?"

"I told him."

"Then why doesn't he write? Do you think . . . could he have found someone else?"

"Don't be foolish. Lafe's only trying to protect you."

And himself, the old maid thought as she restlessly rose and returned to the window. I've a feeling Lafe is a cautious man. In his way as selfish as Judith. Her eyes wandered down to the street. The car was there and Briggs was getting down from behind the wheel. "William's home," she told Judith. "Better give me the locket."

She returned the locket to its hiding place and left the girl to her husband. An hour later, as she was decanting the dinner wine, Gerda bustled into the kitchen. Her wide stolid face showed unusual animation. "It's the missus," she told Elizabeth and Cookie. "She's gone out."

"Mistress," Elizabeth corrected. "Did Mr. Meredith accompany her?"

"Said to tell you he's taking the missus—the mistress—for a walk."

"Land's sake!" Cookie exclaimed. "First time the mistress has set foot out of this house for months. How did she seem, Gerda?"

"Put out. Face like a thundercloud."

William had taken Doctor John's advice and put his foot down. Each day he came home from the office and took his wife for a walk in the park. Judith sulked but the exercise did her good. William seemed relieved about her but shortly he had another worry. A wire arrived from his son George. Without waiting for parental consent the boy, in the company of four classmates, had left Harvard and crossed the Canadian border. The letter that followed said that they had enrolled in an officers' training school in Toronto. George also made clear that if his father tried to force him to come home he would run away and go to England. William was beside himself.

"That silly boy," Judith said to Elizabeth. "Why on earth

would George do a thing like that? I suppose he thinks war is romantic."

"Another type of romance, I think. He's running away."

"From his father?"

"From you."

"George pays no attention to me. When I'm around he hardly ever speaks."

"You have a way with men," Elizabeth told her drily. "George is in love with you. He's too honorable to stand the thought of coveting his father's wife so . . ."

"Silly boy!" Judith repeated but she looked faintly pleased.

Blows continued to rain on William. A few days after he learned his older son was in the Canadian forces his younger was brought home by a stern headmaster in disgrace. William, Alan, and the headmaster were closeted in the study and it was a stormy session. Through the door voices could be heard raised in anger. Elizabeth wished her cousin would use the library. There she would have been able to hear every word from her post in the cloakroom. At dinner William, his brow furrowed, announced that Alan would not be returning to his school and another would be selected for him. Alan was not in the dining room. He'd been banished to his room and it was several days before he reappeared. Elizabeth questioned Judith and found William had told her some of the details.

"Alan was skipping school," Judith said indifferently. "Forging his father's signature on notes excusing his absence."

"Surely he wouldn't be expelled for that."

It was clear Judith was not interested but she thought for a moment. "William said there was something else but I didn't ask him what. I don't like the boy anyway."

Elizabeth loathed him and would have been glad to hear more. Patience, she thought, and a week later her patience was rewarded. It was early evening. Judith had retired and William was in his study. In answer to her tap he called, "Come. Oh, Elizabeth. What can I do for you?"

Without waiting to be asked she settled herself in the chair opposite him. "It's Sally."

"What about her?" He waved at a pile of papers on his desk. "I've a great deal of work to catch up on."

"She has a complaint."

"Why didn't she come herself?"

Elizabeth bent her head to hide a look of satisfaction. "It's a . . . rather a delicate matter."

Putting down his pen, he regarded his cousin bleakly. "Surely you can handle it yourself. Your job is to keep this house running smoothly. I'm a busy man, Elizabeth, and I have a great deal on my mind."

"I'm aware of that and I hesitated to bother you but . . ."

"*What* is Sally's complaint?"

"Alan."

"There can be no possible connection between my son and a maid."

"Sally tells me that Alan has been molesting her."

"Ridiculous! Another person maligning my son. That intolerable headmaster sat right where you are and had the temerity to call my son a thief." William checked himself but it was too late. More slowly he continued, "This is a confidential matter, Elizabeth, and I shouldn't have blurted it out that way. Don't get any idea there's truth in the man's allegations. Alan explained it. The boys who were involved have a down on him and so does the teacher who pretended to find the money and watches in Alan's locker. An outright case of slander. You should have seen that headmaster back down when I threatened to bring suit against him and his school."

William paused for breath and Elizabeth made a sympathetic sound. He said flatly, "Sally is lying too. What did she say about my son?"

What Sally had actually said was, "If that young bastard doesn't keep his hands off me I'm quitting. I'm a decent girl and don't have to take this. Everytime I turn my back he's grabbing my ass and sticking his hands up my skirts!" Diplomatically, Elizabeth watered it down. "Sally says Alan is putting his hands on her."

"Fire her!"

"I can do that but it will be difficult to replace her. Sally's a good upstairs maid and she can also help out downstairs in a pinch. It will take two girls to do her work."

"Two girls, eh?" William's shapely hand rubbed at his chin. "Perhaps we'd better not be hasty. Do you feel she's telling the truth? Alan's a mere child."

"He's over seventeen."

"I keep forgetting. He seems so young to me. Yes, he's becoming a man. I'll have a talk with him. Send him down. And assure Sally she won't be bothered further."

Elizabeth did his bidding and as she left Alan's room to find the maid she wondered if the fact that Alan had been playing hooky, the stolen watches and money, and the harassing of Sally had a connection.

At that moment Alan was mulling over that thought himself. He slipped a striped bathrobe over his pajamas and brushed his wavy hair. What could the old man want now? He'd managed to wriggle neatly out of that headmaster's accusations and his father was only too glad to accept his explanations. Probably have to go through the whole business again. What a bore! Alan half wished he could have told the old man the truth. The look on his face would have been worth it. Sure he'd swiped the watches and money from those dumb kids. He had to have them. Everything of value he had himself had been pawned. He'd considered sneaking things out of the house and down to the pawnbroker but he hadn't dared. The old man had an eagle eye and so did the damn crabapple. And how Cousin Elizabeth would love to snitch on him!

It was all the fault of that whore. When he'd picked her up he'd been in seventh heaven. Finally a girl who was willing. Not that Maggie was that young: she must be twice his age and had a couple of little brats by God knows who. But Maggie was plump with big tits and she'd forgotten more about lovemaking than most women would ever know. God, how he'd wallowed in that body! But Maggie wasn't doing it for nothing. As she told him, pay first, then screw. His allowance had been devoured by her, most of his possessions had been pawned for her, and then he'd had to steal for her. And got caught. That fart of a headmaster had marched him home and even though he'd been able to convince the old man he'd been framed he still had been banished to this room for a couple of days.

As soon as Alan got a chance he'd gone back to Maggie in that dirty hole in Hell's Kitchen. The bitch had *laughed* at him. Where's the money? she taunted, a rich kid like you should be able to come up with something. Alan had tried to force her but she was bigger and stronger. Contemptuously she backhanded him and pointed at his erection. Bring the pecker back, sonny boy, when you got the money. Wild with frustration he had another go at Sally. He hadn't got anywhere and she threatened to squeal on him.

Putting down the hairbrush the boy regarded his plump face in the mirror. Could Sally have ratted to the old man? No, she wouldn't dare. His father would throw her out on her ear.

Whistling a snatch of ragtime, Alan went jauntily down to the study. One look at his father's stern expression and all levity melted away. "Sit down, son," William said heavily. "It's time we have a man-to-man talk. Elizabeth tells me Sally is ready to leave because of you. Are her complaints valid?" Alan hung his head and his father's voice softened. "Don't be afraid to own up. This is partly my fault. I've neglected to talk to you about . . ." The Adam's apple in William's thin throat bobbed up and down and he flushed. "Sex. You're a young man now and have all the instincts of one. If I remember correctly I did speak to both you and George about this several years ago but perhaps you were too young to understand."

Bloody old fool! He'd understood all right. The old man figured he was lecturing a lousy virgin. And listen to the old goat ramble on—could even make sex sound dull. Keep yourself for your pure wife! What a bunch of baloney. And the old devil had a hell of a lot to talk about. That girl upstairs was knocked up higher than a kite. Did his father think he was deaf? Night after night the bedsprings in Judith's room squeaking. Not now though. The old man was having to do without. But Alan assumed an expression of respectful attention and William became more confident.

"There is one other matter I must warn you about. Unpleasant but for your protection. I'm speaking of social diseases. Diseases that can be contacted by being ah, indiscriminate. Do you know anything about this?"

Sure, good old clap. But give the old boy the answer he wants. "Our gym instructor told us about syphilis and gonorrhea, sir."

"Good." William passed a handkerchief over his bald pate. The room wasn't hot but he was sweating. "I must be blunt. I've no wish to frighten you but the results of those diseases are horrible. They rot not only the body but the mind. Once contracted they're a death sentence. Strong men sometimes live long enough to go insane. There, there, son, bear up."

Alan had ducked his head to hide a grin. Jesus! hadn't the old goat heard about condoms? William was now mopping sweat from his upper lip. "I'm sorry to frighten you but you can see why you must wait for marriage for . . . ah, sexual enjoyment. You can't stoop to dalliance with loose women."

Well, that tears it, Alan thought, no more attempted seduction on the home front. He'd have to look elsewhere. Find a little tart not as commercially minded as Maggie. He told his father earnestly, "It's good of you to explain so clearly, father."

"My duty, and most unpleasant for both of us. I think I may now rely on you to be more circumspect. Although I do not hold you responsible for the needs of your body I must take steps to see you are in a position where temptations are removed until you learn to control yourself."

"What do you mean, sir?"

Picking up a folder, William slid it across the desk. "This boarding school in Vermont. I've been considering it and this business with Sally has made up my mind. It's run along military lines and maintains strict discipline. I'll speak with the headmaster and enroll you for the spring and summer term."

"I'll have no holidays, sir!"

William's thin lips moved in a wintry smile. "With the number of holidays you've had playing hooky I don't consider you're hard done by. You must catch up on your grades. I'm hoping you'll follow your brother to Harvard and right now your marks won't qualify. I realize this is bitter medicine, Alan, but you must learn to take responsibility for your own mistakes. If you'd paid more attention to your studies and less to maids there would be no necessity for it."

Alan sprang to his feet, his mouth quivering, and his father came to him and put an arm around his shoulders. With his free hand, William affectionately ruffled the boy's hair. "I'll miss you, son."

To Alan's amazement he felt tears springing to his eyes. He'd miss the old man too. Not many people seemed to like him. The boys at school, the masters, the people in this house—none of them gave a damn about him. George liked him but George was in Canada. He buried his hot face against his father's shoulder. No sense in arguing. When the old man was in this mood nothing could sway him. "I'll miss you too, father," he muttered.

William hugged him and then pushed him gently away. "Off you go to bed. Don't worry, son, this is all part of growing up."

As Alan went upstairs his steps lagged. He was going to be banished to a school that sounded like a lousy prison and whose fault was it? That snitch Elizabeth. If she hadn't encouraged Sally, the girl would never have had guts enough to squeal on him. Vermont! Flaming with rage he ran up to the third floor and banged his fist on Elizabeth's door. A light was burning in the room and her tall figure was darkly silhouetted against it. He couldn't see her face.

"Figure you're smart, don't you? Couldn't wait to go down to the old man and get his back up. He's sending me to Vermont and it's your fault."

"No, Alan, it's your own fault."

"You hate me, don't you?"

"I feel much the same about you as you do about me."

"I'll tell you how I feel about you, crabapple. One of these days I'm going to be boss here and the first thing I'm going to do is kick Cousin Elizabeth's ass out. No leeching on me like you do on my father."

"You're third in line. If anything happens to your father Judith and George are ahead of you."

"Don't pin your hopes on Judith. No matter how gone the old man is on her he'd never will her this house or the business. They'll go to his sons. And George is off to war. He may not come back. I'm going to get you, cousin, if it's the last thing I ever do!"

After Alan dashed down the stairs Elizabeth stood in the doorway, chilled by the thought of William's younger son in control of the family money and her grandfather's house.

— 11 —

On the seventh day of May the British steamship *Lusitania* was torpedoed ten miles off Kinsdale Head, Ireland. Within twenty minutes she sank taking with her over 1,100 people. One hundred and twenty-eight of the casualties were United States citizens and included Alfred G. Vanderbilt, the theatrical producer Charles Frohman, and the authors Miles Forman and Elbert Hubbard. In the United States, popular feeling against Germany rose to a high pitch and a strong sentiment developed for declaring immediate war against Germany. However, President Wilson chose a diplomatic course and sent Germany a note asking for reparation. The Germans refused to accept responsibility for the deaths of the Americans but did agree not to sink passenger liners without warning.

Among those lost on the *Lusitania* was Cynthia Stokes, wife of Doctor Edward Stokes of New York City, daughter of Sir Andrew and Lady Chalmers of London, England.

For a time the Stokes family held on to the slender hope that Cynthia might be among the survivors, but on the evening of the eleventh day of May Aunt Van telephoned William Meredith. He took the call in the study with Elizabeth hovering over him. Putting the phone down, he turned a haggard face to her. "It's been confirmed. Cynthia is dead. Those bastards! A passenger ship, unarmed, full of women and children. Now I agree with George. He was right to enlist!" Putting both hands flat on the desk, he pulled himself up. "I must go to the Stokeses'. Aunt Van says Lavinia and Edward are in bad shape."

"Would you like me to go with you?"

"No. You stay with Judith. Don't tell her about Cynthia. Time after the baby is born for her to know."

After seeing him off, Elizabeth went in to dinner. On the long table only one place was laid. A few days before, Alan had left for Vermont and Judith, as usual, would have a tray taken to her room. Elizabeth worked through salad and soup eyeing William's place at the head of the table. The other chairs were slender and fragile looking but the master's reflected his position. It had a high back and carved arms and was solidly imposing. She wondered, as she often did, how it would feel to sit in that chair, to know it was rightfully hers. Gerda brought in the main course and Elizabeth accepted a large helping. Too bad William was missing his dinner, he liked a steak and kidney pie. It was one of Elizabeth's favorites and she poised her fork over the steaming plate in anticipation.

As she lifted the fork a sound came from the hall, a muffled cry followed by a series of thuds. In seconds she was out of her chair, racing toward the staircase. Sprawled at the foot lay a crumpled figure. Cookie and Gerda hurried up. "What's this?" Cookie asked. "Lawd, it's the mistress! What happened?"

"I've no idea." Elizabeth knelt beside the girl.

Judith's lashes fluttered and then lifted. The violet eyes were wild with fear. "I tried to come downstairs and tripped on my robe. Elizabeth, I hurt myself!"

Sally was running down the stairs but Elizabeth concentrated on the girl at the foot of them. "Where does it hurt?"

"My stomach. Oh God! It hurts. Elizabeth, save me!"

Cookie was wringing her hands. "We better get her up to bed, miss."

"No. We daren't move her. Sally, fetch a blanket. I'll phone for Doctor John."

The butler at the Stokes house told Elizabeth the family had just left. Mrs. Stokes had insisted on going to her brother's summer home on Long Island. No, Mr. Meredith had gone with them and so had Mr. Edward. "Phone the Flanderses," Elizabeth ordered. "Tell them Mrs. Meredith has had a fall. Tell them to send Doctor Stokes and Mr. Meredith back here the minute they arrive. Hurry! This is an emergency."

She tapped the base of the telephone, trying to think what to do. Cookie, still wringing her hands, called, "What are we to do, miss?"

"I'd better call for an ambulance. We'll have to get her to a hospital."

Gerda had dropped to her knees beside Judith. Her hands moved over the writhing girl. "No time. Missus has gone into labor."

Turning to the cook, Elizabeth asked, "Do you know anything about this sort of thing?"

Shaking her head, the cook started to cry. Elizabeth called, "Sally?" The maid's face had a greenish tinge and the look she gave was all the answer required. It was Gerda who said quietly, "I know a bit, miss."

Gerda was the youngest woman there. "How?" Elizabeth demanded.

"I'm the oldest of nine children, miss. Had to help my mum birth the last three."

"Do your best, Gerda. Tell us how to help."

Gerda took control as though birthing a child on the floor was an everyday occurrence. Cookie and Sally were sent to tear sheets into strips and Elizabeth knelt opposite Gerda and did what she was told. It seemed hours before they took the tiny mite from Judith's heaving body but afterward Elizabeth found the child had been born in twenty minutes. Gerda snipped the umbilical cord and deftly knotted it. She slapped the baby on its bottom and it gave a weak squall. Swaddling it in towels, she handed the child to Cookie. "That was an easy one. Should have seen the trouble my mum had. We better get missus up to bed, miss. Can't leave her here."

Elizabeth tried to lift Judith but she only got in the way. Pushing her aside, Gerda lifted the girl in brawny arms and they were dispatched in the lift with a green-faced Sally. Cookie followed them, gingerly holding the baby.

When Doctor John and William hurried in they found Elizabeth slumped on a chair beside the marble-topped table. A decanter of brandy sat at her elbow and she clutched a glass. She was quite drunk.

"Judith?" William panted.

"In bed."

"The baby?"

She straightened and nearly fell off the chair. "You have a daughter."

It took both her cousin and the doctor to get her into the lift.

She rode up to the second floor on the cushioned bench amid the gleam of brass and the richness of mahogany fittings. Doctor John hurried to Judith but William lingered for a moment before he pressed the button for the third floor. "You saved my wife and child, Elizabeth, I won't forget it."

Before the lift reached the third floor, she'd passed out. Cookie and Sally undressed her and put her to bed. They were more shocked by a drunken Elizabeth than they had been at watching the downstairs maid act as midwife at the birth of the mistress's child.

Except for a few bruises, Judith was none the worse for her ordeal. She recovered quickly and by the time she was allowed up she was again slim and lovely, with a flush of rosy color in cheeks and lips and the blond hair shining.

Her baby wasn't as well. As Aunt Van said, the child, named Alicia Emma, was a poor puny thing and for a time Doctor John despaired of saving it. Judith was unable to nurse and a wet nurse was called in, but she proved more interested in the liquor cabinet than her small charge. A furious William sent her on her blowsy way and Doctor John came to the rescue with a trained nurse. Her name was Mrs. MacIntosh but she asked to be called Tosh. She was a widow, a small woman with sad eyes, a limp, and hands disfigured with puckered scars. She'd tried to pull her two children out of a burning house and had failed. With dedication and skill Tosh strove to save the life of Judith's baby. Gradually she won the fight. William was delighted, but although Judith pretended the same delight Elizabeth sensed the girl wasn't concerned about the baby. When the two women were alone Judith's conversation was only about her lover's return from Canada.

In June Lafe Norton did return to the city but that event was eclipsed by George Meredith's leave. It was to be his first and his last leave in New York. Shortly his regiment was due to embark for England from Halifax.

"So soon?" William asked. "You can't be even half-trained."

George smiled grimly. "We'll finish up in England. No time to waste, sir. Casualties on the Western Front are high and they need replacements."

William brooded about replacements. More men to take the place of mangled bodies scattered over No Man's Land, hanging from barbed wire, coughing lungs out in field hospitals. But he was resigned to his son's decision, and after the outrage of the *Lusitania* he understood it. William was proud of the tall artillery officer in the immaculate uniform. From George's visored cap to his polished shoes he looked every inch an officer. A bushy mustache made the boy look older.

Spurred on by Judith, Elizabeth finally took her courage in both hands and asked permission for Lafe to dine with them. William brushed her aside, not unkindly but firmly. "There's no time, Elizabeth. George will only be with us for a few days."

William's friends who a few months before had showered attention on Lafe had no time for him either. They'd been amused by the young man, and perhaps if he hadn't left New York he might have become one of them. But memories are short, Lafe was unimportant, and they had their own problems. Only Doctor John was still in the Stokeses' gracious brownstone. Edward, quiet and withdrawn in his grief, was in England. He had enlisted as quickly as he could in the British Medical Corps. Lavinia, after having blamed her son and husband for Cynthia's death, was tucked into a rest home suffering from what was tactfully referred to as nervous problems. Capricious Aunt Van, after discovering Lafe wasn't Elizabeth's suitor, showed no further interest. Lafe's social star had risen, shone briefly, and then set.

As Lafe Norton bitterly told his friend Alfie, he'd been used as a performing dog, thrown a few bones, and then been kicked back to his doghouse. Alfie ordered more beer, slapped the younger man's shoulder, and said, "What'd you expect? You said you got in the back door. So they cooled off on you. Got to remember grand people like the Merediths and Vandercourts got no use for the likes of us."

Lafe telephoned Elizabeth but she told him she could do nothing. When he argued she promised to try again after George left. As she put down the phone she smiled. It would do no harm to let the young lovers stew for a while.

Because of the brevity of George's leave, the date for the baby's christening was moved up. William decided that in view of Elizabeth's courage at the time of his daughter's birth she was to be godmother. She told him the truth, that Gerda was the one to be rewarded. She wasn't trying to be modest but she knew it wouldn't do to set the servants against her. William pooh-poohed the notion of a maid delivering his daughter but he did give a small gift of money to Gerda. Also, in a rare burst of generosity, he sent Elizabeth to select a suitable outfit for the christening.

Elizabeth arrived at the church resplendent in clothes she had yearned to wear at William's wedding—a watered silk gown and an ostrich-plumed hat. Cradling the baby swathed in the Meredith christening dress and shawl, she took her place at the font with Albert Flanders, who was to be godfather, at her side. The weather smiled and sunlight streamed through stained glass windows. Pools of colored light fell over the pews, bathing the spectators in variegated hues. Aunt Van, Sophie, and Charity had yellow faces and saffron tinted clothes, in the front pew the Meredith family looked like corpses with bluish lips and gray blue skins. Doctor John's ruddy face was even redder and Uncle Herman's silky beard pinkened.

The baby started to whimper and Elizabeth gently rocked it, gazing down at the fragile hairless skull with a delicate tracery of blue veins. Milky blue eyes stared up and the child's mouth opened wider. The poor creature didn't even cry like a normal baby, the sounds coming from her more like the mewling of a kitten. Surrounded by friends and relatives, under the cold glass eyes of angels and saints, William and Judith's daughter was given the names of her grandmothers, Alicia for William's mother, Emma for Judith's.

After the church ceremony Aunt Van provided a buffet dinner for the guests. Once away from the church Elizabeth received scant attention but Judith, charming in tulle and satin, with the baby in her arms, was the star. With the birth of William's child and the circumstances of that birth, Judith was finally and completely accepted in the inner circle.

"They look exactly like a madonna and child," Sophie Vandercourt breathed in Elizabeth's ear.

Elizabeth was helping herself to food at the buffet. She glanced at the other spinster, noted sardonically that the woman's heavy lenses were misted with emotion, and agreed. Silently she laughed. Some madonna! Judith was more a Mary Magdalene.

As soon as she'd eaten, Elizabeth, unnoticed and unmissed, took her leave. She made her way home on foot and found there the true heroine of Alicia Emma's birth. Gerda, her skirts hiked up, was scrubbing the kitchen floor.

The final day of George's leave arrived and his family escorted him to Grand Central Station. Alan had received a few days off from his despised boarding school and Alicia was in the care of Tosh.

To Elizabeth's surprise none of the other relatives or friends were waiting under the barrel-vaulted ceiling of the rotunda. She decided William must have requested that the family be allowed to say goodbye to George alone.

George had already received the family's parting gifts—expensive binoculars in a leather, gold-fitted case from his father, more gold in a wristwatch from Alan, more leather surrounding a family photograph taken the week before from Judith, and a more humble gift from Elizabeth. No gold or leather. Simply a knitted khaki scarf and matching gloves. George had seemed pleased with everything but he'd lingered longest over Judith's gift. From the photograph the family stared out, all of them except the baby and George wearing strained self-conscious smiles. George's lips under the bushy new mustache were set in stern lines.

On the platform they clustered around George, conscious of the stares from the people around them. In the trim Canadian uniform George was a novelty. Two small boys in caps and knickers gaped up at the tall officer but scuttled back to their parents when he bent to speak to them. A stout man with the strawberry nose of a heavy drinker shouted, "Give them Huns hell!" A trio of girls, looking like a posy of flowers, hung from a train window, smiling coquettishly.

Conversation was stilted. Everything that could be said already had been said. George was ill at ease, obviously wishing it was over and he was headed back to Canada. Then the crowds around parted like the Red Sea and with Aunt Van in the lead their friends arrived. It seemed to Elizabeth that everyone they knew in the city was there. They chattered like magpies, their chauffeurs laden with farewell gifts. One by one the chauffeurs deposited the gifts at George's feet, tipped their hats, and withdrew. When the last one stepped back George looked like a khaki clad idol with offerings of fruit, bottles of champagne, brandy, and baskets of flowers hiding his polished boots.

A tribal ritual, Elizabeth thought, everyone acting as though they'd gathered to see a friend off on the Grand Tour, laughing and joking and talking as though George was off on a luxury trip instead of to the trenches of the Western Front. The only sober face was George's, tight-lipped and pink with embarrassment as he gazed down at the blossoms, the glint of gold foil, the baskets heaped with fruit. Doctor John came to the rescue, stooped for a squat brown bottle, handed it to George with a flourish, and told him, "Brandy. Good for the stomach. We'll look after the rest."

At his direction the chauffeurs returned and awkwardly bent to retrieve their burdens. Some ragged immigrants shoved closer, the women and children openmouthed at the bounty before them. Vainly their men tried to pull them back. In the gilded ribbons and gold foil, Elizabeth mused, they must think they're seeing exactly what they dreamed this country was going to offer them, what the noble but empty words on the Statue of Liberty promised them. No mention on that welcoming lady of hunger and cold and filthy tenements. The immigrants crowded closer and the chauffeurs began to shove back. All color had drained from George's face and he looked exhausted, "Let them have it," he ordered.

And so the huddled masses from other shores, many still homeless and hopeless, snatched the bounty without thanks, hugged bottles to their breasts, clutched bouquets to hungry bodies, fought each other for fruit.

The conductor was calling and George bent to kiss the ladies' cheeks, gravely shook hands with the men, dropped a light kiss on Alicia's ruffled bonnet. The baby started to mewl but in the noise from the engine, the voices calling farewells, the tiny sound was lost. For an instant the whole scene slowed and then stopped as though a moving picture had suddenly halted. As in a dream Elizabeth saw the gleam of light catching George's visored hat, the rich leather of the Sam Browne belt, sunbursts of brass buttons. The slipping of his father's determined cheer showing the anguish it had concealed, the cinders speckling the ladies' hats, light colored gowns, white gloves. The nape of George's neck, thin and young and vulnerable, as he bent to brush his lips over Judith's glowing cheek. The look of grief in Doctor John's eyes, Uncle Herman dozing standing up, supported by Nina and Estelle Standford.

Then George was gone, briefly reappearing at a window and lifting a hand in farewell. The ladies were wiping their eyes with lace trimmed hankies, the men stood like soldiers, Tosh took the baby from Elizabeth, the train heaved and rattled and moved off, smoke and cinders veiling George's face.

Something is over, Elizabeth thought, done and dead. She had no idea what it was that had been lost.

Hankies were tucked away, the men replaced their hats, they all went up to the rotunda. The men walked ahead, gathered around William and Alan, then the women in swirls of perfume, rustles of silk, a bobbing of tulle, flowered and plumed hats. Tosh, cradling the baby, and Elizabeth brought up the rear.

They moved across the rotunda, the chauffeurs forming a wedge-shaped platoon to shield their employers from the jostling of common people. New York royalty, Elizabeth thought wryly, and then saw Judith turn, caught a glimpse of mutely imploring eyes. Then Elizabeth saw him. Lafe was standing against a pillar next to a beggar wearing dark glasses, holding out a tin cup. Lafe was bareheaded, his shabby hat clutched in both hands, his hair a defiant banner in the light streaming down from high windows. The group of men passed him without turning a head and then the women fluttered by, high heels beating a staccato rhythm. Aunt Van's sharp eyes spotted him and she lifted a hand in a curt wave but didn't pause.

Gesturing to Tosh to go ahead, Elizabeth fumbled in her purse and stopped at Lafe's side. The coins tinkled as they dropped into the beggar's cup and she hissed, "Are you mad?"

The beggar straightened, the dark glasses swiveling toward her. "It's me eyes gone wrong, mum, not me head."

"I wasn't talking to you," she said but he was gone, his cane sweeping over the floor. She darted a look at Lafe, noticed he was thinner, with his dark suit hanging loosely from his big frame. "At a time like this standing here like a beggar, your hat in your hand."

"I am a beggar." He pushed the hat out, upside down. "Fill it with Judith. I must see her."

"There's no place you can meet. Be patient."

She turned away but his fingers closed painfully around her wrist. His left hand, she thought, the overlong little finger, crisp red hair growing down to the knuckles, a frayed shirt cuff slipping down over his wrist. "Tomorrow. The Oasis. If you don't bring her I'll go to the house and kick that damn door down."

"What time?"

"Twelve."

"We'll be there. But you're a fool."

He released her and she trotted to catch up. A policeman obligingly held up traffic while gleaming limousines pulled away. William's car was in the lead, rolling sedately up Park Avenue as though leading a funeral cortege. Elizabeth sat beside a slouched and damp-eyed Alan facing William and Judith. It *was* like a funeral and here in the hearse was the corpse. William looked as bluish as he had in the church bathed in light pouring through a saint's robe. Judith sat with her head bowed, showing silent sympathy for her husband's suffering. She lifted her eyes once, fixed them on Elizabeth with such a blaze of intensity that the older woman turned and gazed out of a window. She stared at a team of perfectly matched Clydesdales hauling a brewery dray but didn't see them.

What manner of woman are you, Elizabeth wondered. Without any effort you've captured the affections of three men—William, his son George, and Lafe Norton. Lafe standing against a pillar like a mendicant risking all my careful plans for one glimpse of you. Lafe! With his shabby clothes and frayed cuffs, with his flaming hair and tender mouth and strong body, with my heart . . .

I'll see him tomorrow, Elizabeth thought sadly, but I'll wager he won't even look at me.

— 12 —

The Oasis hadn't changed since the day Elizabeth had met Lafe Norton there. They sat at an oak table against a white painted wall on red and white cushions with the menus balanced on the backs of tiny china camels. The change was in the three people gathered around the table. Food was set before them, and pots of tea, but Judith and Lafe ignored it and Elizabeth merely toyed with a meat pie.

Lafe was dressed exactly the way he had been the first time, in shabby tweeds, a turtleneck sweater. Some of the women at nearby tables cast approving looks at him but he had eyes only for Judith Meredith. They didn't touch each other but their eyes locked and passion arced across the table, a feeling so strong that Elizabeth felt if she stretched out a hand she would receive an electric shock.

Lafe kept his voice low. "Judith, we have to be together."

"I remember that hotel room in Boston," Judith breathed.

"This is New York, not Boston," Elizabeth said sharply. "Judith's pictures have appeared on the society pages. She'll be recognized."

"When?" the girl asked her lover.

"Tomorrow. One in the afternoon. My flat." He scribbled on a scrap of paper and tucked it under her handbag.

Elizabeth picked up her cup and found her fingers were trembling. "Both of you are insane. What if she's recognized? Word will be sure to get back to William." She appealed to Judith. "What about your baby daughter?"

"*William's* daughter." For the first time since they'd entered the cafe Judith looked at the other woman. "Anyway, Lafe's supposed to be your friend, not mine. If we are seen, all I'll be guilty of is helping you to meet him. It will be *your* reputation ruined, not mine." She patted Elizabeth's hand. "Do it for me, dear. What difference does your reputation make?"

My life, Elizabeth told her silently. All the careful plans for-
mulated over the months were in danger of being foiled, not by
William, but by these reckless idiots. With her reputation ruined
she would no longer have a claim on her grandfather's house or
her cousin's charity. "I won't do it," she muttered.

"You have to," Judith told her coldly. "You have no choice.
One word from me and William will no longer need your ser-
vices."

Avoiding Elizabeth's eyes, Lafe got to his feet and politely
bowed to both women. Judith and Elizabeth watched his broad
back as he made his way to the door. When he was gone, Judith
turned back to Elizabeth, her mouth forming a pretty moue.
"I'm sorry I had to threaten you. I really didn't mean it, dear.
You want to make me happy, don't you? You promised you'd
help."

Elizabeth simply bent her head in agreement, meekly accepting the girl's apology. Be meek, she reminded herself, but be
patient.

Lafe's home was on the third floor of a run-down brick
building and was no more a flat than Elizabeth's room had been.
The single room had a brass bed with sheets and dingy blankets
drawn over its lumpy mattress. Against a wall stood an old stove
and near it a shelf supported a few pans and dishes. The only
other furnishings were a table and a single wooden chair. The
table was covered with books, magazines, piles of paper, and a
typewriter. Lafe's few clothes hung from pegs and the two uncur-
tained windows were covered with green blinds. One blind had a
long diagonal tear through which light filtered, casting a greenish
hue. The room smelled of cigar smoke and cooking fat.

Elizabeth stood beside the door watching Judith unpinning
her hat, Lafe taking it from her and setting it on the cluttered
table. She glanced around the room, the inanimate objects seeming to sneer at her. The bed beckoned mockingly. She looked
directly at Lafe and he had the grace to blush, hot color seeping
over his collar and dying his face almost the shade of his hair.

Judith made an imperious gesture. "Do some shopping,
Elizabeth. There's a good girl."

Backing out the doorway, Elizabeth muttered, "I'll be back
in two hours."

She felt her way down the poorly lit staircase, moving as the beggar had. Outside sunlight struck harshly, momentarily making her as blind as he was. She wandered along the sidewalk, turning into stores, making small purchases, filling her crocheted shopping bag. She had no idea what she was buying. All she could think of was that room, that bed. Pictures moved through her mind, naked figures entwined on a lumpy mattress, white bodies writhing in green light like strange underwater creatures mating. Spasms of jealousy, almost physically painful, clawed at her, and humiliation nearly overwhelmed her. She staggered and put out a hand for support, smearing her white glove on the dirty brick wall. A man moving past stuck out a helping hand. "You sick, lady?"

Shaking her head, she pushed away from the wall and turned into another store. After a time she found she'd wandered into a park. Her head began to clear and she sat on a bench watching a ferry breasting the river, hearing the hoot from its whistle, seeing two small boys throwing a stick for a dog.

She tried to brush the filth from her glove. They've soiled me, she thought, dirtied me as those bricks dirtied my glove. Forced me to watch their lust as though I'm nothing . . . as though I'm a . . . a poor relative.

The thought steadied her. That was exactly what Cousin Elizabeth was. Carefully and coldly, setting all emotions aside, she began to plan. By the time she got back to Lafe's room she was herself: competent, cool, decisive. Lafe admitted her. He wore no jacket, his shirt was open at the neck, the sleeves rolled above his elbows. His feet were bare. Judith, in pretty disorder, was perched on the bed, brushing her hair with a man's brush.

Pushing past Lafe, Elizabeth turned the wooden chair around to face the bed. At her gesture he sank down next to Judith. "We must talk," she told them.

Judith's hands wove patterns through her hair, ivory against gold. She threw back her head and her eyes were moist violets. "He's leaving again," she told the older woman brokenly. "In September he's being sent abroad."

"Jenkins didn't work out," Lafe said tersely. "I heard this morning. Elizabeth, we *have* to be together. There's so little time."

Judith broke down and he gathered her in his arms, her

damp face pushed against the hollow at the base of his strong neck. Blond hair threaded through crisp red tufts on his chest. Elizabeth took a deep breath. The room still smelled of cigar smoke and cooking fat but now there were the odors of Judith's perfume and the sweat from lovemaking drying against their warm skins. On the shelf near the stove was a basin of water, soap skimming on a tepid surface, a towel flung beside it.

"You can't meet here again," Elizabeth told them crisply. "Too risky. There has to be another way. Lafe, will you have time off before you leave?"

"The editor's giving me August off. To wind up my affairs." He glanced ironically around the room. "That won't take long."

His arms dropped away from Judith and she brushed back her hair. The buttons on her bodice were undone and she started to do them up. Rosy flesh bulged from the gap. The lovers gazed at Elizabeth as though she were the teacher, they the students. Hope began to move in the depths of their eyes.

Elizabeth placed a hand over her eyes as though she were deep in thought. The minutes dragged out and then she said slowly, "We must get out of the city. Lafe, is there a place you can go where you won't have to stay in a hotel?"

"Sure, I've three summer homes waiting for me."

"Be serious."

It was his turn to think. After a time he nodded. "A friend has a cottage in Atlantic City. I think he'd lend it to me."

"That's where William and I honeymooned," Judith cried.

Elizabeth smiled benignly. "That's our answer."

Lafe frowned. "How do you mean?"

"Judith and I will go to Atlantic City for August. You can stay at your friend's cottage. During the daytime we'll behave discreetly. At night—" She waved an expressive hand at the bed.

The hopeful light faded in Judith's eyes. "It won't work. Even if William agrees he'll insist on coming."

"We'll use the baby. The sea air will do Alicia good. And something else. Judith, have you allowed your husband to come to your bed since the baby was born?"

"Of course not! I've been true to Lafe."

God! What a simpleton! How could Lafe prefer this trite girl to a woman like herself? "We can use that. Now, this is how we handle it."

She bent forward and so did they. With their heads close together, speaking in low voices, they looked and sounded like conspirators plotting to commit a crime.

When they were safely home Elizabeth emptied her shopping bag and found she had bought a child's rattle, two copies of the *Saturday Evening Post*, a bottle of lavender scent, a celluloid powder box depicting Cupid shooting an arrow through a heart, a box of cheap chocolates, and three rank black cigars. She gave the scent, the magazines, and the chocolates to the maids. The rattle she took up to the nursery. She pleased Briggs by handing him the cigars. The powder box demonstrating true love she threw into the rubbish bin.

When William wouldn't hear of the projected trip Judith didn't argue, she didn't even weep. Following Elizabeth's instructions the girl went to bed in a darkened room, a cold compress on her brow. Her husband waited but she made no move to leave her bed. On the evening of the third day he took his problem to Doctor John, not at his office but at his home.

He found the doctor seated before a cold hearth in the study of the quiet brownstone. Ranged on the mantel were family photographs—his parents, his son Edward as a chubby schoolboy in knickers and cap, a recent one of Edward in a British uniform, Edward's wedding photograph with his fragile Cynthia at his side, John and Lavinia's wedding picture, and a striking profile shot of the lovely Lavinia.

William studied the mantel and then looked sadly down at his friend. "You've enough worries of your own. I've no right to bother you with mine."

"You've every right. That's my job. Sit down and tell me."

William told him, quickly and concisely. John Stokes's big head bobbed in nods over his massive body resembling a wise Buddha. William's voice became shrill. "She doesn't love me."

Of course Judith doesn't, John thought, everyone but you knows that. There's only one reason an attractive girl like your wife takes a man of your age and it isn't love. Aloud he reassured. "Of course she loves you. And where's the harm in Elizabeth and Judith taking little Alicia to Atlantic City? God knows if I could I'd get out of this city myself. The heat is unbearable."

"She could go to Aunt Van's summer home or to Albert and Nina's."

"She could but obviously she doesn't want to."

"Judith doesn't want *me*. I told her I'd take time off and come with her but she doesn't want me even on weekends." William repeated, "She doesn't love me."

"Did she tell you the reason for this trip?"

"She said she wants to get away from everything, from the city, from me. Says she has to in order to regain her perspective."

Templing his fingers, the doctor gazed down at them. He lowered his voice. "What are your relations with your wife?"

"What relations?"

"You know what I mean."

A hot flush rose over William's high collar, flooding the stark planes of his face, making his eyes colorless. "I don't discuss that with any man. Not even a friend I've valued since I was a boy."

"I'm not asking as a friend. I'm asking as a physician."

"Sorry, John." William looked studiously at his shoes. "There aren't any."

"Since?"

"Last Christmas. When Judith found she was pregnant."

"Not after the baby—"

"She locks her door."

"Ah!" Spreading his hands, the doctor said gently, "There's your answer. It isn't lack of love, William. Judith is afraid. An unwanted and difficult pregnancy, then a terrifying birth without a doctor. Having to rely on three servants and an old maid. Let her go. A month in the sea air, a month to think it out. I guarantee Judith will come back a new woman."

"And I shouldn't go? Not even for a weekend?"

"Don't go at all. Elizabeth will be with her and she's competent."

"Yes, she'll take good care of Judith and the baby. Very well, John, I'll take your advice." He glanced up at the mantel. "How is Lavinia?"

Abruptly, John heaved his bulk up and went across to the liquor cabinet. He wavered and for the first time William realized the doctor was far from sober. He took the glass from John but didn't lift it to his mouth. He watched the other man slump back in his chair, toss down half the whiskey. "No better. I despair of her sanity. First she accused Edward and me of murdering Cynthia, now she refuses to believe any of it ever happened. Every week I go to see her and usually Nina comes with me. She's a godsend. Handles Lavinia better than I do."

"She still won't admit Cynthia is dead?"

"I'm sure somewhere in her mind Lavinia knows the truth but she keeps up this fiction. The *Lusitania* never sank, Cynthia's safe in England, soon she'll come home with the baby. Lavinia's room is piled high with baby clothes she's making. Talks about nothing but Cynthia and the baby. I try to break through but . . ."

William waited for a moment and then asked, "Any word from Edward?"

"Last letter said he was expecting to go to France soon. Probably there by now. In some field hospital. What about George?"

"Haven't heard from him. I suppose he's on the high seas." Setting down his untouched glass, William leaned forward. "Do you think we'll be pulled into this war?"

"Inevitable. The only question is when."

"The Germans did promise not to sink any more passenger liners."

John gave a harsh bark of laughter. "You think they'll keep a promise? Bastards who torpedoed a liner and killed hundreds of women and children?"

"Does Albert still think we can stay neutral?"

"All Albert thinks about is himself and that new mistress of his." John's lips curled, making clearer than words his opinion of his handsome brother-in-law. "Nina's a fine woman. Albert should be horsewhipped!"

Abruptly William reached for his glass and drained it. "War can't do much more to us, John."

"What about Alan? Is he threatening to run away and join the army?"

"Not yet. Perhaps the war will be over before he's old enough."

Reaching for the bottle, John refilled their glasses. "Let's pray it is."

They sat and drank in silence, the empty house stretching out around them. They stared into the cold hearth, thinking of their wives and sons. The line of faces on the mantel, all smiling, gazed down on the aging men, together but each quite alone.

— 13 —

Atlantic City! Great hotels lining the boardwalk, wide porches with wicker sets and rocking chairs, flags flying from cupolas, and in the evening the glimmer of bulbs strung along the eaves. Beyond the boardwalk beaches stretching to slow white-topped breakers of cornflower blue, sand dotted with family groups, fathers and mothers and nursemaids and children taking shelter under hotel umbrellas. Men in striped bathing costume, young women daringly exposing inches of white skin under the knees of skirted pantaloons, older women hunched under beach umbrellas, their heads balancing broad-brimmed hats, their bodies swathed in layers of linen and gauze. Wicker chairs with surrey tops trundling along the boardwalk pushed by bored porters. Colors blazing everywhere, women's gowns of pink and green and yellow, the garish red and blue of brass bands playing in pavilions, vivid balloons in children's hands. Smells. The tang of salt, odors of peanuts and popcorn, richer odors of steaks and roasts and broiled fish wafting from hotel kitchens.

Judith and Elizabeth and baby Alicia in Atlantic City in August. In the dining room of their hotel. Here the predominant color white. White curtains on long doors moving in a sea breeze, white crockery on heavy hotel linen, ladies' white dresses and hats, gentlemen's ice cream suits, boys in white and blue sailor suits, small girls in white dresses sashed with velvet and satin. Judith and Elizabeth in ensembles bought that morning at a boardwalk store. Elizabeth all in white, Judith's gown and hat and parasol trimmed in ice green. Between them the baby in a wicker basket, wrapped to her pointed chin in white ruffles.

Tea was being served, high English tea, by trim waitresses from walnut tea wagons. Mothers and fathers and well-behaved children, older men and women, bashful honeymooners, decorously selecting hot crumpets, scones, whipped cream, pots of preserves, slices of iced cakes. Elizabeth and Judith sipped China tea and tried not to look toward the entrance of the lobby, tried not to appear to be waiting. They made stilted conversation and showed interest only in each other and the sleeping baby. Then, without looking, they knew Lafe had arrived. They could tell by the turning heads of the other guests, the cessation of murmuring voices, the hands holding heavy silver cutlery momentarily stilled.

Elizabeth glanced around and played her role in a high clear voice. "It's Lafcadio Norton. What a surprise!"

Judith turned her head. "So it is. Whatever can Mr. Norton be doing here?"

Lafe was threading his way among the tables. His red hair gleamed under the tinkling chandeliers, the high fluted ceiling. He too was all in white—suit, shirt, shoes, and spats. The only touches of color were in the narrow blue band on a stiff straw hat, the dark blue stripes in a white tie. The clothes were new but they rode his rangy frame as his tweeds did, as though they were a part of him. He played his part well. The start of surprise when he saw the women, a moment of hesitancy, then a slow turn toward their table. He greeted Elizabeth first, then a more formal greeting for her companion. He bent over the basket, gravely admiring the baby. Alicia stirred and peered up with solemn skimmed-milk eyes, looking with the hairless skull and wizened face more like an ancient toothless woman than a baby.

Elizabeth invited Lafe to join them and he did, carefully placing his new hat on a chair. Polite waitresses brought their orders and they nibbled and sipped while they made small talk that might be expected from a chance meeting of acquaintances. Judith asked if Lafe was staying at the hotel and he told her no, he had use of a friend's cottage. He enquired after William and George and Alan. He mentioned the Vandercourts, the Stokeses, the Flanderses. He asked if they had any news of Arnold Standford's condition and about Edward Stokes and Ronnie Grant. He spoke of Antonio and his wife Maud and their infant son. He drank his tea, refused more, and rose. A handsome young man briefly meeting two ladies.

Lafe was saying something but Elizabeth's attention was elsewhere. Across the room was a group of elderly women. Most of them were intent on laden plates but one of them was paying no attention to food. A stout cane was propped beside her chair but she sat with an erect regal posture. Under a filmy hat brim snowy hair swept up like a crown. Her cheeks were round and pink and she had startling unfaded blue eyes. Those eyes were unabashedly moving from Lafe's tall figure to demure Judith and then to herself. Elizabeth met that sharp blue gaze and she turned abruptly back to Lafe and Judith. "I beg your pardon, Judith. Were you speaking to me?"

"Mr. Norton has offered to give us dinner at his cottage."

"Bachelor style, I"m afraid," Lafe said.

Elizabeth raised her brows in question and the girl said slowly, "I should be delighted to go."

"We can't be late," Elizabeth told him. "The baby must have an early bedtime."

"Shall we say six then?" He added rather grandly, "I'll send a car for you."

At six the taxi was waiting and as Elizabeth followed Judith down the shallow steps she was conscious of the intent gaze of the white-haired woman, now seated on the shady veranda. Handing the baby to Judith, she got in the car at her side. As they rumbled away she noticed that although purple wool cascaded from the woman's lap, her knitting needles were not moving.

The borrowed cottage sat with its unpainted back to the road, its windowed front facing the sea. Lost to sight were the lines of hotels and the piers and the boardwalk. Here were only deserted dunes with gulls, sandpipers, and dune grasses. On the badly slanting boards of the stoop Lafe was waiting. He'd discarded his hat and jacket, shoes and spats, and removed his collar and tie. Around his waist a linen tea cloth was pinned and before taking the baby's case from Elizabeth he wiped his hands on the towel.

Inside, the floors sloped as badly as the stoop and the place was neat and clean but bare. Lafe carried the wicker basket into

a tiny bedroom and Elizabeth lifted the child onto a blanket in
the middle of the bed.

In the living room Judith was exclaiming over the table, set
in the middle of the sloping floor, covered with a white cloth, set
with mismatched china, and centered with a jelly jar holding wild
daisies. "How charming! How you must have worked. Flowers
too!" With a graceful movement she unpinned her sailor hat,
looked at the hatpin cunningly fashioned as the head of a white
and yellow daisy, and set the pretty trinket among the living flowers. Joyously she smiled up at her lover. "This afternoon you
even noticed my hatpin."

He hugged her. "I'd like to say yes but all I noticed was you.
I had to fight not to stare."

Elizabeth paused in the bedroom doorway to stare fixedly at
the daisy hatpin in the jelly jar. "Did either of you notice that
woman who was staring at us in the dining room?" Golden and
red heads shook and she continued, "An old woman with white
hair and a cane. When we got into the taxi, Judith, she was on
the veranda and she was still staring."

"I certainly don't know her."

"She may know you. When I write to William and Aunt Van
I'll mention we've seen Lafe. Better safe than sorry."

The girl bubbled with laughter. "Cautious old Elizabeth.
Seeing a spy in some busybody with nothing better to do than
watch people."

Then Lafe proudly served dinner, an odd one but surprisingly well cooked. Boston baked beans, curried chicken, and
a cold lemon souffle. White wine pouring from a long-necked
bottle, Judith sparkling, Lafe devouring her with his eyes, Elizabeth intently looking at the daisy hatpin.

When Lafe stood up and started to gather up dishes, she
made a shooing motion. "That's woman's work. You two go
along and walk on the beach before sunset. I'll clean up here."

They didn't protest. Judith reached for her hat but Elizabeth
told her, "Take your parasol. You'll be more comfortable and
there's no one around to see you."

She watched them wandering along the beach, Judith's arm
linked with Lafe's, Lafe balancing the dainty parasol in a big
knuckled hand. After a few steps the girl stopped, stood on one
leg like a stork, and laughed up into his face. He sank to his

knees, removed one slipper, then the other, and they broke into a run, racing along the beach, Judith's hair working loose and blowing back, ruffled skirt molding her body. White gulls wheeled in a blue sky; white breakers foamed on the beach, hesitated, and then retreated, leaving strands of seaweed and small sea creatures on the wet strip of sand.

When they were out of sight, Elizabeth went to the bedroom. It was as bare as the living room. A white painted chest, a wardrobe, the bed with the sleeping baby. She opened the double doors of the wardrobe. A tweed suit, the new white jacket hung from hangers. On the shelf above was the straw hat with the blue band. Standing on tiptoe she ran a hand over the shelf. Then she closed the doors and went to the chest. In the top drawer shirts and some collars, in the second neatly folded socks, handkerchiefs, the white spats. In the third a pile of underclothing. Under the cotton drawers she found what she was looking for.

Pulling out the blue metal box she looked down at the cover. On it was the head of an Arab, a bold hooked nose, a red burnoose. She slid back the cover and examined the rubber sheaths. Then she went to the living room and lifted Judith's hatpin from the jelly jar. Her hands moving like a surgeon's, with care and deliberation, she pricked each sheath with the sharp pin. The metal top slid back into place, the box disappeared under Lafe's underwear, the drawer closed. Only then did she step to the bed and bend over the baby. Gently she straightened the head on the reed-thin neck, drew a corner of the blanket over the shoulders, and went to replace the hatpin.

When they returned, their stockinged feet covered with sand, their hair windtossed, their faces flushed and laughing, Cousin Elizabeth was seated at the table engrossed in the pages of the *Saturday Evening Post*. She lifted her head and smiled but the smile wasn't directed at them. A more observant pair might have thought the old maid was beaming at the daisies in the jelly glass.

That night in her spacious room Elizabeth bathed the baby, fed her, arranged a blanket over one end of the crib so the breeze wouldn't chill the child, and tilted the desk lamp so the light didn't fall across the pointed face.

She composed letters to Aunt Van and William. Casually she mentioned Judith's and her surprise at meeting Lafcadio in the dining room of their hotel. She told both of the tea they had given Lafe and the dinner they had taken at his cottage. She said how happy Lafe seemed to be posted overseas. Then she gave details on Judith and Alicia, how in the brief time they'd been away both were looking healthier. Into the envelopes she slipped colored postcards of their hotel with windows circled and legends inked in, saying this is Alicia's and my room, this is Judith's.

Her insurance taken out, Elizabeth proceeded to bathe and turn down her bed. The sheets felt crisp against her skin, the air cool enough to pull up a light blanket. She lay still, watching the slow drift of white curtains at the window, listening for sounds from the adjoining room. All was quiet but she knew Judith was not in bed. As clearly as if she could see through the wall she knew Judith was seated at a window, her chin propped on a hand, impatient for full dark.

Later she roused briefly and could no longer see the curtains. The room was velvety black. But she heard the soft closing of a door, the cautious pad of silk clad feet along the hall. Judith, her slippers in her hand, creeping down the rear stairs to her lover. Elizabeth's mind followed them as they moved through velvet darkness toward the cottage in the drift of deserted sand dunes.

She went back to sleep, her cheek pillowed against a hand, her lips curving in a contented smile. She dreamed of a handsome sheik riding a black horse across white sand. A hooked nose curved boldly out from under the folds of a red burnoose. Through the burnoose a hatpin was stuck at a jaunty angle. The daisy head bobbed like a battle banner.

The days in Atlantic City passed slowly, lazy in golden light, the swell of slow breakers, the blue of sea and sky. Judith's and Elizabeth's life fell into a routine. They remained in their rooms until noon, breakfasting from trays, dressed for a light lunch, and then went to the beach. There Elizabeth drowsed under an umbrella with the baby in the wicker basket at her side, rousing to watch children building sand castles, bathers laughing and shouting from the surf.

Elizabeth didn't see Lafe. During the day he kept away from

the hotel and beach area. She pictured him at the cottage among the deserted dunes waiting for darkness and Judith. One afternoon Elizabeth met the white-haired woman who had stirred feelings of unease. She was dozing under the umbrella when the tinkle of ice cubes against glass wakened her. She opened her eyes and saw a waiter setting down a tray of lemonade and glasses beside her. Behind him was the tall, regal woman swathed in sun hat and veils, supported on one side by her cane, on the other by a sour-faced maid.

"May I?" the woman asked and pointed with the cane to the other chair.

"Of course."

Jumping up, Elizabeth helped the maid lower the old woman into the chair. At a gesture from her employer the maid stalked down the beach and came to a halt, her arms folded, to look with disapproval at the bathing costumes of a young couple playing in the surf.

Elizabeth's uninvited companion propped the cane against the table, adjusted a gauze scarf, and told her, "I thought a cold drink . . . you might find it refreshing."

"A kind thought." Elizabeth poured from the frosty pitcher. "I'm Elizabeth Meredith."

"I know. I took the liberty of enquiring at the desk." A gloved hand reached across the tray. "Abigail Porter." The startling eyes waited and then the woman sighed. "I see the name means nothing to you. I once knew Peter Meredith. You are related?"

"He was an uncle."

"Peter had a son. William."

"You know William?"

"I met him a couple of times. Years ago." Again the blue eyes studied Elizabeth's face. "You're Leon's daughter."

"You knew my father?"

"When I was young." She smiled and for an instant the years vanished and Abigail Porter looked like a girl. "Long ago Leon was my beau. We had hopes but . . . my parents decided against him. Leon was romantic and dashing—"

"And an artist."

"And as such suspect. So I was married to a solid man, a

businessman. I've often wondered . . . I'll never know now. Hector was a good husband and a fine father. But he was nothing like Leon. When I saw you in the hotel I said to myself, she's the picture of Leon Meredith." Bending forward, Abigail examined the baby. "Sickly. Possibly never will be strong." She waved a gloved hand at the water. "Hers?"

"Yes. She's William's wife. Her name is Judith."

The young couple Mrs. Porter's maid had been glaring at dashed past the table. The man was chasing the girl. His striped bathing costume clung wetly to his body, outlining his maleness. Both women quickly lowered their eyes. When Elizabeth glanced up she saw her companion staring at Judith. "Second wife," Mrs. Porter corrected. "Georgia Vandercourt mentioned her."

"You're a friend of Aunt Van's?"

"We belonged to the same bridge club for a number of years. Not now. I'm too crippled with rheumatism to get around much. William's wife is a beautiful woman."

Abigail was correct. No longer was Judith a lovely girl, suddenly she was a beautiful woman. Her dark blue bathing costume was as modest as the other women's but it molded damply to every curve, outlining high swelling breasts, narrow waist, luxuriously plump hips. Her rose tinted flesh seemed to burst from the throat of her tunic, rounding her arms and lower legs with dewy flesh. Under the ruffled cap her face was happy and smiling, her eyes reflecting content. Judith was replete with lovemaking, full to the brim with satisfaction, soaking in the sun and salt air and sending them back in sensual somnolent bursts.

So engrossed was Elizabeth that Mrs. Porter's next question caught her off guard. "That young man I saw you with in the dining room—he's *her* friend?"

"No," Elizabeth said sharply. Too sharply. Stretching out a hand for her glass she took an icy lemon sip. "My father and his were friends. He's only slightly acquainted with Mrs. Meredith."

"Indeed." Mrs. Porter seemed to change the subject. "A husband should accompany his wife on holiday. Hector always stayed close by my side and I wasn't thirty years his junior. That man with red hair—he reminded me of your father. Not in looks but in something reckless about him." She smiled again and turned the pink cheeked face to Elizabeth. "I'm old, my dear, my husband is gone and so are two of my children. I have grand-children and three great-grandchildren but they aren't close to me. I can't move around much and because I'm old and helpless the young feel I'm stupid. But old lonely people see a great deal more than those with full lives. In your face I see Leon. Not your expression. Leon had a quality of . . . innocence."

"I haven't been allowed that, Mrs. Porter. Father had my mother to shelter him. I have no one."

Mrs. Porter made a move to rise and her maid came swiftly to her side, her heavy shoes kicking up small bursts of sand. Elizabeth helped the old woman up and for a moment Mrs. Porter clung to her arm. "Will I see you again?" Elizabeth asked.

"I doubt it. Baker and I leave early tomorrow. Perhaps in New York, some time." The hand dropped away but blue eyes swept once more over the younger woman's face. "Take good care of William's wife and his child. Life can be most unkind to the young and beautiful."

Watching the woman's laborious departure, Elizabeth thought: she knows. Somehow Abigail Porter had looked beyond the charade in the dining room and seen the truth. She knows Lafe and Judith are lovers. After a moment Elizabeth shrugged. Mrs. Porter might suspect but she had no proof. And Elizabeth, with those letters to her cousin and his aunt, had protected herself.

Turning back, Elizabeth saw Judith trotting up from the water. She held the hands of two tiny children. Their plump mother trailed along behind, gathering up pails and shovels. Turning the toddlers over to their mother, Judith dropped breathlessly in the chair recently vacated by Abigail Porter. She poured a glass of lemonade and thirstily gulped it. "Umm, good! Was that the spy you've been so worried about?"

"She's met William and she once played bridge in Aunt Van's club."

Judith stretched like a cat full of cream and yawned, momentarily exposing small perfect teeth and a red tongue. "What does it matter?"

Elizabeth gathered up her parasol, her novel, and the wicker basket. "It doesn't," she said flatly.

Judith yawned again and rubbed at her eyes. "I'm going to

have a bath and then a nap. The sun and water exhaust me."

So do the sleepless nights, Elizabeth told her silently. She followed Judith over the beach to the boardwalk but she was thinking of Abigail Porter and her youthful eyes. She didn't dwell on the covert warning about Lafe and Judith. She thought of Abigail and her father when they were young and innocent and in love. They'd lost each other but in the end both might have gained. Perhaps, Elizabeth mused, the memory of lost love and youth might be more rewarding than reality ever could be.

On the evening of their last day in Atlantic City Elizabeth rebelled against the long lonely hours caring for the baby. She paid a chambermaid to stay with Alicia and made her way out to join the gay throngs of the boardwalk. Pennants and flags whipped in the breeze, wicker chairs trundled through pedestrians, children whooped and crowded around amusement areas. Elizabeth paused beside a theater and found that *Dr. Jekyll and Mr. Hyde* was being shown. The girl in the glass enclosure enticingly held up a loop of tickets but Elizabeth shook her head and wandered on. She stopped at a fortune-telling machine and put in a penny. A brightly painted figure moved jerkily and slid out a card. "You're lucky in love," the printing read. Elizabeth's mouth jerked in a bitter smile and she put a coin into a claw machine. Working the wheel she tried to ensnare a red glass heart but it skidded and released into the chute a tin seahorse. Stopping a boy in a sailor suit, his hands sticky from salt taffy, Elizabeth gravely held it out. He made a disdainful face and raced away. She pinned it on the bodice of her white gown.

She strolled past freak shows, penny arcades, looking incuriously at lurid pictures of a Bearded Lady, Siamese Twins, a man in a lion pelt bending a steel bar over his knee. Barkers shouted hoarsely and ticket sellers mutely implored but she continued on her meandering way.

From a lighted pavilion music beckoned and she crossed a strip of sand to stand and watch and listen. Perspiring Negroes in red and blue uniforms were determinedly working at "Tipperary." Beside Elizabeth was a middle-aged couple. The woman said something and Elizabeth caught a crisp English accent. The man took her arm and led her away. Elizabeth thought the woman was weeping. Somewhere in the crowd a man's voice picked up the refrain. "It's a long way to go," he sang off key. Under military caps dark faces gleamed with sweat and the gleam was picked up in shiny trumpets and cornets, tubas and saxophones. The tempo changed and the band played another tune. After a moment Elizabeth recognized it. "Wall Street Rag." Her heartbeat quickened and for an instant she was walking with Lafe through falling snow, her hand warmly cushioned against his body, happily humming the tune with him.

Then she saw him and thought it was only a memory image. His face, under the stiff brim of the straw hat, wavered over a woman's wide hat. Their eyes locked and Elizabeth thought those eyes were exactly the same shade as the ice green trim on Judith's new gown. Then his hand was cupping her elbow, leading her to a wrought iron table. Dreamlike she sat, saw a hand with crisply curling red hair set down a metal bowl. In a paper cone was a yellow mound of sherbert. Her eyes were fastened on the pavilion but she knew he had seated himself across the table. His voice cut across ragtime. "I was thinking of that night I walked you home from the Vandercourts. You were remembering it too."

"I wish I could forget."

They faced the pavilion, neither of them looking at the other. His voice was part of the music, part of the night, part of the dream. "You don't choose your love. It's forced upon you. As it was with me, Elizabeth. Across a drawing room I saw Judith, I loved her. I love her now. I'll never stop."

"You let her marry another man."

"Again I had no choice." The musicians finished the rag, mopped at wet faces, picked up their instruments, and bleated out a sugary waltz. "Can you picture Judith living in that room of mine? No pretty clothes, no servants, no jewels. Giving up wealth for love."

"I could."

"I know. You'd make one room a home, go out to earn money to keep it going. But a man doesn't choose a woman for worth, Elizabeth. I know exactly what Judith is. She's a younger, smarter, more beautiful Emma Arnold. Capricious and immature and . . . she could be treacherous. But I love her."

Elizabeth's hand brushed the bowl of sherbet, the metal cold and sweating against her skin. She was chilled but she didn't move. She waited and finally he said, "I know women but I don't know you. I've met only one other woman who's an enigma. Nina Flanders. I even found a clue to her. In her older daughter. When I was still accepted in the Merediths' circle Susan confided that she wants to be a lawyer. Albert Flanders won't hear of it but Nina is encouraging her."

"Do you think Susan will win?"

"With her mother's help she will. If Nina had been born later she would never have been satisfied to be merely a wife and mother. Her daughter will have what she couldn't. Maybe the time is coming when women will be able to choose. When they will have careers like men."

"And because they're unmarried, won't be set aside as I've been to look after other women's children?"

"That too."

The crowd around the pavilion was dispersing. It was full dark. Family groups trailed away to lighted hotels, fathers carried toddlers, mothers hauled along whimpering children. A sickle moon was rising, tracing a silver path across dark water. The band members put instruments in cases, opened the top buttons on tunics. Red and blue, Elizabeth thought, the red of blood, the blue of death, the shining brass a mockery of what happiness might have been.

"I'm going to write a book," Lafe told her. "A good book. You'll be in it."

"How will you portray me?"

"I've no idea. But in time I'll know." He rose abruptly. "Judith will be waiting. Our last night. Elizabeth, be kind to her."

She made no promise. Side by side they wandered down the boardwalk. The stalls were closing, porters with push brooms were sweeping up debris—waxed paper, wrappers from salt taffy, cones from ice cream.

They spoke only once. Lafe said, "From here it's hard to picture war."

In front of her hotel Elizabeth paused long enough to unpin the seahorse from her bodice. She gave it to him. "A souvenir of Atlantic City. Put it in your book."

As she mounted the steps to the veranda he was already eagerly rounding the corner of the hotel. Somehow, Elizabeth knew with certainty that she would never see Atlantic City again, never see Lafe Norton again. But she would remember. The memory of lost love.

The next morning as Judith, Elizabeth, and the baby boarded the early train the fine weather broke. Low clouds blew in over the Atlantic, releasing a fine rain. Elizabeth fully expected Judith to look as sad and dismal as the morning but the girl seemed sleepy, satiated, relaxed. For a time Judith dozed against a mass of pillows and Elizabeth sat in a corner of the opposite seat, the baby's wicker case at her side, her head resting against the plush back. Telephone poles and frame houses fled by, rain oozed down the window pane. After a time Elizabeth slept.

She woke to find Judith watching her, violet eyes wide and alert. Now, Elizabeth thought drearily, I'll be forced to listen to a tale of grief and loss.

"He may not come back," Judith began and Elizabeth thought, here we go.

"He's only going to England."

"Lafe says he's not going to sit in London on his hands. He intends to go to France, perhaps right into the front lines. Do some firsthand reporting. He's so daring, so adventurous."

Silently Elizabeth agreed. Lafe wasn't the type to sit and wait. Judith fiddled with the saucy sailor hat, pulling out the hatpin and then driving it back in. "Bullets," the girl said, "don't know the difference between a soldier and a war correspondent."

Again Elizabeth silently agreed but Judith was really being philosophical. "Did you make any plans for the future?" Elizabeth asked.

"When Lafe comes back? Yes, we had long talks. We agreed we'd have to be together. Lafe said he'll take me away, maybe out west, where we won't be known. We'll make a new life."

"And Alicia?"

"William can keep her."

"William will never agree to a divorce."

"We know that. He's so *stuffy*. He'd be afraid to soil the sacred name of Meredith. But we'll go anyway."

"What will you live on?"

"Lafe says love will find a way." Leaning over, Judith touched the baby's head. "I do believe she's finally getting some hair. Blond, like mine."

Elizabeth looked down at the few colorless hairs on the blue veined skull. "Lighter I should think."

"'Her color's much better. William will be pleased."

Warily, Elizabeth regarded her. Lafe had said his love could be treacherous and Elizabeth had a hunch fresh treachery was on the way. Reaching into the hamper the hotel had packed, she offered the girl tea from a thermos, sandwiches wrapped in waxed paper. Judith accepted tea but waved the food away. "I'm tired of hotel food. I can hardly wait to sit down to one of Cookie's meals. She cooks divinely." Casually she added, "I must be nicer to William. He's been such a pet and I have treated him badly."

Elizabeth spilt tea in her lap and mopped it up with her handkerchief. She clenched the sodden linen into a ball. "What do you mean?"

"He does have a right to husbandly privileges."

"But you said . . . Judith, you promised Lafe you'd never allow William to return to your bed!"

"That was before I knew Lafe intends to be a hero. If anything happens to him . . . Oh, I love Lafe and it will be an ordeal but . . . If Lafe is killed and I lose William I'll have nobody."

Elizabeth carefully spread the handkerchief on the seat to dry. It gave her the excuse to lower her eyes to hide the rage in them. Judith was going to spoil everything again. "I'm sorry," she said aloud. "What did you say?"

"I asked if you don't agree I'm doing the right thing?"

With an effort, Elizabeth smiled at the girl. "You must make your own decision, my dear."

Judith didn't require Elizabeth's agreement. Her mind was made up. When the train pulled into Grand Central, William, with Briggs hovering behind him, was eagerly waiting. He took them home, the child in his arms, Judith clinging to his arm laughing deliciously up at him. That night when he tried her door it was unlocked. Ecstatically he slid into her bed and gathered to his stringy body the bountiful crop nourished in golden light, blue sea, and the warmth of a younger man's love.

Elizabeth tiptoed down the stairs and applied her ear to the door of Judith's room. The springs on the huge bed were lustily squeaking. Swearing under her breath, she returned to her tiny room.

— 14 —

It wasn't until the middle of October that Elizabeth found her plans were bearing fruit, but a strange type of fruit. One cold stormy morning she carried a breakfast tray up to Judith's room and found the girl wide awake and pink cheeked against a pile of pillows. Elizabeth unfolded the short legs, set the tray over Judith's lap, and pulled back the silk drapes.

Touching the single rose in a bud vase, Judith beamed up at her. "Dear Elizabeth, you never forget. How thoughtful you are."

"You're in high spirits this morning."

"The best." Judith cut a slice of ham into bite-sized pieces. "A letter from Lafe again yesterday. How clever you are! Waiting for the mail every afternoon. William will never suspect, will he?"

"Not if I can help it. How was Lafe?"

"Fine. He asked to be remembered to you. He sounds so gay, so happy. Sometimes I think men *like* war."

"Lafe is furthering his career. Those articles of his are outstanding."

"I never read them but William mentioned last night how exciting they are. He said Lafe is becoming well known in New York." Breaking off a piece of toast, she heaped it with cherry jam. "I'm eating for two," the girl said casually.

Elizabeth's suddenly weak legs took her to the chair beside the bed. She sank into it, her elbow rocking the pink shaded lamp. "You're pregnant?"

"Watch out! You'll break the lamp. Yes, over two months. I told William last night. He's delighted."

Elizabeth didn't have to count. "Lafe's child."

"My darling's." A small hand inched under the tray and tenderly patted the blanket over her stomach. For an instant Elizabeth saw that same hand, balled into a fist, beating the bulge that had marked Alicia. "I hope it will be a boy. Lafe's son."

"How can you be so calm?"

"Why ever shouldn't I be?"

At a loss for words, Elizabeth stared at the younger woman. "It will be born too soon."

Pouring coffee, Judith added cream and two heaping spoonsful of sugar. "Alicia was born ten days too soon."

"You had a fall."

"A fall can be arranged. Perhaps I'll trip over a chair." Judith giggled. "Don't look as though the end of the world is here."

"This baby may look like Lafe," Elizabeth told her grimly. "There has never been red hair in the Meredith family."

"Maybe there is in my family."

"Is there?"

"No." Giggling again, Judith reached for a slice of toast. "I'll tell William my grandmother or aunt or someone had reddish hair. Mama will back me up."

Elizabeth's eyes narrowed. "How will you explain the Allenby finger?"

"Who's going to notice a child's finger? Only you and me. Don't scowl like that, you'll get wrinkles." Judith chewed reflectively. "I feel so well. No morning sickness. Just wonderful! This pregnancy," she said prophetically, "is going to be different from the first."

And it was. Judith fairly bloomed. In cunningly cut maternity gowns and concealing jackets she entertained and sallied forth on her proud husband's arm to be entertained. She attended the theater, the opera, dinners and dances, and a gala evening in Chinatown. She teased William and showered him with attention and caresses. Locked into her room she read and reread and fondled Lafe's letters, hiding them with the locket in her secret drawer.

Elizabeth marveled at the girl's duplicity. She also marveled at her cousin. William was shedding his worries and his age like a snake curling away from the discarded husk of its skin. He bought youthful clothes, grew a dashing mustache, wore as his boutonniere a tiny yellow rose.

Then a wire about George arrived and briefly William again was an aging, haggard man. "He's been wounded," he told Elizabeth heavily. "In a British assault on a town called Vimy Ridge. He's been invalided to England. But in this"—he held up the letter that had followed the wire—"he's determined to go back to the trenches as soon as he can." He buried his face in his hands. "It's a terrible thing to say but I wish his wound had been more serious. They'd have to send him home as they did young Arnold Standford."

"You wouldn't want that," Elizabeth protested.

"I spoke hastily. Of course I wouldn't. That poor tragic boy. Only twenty-five, blinded, with half his lungs destroyed. John Stokes says there's no possibility Arnold will ever come out of that nursing home. At least there is some good news."

"Lavinia, you mean."

"John says since he brought her home she seems to be getting a grasp on reality. Now she admits that Cynthia and the child are gone. John's trying to get her involved with charity work or a hobby. Thinks it might hasten her recovery."

"Nina Stokes told me that Lavinia is thinking of starting a home for"—Elizabeth lowered her eyes modestly—"unfortunate women."

He stroked his chin with tapered fingers. "I suppose Lavinia may make some mental connection between unwed mothers and Cynthia and her unborn child. Hard to say. Lavinia and Albert's mother was dreadfully unstable and Lavinia is much like her. It could be beneficial. And Lavinia has her own money, you know. Both Albert and she are very well off. Seems a silly waste of money but that's John's business, not mine." Under his new mustache William's thin lips curved in a smile. "It might be worse. For us, I mean. Alan's doing well in his school and seems to be really applying himself. And Judith! What a comfort she is! Tosh seems to feel little Alicia is gaining ground too."

"She's still frail."

"Soon she'll have a little sister or brother to grow up with. That may make a difference. Judith has her heart set on a boy."

"I know."

"Now I must go up to Judith." His newfound youth seemed to have suddenly returned. Springing up, he pointed at his grandfather's austere portrait. "If we have a son we'll name him Oliver Pendrell. Judith suggested it. Yes, life could be worse."

Not much, Elizabeth thought dolefully as she followed him from the study to continue her work.

For the remainder of 1915 the time flew. The only highlights came in the festive season. On Christmas Day the usual group gathered for the same festivities at the Meredith house. Judith, charming in flowing chiffon with a matching cape, was a cheerful, competent hostess. She helped her husband light the tree, presided over the festive board, later played the piano and led the singers in a high sweet soprano. When the groups of urchins arrived to sing carols, Judith graciously distributed bags of candy and nuts and mince tarts and pressed coins into small chapped hands. But in the middle of the day Elizabeth heard a snatch of conversation that sent her bolting from the drawing room.

She was seated between William and Doctor John with the men chatting across her as though she were an end table. John was eyeing Judith, who was leaning against the mantel. In spite of her full figure she was elegant and graceful. Her hair was smoothly dressed and a corsage of her favorite roses was pinned to the cape. "What did I tell you?" the doctor gleefully asked William. "Your wife came back from Atlantic City a new woman."

William nodded fervently. "You have a habit of being right. I'm so happy I listened to you. I owe everything to you and that holiday." Lowering his voice, he whispered, "I would even swear I owe this baby to that wonderful month." Suddenly remembering Elizabeth, he turned to her. "Wouldn't you say this child is the direct result of your little holiday?"

Elizabeth had a sudden vision of her hands holding Lafe's sheaths, delicately pricking each in turn. She opened her mouth to answer but to her consternation all that came out was a wild howl of glee. Quickly she turned bubbling mirth into a choking spasm and clapping a hand over that traitor mouth she fled from the room. In the kitchen she clung to the drainboard, her face scarlet, her eyes streaming tears.

Dropping a wooden spoon, Cookie bustled over. She pounded Elizabeth's back and offered a glass of water. "You are in a state, miss. Are you laughing or choking?"

"A little of both, Cookie."

"Did someone make a joke then?"

"Yes indeed, someone made a joke."

A second and unkind joke was played on Elizabeth by fate. The Standfords had invited her to their soiree on the final evening of the year but she declined. She'd had all she could stomach of Judith, of William watching his wife with adoration, of Doctor John watching her approvingly, of Sophie Vandercourt gazing at her friend with damp worshiping eyes. Elizabeth was sick to death of hearing Judith called beautiful, gracious, kind, wonderful. So Elizabeth told Estelle Standford she wasn't feeling well and this was the truth. For several days she'd suffered from a throbbing pain in her side. She shrugged it off, thinking it was the amount of work she'd been doing.

New Year's Eve found Elizabeth alone in the huge house without even a servant for company. She went to her room early, taking with her a bottle of chilled champagne. On the stroke of twelve she uncorked the bottle and proposed a silent toast. As soon as the glass was empty she went to bed but managed to empty the bottle before she drifted off to sleep. At five in the morning she woke with her head throbbing and a furnace in her stomach. At first she blamed it on too much champagne but an hour passed and the pain got steadily worse. I'm in trouble, she told herself as she stumbled out of bed to the bathroom. She vomited until she was dry-retching. She called for help but the household was sleeping soundly. She tried to drag herself to the nursery and Tosh but collapsed in the hall.

At seven when Cookie came yawning down to start breakfast she found Elizabeth unconscious on the cold floor. Doctor John was yanked from bed and arrived with a gigantic hangover he'd truly earned. He wasted no time summoning an ambulance but rushed Elizabeth to the hospital in his own car. Her appendix was on the point of rupturing. Fortunately a competent surgeon was on duty and he operated as soon as she was wheeled into the operating room. For a time Elizabeth's life hung by a thread. Finally her strong body and stronger will turned the tide. Until she was out of danger both Judith and William stayed in the hospital.

Elizabeth was in the hospital for over a month. She had visitors. All the ladies came bearing gifts of flowers, magazines, novels with bright covers. Aunt Van brought a basket of fruit and as she methodically devoured the gift herself she filled Elizabeth in on the latest gossip.

"Marilou Flanders," she said thickly around a mouthful of dates. "Told you she was going to be a trial, didn't I? Now don't breathe a word of this but I hear one of Nina's maids found the little minx and the boy next door down in the coal cellar. And they weren't counting coal! Caught right in the act and Marilou not twelve yet. Boy's older, a big lout, and Albert was all for using a horsewhip on him. Took Nina and the cook and the chauffeur to pull Albert off the lad." Aunt Van began to peel a banana. "Mark my words, that minx has just started! Before she's much older she'll turn her parents' hair snow white. Poor Albert." Unaware of the irony, she added, "Marilou's just like him."

Elizabeth wished the older woman would finish the fruit and leave but Aunt Van was still going strong. She was working on a bunch of grapes and the next tidbit. "Hear about Arnold Standford? No? Suppose William thought you being so weak and nearly dying it might upset you. Maybe I shouldn't tell you but you're sensible and you don't even know the boy all that well." Lowering her voice, she said dramatically, "Tried to do away with himself. Put a belt around his neck and jumped off a chair. If the hook he'd fastened it to hadn't worked loose Arnold would be dead. Mercy of the dear Lord he isn't. Estelle and Horace are taking it hard. Both of them look older than I do. What is this world coming to?"

Even Aunt Van had no answer for that. Having run out of bad news and fruit she took her majestic departure. Elizabeth was thankfully settling down for a nap when the door inched open. She sighed but it was Judith. "Are you too tired?" the girl asked.

"Not to see you."

Closing the door, Judith smiled sympathetically. "I met Aunt Van on the way in." She darted a look at the pretty fruit basket. It contained a few grapes, a banana peel and two apple cores. "That awful woman! The nurses should have sense enough to keep her away from you. Here, a little gift from William and me."

"You shouldn't have! You're spoiling me. All those flowers and those books."

"Open it, dear."

From a nest of tissue paper Elizabeth lifted a fluffy bed-jacket. "How lovely."

"There's something else. Under the tissue. So you'll remember me."

Elizabeth snapped up the lid of a tiny plush box and gasped. "A watch! I've never had a watch. I've never seen such a beautiful thing!"

Judith pointed at the circle of enamel flowers ringing the face of the lapel watch. "See. Forget-me-nots." Elizabeth's dark eyes were brimming with tears of surprise and weakness. Judith thought they came from gratitude. "Don't cry. Here, let me pin it on your nightie."

Holding out the gown until she could look down at the pretty trinket, Elizabeth said slowly, "I'll wear it all my life, Judith. And I'll never forget you."

Both promises were kept.

When Elizabeth was sent home she was told sternly she was to lift nothing heavier than needlework. She obeyed and managed to run the house efficiently from a comfortable chair, going back and forth to her room on the tiny lift. Her strength returned so slowly that when Judith went into labor on the seventh day of May Elizabeth was content to sit as a spectator in a corner of the girl's room. This time there was no lack of helpers. Doctor John was assisted not only by Tosh but by his own nurse, Gerda and Sally ran up and down the stairs, and in the hall William paced.

Judith's labor lasted over six hours and Elizabeth didn't once leave her chair. Stolidly she worked on a pram cover, covering the linen with a shower of forget-me-nots copied from her new watch. The girl's contractions became closer together and as dusk settled over the city Lafe's child arrived, screaming and fighting its way into the world. Putting her needlework aside, Elizabeth went to peer over the doctor's beefy shoulder.

"What a size," the doctor grunted. "Look at these shoulders. Must be a boy."

Elizabeth didn't look at the shoulders. She was staring at a cockscomb of flaming red hair. Returning to her corner, she contentedly picked up the pram cover and took a delicate stitch.

Beaming, the doctor turned with the baby in his hands. No need to spank this bottom. The child was bellowing. "Elizabeth, better tell William he's got one of the biggest girls I've ever delivered. Weighs ten pounds if she weighs an ounce."

Elizabeth found her cousin leaning against the bannister at the top of the stairs, a frond of Boston fern sketching a pattern against his back. He jumped and turned a haggard face to her. "Judith's fine, William. You have another daughter."

They waited until the door opened and Doctor John waved them in. The room had been neatened and aired, the bed freshly made up, a nurse stood like a sentinel on either siof the bed. The bed where Uncle Peter and William had been born. The bed where Elizabeth's father had been born. The bed where Lafe Norton's bastard had just been born. A wanly lovely Judith was propped up against silken pillows, smiling at the child in Tosh's arms and then at her husband. "Our daughter, darling," she whispered. "Do you like her?"

Gently one of William's tapered fingers touched the thatch of hair. "Red. Your mother will be pleased. In her last letter Emma mentioned her Aunt Lucy had auburn hair and she was hoping our child would have red hair too." Elizabeth caught sight of the little finger on a starfish hand. It was almost the length of the next finger. She turned to look at her cousin but William's expression was bemused as he watched the charming tableau of mother and child. "My cup runneth over," he quoted solemnly.

"You're a lucky man." Doctor John clapped a hand on his friend's shoulder. "Two fine sons and two little daughters. What about this latest drop in your cup? Did you pick a girl's name?"

Judith lifted her head. "She's to be named for her great-grandmothers. Mariette Annabel."

"Good family names," the doctor told her.

William bent closer. "Darling, I believe she has your eyes."

"That's a shame." Judith gazed directly at Elizabeth and one eyelid flickered in a barely perceptible wink. "I was hoping she'd have her father's."

Elizabeth pushed the pram cover into her workbasket and left the room. Judith had successfully hoodwinked both her husband and Doctor John, but they were men and not difficult for a pretty woman to deceive. Wait until she hit the real test. The women! Aunt Van and Nina, Lavinia Stokes and Estelle Standford, and Grace Grant. One of them would surely notice the finger and put it and the flaming hair together and come up with Lafcadio Norton. They would know the girl baby in the Meredith cradle was illegitimate.

Eagerly Elizabeth waited for the day of the reception and the denunciation. She watched as Judith carried the child around the drawing room, pausing to display her new daughter proudly to each woman. Estelle was engrossed in her own worries and merely admired the baby's size and health. Lavinia pointed her nose at Mariette but her lushly lashed eyes were vague and indifferent. Nina merely looked, smiled, and nodded. When Aunt Van's turn came Elizabeth was close to praying.

Taking the child on her lap, Aunt Van stared down at her. "Did better this time, Judith. Big baby. Red hair, eh? William tells me Emma is real set up because the baby has her Aunt Lucy's coloring. Never cared for this color hair myself but there's some who like it." Bouncing the baby, she said eagerly, "Have to tell you what the Greggs' cook told my Aggie, ladies. Don't breathe a word of this but—"

Elizabeth didn't wait to hear what the Greggs' cook had told Aunt Van's. She stalked from the room and stopped by the marble-topped table in the hall, fighting down a desire to batter her head against the wall. No longer did she feel angry, just old and tired and defeated. Judith had won and Lafe's bastard was going to pass as William's legitimate daughter.

That year autumn came early to the city. In early September the leaves in Central Park were turning bright russet and yellow. By October those leaves were sodden piles stirred by gales pounding in from the Atlantic and bringing with them icy rain and sleet.

One morning as Elizabeth sat at her desk, the butler's pantry was so damp and chill she was glad of the clanking radiator behind her. She bent over the desk, her account books pushed to one side, pasting items into a new album. It was devoted to Judith and there was a pile of trophies to prove the girl's social prowess. In the months that followed Mariette's birth Judith had taken her place in the social scene with a vengeance.

Picking up a clipping, she smiled sourly. Judith at a garden fete in July, smiling into the camera from under the droopy brim of a picture hat. Scattering the pile, Elizabeth chose one at random. This time Judith wore a trim suit and a tricorn hat. In a gloved hand she held a beribboned bottle and behind her loomed the prow of William's newest freighter. Elizabeth read aloud the caption under it. "The lovely Mrs. William Meredith graciously christens the latest addition to the Meredith Lafroux Shipping Line. This ship bears her name and is called the *Judith Two*." Blah, blah, blah!

The next clipping brought a wider smile to Elizabeth's lips. Although Judith was in the picture, this time she wasn't the main target of the camera. It was a wide-angled shot of an old brownstone in the Village. Across the dooor stretched a broad ribbon and Lavinia Stokes, shears in one hand, stood in profile, her scimitar nose proudly etched against the massive door. A discreet bronze plaque informed viewers that this was the "Cynthia Stokes Home for Unfortunate Women." Ranged on the steps was a group of society matrons, beautifully dressed and smiling. Judith was between Aunt Van and Nina Flanders. On the walk below them, ragged shawls pushed up and skirts hiked over swollen bellies, a knot of the unfortunate women huddled. Most of them could not, in truth, be so described, they were merely adolescent girls bearing the results of quick scuffles under tenement stairs, of tumbles in the underbrush of parks. They stood meekly, like a herd of cows, waiting for the ribbon to be snipped and the haven's magical door to open.

Elizabeth had had the details of the haven from Aunt Van. What waited for the unfortunate women within that door was more misfortune. The matron had a high bridged nose and a mouth like a steel trap. She'd been lured from her job as a guard in a woman's prison. The house had been renovated and was clean and warm, the bedrooms made into dormitories, the kitchen full of modern appliances. As each girl entered she would be led to the bathroom, deloused, issued a shapeless sack made of long-wearing cotton, and assigned her duties. The expectant mothers weren't going to be coddled. They would work hard— scrubbing, washing, cooking. For entertainment they would receive religious instruction each Sabbath from a minister who would rant about scarlet women and bring the threat of fire and brimstone and damnation down on their bowed heads.

Before each girl was accepted she had to sign a form relinquishing all rights to her child. When a baby was delivered, the mother wouldn't be allowed to see the face of her child. The babies would be whisked away to an orphanage in Queens.

Life is unfair, Elizabeth mused as she pasted the clipping in the album. Here is Nina Flanders whose husband might well have got one of these girls pregnant, whose twelve-year-old daughter was busily sinning as they had. Here is sly Judith Meredith whose second daughter is a bastard. All these women smugly sitting in judgment on the frailties of poor immigrant girls.

She was reaching for another clipping when Gerda called from the doorway, "Just took breakfast up to the missus, Miss Elizabeth. She wants you up there right now."

In Judith's room sleet was scratching on the panes and a cold breeze whistled through an open window. Elizabeth hurried over to close the window. "Brr," she told the girl cosily snuggled in the huge bed.

Judith was feeding her dog tidbits from the tray. "It is cold but I don't mind. It will give me a chance to wear my new coat."

The coat she mentioned was William's latest gift. Gifts from her husband fairly rained on Judith. He'd bought her not only the luxurious sable but a Japanese kimono lavishly embroidered with silk, a wide bracelet ringed with diamonds, the tiny dog curled against her knees. Elizabeth admired the other gifts but the Pekinese she detested. Winky Pooh had long silky hair, the bulging eyes of a rock cod, a lineage as blue-blooded as the color of the satin ribbon above his ears, and a treacherous nature. Elizabeth and the servants loathed the animal. He invited caresses and then nipped savagely at the stroking hand. He broke wind constantly, overate, made messes on priceless old rugs.

Keeping a wary eye on Winky Pooh, Elizabeth gathered up a dinner dress carelessly tossed over a chair. Pulling back his lips, the dog snarled at her. Judith patted the brute and crooned, "Don't be a naughty baby." She extended a bit of bacon and it

was snapped out of her hand. "And don't glare at him like that,
Elizabeth. You make him nervous."

I'd like to do worse than that to him, Elizabeth thought as
she bent and scooped up filmy underclothes. At one time she'd
have spoken the words aloud but now she was careful what she
said to Judith. As the girl had moved into her rightful place in
society her attitude had changed. No longer was Judith willing to
confide in Cousin Elizabeth, no longer did she talk about Lafe
for hours. Judith was now cool and detached and measuring.

Giving the dog the last morsel from her plate, the girl
glanced at the wet window pane. "I like this weather better than
summer. In August I thought I'd die from the heat. It was much
hotter this year than last."

"In August of last year we were in Atlantic City."

"I keep forgetting that. What are you fussing around for?"

"The laundress will soon be here and I haven't sorted the
linens yet. I'll take this up and do it now."

"Leave it. I want to talk to you."

Elizabeth obeyed and moved closer to the bed. The dog
lifted his silky head and growled at her. "That letter from Lafe
yesterday. Was there bad news in it?"

"I don't know. I haven't opened it yet." Judith fondled the
dog's ears. "Funny, sometimes I have to open my locket before I
can remember Lafe properly. He keeps getting dimmer and dimmer, like those old pictures. Fading away until you can only see
outlines of faces. I still adore him . . . but. . . . Speaking of heat,
do you know what William has promised? A summer home next
year. There's one near Aunt Van's that's perfect. A sun room
looking right over the water. How wonderful it will be to get
away from the city, and it will be so good for Alicia and Mariette. And I'll be able to entertain. Picnics on the beach and we'll
have a boat. I should love a boat."

"That sounds nice," Elizabeth murmured. Although Judith
might hate William's lovemaking she most certainly was enjoying
being Mrs. William Meredith.

"William's such an old sweetie. Mama warned me he might
be stingy but he *isn't*. Anything I want he's happy to give me."

You should see the old sweetie going over the household
accounts, Elizabeth thought wryly. He complains constantly
about the amount of food consumed, the bills, the servants'

wages. But Judith never saw that side of her doting husband. William saved it for Cousin Elizabeth. "Anything else?"

"Why are you so short this morning?" Pouting, Judith stroked Winky Pooh, who promptly broke wind. "Come over here and sit down. Winky Pooh won't hurt you."

Edging over to a chair, Elizabeth perched on the edge of it. "Yesterday Winky Pooh bit Briggs's thumb to the bone. William had to take a taxi to work this morning."

"Briggs frightened my little darling. He's so sensitive." She directed violet eyes at Elizabeth. No longer were they dreamy, just clear and calculating. "Dear Cousin Elizabeth. Don't you ever get tired of looking after someone else's house?"

This question sounded a warning bell. "In a way this is my home," Elizabeth said carefully. "My grandfather built it and my father was born in that bed."

"I know that, dear, but it's not really, you know. It's William's and mine and our children's. I was telling the old sweetie yesterday that we'd been thoughtless and cruel allowing you to waste your life taking care of us. I said to him, William, we must make it up to Cousin Elizabeth. William agreed."

Yes, William most certainly would agree. Elizabeth picked her words with care. "You're busy with your social life, Judith. How could you do my work? See the house is running smoothly, look after the children?"

Shoving the dog away, Judith sat up against her pillows. "I've thought it all out. Nina and Aunt Van and Lavinia manage and they're as rushed as I am. With that new home she opened Lavinia is even busier. My babies are no problem. Tosh does a splendid job and she's devoted to Alicia and little Mariette. If we find she can't cope we'll hire a nursemaid to help her. And William promised a housekeeper, an older woman with some education so she can look after the household accounts." Judith reached a pink hand out. "Don't look so downcast, dear Elizabeth. William and I are trying to do something nice for you, not trying to hurt you. And just listen. William has agreed to set you up in business."

"What kind of business?"

"Dressmaking, of course. You're so clever in no time you'll be hiring help. Maybe have a little house all your own. Don't try to thank me. I can see you're overcome."

Elizabeth had bent her head to hide her outrage. Employees
in her dress shop. A house of her own. All she'd have would be
unrelenting toil for small wages, a single room with a hotplate
and a dirty bathroom shared with other lodgers. In a muffled
voice she asked, "When do you want me to leave?"

"You *are* hurt. We—William and I—are *not* trying to shove
you out. This has to be your own decision. Take your time and
think about it." She added, her words suddenly chill, dropping
with tinkling sounds like icicles being broken from eaves, "Take
at least a month. I'm sure you'll agree with us, Cousin Elizabeth."

Elizabeth played her last card. "Lafe's letters?"

"I'll write and tell Lafe not to send any more letters here. In
the meantime I'll watch the mail and catch them. Don't worry
about it." Turning her head, Judith started to play with the dog.

She's dismissed me, Elizabeth thought, dismissed me as she
would a servant. Stunned with shock she stared down at Judith's
bright head. Judith had shown her kindness when she'd been so
ill in the hospital. Surely that kindness hadn't been mere calculation? She found herself appealing to the girl. "You have so
much," Elizabeth said brokenly. "You're young and beautiful
and have a devoted husband and two children. All I've ever had
were work and loneliness. Judith, life isn't just enough money to
get by on. My life is centered around this house. My grandfather
built it, my father was born here, and . . . I love this place. Don't
take that away from me. Please, I'll do anything but don't send
me away—"

"*Really.*" The girl turned to face her but it wasn't the Judith
Elizabeth had known. This was Emma Arnold—cold and
haughty and cruel. "You're embarrassing me by begging. Mama
was right and I should have gotten rid of you when I married
William. I needed you then but now you're of no further use.
You've one month to accept William's offer or I'll see you leave
here without a cent. Do you understand?"

Elizabeth understood. Lafe had been correct about his beloved. Judith was a more beautiful Emma with her mother's capricious, treacherous nature. Judith no longer wanted Elizabeth
perched on her shoulder like a conscience, no longer wanted a
witness to adultery in Atlantic City.

Methodically, Elizabeth sorted the laundry. Just as methodically her mind worked. She had one factor in her favor. Judith, no more than Lafe, fully realized what kind of woman Cousin Elizabeth was.

The time had come to fight the war. Elizabeth carefully considered the secret drawer full of Lafe's letters and containing the damning gold locket. She could lead William to this but her cousin would not only find evidence exposing his wife but also evidence of his cousin's perfidy. William would throw her out without a qualm.

Setting aside a pile of sheets, she started to count pillow slips. She must not use the contents of the secret drawer. She gnawed her lower lip. There had to be a way by which only Judith would suffer. Suddenly she had it. There was an element of risk to herself but she had to gamble. She paused, a pillow slip in each hand. It needed precise timing, the right set of circumstances, and time was short.

Cousin Elizabeth began to count towels. She was not religious and tended to scoff at a merciful God, but as added insurance she directed a prayer to an unknown deity who might feel compassion for old maids and poor relations.

Cold air moved in from the Atlantic, seeping through the narrow caverns and turning the sleet to snow. Toward the end of October Judith attended a charity fete and had to stand for nearly an hour on a platform exposed to the wind and snow. She came home sick and chilled. Doctor John, summoned by an anxious William, pronounced the onset of grippe and advised bed rest. For two days she suffered from fever and muscle aches. On the third she was improved but at Elizabeth's urging remained in bed.

Elizabeth did some mental arithmetic and decided the unknown deity might be answering her prayer. Accordingly she set her plan into motion. On her way up to the sewing room at twenty minutes after two she stopped in Judith's room. The girl was snuggled in bed, Winky Pooh at her side, drowsily leafing through a magazine.

"How are you feeling?" Elizabeth asked.

"Some better but my throat's still raspy."

"I'll fix some hot water and honey."

"Sally already did but it doesn't help."

"Try and rest. I'll look in later."

"Elizabeth, wait. Don't forget to check the mail. It's about time for a letter from Lafe."

"Do I ever forget? I've some sewing to do but I'll be down in time to check it."

She climbed the stairs to the fifth floor, her heart thudding. In the sewing room she glanced at snow-shrouded windows and turned the radiator up full. Then she settled at the work table, unpinned her lapel watch, and put it in front of her. She picked up a dress she was making for Alicia for the Christmas season and looked it over. It was nearly finished, every frill and ruffle carefully stitched, and all that had to be done was some embroidery at the throat. She held it up, thinking the pale blue should be flattering to the child's flaxen hair and china blue eyes. Alicia was still a listless child and at seventeen months showed no desire even to crawl. Mariette was the direct opposite. She was a vividly pretty baby with her mother's huge violet eyes and a mop of red gold ringlets. She was Tosh's pride and joy and the nurse delighted in showing everyone how strong her darling was. She'd hold the baby in her lap and beam when Mariette planted her feet firmly and pushed herself erect.

Selecting a strand of deep pink silk, Elizabeth began to embroider a rosebud. She found her hands were shaking. Searching through the drawer she found her pack of cigarettes and smoked one. Then she opened the window to air the room and wind came whistling in, bringing snowflakes that briefly shone like stars in her dark hair. She settled back in the chair, her eyes closed, waiting for time to crawl by.

When the hands of her watch stood at fifteen after three she took off her shoes and stealthily crept down the stairs. She was in luck. There was no sign of Sally. She slid past Judith's door and made her way until she stood at the turn of the stairs and could see the marble-topped table in the lower hall. The unknown deity was still on her side. The top envelope on the silver salver bore a large bold handwriting she knew as well as she did her own. Quietly she retraced her steps, pausing to press an ear against Judith's door. She could hear deep slow breathing. Judith was sleeping away the afternoon.

Back in the sewing room she sank as breathlessly in her chair as though she'd been running. William was always home at four sharp. He'd go directly to his study where Gerda, always faithful to the minute, would deliver the paper and mail. The danger point could come within the next hour. If Judith should rouse, notice the time, send Sally up the sewing room . . . sleep, Judith, she urged, sleep soundly.

Judith slept and Elizabeth waited. At fifteen minutes after five she rose, stretched her stiff back, and put her shoes on. Then she picked up the forget-me-not watch, set the hands back, and stopped them. This time there was no need for stealth. On the third floor she found Sally working in the linen room. "Everything in order?" Elizabeth asked.

"Two buttons torn off one of Mr. Meredith's best shirts, miss."

Elizabeth examined the garment. "That laundry is getting careless. I think we'll change to another. Put this shirt in the sewing room and I'll fix it." She asked casually, "Has Mrs. Meredith needed anything?"

Ribbons on the maid's cap bobbed as she shook her pretty head. "Been quiet all afternoon. I looked in on her a while ago and she's sleeping like a baby."

Elizabeth went directly to Judith's room. The girl was still asleep but Winky Pooh had deserted her and was curled up in his cushioned basket. Elizabeth put a hand on the girl's smooth brow and long lashes quivered and lifted. "I didn't mean to wake you. Your skin feels nice and cool now. No fever. How do you feel?"

"My throat's not as sore." Judith stretched luxuriously. "I think I'll get up for dinner."

"That's not wise and you'll worry William. Best to wait until morning."

"I suppose so. Oh, was there mail from Lafe?"

"I've no idea. I'm going down to look now."

Sitting up abruptly, Judith pointed at the French clock on the mantel. "Oh my God! Elizabeth, it's after five!"

"That clock's wrong. See my lapel watch. You know how accurate it is. Twenty-two after three."

Shoving back the comforter, Judith ran across and snatched her watch off the dressing table. "It isn't wrong. Let's see your watch. Elizabeth, it's stopped. Oh God, William has the mail!"

"Get back in bed this minute. You'll catch your death. Calm down, dear."

"Calm down!" She glared up at Elizabeth. "What if William is reading Lafe's letter?"

"Think. Gerda takes him the mail shortly after four. If he had a letter from Lafe do you think he'd still be downstairs?"

With a sigh of relief Judith slipped back in bed and allowed Elizabeth to plump up her pillows. "No, there wasn't a letter today. If there had been William would be up here ranting and pawing the ground. But such a scare. You mustn't miss the mail again."

"I'll only be here a little while longer, dear. I've decided to accept your offer and start my own dressmaking business. But until I do leave I'll be very careful. From now on I'll take my alarm clock with me. I should have realized how long I was working but I was trying to finish that blue dress for Alicia and—"

"Do be quiet," the girl snapped. "You have been careless but no harm's been done." Judith yawned widely and snuggled down. "Tell Cookie all I want for dinner is some of that chicken broth. Perhaps some fruit. After William has dined ask him to bring up that new novel. I left it in the drawing room."

Elizabeth delivered the order to the kitchen and as she returned to the hall she gazed at the closed door of the study. At that moment it opened and William poked his head out. "Elizabeth. I thought I heard you. Come in and do shut the door."

On the desk a glass of whiskey and soda sat untouched, a cigar smoldered in an ashtray. The pile of mail sat on the unopened paper. On the blotter was a letter opener, an envelope addressed in a bold hand, and several sheets of notepaper. William's appearance of second youth had waned. His expression was unrevealing but his skin was chalky and as he turned his head his cousin noticed for the first time that the fringe of hair was speckled with gray. Staring down at the blotter, he said slowly, "That Norton chap. You know him much better than I do. Does he strike you as the type to play practical jokes?"

"Not really. Lafe has a sense of humor but . . . William, I can't really say I know him that well. I saw him only a few times when he was here or at Aunt Van's."

William reached out a hand, hesitated, and then picked up the sheets of notepaper and passed them across to her. "Read this."

The letter began, "My dearest love." She read slowly. A

love letter and written as one would expect a man with literary aspirations to word it. Elegantly phrased, descending a few times to purple prose. She was relieved that Lafe had not mentioned her. That had been a gamble but not a large one. Except for a couple of greetings in his first letters Lafe hadn't bothered to send messages to Elizabeth. As she read she felt her lips form a smile but managed to turn it into a grimace of distaste. Lafe had done a wonderful job. He alluded to his love's "warm ivory thighs" and to "breasts like rose-tipped volcanoes." *Volcanoes!* The letter closed with "and to think, my darling, we now have a living breathing symbol of our passion." That should be clear enough even for Judith's old sweetie.

She put the pages on the blotter. "William, I don't understand."

"Neither do I. It's definitely some grotesque mistake. Elizabeth, could it be possible . . . now, don't take offense . . ."

"Yes?"

"Could Norton have written that letter to you?"

Elizabeth jumped up, her eyes flashing. "*William*. Are you suggesting that a man I barely know would dare write to me like that? What kind of woman do you think I am?"

"I'm truly sorry. Do sit down and compose yourself. I know you're a respectable woman. A lady above reproach. I was grasping at straws. Trying to find a way out of a nightmare." He paused and then said tragically, "That letter is addressed to my wife."

"*Judith!*"

"That's why I asked if he could be a practical joker. Making malicious mischief. There must be a rational explanation."

There is, you besotted fool, Elizabeth told him silently. Aloud she said, "Is it possible the letter was written to another woman? Could Lafe have mixed two letters up? Sent the wrong one to Judith?"

William smacked the desk so hard the ink stand jumped. "By George, you're right! Perhaps he wrote a few lines to Judith, telling her a little of what he's doing overseas and . . ." His voice trailed off and after a moment the light dimmed on his gaunt features. "No, it would be most improper. Norton would have addressed his letter either in my name or in both our names. To do otherwise would be a direct insult to me."

"That's true. Lafe isn't the type of man to send a letter to a married lady he has seen only a few times. Unless . . ."

"Yes, unless." A shapely hand covered William's eyes. "Elizabeth, I must reason this out. You go along and have your dinner. Tell Cookie I don't care for anything."

Elizabeth sat alone at the long table, pushing food around her plate. Gerda set the main course down in front of her and she smelled the rich odor of lamb in mint sauce and nearly gagged. She pushed the plate away.

Gerda frowned ferociously. "Don't know what's wrong in this house, miss. The missus up in bed and Mr. Meredith closed in the study and you looking like there's flies on your nice dinner. Cookie's gonna see red. Slaved to cook a good meal and—"

"Tell her I'm sorry. I'm just not hungry, Gerda."

"She made your favorite dessert, miss. Chocolate pie."

"Perhaps I'll have some later. Just bring coffee. Gerda, ask Cookie to cut sandwiches for Mr. Meredith. There's beef left from yesterday. And a fresh pot of coffee for him. When the tray's ready, bring it to me. I'll take it in to him."

Closing her eyes, Elizabeth leaned back in her chair. She realized she'd done a terrible thing and betrayed a girl who had shown her kindness and had trusted her. Granted she was fighting for survival, but was that any excuse to destroy Judith? Then Elizabeth realized the futility of her regrets. What was done was done, it was too late to change that. When Gerda carried in the tray she took it to the study, tapped lightly, heard her cousin's voice, and swung open the door. The whiskey glass was empty and he shook his head at the tray. "At least have coffee, William."

"No. But don't leave. I need your advice."

"In a matter like this I can't advise you. I'm too close to Judith."

"I know you're devoted to her. But I'm confused. My mind is whirling around like a squirrel in a cage. I need help."

Folding her hands, Elizabeth bowed her sleek head. "You need advice from a person not so close to your wife. Someone older and wiser than I."

He splashed whiskey into the glass and took a gulp. "I'd better go to John Stokes."

"When it comes to something like this men tend to be harsh,

believe the worst. I was thinking of a woman."

He stared into the glass. "Call Aunt Van."

Elizabeth telephoned the Vandercourt house. It proved to be Aunt Van's night to host her bridge club and there was a lengthy delay before she'd even come to the phone. When she spoke her voice was sharp with impatience. "Really, Elizabeth, how can you be so thoughtless. I'd expect better sense from you." She lowered her voice to a hoarse whisper. "We have a grand slam. Whatever you want will have to wait."

"It can't. This is an emergency. Aunt Van, William *needs* you."

She'd used exactly the right words. There was a pause and then Aunt Van said, "I'll be right there. Sophie will have to sit in for me."

As Elizabeth replaced the receiver, William looked bleakly up at her. She nodded and he said forlornly, "I know I ask a lot from you but will you . . . can you explain to Aunt Van?"

"May I show her the letter?"

"No."

"She'll have to see it."

"I suppose she will." He pushed the sheets over and she gathered them up and replaced them in the envelope. As she left the room she glanced back. No longer did William look exactly like their stern grandfather. He huddled in the big chair, his shoulders bowed, the sprightly mustache appearing to droop. The youthful suit and bright tie were a travesty of youth. For an instant she felt a rush of pity. Then she shrugged. Pity was an emotion not allowed a poor relative. Pity had never been shown to her father, or to her.

Elizabeth waited in the hall for the next pawn in the dangerous game. She hadn't a long wait. As the Vandercourt Packard pulled up, Elizabeth flung the door open. Aunt Van, without waiting for Henry's assistance, bounced out of the car and trotted up the walk. In the bulky Persian lamb coat she looked like a teddy bear. A matching toque was tilted over one gleaming eye. Taking the coat, Elizabeth brushed at the snowflakes covering it.

"Don't fuss, Elizabeth. What's wrong? Is the boy ill?"

"Come into the library. We wouldn't want the servants to hear this."

In the library two lamps cast a mellow glow over white walls, leather, regimented lines of books. Sinking on the long sofa, the older woman asked in a whisper, "Judith?"

Elizabeth pulled the envelope from her sweater pocket and Aunt Van grabbed it. She took her time, scrutinizing the envelope, extracting the pages, reading. As she read her lips moved. She dropped the pages into her lap and leaned forward, her eyes glowing with triumph. "The slut. The wanton. That whore! I told you so. Remember? I said, mark my words, Elizabeth, that poor deluded boy will rue the day he didn't take Aunt Van's advice. And everyone thinks that hussy is a saint. Aunt Van never did. Didn't have *me* fooled for a minute." The woman was so excited that saliva spewed in a fine mist from her mouth. "Lafe? That's that Norton man, isn't it? The reporter. That friend of yours."

Lifting her chin, Elizabeth said primly, "Lafcadio is no longer a friend of mine."

"Has William sent that slut packing?"

"No. He can't believe it. He's dazed. Doesn't know what to do. That's why he called for you."

"He came to the right person. I'll tell him what to do." Aunt Van heaved herself up. The toque dipped further over her eyes and she pushed it back. "Mark my words, when news of this gets out William won't be able to hold up his head." She surged toward the hall. "Where is he?"

"In the study."

Aunt Van didn't bother knocking. She marched in and took a fresh glass of whiskey from William's hand. "You don't need this."

He stared into her face. "What do you think?"

"I think you'd better get up and throw that woman out of this house. And that brat of hers too."

He appeared to shrink in size. "Aunt Van, I know you're fond of Judith. Don't you think there's a chance she's innocent?"

"I can read and so can you. What do you want—to be confronted with them in your own bed?"

He straightened and said harshly, "This is no time to jump to conclusions. Sit down, Aunt Van, and let's reason this out."

Aunt Van glowered but she did sit down. Elizabeth stood behind the chair, one hand resting lightly on its back. "Start reasoning," the older woman ordered.

"If this is true there'd have to be an opportunity. There's

been none. Judith has never even gone shopping alone. It's impossible."

"Nothing is impossible, dear boy. But I grant you it does seem unlikely. Hmm, let me think." Propping her chin on a hand, Aunt Van looked into space. Then her mouth pursed and she pounded the arm of her chair with a pudgy fist. *"Atlantic City."*

"No," Elizabeth said. "I was with her."

"Come around where I can see you. Hate anyone breathing down my neck. That's better. Now, Elizabeth, think. That letter you wrote me last August. You did say this Norton man was in Atlantic City. That you and Judith saw him."

"Of course we saw him. Twice, Aunt Van. The day after we arrived he came to our hotel and we gave him tea. That evening he gave us dinner at his cottage. We didn't stay long because Alicia had to be put to bed."

Small shrewd eyes probed at Elizabeth's dark ones. "And Judith didn't see him again?"

"Neither of us saw him again."

"Did you and Judith share a room?"

Elizabeth opened her mouth but William snapped, "Of course they didn't. Judith needed unbroken rest and Alicia was in Elizabeth's charge. They had adjoining rooms."

"I see. Cousin Elizabeth, did you ever enter Judith's room at night?"

"There was never any reason to. And I was tired. Sea and sun can be enervating. I had full care of Alicia and by night I was exhausted."

"And there's your opportunity, William. I know those resort hotels and so do you. Like Elizabeth, most of the holidayers are tired at night. They go to bed fairly early and sleep like the dead. How difficult would it have been for your wife to slip out and meet this Norton?"

He shook a stubborn head. "Until that time Judith had only seen Norton a few times and I was always with her. No woman is going to set up an assignation to meet a total stranger in Atlantic City."

"A total stranger." Aunt Van seemed to like the taste of the words. Her lips moved as though she were chewing. She looked up at Elizabeth. "Exactly how did you meet this Norton?"

"We met when I was about nine. Our fathers were friends and Lafe came to—"

"Last year?"

Dutifully Elizabeth recounted the meeting in the Oasis. While she spoke Aunt Van's tiny fingers drummed on the arm of her chair. "And you say Judith insisted on this restaurant in the Village?"

"She didn't actually insist. When I said I didn't like the looks of it she said we'd go inside and if I still didn't like it we wouldn't stay. But it was quite a respectable place, Aunt Van."

The older woman gave her a pitying look. "You're such an innocent. That woman took you in as completely as she did William. Elizabeth, can't you see you were *used*?" Aunt Van turned to the man behind the desk. "Dear boy, it's obvious that woman insisted on marrying you when she already knew this Norton. She duped poor Cousin Elizabeth into introducing her lover into your house."

"I refuse to believe that."

"It had to be in Boston." Aunt Van shoved the telephone at him. "Get Emma Arnold. Ask *her*."

He picked the black instrument up gingerly, as though it were a snake. But by the time the connection was made his mouth was firm and his voice cold and concise. "Emma, do you know a man called Lafcadio Norton? Just answer my question . . . you do . . . and Judith . . . a casual acquaintance . . . she met him where? no, I won't explain my reason . . . no, Emma, I'm not angry with you . . . now, don't cry . . . in time you will. Goodnight." He hung up and said heavily, "They met in Boston. Before our marriage. Emma said quite casually."

"Casually," Aunt Van hooted. "Well, dear boy, it's clear now. That woman married you for what you could give her. As soon as she could she used Cousin Elizabeth, this poor unsuspecting lamb, to see the man. She went to Atlantic City for only one reason and used poor Elizabeth again. She's wicked and an innocent like Elizabeth couldn't possibly see through her. It takes an experienced woman like me to know what she is." On tiny fingers she counted, her rings sending sparkles of light. "Mariette is *his* child."

"No!" William cried. "She's mine."

"Elizabeth, bring that baby down here."

Elizabeth didn't move until William jerked his head in assent. In the nursery she found the children and their nurse asleep. Tosh woke immediately, pushing back her elaborate nightcap. "Miss Elizabeth?"

"Mr. Meredith wants me to bring down Mariette."

Tosh reached for a flannel robe. "At this hour?"

"His aunt is with him. Mrs. Vandercourt would like to see the baby."

"Getting the wee lassie out of her crib at this hour? Doesn't seem right."

Tosh wrapped the baby in a blanket and handed her to Elizabeth. Mariette slept through this and all the way down to the study. Aunt Van poked a pudgy finger into the warm bundle. "I should have seen it before. She's the picture of that Norton man. Look at that hair, William."

"Judith explained that. Her Aunt Lucy—"

"Fiddlesticks. My, but Judith's a clever minx. Had me fooled too. Never was any Aunt Lucy. Emma must have been in on it too."

Aunt Van poked at the bundle again and the baby opened violet eyes and let out a howl of protest. William took her from Elizabeth's arms, rocked her, and then pulled a contented thumb from the rosy mouth. "Aunt Van, this child is *mine*."

"My boy, you're simply being stubborn, unwilling to admit what a mistake you made in going against my advice and marrying that woman." Sinking into a chair, Aunt Van stared into space. "Let me think and I'll give you proof. The Allenbys. There was something . . . some queerness. Hazel . . . now, what was it? So long ago. Hazel and I were only girls."

The room was quiet, the silence broken only by the crooning sound William was making over the baby. Then Aunt Van's hands clapped. "I never forget. The Allenbys had a deformity. Hazel had it and so did her brother Robbie. The little finger. Long, almost as long as the next finger. Let's see that baby."

Lifting a starfish hand, Aunt Van spread it, showing the finger to William. Her voice was husky with compassion as she whispered, "My poor boy, *now* do you see it?"

William saw. He thrust out his arms so abruptly the child nearly fell. Elizabeth rescued the baby and clutched her to her breast. He looked as though a sculptor had carved his figure from granite. "Get her out of here," he grated. "Get that . . . that thing out of my sight."

"Elizabeth, wait," Aunt Van ordered. "William, you know what you must do?" His head jerked and she said gently, "Elizabeth mustn't be here. She loves that woman and it would be too hard for her. She's suffered enough." She swung to face the spinster. "Have you anywhere you can go for a little while?"

Gratefully Elizabeth nodded. The gratitude was genuine. "I've a friend in New Rochelle. A librarian. Should I . . ."

"Go to her."

"When will I come back?"

"When William sends for you."

Before the door closed Elizabeth saw her cousin collapsing in a chair, his aunt bending over him. She took the baby up to the nursery. Tosh had not returned to her warm bed but was sitting in a rocking chair, a shawl draped over her bony shoulders. Taking Mariette, she tucked her tenderly back in the cradle. Elizabeth stood over Alicia's crib gazing down at the pointed face framed in flaxen hair.

"I hope Mrs. Vandercourt was satisfied," Tosh said frostily.

"Yes," Elizabeth said softly. "She was satisfied."

In her tiny room she opened the commode and extracted a pack of cigarettes from the chamber pot. The commodes and china sets had been removed from the other bedrooms but in this one, seldom used, they'd been overlooked, Elizabeth used the pot as an oversized ashtray. There was no use in trying to sleep so she perched on the edge of the bed and smoked a cigarette. She pictured the unsuspecting Judith in the room on the second floor. Elizabeth was fighting the desire to go to the girl, to warn her. She shrugged. Let her sleep. The wheels had been set in motion and from the moment that Aunt Van had been brought into it the girl was doomed.

Where would Judith go? Then Elizabeth relaxed. Emma Arnold would have to take her daughter and grandchild in. Judith and Mariette would be cared for. Closing her eyes, Elizabeth pictured all the roles Judith had played. The composed beauty in the drawing room the first time she had entered the Meredith house; the warm and generous bride who had lavished attentions on her husband's cousin; the querulous semi-invalid before Alicia's birth; the recently devoted wife and society matron. Now Judith Meredith would have another role to play, that of unfaithful, discarded wife, mother of an illegitimate daughter, a woman shunned as a pariah by former friends, dependent on a flighty, duplicitous mother.

In vain Elizabeth tried to picture the cold haughty Judith who was ready to discard her like a pair of used bedroom slippers. But her clearest memories were of the girl's many little kindnesses to her and of a crumpled form at the foot of the stairs and a terror-filled voice begging Elizabeth for help.

Even if I wanted to, Elizabeth thought, I can't save Judith from what is going to happen to her as soon as I leave this house. I swore vengeance on all the Merediths for what they did to my father . . . and *me*. Part of that vow is accomplished. William is in agony and Judith soon will be.

Somehow Elizabeth found that revenge wasn't as sweet as she had thought it would be.

— 15 —

The next morning before the household was stirring Elizabeth packed her carpetbag and summoned a taxi. She phoned New Rochelle from the station and found Nettie Towers was pleased to have an unexpected guest. Nettie even took a day off so she could meet her friend and take her to the neat old-maidish cottage.

Elizabeth spent eleven agonizing days in that cottage. Nettie, as fluttery and foolish and girlish as she'd been when they'd attended school, tried to be the soul of hospitality. She took Elizabeth to church, to church socials, to a potluck supper in the church basement. Nettie introduced her friend to her small circle of cronies and Elizabeth spent long hours playing whist and chatting with a gaggle of old maids and widows known collectively as "the girls." The girls, regardless of differences in age and physical appearances, had two qualities in common. They were completely, unbelievably boring, and all cherished a passionate attachment for their spiritual leader. After meeting Reverend Philpott Elizabeth was at a loss to understand the reason for all the passion. He was in his sixties, tall and gray and stooped, with buck teeth. He reminded her of an aging gray rabbit.

In this society Eliizabeth felt stifled. By the eleventh day of her exile she felt close to desperate. It was Sunday and after the morning church service she persuaded Nettie to allow her to prepare dinner. She didn't like cooking but it would get her away from her hostess for a time. She settled Nettie in the prim parlor with a Bible on her knees and a photograph of Reverend Philpott, smiling his toothy smile, at her elbow and thankfully escaped to the kitchen. She baked a ham and made a casserole of scalloped potatoes. Then she seated herself at the table and began to chop onions for salad. She found tears oozing from her eyes and couldn't decide whether they were caused by fumes or her own situation. If Nettie fluttered in with one more asinine remark about church, the minister, or the girls, Elizabeth knew she would fling the salad bowl through the neatly curtained window.

The door did open and Nettie fluttered in. She was even more agitated than usual. "A big foreign car," she whispered dramatically. "And a chauffeur. Elizabeth, he's coming up the walk."

Weak with relief, Elizabeth reached for a dishcloth and dabbed at her wet eyes. "That will be Briggs." Without removing her apron she went to the door. Briggs stamped snow from his boots and gratefully entered the warm parlor. Muffled in a greatcoat, the big man dwarfed the room. Pulling off heavy gloves, he blew on his fingers and then pulled an envelope from his pocket. "From Mr. Meredith, miss."

Aware of Nettie at her elbow, Elizabeth tore the envelope. It contained only three words. "Come home, Elizabeth," William had written.

Nettie read it and sighed. "Isn't that too bad? Just when we were having so much fun."

"Very sad," Elizabeth lied. "Briggs, you looked chilled to the bone."

"That I am, miss. Cold drive. Wish Mr. Meredith would get a car where I could sit inside. The Panhard is fine in summer but in this weather a man comes close to perishing. Could use a mug of tea."

Nettie eagerly offered not only tea but hot food and fluttered Briggs away to the kitchen. Elizabeth declined dinner and went to her room to pack. Taking a pile of underclothes from the bureau, she slid them into the carpetbag. She had no inkling what her reception would be when she returned. Like a gambler, she had risked everything on Judith's reaction when she was confronted by William and Aunt Van. The girl was treacherous. She could have betrayed Elizabeth, told her husband and his aunt that Elizabeth had not been hoodwinked but had aided and abetted the lovers. On the other hand Elizabeth felt confident that she had persuaded Judith that the lapel watch had stopped, that she had innocently allowed the letter to reach William. Even if Judith had talked, would either Aunt Van or William have believed her? They might think it venom and spite.

Soon enough she would know. Pushing in the last garment, Elizabeth snapped the bag closed. As soon as Briggs had finished his meal, she insisted on leaving. Nettie, wrapped in a fluffy scarf, came to the car with them. Pecking a kiss at the other old maid's cheek, Elizabeth seated herself and Briggs pulled a warm rug over her knees. Along the row of cottages, all similar to Nettie Towers's, starched curtains were pulled back and curious faces peered out. One of the girls came boldly out on her stoop to stare. Briggs heaved his big frame behind the wheel, the car drew away, Nettie and the other girl waved furiously. Elizabeth waved back. New Rochelle fell behind and the car picked up speed. Elizabeth fingered the speaking tube, wondering if she should pump Briggs about his master's state of mind. She decided against it. Even if Briggs knew anything, she doubted if he'd tell her. In every sense, he was his master's man.

The Panhard, driven faster than usual by a cold and miserable chauffeur, ate up the miles. They arrived at the Meredith house in good time and Elizabeth dropped her bag in the hall and went to the kitchen. The scullery maid was peeling vegetables at the sink and the two maids and Cookie were seated at the long pine table drinking steaming cups of tea and eating slabs of pecan pie. As the old maid pushed open the baize door they sprang guiltily to their feet. Smiling, Elizabeth waved them back. She took off her coat and draped it over the back of a chair. Then she sat down with them. "That looks good," she told the cook.

A flustered Cookie sprang up again for a plate and cup. "Don't think we're idling in our time, Miss Elizabeth. All the work's done and I thought we'd have a sitdown and some tea."

"Perfectly all right," Elizabeth assured her.

"Now if we'd known you was coming back . . ."

"Didn't Briggs tell you?"

"Briggs's been down with Mr. Meredith at his club, miss," Sally volunteered. "Haven't seen hide nor hair of them since the day you left."

"Mr. Meredith isn't home?"

Cookie scowled. "Might have known Briggs wouldn't say nothing. Can be real closemouthed, that man. Mr. Meredith sent a message. Said he'd be home after work tomorrow."

"I see." Elizabeth sipped strong tea and wondered how to get the servants talking.

There was no necessity. Gerda began, a stream of words that reminded Elizabeth how fanatically religious the girl was. "That scarlet woman. Bringing shame down on every one of us. I'm thinking of handing in my notice."

Sally was more tolerant. "Come, Gerda. All she did was have a little fun on the side. I feel kinda sorry for the mistress."

Gerda bristled but Elizabeth intervened. "Has Mrs. Meredith left?"

"Went the day you did, miss," Cookie told her. "Mr. Meredith came downstairs early and sent Gerda up to see if the mistress was well enough to come down to the study. When she come down I saw she was feeling better but she looked puzzled. She went into the study and the door closed—"

"Mrs. Vandercourt wasn't here?" Elizabeth interrupted.

"She stayed late the night before but Mr. Meredith was alone in the study. What was I saying? Oh, they was in there maybe an hour and then the master comes out and tells Gerda to pack a bag for him for about a week. He says give it to Briggs and both of them will be down at his club. He tells Gerda not to worry, to tell the staff to carry on as usual."

"Looked like death, he did," Gerda blurted. "And no wonder. After he left that scarlet woman comes out and goes upstairs. She looked funny too, kind of like she didn't know what she was doing. She called Sally and—"

"I'll tell about this," Sally said firmly. She turned excited eyes on Elizabeth. "I didn't know what was going on, miss. Mrs. Meredith comes running upstairs, her face real red and she says, Sally, you get Gerda and bring down my trunks. So we did. Had an awful time lugging them down them stairs too. Mrs. Meredith was standing looking around her pretty room like she never saw it before."

"Was she crying?" Elizabeth asked.

"No. She just kept looking around, kinda shaking her head. Then she orders us to pack her things. Mrs. Meredith packs an overnight case herself. Just stuff to sleep in. By then she seemed to have calmed down some. We didn't dare ask questions."

"I didn't need to," Gerda said sternly. "Written all over her. A Jezebel who was found out. When we got everything packed she tells us she'll send a carter for the trunks. Then she goes up to the nursery and we heard her arguing with Tosh. We couldn't hear what Tosh was saying but that woman was screeching her lungs out. Ordering Tosh to pack the baby's things, the little one I mean. Tosh started to howl but she packs up the baby's stuff and that woman brings the wee one down all wrapped in blankets. She tells me to carry that dog and I try to pick it up and it bites at me. So she pushes the baby at me and picks up that beast herself."

For a moment the servants were silent, looking glumly into their cups. Then Cookie said quietly, "That's about all, miss. I phoned for a taxi and the mistress gets into it with her little bag and the dog and the baby. I ask where she'll be and she says she don't know. I started to cry. I just couldn't help it. I was that upset." Cookie's voice broke and she dabbed at damp eyes with a corner of her apron. "Then she reaches up and kisses me right on the cheek and I smell that pretty perfume and I cry harder. She tells me it's all right and not to worry—"

"*I* wasn't worrying." Gerda sniffed. "Jezebel."

"No," Cookie said sadly. "Just a heedless girl led astray. What'll happen to her and Mariette, miss?"

Elizabeth shook her head. Gerda poured more tea and said sourly, "Big question is what's to happen to us."

"What do you mean?"

"No way we can stay on in this house, miss. We're decent women, from decent families."

"Don't bother Miss Elizabeth with this," Sally said sharply.

"With what?" Elizabeth looked around the circle of faces. "I think you'd better tell me."

Cookie's neat gray head bobbed. "Servants' gossip, miss. That cook of Mrs. Vandercourt's—"

"Aggie?"

"The same. Comes over all high and mighty and tells us we're living in a den of iniquity. That our mistress is no better than a . . . a whore. That Mariette is a—Miss Elizabeth, I'm only using the words Aggie did—is a bastard and there's some think the other little girl is too. I shut her up. I up and says Aggie, Miss Elizabeth's coming back to this house. Everyone knows what a good, respectable woman she is. I told Aggie if Miss Elizabeth stays under this roof it proves Alicia is a Meredith and this is no den of iniquity. Aggie didn't argue none about that."

Sally, Gerda, even the kitchen maid, nodded in agreement. "You were quite right to reprimand Aggie," Elizabeth told the cook. "I give you my word Alicia is a Meredith, and Mrs. Meredith and the other child are no longer in the house."

"Good riddance to bad rubbish," Gerda stated righteously. "But they left the stench of sin behind them. Sinners in the eyes of the Lord."

Getting to her feet, Elizabeth looked sternly down at the maid. "It also says in the Good Book that the one without sin may cast the first stone. Gerda, I want to hear no more about Mrs. Meredith or Mariette from you. If I ever do you're discharged. Do you understand?"

The chastened maid nodded her head and Elizabeth left the kitchen. As she carried her bag up to her room she felt lightheaded with relief. So, tongues were wagging. It would appear that William now needed her. Her continued presence in the house would give it a much needed aura of respectability. If she were to leave tongues would wag even harder.

She smiled, a wide, delighted smile. The time had come to demand some respect from Cousin William. She lit a cigarette and inhaled luxuriously. At that moment a tap sounded on the door. Hastily she stuck the cigarette in the chamber pot and pushed it back in the commode. She opened the door a crack and saw a flushed and breathless Cookie. "Clean forgot, Miss Elizabeth. Mistress left this for you. Says to me, give this to Miss Elizabeth."

Elizabeth took the crumpled envelope, thanked the cook, and closed the door. Perching on the edge of the bed, she examined the flap. It hadn't been tampered with. She slit it open and pulled out a single sheet of notepaper.

Dear Elizabeth,

All is discovered. That dreadful old woman has influenced William and he is throwing me out. He isn't allowing me to take my jewels or clothes. I regret I ever became involved with Lafe. Now that I have lost my husband I realize how fortunate I was to marry a man like William. But, alas, it's too late for regrets. I see no reason for you to be hurt too so I concealed your part in this affair. From the beginning you did advise me against seeing Lafe. I love you very much and I wish you the best. I'm leaving my dressing table for you. I know you have the forget-me-not watch to remind you of Judith but it has proved a traitor and ruined me so I know you must hate it.

Your loving friend,
Judith

By the time Elizabeth had read the short letter her eyes were brimming with tears. Capricious Judith, first ruthlessly ordering her from the house and then protecting her from William's wrath. Ready to throw her to the mercy of a cold world and then leaving her that lovely dressing table. Judith, who was neither good nor bad but a combination of both.

With shaking hands she took out the chamber pot and set it on the floor. Striking a match, she touched flame to a corner of the envelope. After it was burnt she did the same with the letter.

At four sharp the following afternoon William returned to his house. At ten after the hour he sent for Elizabeth. When she joined him in the study he greeted her warmly, asked courteously about her visit to New Rochelle, and, much to her surprise, proposed she have sherry. As she sipped she studied her cousin. Since last she'd seen him he'd regained his composure but it was evident that his second youth had vanished with his wife. The stylish clothes had given way to a black tie and a sober gray suit, the white in the fringe of hair was more pronounced, there were deep hollows under his cheekbones, his eyes sunken and rimmed by shadows the same shade as his suit. He'd shaved off the mustache and his long upper lip looked naked.

Elizabeth assumed an air of sympathy. "How have you been, William?"

"It's been a difficult time, Elizabeth. The saddest period of my life. No one has said anything directly to me but I've seen the glances and heard the rumors. You wouldn't believe what people are saying."

"Gossip can be brutal, but people will tire of it. Something else will happen and all this will be forgotten."

"I'm afraid it isn't as simple as that." He brushed a tapered finger over his upper lip. "I don't like to distress you but I think you should be aware of the situation. The rumors say the reason George enlisted was that his stepmother was making advances to him. There's talk about little Alicia not being my child." He looked pleadingly at his cousin. "This isn't the truth."

He hadn't uttered his last remark as a question but she knew it was. "Not one word of truth. Judith did *not* make advances to George. She hardly noticed the boy. And Alicia is *your* child. You know that."

"I do. But this is the first time scandal has ever touched our family. I have no idea how to cope."

"You must do your best. As I said, this will pass."

He managed a wan smile. "I've been talking with Aunt Van. She's been most supportive and has done her best to quell gossip. She made a suggestion."

Hastily, Elizabeth lifted her glass to hide a smile. She could imagine Aunt Van quelling gossip. Somewhat similar to throwing gasoline on a fire to put out the flames. "What did she suggest?"

"A solution that involves you. Aunt Van feels that if you would consent to act as mother to little Alicia, these vicious rumors will die. As she mentioned, you are regarded as an upright, God-fearing woman."

William waited and Elizabeth let him wait. An upright, God-fearing woman, she thought cynically. Translate that and it comes out a prudish spinster. When she didn't speak he continued, "Aunt Van says that if you will raise Alicia and attend to her debut in society people will cease to question her right to the name of Meredith. You are quiet, Cousin Elizabeth. What are you thinking?"

"You know how devoted I am to you and to Alicia. But, William, I don't believe I can remain in this house."

Alarm flashed across his face. "You said you didn't believe that George . . . or about Alicia."

"I most certainly don't. My reasons are personal. I'm fond of Judith too and it will be painful for me to stay on here. Also, there's my age to consider."

"Your age?"

Leaning forward, she set her glass on the desk. He reached for the decanter and refilled it. "I'm thirty-eight. To raise the child and help her enter society will take about twenty years. Approaching sixty I may find myself homeless and penniless."

"Come now, you know better than that. You'll always have a home with me."

"You're sixteen years my senior. What will happen if you . . ."

"Die? I see. George will certainly see my wishes are carried out."

"George is on the Western Front."

He flinched. "Yes. You don't get along well with Alan, do you?"

"No."

"Some insurance is needed. I could mention you in my will. Set aside an income for you."

"I was thinking of more immediate insurance."

"A little nest egg?" He gave her an indulgent smile. "What sum do you have in mind? Five hundred? Perhaps even a thousand?"

"Five thousand."

William nearly leaped from his chair. "That's a *great* deal of money.

"Divide it by twenty years."

He looked as though he were in physical pain. After a time

he said slowly, "Looking at it that way . . . very well, Elizabeth. I'll arrange for a trust fund—"

"No."

"Then let me arrange for a safe investment. After all, with your father's carelessness in money matters I don't—"

"William!" Elizabeth made no effort to hide her anger. "I don't wish to hear further about my father."

"Indeed. I had no idea you were so sensitive. How do you wish the money."

"In cash."

"Tomorrow I'll make arrangements with my bank." He added hopelessly, "I suppose you'll expect your present salary to continue."

"Of course. As Alicia's surrogate mother I'll need to look after myself, dress properly. I certainly can't spend the nest egg for my old age on that."

His eyes narrowed. "Any other requests?"

"Only one and it doesn't concern money. As I'll be permanently in this house it will be awkward to stay in the room I have now. It's too small."

He sighed. "You are thinking of the large room at the front. The one you mentioned before."

"Yes."

"It's yours. Move into it as soon as you wish. I'll have Briggs bring down your parents' furniture."

"Thank you," she said demurely. Draining her glass, she rose. "I assure you I'll do my best with Alicia and the house."

"And your best is very good," he said wryly. He leaned back in his chair and smiled slightly. "I've a feeling I may have misjudged you, Cousin Elizabeth. You may have the makings of an astute businesswoman. Now, I have two requests. I never want to hear my . . . my former wife's name mentioned again. And, under no circumstances are yellow roses to enter this house."

"Agreed. But for my peace of mind, William, I must ask you one last question."

"Yes?"

"Do you know where Judith went?"

"No."

"Could she be with her mother?"

For a moment she thought he wouldn't answer. Then he said grudgingly, "No. I've spoken to Emma. Braced her, as Aunt Van insisted, on her part in this intrigue. Emma admitted to me that Judith begged her to mention red hair but wouldn't give a reason. I still don't think Emma is wholly innocent but she begged and wept when I threatened to cut off her allowance. Finally I told her it would continue but if I ever found she'd given shelter or aid to that . . . to her daughter or her child I would never give her another cent. Take my word, Elizabeth, they're not in Boston."

As his cousin rose he cleared his throat. "One moment, Elizabeth. I find it difficult to express emotions properly but I want you to know . . . I'm most grateful to you. There have been times in the past when perhaps I didn't show sufficient interest in your welfare but that is now changed. I'll always remember your loyalty and devotion during this trying period." He flushed and murmured, "I want you to know this."

Amazed at William's fumbling attempt to apologize, Elizabeth managed to nod and left the study. Truly this was a side of her cousin she'd never before seen. As she mounted the stairs she thought bleakly, no, Judith and Mariette are not in Boston. William had effectively cut off even that dubious haven for them. Driven by guilt she went to Judith's room. Except for a few padded hangers the wardrobe was empty and the drawers of the chiffonier contained only tissue linings. In the secret drawer of the dressing table that she now owned was only a crumpled pink ribbon. Elizabeth sniffed. The only indication of Judith was a lingering odor of her perfume.

Quietly closing the door behind her, she made her way up to the third floor and looked her new bedroom over. The bed was lovely but the canopy and bedspread would have to be replaced. In front of one window she'd put her black and scarlet escritoire with her father's leather chair beside it. The table with the green stone top would look well beside the bed. She touched the walnut dressing table. That would have to go up to the attic. The secret drawer in Judith's dressing table would be an ideal hiding place for cigarettes. Wandering over to a window she touched a curtain. Quite worn. She'd make up new curtains to match the bedspread. Lavender. Or perhaps pale yellow. She glanced down at the street. Much different from the view of the bleak garden and the rear of the house she'd had to look at from her old cramped room. Then with a sigh of satisfaction she took down a floral picture hanging on the wall opposite the bed.

"At last," she said aloud to the shade of her father, "your paintings will hang in your home. This room is only a beginning. In time they'll be where they should be. William's settlement is only a down payment on what they owe us."

Feeling a little better, she went down to the kitchen and Cookie.

Both William and Elizabeth kept their word. Within a week five thousand dollars was transferred to her name. Elizabeth set out to do her best and, as her cousin had remarked, her best was very good indeed. Under her supervision the house ran smoothly. She checked the welfare of Alicia frequently, although it took little of her time. Like a hen with one chick the widowed nurse hovered over the baby.

Elizabeth coddled her cousin and saw he received proper food and rest. In a short time he had gained a few pounds, the dark circles around his eyes diminished, and color crept back into his face. After a while she approached him about entertaining. Fearing snubs, William proved balky. His cousin shrugged off his fears. "Your true friends will rally around," she told him. "We won't worry about the others. In time they'll come around. It must be done. We can't look as though we're hiding."

He reluctantly gave his consent and Elizabeth organized a series of dinner parties. Not one person invited refused the invitation. They came to show sympathy and support or from outright curiosity. They left with admiration for the Meredith family. Elizabeth proved to be a considerate hostess and superb food, excellent wine, and lively conversation made her dinners enjoyable. As often as possible she brought Alicia down to the drawing room for a few moments before dinner. Elizabeth was conscious that the child's hands were covertly examined but she thought, let them look, Alicia's little finger is normal.

With lack of fresh fuel and Elizabeth's unflinching presence gossip slowed, then died a natural death, and when invitations began to flow in she knew she'd won. She went with William to

dinner parties, to theaters, to the opera. Gradually the ladies'
attitudes toward the poor spinster cousin began to change. They
almost, but not quite, accepted her as an equal. She went to their
bridge parties, on shopping expeditions, to charity bazaars. Lavinia Stokes, in a burst of uncharacteristic expansiveness, conducted Elizabeth through her home for unfortunate women.
Elizabeth was cautious. She dressed well but plainly, did not presume, gave well-turned compliments, and always was a model of
diplomacy.

Christmas came and this year Elizabeth helped William light
the tree. She presided over dinner and distributed gifts to the
caroling children. The culmination of the busy months came on
New Year's Eve when William escorted her to the Standfords'
party. Elizabeth was handsome in midnight blue velvet ornamented by a single strand of perfectly matched pearls given to
her by a grateful William.

Doctor John traditionally offered the toast of the New Year.
He raised his glass, uttered jovial wishes for peace, prosperity,
and happiness, and his friends, content and secure in their little
world, echoed them. A few moments later in an aside to William
the doctor was far from jovial. Elizabeth overheard and some of
her happiness dimmed.

"Personally," the doctor said solemnly, "I think we're in for
one hell of a 'seventeen.'"

"It can't be much worse than 'sixteen," William told him.
"Anyway, it looks as though President Wilson may bring about
his 'peace without victory.'"

"I'll grant you he's doing his best but Great Britain has re-
jected his terms. They're too favorable to the Germans."

William clapped his friend's heavy shoulder. "Don't be so
gloomy."

But John Stokes was right. In January Germany announced
unrestricted submarine warfare would be waged against all shipping to and from Great Britain. In February two of William's
freighters were sunk. One was the *Judith Two*. On April sixth the
United States declared war on Germany. On that day William
sustained a blow much more grevious than the loss of his ships.

The night before that fateful day Elizabeth had spent hours
in the nursery with Alicia and Tosh. The child had a delicate
chest and was feverish and restless with a bout of bronchitis. At

lunch Tosh had looked at Elizabeth's drawn face and had sternly ordered her to her room for a nap. Shortly after four Elizabeth roused, realized William would be home, and got up. She paused beside the window, pulled back fresh lavender silk, and gazed out. A boy in the uniform of the telegraph office was propping his bike against the lamp standard in front of the house. His cap was tilted back and he appeared to be whistling. He headed up the steps and she lost sight of him. She stood like a statue. George, she thought. For an instant she saw George at Grand Central, the train behind him, the bevy of girls leaning out of a window. She saw his face pink and embarrassed as he gazed down at the gifts heaped at his feet. Not an idol, Elizabeth thought with hindsight, but an offering to the god of war. A mere boy in a soldier suit with an Adam's apple jerking in a thin throat, the nape of his neck young and pathetic and vulnerable.

Without waiting to tidy her hair she pulled on a dressing gown and ran down the stairs. William was in the hall, the telegram in one hand, his expression dazed. "He'd have been twenty-one next week," he told Elizabeth. He held out the yellow sheet. "They're giving him medals. The French . . . the British. They'd killed my son and they're giving me scraps of metal and ribbon."

He swayed and Elizabeth rushed to support him. She screamed for Cookie and they managed to hold him until Briggs came to their aid. William made no demur when they put him in the lift, no demur when Briggs undressed him and put him to bed. Elizabeth hurried in with a bottle of brandy but William shook his head. His eyes were closed and his lips bluish.

"My life is finished," he whispered. "I've nothing left to live for."

Oh God, Elizabeth thought, all that stands between me and Alan now is this man. "William, you must bear up. There's little Alicia and Alan."

He turned his face to the wall. "Take charge, Elizabeth."

She took charge. Wires were sent to Alan's school, to out-of-town friends. She made phone calls. Answers began to pour in—telegrams, letters, cards. The hall and front drawing room were crowded with baskets, boxes, vases of flowers, mute offerings of sympathy. Competently, Elizabeth handled everything. She sent notes of gratitude, answered the telephone, dispatched the flowers to hospitals and Lavinia's home for unwed mothers. She found time to spend with William, vainly trying to rouse him from apathy. In desperation she sent for Aunt Van.

Aunt Van came down from William's room shaking a baffled head. "Can't do a thing with the boy. He's crumbled. First that wife of his, now this . . . Elizabeth, you must *do* something or we'll lose him."

After Aunt Van left, more flowers arrived. Elizabeth took one look at a bouquet of tiny yellow roses and told the delivery man to leave it on the doorstep. There was no card and she sensed it came from Judith. She called Briggs and told him to get rid of it.

"Where?" he asked.

"Put it in the rubbish bin. Don't bring it through the house."

Then she lifted her chin and went up to do something about William. His face was still turned to the wall. "Talk to me," she pleaded. "Don't bottle it up." There was no answer and she asked, "Would you like to have Alan come and sit with you again?"

"Leave the boy alone," he whispered. "He's mourning his brother."

Much to Elizabeth's surprise Alan seemed to be doing just that. She'd never considered that Alan cared for anyone but himself. "He is," she said abruptly. "And you're not helping him."

"I can't even help myself. George was alive . . . now he's dead. I can't claim his body . . . give him a Christian burial. There's no feeling of . . . of finality."

An inspiration came to Elizabeth. "This isn't fair to George, to the people who knew and loved him. They must be feeling the same way. William, you must have a memorial service."

His head turned and sunken eyes stared up at her. "Where? Our church?"

"Perhaps it should be in the chapel at Harvard."

Harvard had been not only William's alma mater but his father's. He pushed himself up on an elbow. "Hmm, yes, I believe I should. His teachers, the other students . . . Elizabeth, you're right. Respect for my son's memory."

"Perhaps you might consider a lasting tribute to him. What about a scholarship in George's name?"

"A fine idea." Pushing the bedclothes aside, he perched on

the edge of the bed, his flannel nightgown outlining stringy thighs. "Or a gift to the chapel."

She left him, knowing he would now stir himself to make arrangements. In record time William had arranged for his gift to Harvard and the memorial service was held. It was attended by students, teachers, relatives, and friends. The chaplain gave a stirring address, lauding George Peter Meredith for his valor and gallantry, for the honors heaped on him by the British and French. His voice sank as he mournfully spoke of the loss of a fine young man with the promise of a brilliant future. He ended his address by predicting that now their country had joined the struggle against the godless hordes other young Americans would be following George Meredith's example. His sacrifice, the chaplain intoned, shall not be in vain.

Elizabeth's dark eyes were fixed on the memorial to George. William had chosen a stained glass window depicting a slender, rather asexual figure wearing armor and a helmet and holding aloft a flaming sword. At its feet groveled a creature that might have been either a snake or a lizard. St. George and the dragon? The main thing was that it had turned the trick. William was going to recover. Though saddened, Elizabeth felt no deep sorrow. That moment had come and gone as she looked from the window and glimpsed the boy arriving with the telegram. In her memory George had receded; a pleasant young man but not much more. She had only one regret. She wished it had been Alan.

After the service they straggled toward the cars. In the lead was William, the chaplain holding one of his arms, Aunt Van tightly clasping the other. Elizabeth let the rest go ahead and fell in at the end of the line. To her surprise Alan waited and fell into step with her. From the corner of her eye she regarded his round face, the lock of hair falling over the brow, his eyes puffed and reddened. Then the fleshy lips moved and he whispered, "Two down, Cousin Elizabeth."

Elizabeth went rigid with shock but she got the message. As she reached the car she thought, "I must take good care of William. Very good care indeed."

Six weeks after Alan returned to school William received a call from Vermont that sent him hurrying north. He had a painful session with the headmaster and then picked up his son at his dormitory, arranged for the luggage to be sent to New York, and told Briggs, "Take us home."

Replacing the speaking tube, he turned his back on his son, and gazed out of the window. Alan huddled in the corner, his own face averted. For a long time neither spoke and then Alan muttered, "You haven't said a word to me, father, not one word. You won't even listen to my side."

"I listened to you when you were expelled from school in New York. You probably were lying then. I want no more lies."

"But—"

"No excuses. My answer is on your face."

Alan clenched his hands together, willing them not to touch his face. God, how it hurt! One eye swollen shut and every shade of the rainbow, bruises all over his cheeks, a long gash across his upper lip. How in hell was he going to get out of this one? He'd never seen the old man like this before. He was terrifying. "Father, please listen," he begged.

William swung on him. "No, you listen. Those grades I was so proud of—all lies."

"I didn't lie. You saw the report cards."

"The headmaster showed me the exam papers. You cheated and they knew you were cheating but couldn't catch you out until the last one."

Alan clutched at his father's sleeve but William wrenched his hand away. "Father, I was trying to make you proud of me. I don't learn fast. I wanted to please you."

"So you cheated to please me and then you got into a fight with another boy. Over a tawdry waitress, a loose woman." Taking a deep breath, William looked directly at his son's bruised face. "I might have been able to stand the cheating, perhaps even that woman. I wouldn't have faulted you on a fight but"—he lowered his voice as though Briggs, through thick glass, might hear him—"I can't stand the fact that you ran from that fight. The other boy had to chase you. You whined and begged and cried—didn't raise a hand against him. A Meredith—a cheat, a liar . . . a coward."

"I know what you're thinking. George would never have done it. I'll bet you're wishing I was dead and George alive."

"I don't wish death on anyone. But I will tell you this. All your life I've loved you more than I did your brother and I couldn't help myself. Now I find I lavished affection on the son who doesn't deserve it. George was fine and honorable. You . . . you're despicable."

Alan groaned. "Father, what are you going to do? If you send me back to school I promise I'll be different. I'll work and bring up my marks so I can go to Harvard. You'd like that."

"Once I would have. Now I know no school will accept you. Harvard certainly won't. There's only one course, son."

The use of the word *son* and William's milder tone raised fresh hope in Alan. The old man was weakening. Maybe he could still pull this off. "I'm nineteen, father. Maybe I could enter the business. Learn how to handle it, start at the bottom. I promise I'd work hard, sir."

"Nineteen. The same age as George was when he went to Canada and enlisted."

Alan's uninjured eye slid warily sideways. He studied his father. The old man looked as though he'd been carved from marble. "You aren't considering—"

"Our country is at war and your brother gave his life for that war. As soon as your face heals enough that you won't shame me, you're enlisting."

"No. I might be killed. *Father.*"

"I understand that the army either makes or breaks a man. We'll see what it does to you."

"I won't." Alan struck the seat with a clenched fist. "You can't force me."

"Don't fight me, son." With a touch of grim humor William added, "Save that for the enemy."

Alan knew he had lost and Elizabeth, much to her delight, soon knew he had too. She hoped Alan would shortly be sent to the Western Front and the Germans would solve her problem with William's younger son. But he had an unknown deity looking after him too. Perhaps one who was kind to liars and cowards. He spent the war years not on the Western Front but in a quartermaster's corps in Kansas. It was an ideal location for a young man with his qualifications. He made money from stealing supplies and, learning from past experience, did it so skillfully he was never caught. He was even wounded but managed to hide this from his father. Alan conceived a passion for the young wife of a middle-aged farmer and was caught in a barn humping the girl. There was no time to pull on his uniform and he took off over the fields. As the farmer later boasted, hitting a bull's eye on that big white ass with his shotgun was as easy as shooting ducks in a barrel. Alan's buddies arrived at the hospital bearing a star cut from cardboard, plastered with ribbons, and bearing neat letters conferring on him the Order of the Flying Fuck.

While Alan Meredith fornicated and stole in Kansas, America went to war.

— 16 —

Elizabeth knelt on the landing beside the bannister arranging white and purple lilacs in the pottery urn. Inhaling their dewy fragrance, she picked up the last bough. Sally ran lightly up the stairs and puased to watch her mistress. "My, but they smell good, miss." She rolled her eyes dramatically. "I just came from the kitchen and Cookie and Gerda are having a real set-to."

Elizabeth pulled herself to her feet, stepped back, and critically eyed the flowers. "What about?"

"Don't know, miss. Stuck my head in and then left fast. Cookie don't often get her dander up but when she does—whew. Think you'd better get down before they start pulling hair."

Before Elizabeth pushed open the baize door she could hear Cookie bellowing. "What's going on here?"

Cookie, her face flushed and her usually neat hair looking as though she'd been running fingers through it, swung around. "Miss Elizabeth, is my word law in this room or not?"

Gerda was standing like a ramrod. "I didn't do nothing, miss. Not one thing. All I said was—"

"Don't you go saying it again. Putting a hex on us, that's what you're doing. Bringing bad luck down on this house."

Elizabeth flung her hands up. "Both of you calm down. Tell me what this is about." They both started to talk and she said sharply. "One at a time. Gerda?"

"All I said was bad things come in threes. We've had two and we're gonna have another one soon."

"What bad things?"

Gerda's lower lip protruded sullenly. "Can't say the name, miss, you forbade me to say her name."

"Oh." The maid was thinking of Judith. "And the second, I suppose, was George's death."

"Struck down in his prime by a bolt of lightning, miss."

"Hardly. Men do get killed in war."

"Gonna be a third. Feel it in my bones, I do."

Cookie let out an agonized wail and Elizabeth remembered that the cook's superstition more than matched the fervor of Gerda's religion. "That's enough," she told the maid. "Cookie's quite right. We'll have no more nonsense like that. And I'll allow no more gossiping about this family."

"I'm not a gossip, miss. All I said was—"

"Not one more word!"

Cookie looked gratified and started to straighten her ruffled hair. But storm warnings showed in Gerda's sullen face, a dull unbecoming red seeping over her broad cheeks. Elizabeth stifled a sigh. She'd have to smooth down the maid's ruffled feathers. She held out a small olive branch. "How's that nice young man of yours?" She was being charitable. Gerda's boyfriend was neither nice nor young. The previous autumn he'd come to see the maid and had waited for her in the kitchen. He was a wiry little gent who looked more like the girl's father than her suitor. Joshua wore an ancient serge suit with pant legs short enough to expose the tops of huge boots, and sleeves baring thick red wrists and huge hands. Both hands and feet were out of proportion to the thin body. When Elizabeth had met him he was reading a Bible, his lips moving, and the eyes he'd lifted to her blazed with the zeal of a fanatic.

"Joshua's all right," Gerda muttered.

Elizabeth couldn't have cared less about Joshua but she had

to care about Gerda. Maids with grudges could be trouble-makers. Gently she teased the girl. "Are we soon going to be shopping for wedding presents?"

An odd expression flashed across the broad face. Dread? "Not for a while, Miss Elizabeth."

"Your Joshua told me he has a little farm."

"Near Albany. But Joshua's the sole support of his ma and three young brothers. His dad passed over when he was just a boy. We'd like to be together but I'd only be another mouth to feed."

"That's too bad but I'm sure it will work out."

"You don't know nothing about life, Miss Elizabeth." Gerda waved an expressive hand. "Most people don't live like this. Most of us don't get enough to keep soul and body together."

Was she being impertinent? Elizabeth wondered. No, Gerda was only saying something she sincerely believed. But then, the maid had no memory of poor Cousin Elizabeth smuggling left-overs home to a dingy room, so she simply murmured, "I know what it is to be poor and hungry."

"'Deed she does," Cookie chimed in. "That's what makes Miss Elizabeth so good and kind."

Having restored harmony to the kitchen, she went her way laughing. A hex!

Two days later she stopped laughing. She was in the butler's pantry working on her accounts when Gerda stuck a triumphant face around the door. "Told you so, miss. A man brought her back. She's in the hall."

"She? Who are you talking about?"

"Can't say the name, miss."

Elizabeth, her heart thudding painfully, was on her feet. "Mrs. Meredith?"

Gerda's cap shook violently enough to make the ribbons fly. "The other one."

With Gerda at her heels she ran down the hall. Near the door a man in a checkered jacket was standing. In one hand he clutched a greasy leather cap; the other held the hand of a little girl. The child had red gold ringlets and wide violet eyes. The man shuffled his feet but didn't relinquish the child's hand. "You Miss Elizabeth Meredith, ma'am?"

"Yes."

"Woman told me to bring this kid here. So I—"

"*Who* are you?"

"Drive a taxi, ma'am. Wouldn't take a kid this age as fare but didn't get a chance to say no. Woman pushed an envelope and a dollar bill at me and while I was looking at them she shoved the kid in the back and ran off. Here, guess this is for you."

Tucking the cap under an arm, he fished in a pocket. Elizabeth took the crumpled envelope, realized Gerda was breathing down her neck, and snapped, "Get back to your work."

She waited until the maid stalked down the hall before she looked at the envelope. In Judith's tiny writing was her name and the address. She tore it open. A single sheet of paper and a few words. "Elizabeth, take care of Mariette. I'm sorry. Judith." The signature was a scrawl.

The taxi driver was watching her uneasily. "You know this kid, ma'am? Don't mean to pry but I got a girl about the same age. Wouldn't want to put her in the wrong hands. No offense, ma'am."

"Very decent of you to be concerned. Yes, I know the child. Her name's Mariette and in a way she's related to this family." Elizabeth took a deep breath. "Please help me. Where did you pick up the child? Did you see where the woman went? What did she look like?"

His low brow furrowed in thought. "Picked her up at the corner of East Third and First. Young woman flagged me down. Tall with light hair and—"

"How was she dressed?"

He looked down at Mariette. "Like her, ma'am. Shabby."

Elizabeth nodded. The child's clothes were clean but shoddy and patched. "Go on."

"Nuthin' much to tell. Like I said she flags me down, pushes the money and that envelope at me, and before I know it she's got the kid in the back and takes off at a run. I holler at her but she disappeared in the crowd. Didn't know what to do. First off I figure I'll take the kid to the police station but then I thought, no, I'll bring her here and see what the place is like. Looks okay to me."

"We're not kidnappers or white slavers," Elizabeth told him crisply. She found her purse and handed him a bill. "This is for your trouble."

He took his hand from the child's clasp and she grabbed at his jacket and clung to it. "Sure took a fancy to me. Prettiest kid I ever did see. You'll look after her right?"

"She's in good hands." Elizabeth opened the door and he left. She called Gerda. "Take Mariette up to Tosh."

Scooping the child up, Gerda hugged her. "Hush now, sweetie. Come with Gerda."

As soon as the door had shut after the taxi driver Mariette had started to wail but before Gerda reached the bend of the stairs a chubby hand was playing with the ribbons on her cap. Elizabeth felt like wailing herself. It looked as though Gerda's hex was working. Something was terribly wrong and she had to locate Judith. She stretched out a hand toward the telephone to call William and then pulled it back. He would have no idea where she was. Who might have? Then she decided there was only one person in the city who might have kept track of Judith.

She called the Vandercourt number, breathed a sigh of relief when she was told Mrs. Vandercourt was shopping, asked for Sophie, and asked, "Where is Judith?"

"How would I know?"

"You're the only one she might be in touch with."

"Even if I do know, why should I tell you?"

"Because she may be in trouble."

"She's been in trouble since you threw her out."

"*I* didn't throw her out. Sophie, you must tell me. She sent Mariette to me, and a note. She asked me to care for the baby and she said she was sorry."

Elizabeth heard the intake of Sophie's breath and then the woman whispered, "I'll be right over."

Elizabeth didn't wait in the house. She put on a hat and picked up her purse. When Sophie climbed out of the taxi Elizabeth was standing beside the Panhard, her foot beating out an impatient tattoo. Sophie had dressed hastily, a coil of mousy hair was working loose and a pink slip showed under the hem of her skirt.

Elizabeth wasted no time on greetings. "Where is she?"

"First I want to see that note." Pushing up heavy glasses on her nose, Sophie read it. "This is Judith's writing but her signature . . ."

"The address."

When Sophie gave it Briggs shook an obstinate head. "Can't take you down there without Mr. Meredith's say-so. That's on the Lower East Side."

Drawing herself up to her full height, Elizabeth said icily, "You have the address. Drive as fast as possible."

"Mr. Meredith—"

"Right now you're taking orders from me, Briggs. Drive."

Sophie had already slid into the tonneau. Climbing in beside her, Elizabeth regarded the back of Briggs's head. His thick neck was flushed a brick red but he obeyed her order without further argument. She glanced at Sophie, noticed her eyes were damp, and asked, "Have you visited Judith there?"

"No."

"How long have you been in touch with her?"

"About six months."

Stifling the impulse to reach over and shake the woman, Elizabeth said tartly, "I'm not going to coax answers from you. If anything happens to Judith—"

"She telephoned me. Asked me to meet her downtown. She was dreadfully shabby. Told me she'd sold everything she had left. Most of her clothes. I've been giving her all I could. Mother doesn't let me have much allowance but I gave it all to Judith. I pawned all my jewelry, the pearls father gave me and a couple of rings." Pushing her glasses up, Sophie dabbed at wet eyes. "Judith looks so awful. Thin and haggard. I don't think she's getting enough to eat."

"Has her mother sneaked her any help?"

"That's the first place she went when you . . . when William kicked her out. Mrs. Arnold wouldn't even let her or Mariette into the house, wouldn't give her any money. She said if she did William would cut her allowance off."

"Hasn't Lafe Norton helped her and the child?"

"The last time I saw her I asked her that. After all, he's responsible. Judith didn't answer. All she said was when he came back Mariette and she would be fine. She said he promised to take them away, give them a good home where no one would know about the scandal. When Judith talked about him she seemed so happy." Sophie blew her nose. "Can't we go faster?"

"Briggs is driving as fast as he dares." Elizabeth patted the other spinster's bony knee. "Don't cry. Perhaps we're panicking over nothing. It's possible Judith simply couldn't look after the child any longer. She believes I'll do all I can for Mariette."

Having offered this consolation Elizabeth stared from the window. She could see why the chauffeur had balked. They were rolling along a street that filled her with horror. She knew areas like this existed but she'd never had cause to enter one before. Saloons, pawnshops, secondhand stores, and run-down shops lined cracked pavement. Even the people looked different. There were young men flashily and cheaply dressed, laborers in worn clothes, women in ragged dresses and shawls, other women turning brightly painted faces boldly toward the shining car.

Briggs turned down another street, narrow and covered with filth. Pushcarts lined it, along the curbstone children played in muck, beside the entrances to houses overflowing garbage cans stood. Judith, Elizabeth thought. Judith with her translucent skin and dainty blond beauty on a street like this. Judith with her perfumed body and satins and brocades . . .

"Elizabeth!" Sophie cried.

The car had pulled to a stop in front of a six-story building. Fire escapes draped with bedding clung like iron spider webs to dingy brick. Picking up the speaking tube, Briggs pointed a finger. "That's it. Still want to go in?"

In answer Elizabeth opened the door and stepped out. Rubbish cascaded from an overturned garbage can. "Watch your feet," she warned Sophie. Smells hit her and she nearly gagged. Some of the urchins crowded around the car, staring at the gleaming metal work, the immaculate upholstery, Briggs's gray livery and black leather puttees. Briggs shooed them away and turned a sullen, disgusted face on Elizabeth. "Want me to go in with you?"

She took another look at the building and decided it might be a good idea. Jerking her head, she led the way up the steps. In the dark, foul-smelling hallway she paused and looked around. Briggs moved past Sophie. "Janitor'll have a place down here. Better let me do the talking. Could be a surly cuss."

"You find him and I'll do the talking."

The chauffeur found him and as the man opened his door a

crack she admitted Briggs had been right. He wore grimy underwear, his braces sagging down over his pants. He had a narrow mean face and eyes to match. A strong odor of garlic and beer surrounded him as his narrow eyes insolently looked the women up and down and then shifted to Briggs. "Yuh got the wrong place. This ain't the Plaza, buddy."

"We're looking for one of your tenants," Elizabeth told him. "What name?"

Biting at her lower lip, she considered. What would Judith call herself? Certainly not Meredith. She turned toward Sophie but the other woman shook her head. "Arnold?" she hazarded.

"Ain't no one here of that name." The door started to close and Briggs stuck a boot out and stopped it. The janitor glared up at him. "None of that. Yuh got no right busting in here, yuh bastard—"

The words were cut off abruptly as Briggs reached out hands like hams, grabbed the narrow shoulders, and shook him. "Keep a civil tongue in your head and answer the lady's questions."

"I'll have the police on yuh!"

"Leave him alone," Elizabeth ordered. She pulled out a dollar bill and extended it.

The bill was pulled from her grasp and the man's lips drew back over discolored teeth. "That's more like it but there still ain't anybody here called Arnold."

"The woman we're looking for is young and tall and blond. She has a child around two with red hair—"

"Oh, that'll be the stuck-up bit—" The janitor shot a look at Briggs's glowering face and added hastily, "That's the woman on the second floor. Calls herself Mrs. Brown. Saw her come in a while ago and tried to catch her to tell her she's late with the rent again but she shot upstairs in one hell of a hurry. Didn't see the kid with her."

Sophie tugged at Elizabeth's arm. "Let's get up there."

They climbed stairs littered with filth, and the higher they went the stronger the stench got. At the top a door sagged open and Elizabeth saw a toilet. Like the garbage pail this was overflowing. Stepping over a puddle she held her breath. Her stomach churned and she tasted bile at the back of her throat. She heard Sophie moaning softly.

"Back that way," a man's voice called.

She looked over her shoulder. The janitor, his eyes avid with curiosity, was tagging along behind Briggs. She picked her way down the dark hallway and knocked on the door he pointed at. No one answered. "Should be in there," the janitor grunted. "Saw her running up them stairs like something was chasing her."

Elizabeth turned the knob. Locked. "Have you a pass key?"

He pulled a ring of keys from his pocket. "Right here but ain't using it. No call to. If she wants to see yuh she can open the door." Narrow eyes fastened on Elizabeth's purse. "'Course for another buck . . ."

Elizabeth lifted her chin and told Briggs, "Break it down."

"Okay, lady, you win. But I'm gonna have the police on yuh." Still grumbling, the man selected a key and unlocked the door. He stepped back and so did Sophie and the chauffeur.

Elizabeth swung the door open and entered the room. It looked clean and fresh air streamed through an open window. It was also bare. Against one wall a bench supported a hot plate and a few cracked dishes. In the middle of the floor was a rickety table and one chair. Pushed back in an alcove was an iron bedstead covered with a blue blanket. She heard Briggs mutter a curse, she heard Sophie's stifled scream, she walked stiffly over to the bed.

Judith lay on her back, her arms thrown out, her legs straight and close together. Blond hair was braided tightly around the small skull. Her hands were turned palms up. Both wrists were slashed and the blanket under them was sodden with blood. Violet eyes stared up at the discolored ceiling. The wide brow, uptilted nose, rounded chin, looked as though they'd been carved from alabaster.

Elizabeth stood as though she too had been turned to stone. It was Sophie who sank to her knees, touched the brow, the base of the throat. She fumbled in her purse and held a compact mirror over marble lips. "Too late," she said simply and tenderly closed staring eyes.

Elizabeth was conscious of the janitor's muttering, of Briggs swearing in a monotone, of Sophie's stricken face. She managed to turn away from the bed and spotted two objects on the table, an envelope and a gold locket. She took a few steps, scooped them up, and stuck them in her purse. Then she called to the janitor, "Is there a telephone in this building?"

His insolence had vanished. "Owner had one put in my room. You gotta call the police, lady. Tell them I didn't have nothin' to do with this. Sure, I pushed her for the rent but the owner's always on my back and—"

"You come with me. Briggs, Sophie, you stay up here. In the hall if you'd rather."

She followed the man along the hall, down the stairs. No longer did she see the squalor, smell the rottenness. In the janitor's room she saw nothing but the black telephone. "Out," she ordered. "Wait in the hall. Close the door."

The door closed behind him but she kept her voice down as she gave the operator the number of William's office. Miss Patterson put him on immediately. "Elizabeth? I'm very busy. Is something wrong at home?"

"An emergency. Judith's committed suicide. She slit her wrists. She sent Mariette to the house and—"

"Get a grip on yourself. Where are you?" She gave him the address. "Is anyone with you?"

"Briggs and Sophie Vandercourt. They're upstairs with . . . with Judith."

"You haven't called the police?"

"No."

"Thank God! Let me think."

She clung to the phone, her knuckles white from pressure. It seemed hours before he said, "Get Briggs and Sophie and get out of there."

"William, I can't. I can't leave her like that in this horrible—"

"Listen to me! It's imperative you leave. If it reaches the papers, think of the scandal. This must be handled with discretion. The police commissioner is a member of my club. I'll speak with him immediately and someone will be there to take care of it."

"But we found her. Sophie and Briggs and I. The janitor was with us. He'll talk."

"The janitor will be handled." Her cousin's voice was cold and clear. "Will Sophie talk?"

"I don't think so. She loves . . . she loved Judith."

For the first time since she'd picked up the phone his voice softened. "We all loved her, Elizabeth. Please, for my sake, for Alicia's sake, leave."

Elizabeth bowed her head and obeyed.

The old boys' network really works, Elizabeth thought as she sat at the escritoire in her room clipping an item from a newspaper. It was exactly three weeks after the day she'd stood looking down at Judith's body and in that time the potential scandal had been buried as deep as Judith. The only indication of the suicide was the item she was clipping from the back page of the paper. It contained just a few lines. A woman identified as a Mrs. J. Brown had been found dead at such an address. She had taken her life while apparently of unsound mind. Police were notifying next of kin.

The funeral had been held and Judith Arnold Meredith now rested under a marker calling her Mrs. J. Brown. Other than Sophie and Elizabeth, only a minister with a head cold and a couple of grave diggers had been present. The flowers were as sparse as the mourners. Sophie placed a handful of pink carnations on the coffin and Elizabeth had bought a cross made of tiny yellow roses. While the minister wiped at his nose and mumbled a hasty burial service, Sophie had stood on one side of the grave, Elizabeth on the other. As the two spinsters rode silently home Elizabeth wondered at Sophie's stoicism. Recalling Sophie's easy tears, she marveled at the lack of them. From the moment they'd discovered the body she hadn't seen the woman shed one.

As Briggs pulled up in front of her home, Sophie turned a grim face to her companion. "She shouldn't have died. Judith was a truly beautiful person. Not just in looks but in nature. William forced her out but I know he wouldn't have done it without my mother. She's the one I blame. Mother is a cruel woman. She ruined my life and now she's ruining my brother's. Earl doesn't want to be a banker but mother has spoken and that's what he's doing." Opening the door, Sophie slid out. Behind the lenses her weak eyes blazed with hate. "Mother's going to pay for this. Elizabeth, I swear I'll make her pay." Before she turned away she asked one pathetic question. "But *why* did Judith kill herself?"

Putting the shears aside, Elizabeth stared down at the clipping. She could tell Sophie why Judith had taken her life. The answer to that was in the letter left beside the gold locket. William Meredith and Aunt Van shouldn't pay the price for the girl's death. Lafcadio Norton was directly responsible.

Elizabeth opened the secret drawer in the dressing table. In it was a pack of cigarettes, the locket, and an envelope addressed to Mrs. J. Brown. She didn't bother rereading it. It was short, not a love letter but coldly businesslike. Lafe had told Judith he wasn't coming back to New York. He gave her the reason. There was no way on a reporter's salary he could look after a wife and child decently. He reassured her about her own future. A beautiful woman, Lafe said, could easily find a wealthy protector. As for himself, he too must find a protector. He was going to be married. Not for love, but for the security a wealthy wife could offer. "I'm a writer," Lafe wrote, "a man who has a duty to the public. My fiancée isn't young or even pretty. Anne Louise is five years my senior and has a face like a well-bred horse. But she's a wealthy woman and she adores me." He closed the letter with the only touch of sentiment in it. "My heart will always belong to you, Judith." He didn't mention Mariette.

Clipping the item about Judith's death to Lafe's heartless letter, she slid them into the secret drawer of the dressing table. Then she went to the window and with clouded eyes looked down at the street. She couldn't see properly because her eyes were blurred with tears. They rolled down her cheeks but she made no effort to wipe them away. Futile tears, she thought, tears for her own part in the girl's terrible death. Between Lafe and her they had driven Judith to that sordid death. As she wept, the last lingering traces of affection for Lafe melted away and were replaced with a darker emotion. Lafe was a man she'd known for only a short time, a man without the slightest sense of honor.

Love doesn't stop, she mused, it slips gradually away and sometimes is replaced with a feeling much like hatred. Someday, Lafe . . . someday I hope you pay for this.

— 17 —

After a time Elizabeth was able to shut the odious memory of Lafe Norton from her mind, but she wasn't able to relegate Judith to oblivion. She tried to reason with her conscience. She'd only wanted the girl out of the house, she certainly hadn't wanted her to live like that or to die like that. But as Elizabeth moved through the house she fancied she was dogged by a misty, plaintive ghost mutely reproaching her. There was only one way to exorcise that pathetic shade and try to ease her mind. She had to make every effort to see that justice was done to Judith's small daughter.

Mariette was still in the nursery with Alicia but the child was only there on sufferance. William had no intention of sheltering the child and for that Elizabeth didn't blame him. To raise the child in the Meredith house would only awaken the specter of scandal and rumor. Elizabeth wondered how long it would be before her cousin raised the issue, and that evening she found the time had come. Shortly after dinner William sent for her.

She found him in the study, a book open before him, a glass of brandy in one hand. His expression was much the same as the pictured likeness of their grandfather—chilly and unrevealing. Whether he felt grief for Judith she didn't know. Except when it was necessary to give her details about the funeral, he hadn't once mentioned his young wife. But his fringe of hair was now completely white and he'd aged. Also, shortly after Judith's death, he'd come home with a strange purchase. It was an object d'art, a quattrocento madonna with a gold background. William had hung it himself, opposite his bed, where once he'd placed a photograph of Judith. Elizabeth had hunted in vain for a likeness to the lovely Judith in the madonna's dark face.

Putting aside his book, William rose and poured sherry for her. As he gave her the glass he came immediately to the point. "The child must go, and the sooner the better. I've checked out a couple of orphanages. The one in Queens where the children from Lavinia's home are sent and another on Long Island near New Rochelle. I've decided on the latter."

"They're dreadful places."

"Not as bad as you imagine. The children are treated decently. Adequately fed and clothed. One can't expect a home atmosphere for foundlings. Because of the way the child was sent to you I know you feel responsibility, but you understand it is imperative she leave."

Elizabeth bent her head and stared into the depths of her glass. "I agree but . . ."

"Tell me your thoughts."

There was no use in pleading for the baby. That wouldn't move her cousin. She tried a different tack. "I'm not thinking of Mariette. I'm considering you and your reputation. If your friends find out you've banished the child to an orphanage they may think less of you. Consider you a mean and vindictive man."

"How would they know? None of them even knows about . . . the mother's death. No one knows the child is here."

"The servants know Mariette was sent to us. No matter how we try to hide it they'll know if she's sent to an orphanage. And servants talk."

He raised his brows. "You think our staff would be that disloyal?"

Elizabeth didn't think that for a moment. After the talk and threats she'd made she knew none of the servants would dare. Time for a good lie, she thought. "Certainly they're loyal but it's their nature to gossip. Aunt Van's cook and the Flanderses' servants may hear. It will spread like wildfire."

Rubbing his chin, he said thoughtfully, "What other course is open to us?"

"I've no idea but if you give me a little time perhaps I can work something out. If I find no answer we can put the child into an orphanage."

He picked up his book. "You have two weeks. After that I'll take it into my own hands."

It didn't take two weeks. The next morning Elizabeth found the cook grumbling to the kitchen maid. "What's wrong, Cookie?" she asked.

"That Gerda again. Says she isn't well enough to come down

this morning. Third time this month she's laid in bed and we've had to do her work. You'll have to send Sally down to help."

"Gerda's never been sick before. What's her problem, Cookie?"

"She don't say, Miss Elizabeth, but if I was you I'd give her her walking papers."

This remark from tenderhearted Cookie shocked Elizabeth. Granted Gerda and the cook had their differences but such harshness was out of character. "Fix a breakfast tray and I'll take it up for her."

Elizabeth found Gerda huddled under layers of blankets. The other servants had made their rooms attractive with cushions, knickknacks, and family pictures, but Gerda's room looked like a nun's. All that had been added were a leather-covered Bible on a table and a garishly colored picture of the Crucifixion. The maid's wide face was drained of its usual fresh color and as Elizabeth put the tray down she feebly waved it away. "Not hungry, miss. It's good of you to trouble but my stomach's fair heaving."

Pulling up a chair, Elizabeth sat down beside the bed. "At least you're having tea. Cookie made it the way you like it, good and strong."

Gerda sipped tea and then made a face and hastily reached for the slop jar. As she retched Elizabeth found the answer to Cookie's heartless attitude. She waited until the girl sank back and then asked, "You're in trouble, aren't you?"

"No, miss, I ain't in trouble. I'm a decent God-fearing woman."

Gerda never lied, Elizabeth thought, but perhaps she was giving a literal answer. She worded the question a different way. "You are pregnant?"

"I am, but I'm not in trouble. I'm married and have been since Mr. Meredith gave me time off in the spring. My man and I were churched proper."

Elizabeth recalled that Gerda's Joshua couldn't feed all the mouths he had now and soon he would have two more. She knew the reason Gerda had married secretly. William refused to employ married servants and the maid would lose a much needed wage. This might be the answer to finding a home for Judith's daughter. Tears were running down Gerda's pale cheeks. "Now you'll tell the master and he'll send me away. I don't know what we're going to do. Could you . . . would you not tell him for a bit? Let me earn more money to help my Joshua."

"That would be the same as lying. With your beliefs you can't expect me to do that. I'd like to help you. You're a good girl and have worked hard. Maybe there is a way. How would you like to go home, be with your husband, have your baby, and still receive your wages every month?"

Gerda sat up, her eyes widening. "How, miss?"

"You do like children?"

"'Course I do."

"Mariette needs a good home and Christian people to raise her. Mr. Meredith not only would continue to pay your salary but he'd also provide clothing and anything extra for the child. This would help you and your husband." Elizabeth mentally crossed her fingers hoping William would agree.

"I don't know, miss. Her being born in sin and all. I'd be willing but my Joshua is pretty strict."

"Ask him. Write him now and ask."

Laboriously, Gerda wrote her husband and Elizabeth posted the letter. The answer didn't come by mail. Four days later Joshua sat in the drawing room, perched on the velvet-covered loveseat with his wife by his side. Gerda, clad in Quaker gray and an old fashioned bonnet, loomed over him but Joshua dominated the room. He sat bolt upright, attired again in the serge suit and a collarless white shirt. A Bible poked from his coat pocket and he balanced a black, low-crowned hat on his knee.

"I come as soon as I got my wife's letter," he told Elizabeth. "But before I left I went to my pastor for advice. He told me to talk to the Lord so's I went down on my knees and did just that. The Lord spake to me and says, Joshua, that child was born of scarlet sinners, abominations in Mine eyes—"

"Does that mean," Elizabeth interrupted, "you won't take the child?"

Fire flared in the man's eyes. "Don't hasten the Lord's words, woman! The Lord says to me . . ." Joshua went into details of a long and complicated conversation with that deity ending on rather an obscure note. "Last words He spake were, Joshua, go ye forth and bring My lambs back into the fold." He paused expectantly but a bemused Elizabeth waited to hear what this signified. "So . . . take the child I will. But I warn you I will not abide interference with my raising of the girl. She shall be raised as my own children will be in the word of the Lord my God. I shall feed and clothe her as one of my own. She shall work but not beyond her strength. If I must I shall chastise her—"

"I will not have her beaten," Elizabeth said crisply.

"I do not beat, woman, I chastise. For the good of her soul it may be necessary as the Devil may abide within her." Having disposed of his Lord's will he proceeded to mention a more mundane subject with all the guile of a Yankee trader. "My wife mentioned a sum of money above and beyond her wages. How much will you allow me?"

Elizabeth mentioned the amount and his eyes flashed. "Not enough. Far too little for the work I must do with her."

Elizabeth considered how to handle him. On one hand she was faced with a thrifty William, on the other with an equally thrifty Joshua. She glanced at Gerda's broad face and decided there was no help from that direction. Obviously she was overawed by her small fierce mate. Then Elizabeth lifted her chin haughtily. "I had hoped to place the child with Gerda and you. You are Christians and that influenced my decision. My terms are fair and if you refuse them I shall have no difficulty in finding another family to take the baby in." Shrewdly, she pointed out, "I shouldn't think a merciful God would have urged you to barter money for a child's soul."

His low brow under short bristly hair furrowed in thought and one calloused hand caressed his Bible. Then he bobbed his head. "Through your mouth the Lord has spoken. I will take the child on your terms and rear her."

She pressed her advantage. "You have stated your position and I agree with it. Now I'll give you mine. Twice a year, in June and December, I'll visit your home for a few hours to see her. Also, she must never know the surname she now has, nor of this family."

"Do you promise not to interfere with my raising?" When Elizabeth nodded he said, "Then we are agreed. What name does the child bear?"

"Mariette Annabel."

"Names bespeaking vanity. Her name must be changed."

"Call her anything you wish." For an instant Elizabeth saw her hand holding Judith's hatpin. "Daisy is a good name," she told him.

"Daisy." His thin lips writhed as though he was tasting the name. "A flower. There may be vanity there."

"Joshua." For the first time since the interview had begun Gerda timidly spoke. "My own aunt is called Daisy and she's a good Christian."

Darting a glance at his wife, he nodded. "I shall call her Daisy and will give her my own name. Henceforth she shall be known as Daisy Huggins."

"It has a good ring," Elizabeth said demurely.

The bargain struck, Joshua made a lengthy prayer and the baby was brought down. With Joshua and Gerda, Judith's daughter, now known as Daisy Huggins, left to begin a new life. When William was told he breathed a sigh of relief and without argument agreed to pay the sum needed. He had two terms of his own. "I'll provide for the child until she reaches sixteen and not a day longer. I don't want to know where she is or with whom she lives. You've insisted on this move and if there are difficulties you must handle them. Do you understand?"

Elizabeth understood.

After the United States entered the war in April of 1917 it moved rapidly to raise and transport overseas a strong military force known as the American Expeditionary Force. It was under the command of General John J. Pershing. By June 175,000 American troops were training in France and one division was in the lines of the Allied sector near Belfort. By November of 1918 the strength of the A.E.F. was two million.

America was singing and its doughboys were singing. As they tumbled off troopships at Le Havre they sang "Over There," "How You Gonna Keep Them down on the Farm," and "Mademoiselle from Armentieres." The mademoiselles were waiting. They gave doughboys flowers, warm bodies, in some cases, clap. The soldiers saw "Paree" but many never returned to the farm. Their blood mingled with that shed before them and soaked into the alien soil of ancient battlefields.

In this war patriotism was the watchword. For love of country, for the preservation of their way of life, for a war that would end all wars, they went to battle. On two counts they were wrong. Other wars would follow, and the gentle, slow-paced life they valued vanished during the next two years. When the survivors of the A.E.F. returned to America they found to their shock and bewilderment that their way of life was dead and in its place was the madness and frenzy of the Roaring Twenties.

PART II
Family Matters

— 18 —

The Roaring Twenties actually began in 1918 and ushered in an epoch resembling a roller coaster ride to damnation. Prohibition led to a great increase in gangsterism and drove millions of citizens to habitual law-breaking. Professional criminals soon discovered the wealth to be had in supplying alcohol to the masses and quickly drove most of the amateurs from the arena.

The Lost Generation, returning from the trenches, were bewildered by a world gone mad with sexual freedom and indulgence in vice. Their women were bobbing their hair, raising their hem lines, lowering their morals. Thousands of roadhouses, blind pigs, speakeasies mushroomed and funneled money directly into the pockets of racketeers.

Some young people refrained from joining this wide open life-style, and many came to it reluctantly, but it was then that the Alan Merediths finally came into their own.

In 1918 when Alan returned from exile in Kansas he went about fence-mending with his father. William, still wary after the debacle at his son's school, consented to take him into the family business but gave him only limited responsibility and watched his every move. Alan was careful to give the older man no cause for complaint. He worked harder than he ever had in his life. Time, he assured himself, was on his side. With Cousin Elizabeth the young man was equally cautious. No longer was she simply an underpaid servant. She now acted as mistress of the house and mother of Alan's young half-sister. He realized that during his absence Elizabeth had firmly consolidated her position with his father and William was now much influenced by her. As much as possible Alan avoided her but when they were thrown together he managed to be civil. She responded in much the same manner and outwardly all seemed harmonious. Behind the unspoken truce they watched each other like boxers weighing up an opponent and seeking chinks in the other's guard.

Having lulled his father into a sense of security at work, Alan proceeded lustily with his private life. With the proceeds of his thievery from the army he bought a Stutz Bearcat and made the rounds of the more fashionable speakeasies. His one disappointment was that he couldn't join in the consumption of alcohol. In Kansas he'd tried to keep up with his booze-swilling buddies but after a couple of disastrous drunks found he was violently allergic to liquor. Not only did he break out in a rash but his heart palpitated and breathing was difficult. As an army doctor told him bluntly, "Keep on drinking and you'll die." Alan had no intention of endangering his precious hide so he consoled himself with sex. Everywhere girls were for the taking, nubile and curvaceous and scantily clothed. He wallowed in sex, gorging himself on warm bodies and slick young skin. For a time he was indiscriminate but as the sexual feast continued he became somewhat jaded. Willing girls ceased to interest him and he turned to others harder to get. It became a game. He titillated himself with conquests of the reluctant, and delighted in deflowering virgins. With a combination of good looks, the flashy car, and the Meredith name, he hunted prey successfully. One evening in a speakeasy called the Dead End he met his match.

That night his companions were Ronnie Grant and Aunt Van's son Earl. Ronnie had served overseas and had been wounded. He still limped slightly from shrapnel in his right leg, a limp girls deemed romantic. All of them, even the mousy Earl Vandercourt, were in high spirits. They entered the mortuary, opened the lid of a huge mahogany casket that appeared to be propped against a wall, pressed a buzzer concealed in chaste white satin, and waited while an eye peered at them through a peephole. The satin back, cunningly made into a narrow door, swung open and they entered the speakeasy. Jazz and smoke and liquor fumes belched out to greet them, Friends waved but the young men disregarded their invitations and took a table near the stage. The other two ordered drinks. The only people in New York who knew of Alan's allergy were his father and Cousin Elizabeth. He managed to conceal what he considered an unmanly weakness by carrying his own flask, filled either with water or cold tea, and pretended to scorn bathtub gin and cheap whiskey.

Earl Vandercourt dashed down a glassful of gin and was immediately sloshed. The others watched him with amusement. On the stage a comedian in baggy pants and a straw hat was trying to work through a routine of stale jokes but the audience booed and catcalled. Ronnie gave him a disgusted look and yelled, "Bring on the girls."

Howls of approval rang out and the band burst into a Charleston. As the comedian retired, five girls bounced onto the stage, madly jerking up their knees and wriggling round bottoms. Alan had never seen any of them before and he looked them over critically. They wore short fringed dresses, flesh-colored stockings, and beaded headbands around bobbed hair. Two were redheads, two brunettes, one a platinum blond. More easy pussy, Alan decided, nothing here for him. He poured cold tea from his silver flask.

"Wow!" Ronnie's face lit up. "Get a load of that little redhead in blue."

Banging down an empty glass, Earl flagged a waiter. He hiccuped and said shrilly, "You're out a country mile, Ronnie. Blondie's the pick of the litter."

The band swung into the Black Bottom and the girls gyrated madly. Cuban heels clicked, satin-clad hips swung, fringes flew, flesh jiggled. Alan's predatory eyes slid over them and hesitated on the blond. Her build was perfect for the current fashion, practically no breasts, boyish hips, long slender legs. Then the other girls fell in behind her and she moved to the mike. In a breathless little voice she began to sing "The Bells of St. Mary's." Ordinarily a war song would have been hooted down but something about this girl kept the audience in line. It certainly isn't her voice, Alan mused, she can hold a tune and that's about all. Then he spotted the reason. Despite the peroxided hair, the show-girl makeup, the revealing clothes, she had a quality of freshness, of innocence.

He waited until the song was finished and the girls had pranced into the wings before he jerked his head at a waiter. "That blond," he told the man. "Tell her I'll buy her a drink."

The waiter's fleshy face broke into a wide grin. "Wasting your time, mister, and mine. She don't date."

"Customers?"

"No one." He closed an eye in a lewd wink. "Had a try myself but no dice. Fresh in from Iowa and not putting out. Better have a go at the little redhead. She's a hot tomato."

Alan handed him a bill. "Deliver my message."

The answer came in moments. The grinning waiter delivered it with relish. "Said for you to peddle your papers."

Both Ronnie and Earl brayed with delight. "Our sheik of Araby just struck out," Ronnie hooted.

"You can say that again," Earl agreed.

Alan wasn't amused. A flush worked up his round cheeks and he bit his heavy lower lip. If it took a year he'd lay that bottle blond. From then on he haunted the Dead End. He brought flowers and candy and sent them with his card backstage. The girl, who was called Dania Delong, a name probably as phony as the color of her hair, kept the gifts and told him to shove off. The news of his vain pursuit spread and Alan found himself the butt of jokes and sniggers. He couldn't stop. Night after night he came to the speakeasy, night after night she performed and didn't even glance at him.

He bribed a waiter and got her address. One evening as she left for work Dania found the Stutz Bearcat parked in front of her rooming house. "Taxi, lady?" Alan called and gave her his most charming smile. She stalked past and flagged a cab.

This rejection only whetted his desire and the next night he waited in the shadows near the rear door of the speakeasy. Dania finally appeared with two other girls, said goodnight to them in the alley, and walked in the opposite direction. Stealthily Alan stalked her. She heard him and at the mouth of the alley turned and yelled, "Come one step closer and I call a cop."

"Have a heart," he called back. "I'm half-frozen. At least listen."

She let him approach until they stood in the circle of a streetlight. "Oh, it's you. For God's sake can't you take no for an answer?"

"I can't help myself. Give me a break and have a cup of coffee with me. Look, I bought this for you. One cup of coffee and it's yours."

She glanced at the long string of amber beads he was holding. "Okay, but I warn you—"

He sketched a cross over his chest. "Word of honor. Come on."

As they crossed the street to an all night diner, he glanced at her sleazy coat. "You must be cold. A girl like you should be cuddled up in mink."

"Lay off, buster. I've heard them all. Diamonds and mink and all you have to do, Dania, is come across. I'm from Missouri."

Like hell you are, Alan thought, you're from Iowa and pretty soon I'm going to be pecker deep in good old Iowa corn. Dania gulped her coffee, scooped up the beads, and went home alone. Alan spent four miserable evenings in subzero temperatures before she'd even allow him to drive her home. Out of the corners of his eyes he watched her. Her knees were crossed and the short skirt had ridden up so he could see the gleam of a satin garter, a curved thigh. Weak with lust, he pulled the car to a stop in front of the rooming house and reached for her. She was out of the car like a shot and slammed the door.

"You're like all the rest, buster. Got a rich daddy and a Stutz and figure you can buy anything. I'm a virgin and I'm saving myself. You better come across with something better than a lousy string of beads and some candy."

"What do you want? A fur coat?"

"A wedding ring with a preacher and a license. That's what I want." She flounced up the steps, long silken legs flashing.

"That'll be the day," he yelled.

"So? Peddle your papers!"

Tough, he thought furiously, and with a mouth on her. Probably lost her cherry years ago and only has the box it came in. Slamming the car into gear he drove away. Fat chance of him falling for that game. Let the bitch go!

But he couldn't. At the office he thought of her, at home he dreamed of her. He tried to slake his thirst with other women and failed. Jesus, Alan thought, I've *got* to have that flashy bitch. He lost weight and yearned for her. After another month he

surrendered. With a ring and license Dania and Alan drove to
Maryland. As insurance, so he didn't try to trick her into a false
marriage, she shrewdly took along the club bouncer and the hot
tomato with red hair as witnesses. After the ceremony the
bouncer and the other dancer bedded down in the room next to
Alan and his bride.

Alan had his clothes off in record time. The girl's eyes widened as she looked at his buttocks. "Where did you get all the
scars from?"

He patted the dimpled scars left by the buckshot from the
irate Kansas farmer. "War wounds," he told her grandly.

Then he tore off her clothes and fell on her. To his surprise
he found she had told the truth. Dania had saved herself.
Joyously he deflowered a virgin. But in the cold light of dawn he
wondered how to break the news to his father.

Elizabeth met the bride and groom in the hallway of the
Meredith house. Her dark eyes slid from Alan's flushed face to
his companion, who was bundled up in a cheap little coat and a
cloche hat. "Your father's been worried," she told her cousin.

"I left a message with Miss Patterson." Waving a hand at the
girl, he said airily, "Dania. And this is Cousin Elizabeth."

"Howjado," the girl whispered.

Dania was rigid with terror. As he helped her out of her coat
her thin arms felt like sticks and he had to work them free of the
sleeves. He noticed that Elizabeth was eyeing Dania's dress.
She'd worn her best, a skimpy blue satin with silk fringe, painted
her face as though she was going to face a spotlight, and encased
her tiny feet in sandals. What had made Dania fetching on the
stage of the speakeasy made her look in the Meredith hall like a
cheap floozie.

"Father home?" he asked.

"In the study with the mail and paper. Would you like to see
him there?"

He pushed Dania into the drawing room. "We'll wait here
for him."

Dania stood in the middle of the room staring with awed
eyes at the fire blazing on the hearth, the bowls of flowers on
cherry tables. "It's so big," she whispered. "Everything looks so

old. That woman who let us in, she scares me stiff."

"Don't worry about Elizabeth. She's only a poor relative. Lived off us for years. Jesus, will you loosen up? You act as though you're going to be stood up and shot."

"That's how I feel. Alan, your dad's gonna *hate* me."

He fought down the desire to shake her. The kid's terrified enough now, he told himself, as he guided her to a loveseat. He took her clammy hand and squeezed it. Then he jumped up. His father, with Elizabeth peering over his shoulder, was standing in the archway.

William gave his son a relieved smile. "You had me worried. Where—" As he caught sight of the girl he stopped abruptly and the smile disappeared. Icy gray eyes swept over her, lingered at her knees, and he flinched. Alan glanced down, saw the blue skirt had ridden up displaying a wide satin garter ornamented with a rosette, and above that fully three inches of white thigh.

By now Alan was as nervous as his bride. "Father," he said hoarsely, "this is my wife."

"*Wife!* You can't be serious!"

Trying vainly to pull down her skirt, Dania whispered, "Howjado."

Alan attempted a smile. "We were married in Maryland, sir. Two days ago."

William's eyes drilled into the girl's. Her face was so pale the show-girl makeup made her look like a clown. She was biting Cupid's bow lips. "May I ask your name, young lady?"

"Dania . . . Dania Delong."

"Dania Meredith," Alan corrected.

His father ignored him. "Are you a native New Yorker?"

"No. I've only been here about . . . maybe a year. My home is in Iowa on a farm."

"Do you have a profession?"

"I'm a . . . an entertainer."

"I rather suspected that. What type of entertaining do you do?"

"Sing and dance. I dance pretty good but my voice isn't strong."

"And just where do you do your dancing and singing?"

Moving restlessly, Alan answered. "The Dead End. You

wouldn't know it, sir, but it's quite a fashionable nightspot. Many of the people you know go there. Even Aunt Van's son has been there a couple of times."

"Young Earl? I would imagine his mother is ignorant of that. Is this . . . ah, one of those—" William turned to Elizabeth who was primly perched on the chair near the archway. "I never can remember the names."

"Blind pigs," she told him crisply. "Speakeasies."

Alan darted her a venomous look. You could tell nothing from Elizabeth's expression but he'd bet the crabapple was having the time of her life. "Yes, it's a speakeasy, father. As I said, it's quite respectable." Alan smiled again, this time successfully. "Aren't you going to break out the champagne? Celebrate your new daughter-in-law?"

Unfortunately, at that moment Dania decided to say a few words. "I don't like champagne but I could do with a pink gin."

Elizabeth's lips twitched and William stiffened. "In this house, young lady, gin, pink or otherwise, is *not* served. Alan, I'll speak with you in the study. Alone."

Dania looked desperately at her husband, and Elizabeth came to the rescue. "I was just about to have tea, Dania. Will you join me?"

As Alan followed his father down the hall he heard Dania with unnecessary emphasis saying, "Oh, yes. I simply *love* tea."

In the study William's demeanor changed. He made a whiskey and soda for himself, splashed soda into a glass and handed it to Alan. "Let's discuss this matter in a rational manner, son."

Jesus, another father and son talk. "What is there to discuss, sir?"

"This isn't another of your pranks, is it? I mean, you actually *did* marry this woman?"

"I told you I did." Alan glanced from his father's face to the face in the plush and gilt frame. Two peas in a pod and if George had lived he'd have made the third.

"I believe you mentioned the ceremony was two days ago. I see no problem. It won't be difficult to arrange an annulment. I'll see the woman is fairly treated. A small cash settlement and perhaps she can be persuaded to leave the city and go—"

"It's my turn to ask if you're serious. I married Dania and I love her. There won't be an annulment."

"Come, you're confusing lust with love. There's no possible way you can love a woman like this one. Dressed like a strumpet, her face painted like a street woman. Think, my boy. *This* woman with the Meredith name, bearing Meredith children. Act like a man and admit you've made a mistake."

Color flooded into Alan's face. The old man had hit the nail on the head. He'd married Dania because that was the only way he could lay her, but be damned if this pompous old bastard was going to order him around any more. "Act like a man? When have you ever allowed me to? Pulling me out of school when you could have fixed it some way, forcing me into the army. Taking me into the business but watching every move I make as though my hand's in the till. I married Dania and she's my wife."

William attempted to appease him. "We all make errors. Raising children is far from easy. But this decision will affect the rest of your life. You'll be tied to a woman who sits in our drawing room exposing her private parts—"

"Come up to date. This is the twenties. For God's sake, you're stuck back at the turn of the century. Many women dress like that. Dania is a decent kid. Give her a chance."

"I may be stuck in time but I know a loose woman when I see one. You've done a number of foolish things but I promise you this is the stupidest move you've ever made."

Rage welled up in Alan and his hands knotted into fists. Losing all control, he cut loose. "Maybe I should listen to you. You're an expert on whores. Sure, Judith looked like a lady and even acted like one but she was a *whore*. Brought her lover right into your sacred house. Even tried to shove off her bastard on you. And you've gall enough to insult *my* wife."

Shock and disbelief struggled on William's face. Judith's name hadn't been spoken in this house since 1916. No one dared mention her. His glass fell from a limp hand and liquid spilled across the polished surface of the desk. "I believe," he said stiffly, "an apology is in order."

Alan was on his feet. "It sure as hell is. To me."

"This is your last chance. Apologize."

"*Never.*"

"Your belongings will be packed. You may send for them. Take that . . . that woman and leave my house."

Alan was beginning to regret his outburst. The old man

looked implacable. Hesitantly, he asked, "What about work?"

"Miss Patterson will clear your desk. You can pick up the box when you wish."

For an instant Alan felt sick. Then rage came welling back and he flung the door open. "To hell with you then." He tore his eyes from his father's face and glared at his great-grandfather's portrait. "To hell with both of you!"

William expected the door to slam but it was left ajar. He could hear Alan lunging down the hall, calling his wife. Taking out his handkerchief, William, hardly knowing what he was doing, tried to mop up the whiskey. Later he told Elizabeth to arrange for the removal of his son's personal effects. A few years earlier Elizabeth wouldn't have dared question him but the circumstances had changed. Gently she asked, "Is there no possibility of a reconciliation?"

"Not unless he proffers a full apology. He said monstrous things." William's lips quirked with pain. "I don't like the boy but unfortunately I love him and love can't be turned off like a tap. More and more I think of George. How different life would be if he'd lived. But Alan is my only son and if he does the gentlemanly thing I'll take him back."

"There is Alicia."

"Alicia is a girl."

Yes, Elizabeth mused, Alicia is a girl and completely under my control. How wonderful it would be if she were to become William's sole heir. With this in mind Elizabeth cautiously put out feelers. She had made a practice of cultivating William's spinster secretary. Elizabeth gave Miss Patterson small gifts at Christmas, took her to lunch occasionally, and had even crocheted a bed jacket for the woman's invalid mother. Miss Patterson admired Elizabeth, who sensed she had small regard for Alan. She phoned William's office and asked Miss Patterson how her mother's health was. There was no need to broach the vital subject. Lowering her voice, the secretary said, "There's been a quarrel. Between Mr. Meredith and Mr. Alan."

"I know. Alan isn't at work then?"

"No, and he won't be coming back. Mr. Meredith had me empty out his son's desk. He looked simply dreadful. What a sad thing."

"Tragic," Elizabeth gallantly lied.

When Alan's luggage was picked up she bribed the driver of the van to tell her its destination. A hotel on the East Side. How long would Alan be able to afford even that? He was extravagant and probably every cent of his salary had gone into his car and his women. Elizabeth had no hopes that Alan would hold out long. He'd come weasling back.

Six weeks later she received a call from an excited Miss Patterson. "He just left, Miss Meredith. Came in bold as brass and asked to see his father. They were shut into Mr. Meredith's office for over an hour and then Mr. Meredith came out all smiles and asked me to bring coffee for Mr. Alan. When Mr. Alan left his father had an arm around his shoulders. Told me to put the stuff back into his son's desk. He looks quite cheerful now."

That evening William did look in good spirits as he told Elizabeth the same thing his secretary had. "Alan made a handsome apology, Elizabeth. Told me he was so shaken by his hasty marriage that he had no idea what he was saying. He'll be home in a few days. Do see his room is cleaned and aired."

"And Dania?"

"We'll have to make the best of it. Perhaps you can influence the woman. See she dresses more discreetly and leaves some of that paint off her face."

"Will they be sharing a room?"

"I didn't think to ask. It might be wise to have George's room cleaned too."

"She may find the furnishings a bit old-fashioned."

"If she doesn't care for the room as it is, have the furniture moved up to the attic. Let her redecorate."

Elizabeth winced, thinking of those gracious walnut pieces moved out, but one thought gave her comfort. William certainly still disapproved of the girl his son had forced on him. There was no chance Dania would be allowed to redecorate the entire house. William was stroking his chin and frowning. "Elizabeth, try to keep the costs down. Dania strikes me as a young woman prone to extravagance."

Dania certainly wasn't prone to extravagance but her taste was appalling. Elizabeth winced as she watched the Bokhara rug rolled up and reed mats put down that would have looked at home on a veranda. Graceful walnut gave place to ratty rattan chairs and tables. Where an elegant four-poster had sat was a daybed covered with garish pillows and a long-legged flapper doll. Mellow paneling disappeared under hangings of bright pink fabric. The only item from Dania's previous life was a large cage containing a parrot. With its curved beak and beautiful green and red plumage the bird reminded Elizabeth of Lavinia Stokes. It also had her temperament.

"I call him Polly," Dania confided. She crooned to the bird, "Pretty Polly."

Cocking an evil black eye the bird said clearly, "Go screw yourself."

The girl told Elizabeth indignantly. "It was those lodgers in the rooming house. Figured they were smart to teach Polly dirty things. I'm trying to break him of it." She spoke to the bird again. "Pretty Polly, say booboopadoop."

"Teach your grannie to suck eggs," the bird snarled.

"Bad." Pulling the cover over the cage, Dania spun around. "This room is perfect, Elizabeth. A nice hideaway. Reason I set it up is I'm not going to have to sit down in that gloomy drawing room with old stone face glaring daggers—" She clapped a hand over her mouth. "I'm sorry."

"You should be. Your father-in-law has been decent to you."

"It's just I'm so scared of him. Like I was of you when I first saw you."

"You've nothing to fear from me," Elizabeth told her. It was the truth. She felt no threat from this pathetic child. She changed the subject. "Now you have your room fixed up we must invite a few friends to meet you."

"Whose friends?"

"Friends of the family."

"Old fuddy-duddies?"

"Many of them are younger than William."

"But they're like him aren't they? Going around with their noses in the air like they smell something bad."

"They are rather straitlaced but you must accept that."

"I don't wanta meet them."

"Might as well get it over with, Dania."

"Okay, but I better get a new outfit." The girl fiddled with a platinum spit curl. "Better get my roots retouched."

Elizabeth suggested hastily, "Perhaps I could help you shop."

She did go shopping with Dania and tried to purchase clothes William would consider discreet. Elizabeth held out a navy dress with a chaste collar and cuffs of white linen. The girl shook her head. "It's not me. Too dowdy."

What turned out to be her was pink satin, loops of pink and blue beads that touched the hemline, and a headband beaded with more pink and blue. Before her introduction to the family's friends the girl slaved over her appearance. Platinum hair gleamed, mascara beaded her eyelashes, spots of rouge flared on her cheekbones, a perfect Cupid's bow outlined her lips. A lamb to the slaughter, Elizabeth thought compassionately as she led the way to the drawing room. When they appeared in the archway, dead silence fell. William had shown no mercy. Most of their friends were there. When they saw Dania the women's eyes widened, the men tried to conceal grins, Uncle Herman roused from a doze and dropped his ear trumpet.

Alan, trying to appear at ease and failing, led his wife around the room, introducing her. The only ones who tried to show kindness were Nina Flanders and, strangely enough, Uncle Herman. Nina attempted to chat but Dania, sitting bolt upright at her husband's side, could only manage a hoarse whisper. Uncle Herman was more forthright. "A dancer," he bellowed approvingly. "Likely looking girl. Reminds me of one of those Floradora girls. You're a lucky man, young Alan."

Unable to watch the carnage, Elizabeth came to the girl's rescue. She concentrated on Aunt Van, knowing the right conversational buttons to press. Tearing her baleful gaze from the bride, Aunt Van started to talk. The other guests joined in. Sherry was poured, refreshments served, Dania ignored. When the guests had left, Dania broke into tears and raced up the stairs. William made no comment; he simply looked eloquently at his son.

"I don't give a damn," Alan blurted. "All of you are half-dead anyway. What do Dania and I have to do with people like you?"

"A great deal, son. Like it or not, you happen to be one of us."

That was the last time Alan and Dania allowed themselves to be exposed to mass disapproval. Life continued as though neither of the young people were in the house. Dania kept show-girl hours, rising at noon and promptly leaving. Elizabeth had no idea how the girl spent her time. She guessed Dania might be seeking out the people she had once worked with. The young couple seldom dined at home. After work Alan picked up his wife and they went out for dinner and then to speakeasies. William accepted this with every evidence of relief but Elizabeth would have liked to see more of the girl. She'd warmed to Dania, enjoyed hearing her sing snatches of popular songs, doing the Charleston in the hall, as bright and gay as a butterfly, as easily crushed. It wasn't William or his friends the spinster feared, it was Alan. She knew him too well to think he would remain faithful to his wife.

Then Elizabeth's forbodings became reality. Dania was pregnant, and from the beginning it was a bad pregnancy. Dania was genuinely ill but she refused to visit Doctor John and insisted on going to a doctor she'd seen a couple of times before her marriage. Her boyish body bloated and in no time she looked like a balloon with a tiny head and thin legs and arms stuck on. True to form, Alan wasted no time on a sick, unsightly wife.

"He's got other women," Dania told Elizabeth. "Can't say I blame him. Look at me. A blimp! I'll never get my figure back again."

"You certainly will. Don't worry, I'll look after you."

Elizabeth took her worries to William. "I think we'd better call in a specialist. There's something badly wrong, William." He shrugged and told her Dania already had a doctor, but when Elizabeth insisted he did call another doctor in. "Twins," the doctor told them grimly, "I'm willing to stake my reputation on it. Mrs. Meredith isn't built for it. This is going to be tricky."

It was more than tricky. The night the twins were born Dania came close to dying. Alan couldn't be located and it was William and Elizabeth who paced the hospital waiting room. When Alan finally showed up his clothes were wrinkled and he needed a shave. On one cheek was a smear that looked much like lipstick.

"Where have you been?" William demanded.

"Out on the town. What's the big deal?"

"While you were 'out on the town' your wife nearly died. She's still very weak."

"She comes from strong stock. Let's have a look at the babies."

Alan poked a finger at one baby. "Dania pick names for them yet?"

"Jessica," his father told him, pointing at the larger baby. "And this one is Katherine."

Losing interest in his infant daughters, Alan ran a hand over his chin. "I'd better get home and cleaned up."

William gave him a look of complete contempt. "We'll both go home. I want to talk to you."

Whatever William said to his son produced a subdued Alan. No longer did he leave his wife to make the rounds of the night-spots. Dania's health improved and to her delight she regained her boyish figure. When the twins were slightly over three months old she made an early appearance at the breakfast table one morning. William and Alan had left for the office and Elizabeth was having a second cup of coffee.

Dania investigated the contents of the covered dishes on the sideboard. "Sausages and eggs and bacon. Gee, you people eat a big breakfast."

"You must have had hearty meals on the farm."

Dania settled for coffee and toast and sat down opposite Elizabeth. "Seems a long time ago now. Sometimes I figure I should have stayed there. Funny, when I married Alan I figured life would be a bowl of cherries."

"You've found out they're sour?"

"And how! Let's face it, I'll never fit in with you people. But I did get a promise from Alan. No more kids."

Elizabeth poured coffee for both of them. "We seldom see you before noon. Why are you up so early?"

"Alan's orders. Being the big masterful husband." Dania made a face. "Says this house is gonna be ours some day and I better get off my butt and find out how to run it. I told him I figure that's why we got servants. Pay them to run it, but the big guy's spoken and I better try. Do you mind?"

Of course I mind, Elizabeth told her silently, this is *my*

house and *I* take care of it. Aloud she said, "Not at all. In fact, Dania, it will be a relief. I'll have more time for Alicia and myself. Managing a house like this takes a great deal of energy."

"What about the servants? Don't they do it?"

"Servants are only as good as the mistress. A lax mistress produces a staff who are lazy and wasteful."

The smooth skin between Dania's plucked brows puckered and she said mournfully, "I don't get your drift."

"You will soon," Elizabeth promised.

Under supervision Dania sorted and counted the laundry. Elizabeth perched on a stool and watched. "Damn." Dania held out a hand. "I broke a nail."

Smiling, Elizabeth examined the brightly colored nails. "Better clip them shorter."

The girl threw down some towels. "Why can't Sally do this?"

"Because the mistress must know exactly what goes out of the house and what comes back in. This is good quality linen. It would fetch a fair price at secondhand stores."

Dania's eyes widened. "Think Sally would swipe some?"

"I doubt it but best not to tempt. Anyway, the laundress might." Climbing down from the stool, Elizabeth said briskly. "You've done well. Now we'll go down to the butler's pantry and I'll explain meal planning."

First Elizabeth patiently explained the bookkeeping, then the ordering of food and the preparing of menus. This took until lunch time. After they'd eaten, Dania stretched, stifled a yawn, and said wearily, "Glad that's done. I'm bushed. Think I'll take a nap.'"

"You haven't time. We have to go down to the wine cellar and take a tally of—"

"I am *not* going into a dirty cellar with spiders all over the place."

"Briggs keeps the cellars clean. After that we'll polish silver—"

"Doesn't Bertha do that?"

There was no need for Elizabeth to answer. Bertha was clearing the table. She was a middle-aged, stocky woman who wasn't as strong or fast as Gerda had been but she did her work well. She told Dania indignantly, "Haven't the time, Mrs. Meredith. Too much work here for me anyway. Isn't there, Miss Elizabeth?"

"You manage well, Bertha, but I think Mrs. Meredith takes your point."

Dania's bright head drooped. "What then?"

"Briggs will bring Alicia home from school and you can take her for her walk in the park."

"Doesn't Tosh do that?"

"She used to but now Jess and Katie take up her time. When you get back you must arrange the flowers the florist delivered this morning and check on dinner preparations and—"

Jumping up, Dania threw down her napkin. "I'm not doing it. I don't care what Alan says but I'm not gonna be a drudge while he flits around having fun." She patted the older woman's shoulder. "Sorry, Elizabeth, you're real nice to me but I told you I'd never fit in."

"Alan will be angry," Elizabeth warned, but Dania was gone.

Shortly before dinner Alan's wrath burst over the house. Elizabeth and William were waiting for the young people in the drawing room when sounds drifted down the staircase. William lifted his head. "Lovers' quarrel? Should we wait dinner for them?"

Putting aside her knitting, Elizabeth rose. "I think not."

She wondered how Dania would stand up to her husband but the following day she found the girl was not as soft as she appeared. Instead of turning up for another lesson Dania fell back into her habit of sleeping late and leaving for the day. Elizabeth waited for Alan to take his revenge but to her surprise he appeared to relent and began again to squire his young wife around to their favorite nightspots. He brought presents for her—costume jewelry and a fur jacket. His behavior might have reassured Dania but it left Elizabeth uneasy. Alan was planning something.

The twins were six months old when she discovered what that something was. William was dressing for dinner and Alan and Elizabeth were in the drawing room when the front door crashed open and Dania appeared in the archway. She was wearing a scarlet cloche and dress and her new jacket. Her expression was furious but her voice was cool and controlled. "You bastard. You conniving, dirty bastard."

With great deliberation Alan folded the paper he'd been scanning. "Tsk, tsk, Such language. What has upset my precious little lamb?"

"You damn well know. You're trying to kill me, aren't you?"

Alan darted an amused look at his cousin. "Now what can she be talking about, Cousin Elizabeth?"

"Leave her out of this, you bastard. What a fool I am. Really thought you were being nice to me, taking me out, urging me to drink." Forgetting her recent words, she turned a tragic face to Elizabeth. "The doctor told him another baby might kill me and he's got me pregnant again."

"So that's it." Alan lifted wide innocent eyes. "Accidents will happen, you know."

"This was no *accident*. It was deliberate." Perching on the arm of a chair, she stretched long legs out. "But you're gonna be laughing on the other side of your face, buster. Not only am I gonna live but you're gonna pay. I want a Stutz, dear hubbie, one just like yours. And I want it right away."

Throwing back his head, he roared with laughter. "Want the moon too?"

"Want your dad to throw you out on your ass?"

Elizabeth was glancing from one to the other as though watching a tennis match. Your serve, Alan, she thought. Alan was still grinning. "On what grounds, dear wife?"

The Cupid's bow lips relaxed into a matching grin. "He'd love a grandson. This kid might be a boy. If you don't come across I'm gonna abort it and then tell him exactly why. He's gonna see red, buster."

Elizabeth found she was smiling as widely as Dania. The girl was on the right track. For William this might be the last straw and when the camel's back broke his son might find himself disinherited. She could see the same thoughts chasing themselves across Alan's plump face. Still speaking in low tones, Dania continued, "I'll make a promise. Until this kid is born I'll have to hang around but as soon as it is I'm gonna clear out. Take the

Stutz and make tracks. I was a dumb Dora to get mixed up with you. You're a dirty piece of goods."

"You win, you cheap floozy. I'll get the damn car for you and you better keep your promise. The old man was right when he told me the stupidest move I ever made was to marry you."

"That goes double." Dania stood up and stretched. She picked up her red purse and called back over her shoulder, "You try to get into my room again and I'll crack a chair over your empty head."

Alan's face was like a thundercloud. He turned his venom on his cousin. "Bet that made you happy. Never mind, the old man can't last forever and I'm waiting for you."

Getting up, Elizabeth smoothed down her skirt. "We'll see. Anyway, as your wife just proved, you're not invulnerable."

Alan brought the Stutz, a white one with yellow seats, and Dania swung through her pregnancy with no problems. On August eighth, 1923, William and Judith's wedding anniversary, her son was born. This time William made no effort to locate his son and only Elizabeth was with him when the baby was born.

"A grandson," William whispered as he took the child from a nurse. "He's a big boy, Elizabeth. I do believe he takes after the Merediths. Look at that chin, the lines of the face." He beamed down at his daughter-in-law. "Have you chosen a name for the little chap?"

Dania was propped against a pillow wearing a bright red jacket Elizabeth had knitted for her. Her small face, washed clean of makeup, was young and appealing. "I figured you might like to name him," she said shyly.

"An honor, my dear. Yes, I would like a family name." He handed the child to Elizabeth. "Take a good look at him. He looks exactly like the baby pictures of Uncle Leon."

"My father?" Wonderingly she stared down at dark brown hair and eyes as dark as her own. "William, I believe he does. Are you thinking . . ."

"Hardly. Napoleon Bonaparte is rather extreme." Lifting a tapered fiinger he gently touched his grandson's tiny shoulder. "I hereby dub you Oliver Pendrell Meredith."

"A big name for such a little boy," Dania said softly. "I'd hate to have him called Ollie."

Elizabeth cradled the child to her breast. "Couldn't we call him Opie?"

William smiled indulgently. "While he's small I suppose it would do no harm. When he's older we'll call him Oliver. Better give him to mother now."

Elizabeth's arms tightened. She felt a curious reluctance to relinquish the baby. The other babies she'd held, the children she looked after, meant little to her. But this boy with the Meredith bone structure and her own coloring stirred some dormant emotion. Dania was holding out her arms and after a moment Elizabeth bent and placed the child gently in them.

As she left the hospital she told herself, it will pass, this boy will have no more impact on my life than Alicia and Mariette had, than Jess or Katie. Both William and his cousin were in error. For the remainder of his life Oliver Pendrell the second would be called Opie. And Elizabeth's emotion didn't wane, it increased. She'd broken her vow and once more had allowed herself to love. Opie Meredith, conceived by a drunken mother and a vengeful father, was, in time, to become the focus of her life.

September of 1923 proved to be a fine month, warm enough to be comfortable but lacking the suffocating heat of the previous month. One golden afternoon Elizabeth wrapped Opie in layers of blankets and carried him down to the small garden behind the house. There she found Alicia, sketching, with Tosh seated close to her. At eight the girl was much stronger than she'd been as an infant but was still delicate and nervy. But she was a good child, obedient and nicely mannered, and she showed a talent for art. The sketch she was doing of the maple tree at the bottom of the garden was surprisingly well done.

Tosh gazed searchingly at Elizabeth. "You look tired today, Miss Elizabeth. Did the baby have another bad night?"

"I was up and down with him most of the night. Colic again. Poor little boy. But now he's sleeping soundly."

"I've been thinking . . ."

"Yes?"

"You've taken most of the work with Opie off my shoulders but it's hard on you. You've lost weight and your color isn't good. You should ask Mr. Meredith to hire a helper for me. I'd like to do more but with the twins and Alicia, and I'm not getting any younger—"

"No." Elizabeth's arms tightened possessively around the sleeping baby. "I'll look after him. Since we moved his crib into my room it's been easier. It was running back and forth to the nursery that was so tiring."

"You set a lot of store by this little one." Tosh shook a puzzled head. "It's not my place to say it but . . ."

"Go ahead."

"You've been good to the other little ones but not one of them ever seemed so important to you."

Silently Elizabeth agreed with the old nurse. She was as puzzled as Tosh was about her reaction to Opie. After all, he was Alan's son and she certainly didn't have feelings for *him*. Opie's mother . . . yes, in the time she'd known Dania she'd become fond of the girl. Dania was a shallow little thing but she was bright and gay and amusing. Elizabeth looked down at the face framed in the ruffled bonnet. A lock of dark hair lay on the rounded brow, thick dark lashes rested against flushed cheeks. Opie looked exactly like the baby pictures of her father and herself. There isn't a trace, she assured herself, of either Dania or Alan in that face. But after all the other babies . . . why this one? She admitted she felt little for Alicia, only a sense of duty toward Mariette, nothing at all for the twins. But Alicia had always turned to Tosh for comfort and affection, Mariette had only been in the house for a short time, the twins, particularly Jess, reminded her of Alan. But Opie was different and he needed her. Alan didn't seem to know the boy existed, his mother was too busy with her own life to bother—Opie had only Elizabeth. As for Cousin Elizabeth . . . who cared about her? Her father had but her father was dead. Lafe had pretended to but he had simply used her.

The baby stirred in her arms, his eyelashes fluttering, one dimpled hand fighting loose from the cocoon of blankets. She tucked the tiny hand back and it curled warmly and trustingly around one of her fingers. Yes, he needed her and she needed *him*. She was lonely, starved for someone to love. She didn't care if Alan *had* fathered this child. Opie looked enough like her that he could easily be the son she'd never have, the child she'd never bear. Who can explain the vagaries of the human heart, the rapport that sometimes exists between two human beings? Elizabeth couldn't and she didn't try. All she knew was that Opie was *hers*.

Tosh moved restlessly and Elizabeth looked up. "I'll be fine, Tosh. As long as you can handle the twins we'll make out fine."

"Katie's no problem. Easiest baby I've ever handled. But that Jess is an imp."

"She is a handful."

Jess *was* a handful. She was the larger twin and while her sister was still crawling Jess was walking and breaking every object she could get her hands on. The twins didn't look alive. Jess had olive skin, chestnut hair, and eyes like chips of cobalt. Her sister was plumper with a milky complexion, light brown hair, and her eyes were the color of an April sky.

"Elizabeth," a voice called.

She craned her neck and saw Dania leaning out of an upper window. "Could you come up here for a minute," the girl called.

"I'll tuck Opie into his crib and be right there."

Dania was perched on a rattan chair with one foot propped up on a stool. Her platinum head was bent and she was painting her toenails the same bright color as her long fingernails. She wore a short silk kimono and under it Elizabeth glimpsed a peach slip. The daybed was piled high with lingerie, satin step-ins, a rainbow heap of garters. Three cheap suitcases stood near the wardrobe and another one, spilling dresses, was open on the floor near the window.

Her eyes on the open case, Elizabeth asked, "You do intend to leave, then?"

"Yeah. I've been waiting until I felt up to it and I feel fine now so I'm keeping my promise and clearing out."

Elizabeth sank into a chair near the parrot cage. Polly cocked his bright head and muttered obscenities. "Naughty," Dania told him sharply. "Bad Polly. No matter how I try I can't break him of swearing, Elizabeth. Come on Polly. Say booboopadoop, pretty Polly." The bird spat a four-letter word and Dania shrugged, the kimono sliding off a thin shoulder to expose a lace strap. "Come on, Elizabeth, cheer up. Why so sad?"

"I thought you'd changed your mind. I'll miss you."

"I've got to go. Nothing here for me. The whole mess is my own fault. Figured I was really making a match. Gonna have furs and a big house and drip with diamonds. What I got was a penny-pinching father-in-law who holds the purse strings and a no-good bum for a husband. No use wasting more time. I got a life to live. Sure, there's things I'll miss. Mainly you and the kids."

Elizabeth felt a stab of fear. "What about the children?"

Shifting in her chair, the girl waved her foot in the air, waiting for the polish to dry. "I'm gonna have to make my own way and I can't drag along three little kids. What would I do with them? Anyway, can you picture Alan or his dad letting me take the kids? They'd have every cop in New York looking for me. The kids will be better off here anyway. There's you and Tosh to look out for them and they'll be able to go to fancy schools like Alicia does. But you'll write and let me know how they are, won't you?"

"Of course."

"Think I'm pretty heartless, don't you?"

"It has to be your own decision. Will you go home?"

"Kinda wish I could." Critically, Dania peered at her foot and then put it on the floor and started painting the nails on the other one. "My folks are pretty strict. When I left home they told me not to bother coming back. Meant it too. No, we're heading west."

"We?"

"Joy's coming with me. You never met her. Joy stood as witness when I married that dope Alan. Pretty little thing with red hair and a good dancer too. We're gonna get jobs in Hollywood. Extras maybe, and work our way up. Just think, Elizabeth, we'll get to see Mary Pickford and Doug Fairbanks. Read about their new mansion in *Photocopy*. It's some spread, got acres of gardens and this private screening room. Called Pickfair. Gee . . . maybe we'll get to see it. I can hardly wait. Gloria Swanson, John Barrymore, Buster Keaton, Natalie Talmadge . . ." Her voice trailed off and she lifted eyes gleaming between darkened eyelashes. "Won't that be something? Hey, why don't you chuck it and come with us?"

"Me?"

"Sure, you're one smart lady. Look at the way you run this

big place and you speak so nice too. You could manage Joy and me. Get jobs for us and take a split of our pay. 'Course you'd have to do something about the way you look." Dania eyed Elizabeeth up and down, from her sensible shoes to the top of her gleaming head. "You should put that hem up, it's halfway down to your ankles, and get some decent shoes. Your hair looks not bad in that French roll but it would look better bobbed and marcelled. I can show you how to put rouge and lipstick on so it'd suit your face. Be a heck of a lot more fun than hanging around this old dump looking after a bunch of kids."

Dreamily, Elizabeth looked at the parrot and saw instead sun-drenched boulevards, palm trees, scintillating stars in expensive cars. She pictured herself as an agent, managing movie stars, having a mansion of her own with a swimming pool. Then she jerked back to reality. "I really appreciate the offer, Dania, but everything I want is right here."

Dania shrugged again and the lace strap slid down to join the kimono. She looked not unlike the leggy flapper doll on the bed. "Each to his own, said the old lady as she kissed the cow."

"Have you told Alan or his father?"

"Alan couldn't care less. Hasn't spoken to me in months. His dad? No, I'm still scared stiff of him though he's been pretty nice to me. You tell him I'm gone and tell him he was right. We should of got our marriage annulled. Tell him I'm glad I could at least have given him grandchildren."

"I'll tell him. When do you leave?"

"Early tomorrow morning. Before you're up. I hate goodbyes. Always cry. I've got most of my stuff ready to stick in those suitcases."

"It's an expensive trip, Dania. Have you sold your car?"

"Are you kidding? The Stutz is the only thing I got outta Alan except some cheap jewelry and that ratty jacket. Joy and me are gonna drive west in high style."

"Have you enough money?"

"I got a few bucks and Joy's got some put aside. We'll make out. If we run out of money we'll stop and work for a while. Sling hash or pearl dive—" Dania laughed at Elizabeth's baffled expression. "Work as waitresses or wash dishes, is what I mean."

"I've some savings. Perhaps I could lend you—"

"Uh uh. Like I said, we'll make out. Tell you what, if we do get in a bind I'll yell and you can come riding to the rescue. Okay?"

"I'll do that," Elizabeth promised.

"One other thing. There's no way I can take Polly. I know he's got a dirty mouth but I've got kinda fond of him. You ever had a pet, Elizabeth?"

"Once. Long ago I had a cat. Her name was Sussie. I know how you feel. Would you like me to keep Polly?"

"I sure would. He isn't much work. Just have to clean his cage and see he gets bird seed and water. Maybe you can get him to stop swearing." The girl pulled the kimono up over her shoulder. "Guess you can hardly wait to take these hangings down and get rid of the furniture."

"I've grown rather used to it," Elizabeth confessed. The pink walls, rattan furniture, garish pillows, were a perfect setting for Dania with her cheap finery and bright hair. She'd miss the girl. Dania had brightened up the house and she owed her a debt. Dania had given her Opie. "I suppose we'd better say goodbye now."

"Yeah." Dania padded on bare feet to the wardrobe and started to slide dresses from hangers. "Here, want this doll? Something to remember me by."

Picking up the flapper doll, Elizabeth tucked it under her arm. "I'd love to have it. Thank you."

Dania threw a dress on the bed and ran over to the older woman. She hugged her and raised eyes spangled with tears. "Gee, but I'm gonna miss you. Honest. You been so nice to me. Not like Alan said when we moved in. Told me you were a snake in the grass. Shoulda known he was lying. Elizabeth, you watch out for him. He hates your guts."

Elizabeth's lips brushed the girl's warm cheek. "Don't cry. Your mascara's running. As for Alan, William keeps him in line."

"Anything happens to Alan's dad and you're in big trouble. Gonna tell you this too, Alan's got in with a bad crowd."

Seeking his own level, Elizabeth thought. "What kind of crowd?"

"Gangsters. Oh, I know a lot of wealthy kids figure it's

smart to pal around with them. Figure they're just guys who wear
sharp clothes and have a lot of dough from running booze. But
they're poison, Elizabeth, and they get their dough from lots of
things beside booze. Got their dirty hands into everything, girls
and drugs and gambling. Alan had better watch out."

"Does he see any one in particular?"

"Yeah." Stepping back, Dania glanced around as though
afraid of being overheard. "Young guy about Alan's age. His old
man runs the Lower East Side. He's had a good education and
talks something like you but believe me that guy's the red light
for danger."

"His name?" Elizabeth probed.

"Carelli," Dania whispered. "Leonardo Carelli. They call
him Leo the Lion. Don't know why. He don't look like a lion.
He owns the Dead End and a lotta other clubs. Alan thinks he's
the cat's whiskers. Don't say nothing about this but I figured you
better know."

"I won't say a word." Elizabeth opened the door. "Goodbye, Dania. Be sure to let me know your address and I'll write
and tell you how the children are."

"Soon's we get settled. I'll send postcards too." Cupid's bow
lips lifted in a dazzling smile. "See you in the funny papers."

"No," Elizabeth said gravely, "I'll see you in the movies."

— 19 —

Dania never got into the movies or even to Hollywood.
On the first day of October a telegram arrived from Lees Bluff, a
tiny town north and east of Peoria, Illinois. It was addressed to
Elizabeth and after she read it she stood in the hall, leaning
against the marble-topped table, hearing Dania's voice. "If we
get in a bind," the girl had said, "I'll yell and you can come
riding to the rescue."

Elizabeth went to William's study and opened the door without knocking. He glanced up, saw the expression on her face, and took the telegram. "My dear Lord," he muttered. "The poor child. Could she have been drunk?"

"You know as much as I do. They think she went to sleep at the wheel."

"You said she was traveling with a woman friend. There's no mention of that here."

"Her name was Joy. She was a dancer with red hair. That's all Dania said."

The Merediths never did find out what happened to the hot tomato with red hair. They never knew that Joy had become involved with a young chap in Columbus, Ohio, and had given up the silver screen to marry him and go to work in his father's hardware store. Dania had continued the trip alone, driving long hours, not eating or sleeping properly. A few miles from Lees Bluff she dozed off, careened off the road, and the Stutz sheared off a telephone pole. Dania died instantly.

William's brow was furrowed. "It says they found a note in her purse listing you as next of kin. We'll have to notify her family. Do you . . ."

"All I know is that her stage name was Dania Delong."

"Would Alan?"

"I've no idea."

"Have you told him yet?"

"I came directly to you."

"Yes. I don't think he's going to care. What are we to do? Dania was a Meredith if only by marriage, and she was the mother of my grandchildren. She must have a proper burial." Rubbing his chin, William looked hopefully at his cousin. "I simply can't spare the time to go myself. Possibly Alan could take over but he's inexperienced and I hesitate to leave him in full charge of the business. I know this is asking a great deal, Elizabeth, but could you—"

"I will. I'd have gone anyway. I'll pack. Sally will have to help Tosh out with the babies while I'm gone."

"Do see Dania is . . . see she's properly looked after. I'll see if I can locate her family and let them know."

"They won't care. They disowned her." Elizabeth's voice broke and she turned away. "No one cares."

"You do," William told her gently.

The hamlet where Dania's body waited in a room behind the funeral home was not unlike the Iowa towns that Dania must once have known. It had one street lined with a few stores, horses and carts tied to hitching posts, two grain elevators looming in the background. Even in October it was warm and dusty. Elizabeth selected the most expensive casket available and sent to Peoria for a floral blanket to cover it. Dania was laid to rest in an old cemetery among leaning tombstones. Elizabeth expected that with the exception of the minister she'd be the only person to stand beside the grave, but the town had a heart. The townspeople came to the service, straggling up the dusty road, bringing bunches of flowers from their gardens. They stood bareheaded during the prayers and afterward gravely shook Elizabeth's hand. So young, they murmured, and many of them were old enough to mourn the loss of a young life. So young . . . Dania had been twenty-three.

Back in New York Elizabeth took a taxi from the station and once home, went immediately upstairs. On the second floor she paused and opened the door of Dania's room. The hangings still glared pinkly, rattan furniture still stood on reed mats, but there was nothing of Dania left, no more than there had been of Judith. Both dead, Elizabeth thought, and made her way wearily up to her own room. In the cage by a window Polly turned his head so one beady eye peered at her. On top of the chiffonier the flapper doll sprawled, long legs dangling limply. Memorabilia. A dressing table, a lapel watch ringed with forget-me-nots, a doll, a foul-mouthed parrot. The donors both dead, both dead so young.

She walked toward the cage expecting the bird to spew curses, but Polly was silent, watching her intently. "Dania's gone," she whispered. "She's dead."

The dead girl's voice sounded through the room, a soft crooning murmur. "Say booboopadoop," Polly said in Dania's voice. "Pretty Polly."

"Why couldn't you have said that for *her*?"

Pulling the cover over the cage, Elizabeth sank onto the bed, her face buried in her hands.

Aunt Van spoke around a mouthful of jam tart. "So I told William, I'll speak to Elizabeth. You've been depressed since you got back from Pennsylvania—"

"Illinois," Elizabeth corrected.

"I never can keep those states straight. I'll tell you why you have William so upset. You're too tenderhearted. Look at the way you carried on over Judith and now this girl. I'll admit I'm sorry we weren't nicer to Alan's wife. I suppose it wouldn't have hurt us. But really! Imagine Alan picking up a cheap dime-a-dance girl like that. And Nina Flanders *did* try. She invited the girl ever so many times to come over and see them and the hussy never went."

"Dania was afraid of all of you."

Aunt Van's beringed hand hovered over the cake plate, moving indecisively from a tart to a macaroon. "Do have a slice of cheesecake, Cousin Elizabeth. If I do say so myself, that's one thing my Aggie does better than your Cookie. No? You certainly don't eat enough. You're thin as a rail. And another thing. You're much too conscientious. Oh, I've heard all about you looking after little Opie. Cookie told my Aggie. Running herself ragged, Miss Elizabeth is, Cookie said, working all day and up and down all night with that baby. And him with colic, too. You're perfectly aware William can well afford another nurse-maid. Why do you do it? No, don't bother answering, you're all wrapped up in that child. Why I can't see. Opie's a fine little fellow and *does* favor your father in looks. Let's pray his temperament will be different. Wouldn't want another Leon. Don't glower like that, Elizabeth, you'll surely have wrinkles. How do you like my decor?"

Elizabeth had been dreading that question. Since Aunt Van's Egyptian period she'd redecorated several times but this new one was certainly the worst. Her drawing room now looked like an operating theater, complete with white linen curtains, angular metal furniture, and a white rug. Against the long windows snow drifted lazily and although the room was well heated Elizabeth felt chilled. Instead of giving the expected compliment, she asked a question. "Tell me, no matter what your new decor is, why do you always leave that sofa?"

Patting a wide cushion, Aunt Van smiled. "I can never part from this. My dear departed picked it out. Told me, Georgia, this piece of furniture is perfect for you. How old are you, Elizabeth?"

Caught off guard, Elizabeth had to think. "Nearly forty-six."

"Ah. A dangerous age for women—"

"The menopause?"

Aunt Van choked on her tea. "Really! In my day one didn't say that word. Change of life is bad enough. Hmm, I didn't realize you were that much older than my Sophie. She's thirty-eight. You look years younger than she does. I think both of you are going through the change. Act like it. Have you seen Sophie lately? No? Not many people have. Last few years she's just moped around this house. Only goes out to the library. That's where she is now. I must admit both my older children are disappointments. By this time I expected Earl to be married with children but he isn't even doing well at the bank. I'm told he does his work all right but he's a plodder, not a spark of ambition."

"Perhaps he'd rather be in another profession."

"Nonsense. Vandercourts have been bankers for generations. My dear departed would roll over in his grave if his son wasn't following in his footsteps. And Sophie. I declare, Elizabeth, I don't understand that girl. The way she looks at me. Sometimes I catch her watching me and I literally shudder. Her eyes look queer. Did I ever tell you about my Aunt Louise? Don't bother answering. Of course I haven't. None of us ever mention *her*. Aunt Louise was a spinster too and she was always kind of eccentric but when she reached the change she went completely batty. Imagined her house was inhabited by evil spirits, succubi and incubi and that type of thing. Louise had a lovely home filled with nice furniture and paintings worth a great deal. Anyway, she read somewhere or heard it that evil can't abide water. So she started throwing pails of water around. All over her house. By the time the family found what she was doing she'd ruined it, literally drowned all that expensive stuff." Aunt Van poured more tea and extended sliced lemon. "She had to be committed, of course, and Sophie looks exactly like Louise. Starting to act like her too."

"Sophie is throwing pails of water around?"

"Of course not. Don't be so obtuse, Elizabeth. It's her eyes. At times I feel she's . . . well, unbalanced." Dropping her unbalanced daughter, Aunt Van looked complacently around. "Should get your mind off that dead girl by doing some redecorating. I was telling Charity just this morning, one should try and keep up to date. Can't keep on acting as though it's the nineteen hundreds. William's house hasn't been changed since his grandfather built it and—"

"We like it the way it is."

"Mark my words, when Alan comes into his own he'll change it. That boy's cutting a wide swath. Almost as bad as Marilou Flanders. Now there *is* a minx. Remember? When the girl was only a child I told you she was going to be a trial. Best thing Albert ever did was to send her away to that convent school after Marilou was caught stark naked in the coal cellar with that boy. Should have left her there, she's—"

"Aunt Van, Marilou is nineteen now. Her parents can't keep her walled off forever. She's—"

"She's driving her father mad. Must say Nina is taking it lightly. Spends all her time down at that little office Susan took after she got her law degree. I hear Nina's even learning to operate a typewriter so she can help Susan. Both those girls have been trials for their father—"

"I can't see," Elizabeth cut into the flow of words, "how having another lawyer in the family is a disgrace. I admire Susan's spirit."

"A *woman* lawyer. Susan should be married and raising a family. Fine looking girl. Earl was telling me that Alan was hot on Susan's trail. Of course so are a lot of other young men."

"Susan Flanders and Alan?" Elizabeth frowned. She liked Susan but she wouldn't want her as mistress of the Meredith house. Susan *would* be an adversary.

"Stop that glowering. You are getting wrinkles. You have nothing to worry about, Cousin Elizabeth. Susan told Alan she couldn't stand him when they were children, and she despises him now. Even Alan understood *that*. How is he taking his wife's death?" Elizabeth shrugged and the older woman nodded. "Only to be expected. I'd swear that boy cares for no one but himself. If George had lived I've always figured Susan and he would have made a match. But it's funny how some odd matches are making out. Remember the Standfords and how upset they were when Maud eloped with that Italian, and now both Estelle and Horace are proud as punch of Antonio. Three grandchildren and such handsome ones too, and Horace claims Antonio is a right hand to him in the business. Taken poor Arnold's place. When Ronnie Grant married that girl a couple of years ago his parents were upset. She worked in a five and dime, you know. But she settled Ronnie right down. He was pretty wild but now Ronnie's in the family business. As I keep telling Charity, one must keep up to date."

Elizabeth was watching the older woman warily. When she'd received Aunt Van's summons to tea she'd had a hunch it was for something besides a lecture on her own behavior. This was the second reference in moments to keeping up to date. She put out a probe. "I noticed how attractive Charity looks since she had her hair bobbed."

Aunt Van patted her own high piled hair. "Been thinking of having a marcel and bob myself. You should do it too. Your hair's so thick it must be a bother. Charity is wearing a little makeup too. Bit of powder and lipstick. She has a beau, you know."

Elizabeth hadn't known and she nearly blurted out her reaction. It was high time Charity had a beau. A small fortune had been spent on the girl's debut but even at her own parties the only males to steer her around the dance floor had been older men and a few youngsters pressed into reluctant service. Despite the prestige of the Vandercourt name and the family wealth there had been no takers for Charity's pudgy hand. She asked Aunt Van, "Do I know Charity's beau?"

"No. Roger's from out of town. His name is Roger Pawder and he's a charming—"

"Pawder? Not a common name."

"It's been shortened."

"We once had a kitchen maid named Pawderiski. She had to be discharged for stealing silverware."

"Certainly no relative of our Roger's. Elizabeth, you chatter so much you put me right off my train of thought. Roger is devoted to Charity and the way they met was quite romantic. Charity was in Gramercy Park feeding the pigeons—she's so kind to birds, you know—and Roger was there too. He had no idea Charity was a Vandercourt but he was attracted and struck up a conversation. Well, to make a long story short she brought him home and I was taken with the boy immediately—"

"Where does he come from?"

"There you go! Interrupting again. I was going to tell you
our Roger comes from Des Moines and his father is in the shoe
business. Now, I know when we were girls our parents would
have been fit to be tied if we'd brought home a man like that, but
the world's changed and it's high time. Now, what do you
think?"

Elizabeth was enjoying herself. "Shoe business. Do the
Pawders own a factory?"

Aunt Van flushed. "Not exactly. I might as well tell you.
Our Roger's quite aboveboard about his humble origins. Such an
honest young man! His father is a cobbler. But Roger has a good
education and he dresses and speaks well. I'd swear you'd never
guess he isn't one of us. You know, Elizabeth, I hate to sound
critical but I never realized you were such a snob. After all, *your*
mother was a milliner."

"I'm not a snob. But I can't help remembering you and the
rest of William's friends were absolutely beastly to Dania because
her father is a farmer."

Aunt Van was so affronted she removed her hand from its
questing position over the cake plate. "*Well.* I've said I'm sorry
because we weren't nicer to the girl but Dania can't be compared
to Charity's beau. Roger is a gentleman and Dania certainly
couldn't be called a *lady*. You must keep an open mind. I do
believe it's the change that's making you so irritable."

Smothering a smile, Elizabeth said meekly, "I'm not feeling
myself, Aunt Van. Please go on."

Appeased, the older woman took a peach tart. "Cousin Elizabeth, you must never consider me a credulous fool. I'm well
aware of the danger of fortune hunters. When I met Roger I
thought, I'll check you out, young fellow me lad, and see how
honest you are. So I hired a private investigator and found Roger
had told the truth. He graduated from university and hasn't a
black mark against him. And he is *so* fond of Charity."

While Aunt Van demolished the tart Elizabeth considered
Charity Vandercourt. The girl hadn't improved since she was an
unattractive child. She had her mother's obesity and porcine face
but unfortunately she hadn't inherited Aunt Van's forceful per-
sonality or shrewdness. Perhaps this man was the answer to her
mother's prayer. "He sounds like a fine young man," she said.
"Are they engaged?"

"The announcement will be made at Christmas time. Roger is giving the little dear a ring. Which brings me to a request. I was wondering if you could arrange a little larger dinner than usual. I'm sure William will agree. I can lend you Aggie to help Cookie and a few waitresses can be hired to assist Bertha and Sally." Taking Elizabeth's assent for granted, Aunt Van continued, "Funny about Sally, isn't it? She's such a good-looking girl I thought you'd have lost her years ago. I never hire a pretty maid. As soon as they're trained they usually walk out on you and get married."

"Sally's sweetheart was killed in the war. I doubt she'll ever marry."

"So sad." Aunt Van sighed. "Many girls will be old maids because of that terrible war. But not my Charity. She'll have a husband and children and a wonderful life. Now, about Christmas. I want the Standfords and the Grants and their families invited. I know it will mean a great many children but you already have four in the house."

"We'd be happy to."

"Do tell William about our Roger, but not a word to anyone else. I want this to be a surprise." Settling back, Aunt Van gazed blissfully around the dreadful room. "Roger and Charity will be such a comfort to me. One should have at least one child who is not a disappointment. Poor Alfred and Nina. I wonder what they're going to do about Marilou."

Elizabeth's lips set in a firm line. "Aunt Van, I saw Marilou a few days ago."

"Really? Where?"

"I was shopping and I bumped into her."

Elizabeth had literally bumped into Marilou. She'd been hurrying down Lexington, her arms full of parcels, when a group of young men and women brushed by her. They were talking and laughing, heedless of the middle-aged woman vainly trying to move out of their path. A girl, bundled up in a short gray fur coat, walked right into her. Elizabeth reeled and dropped a package. The girl paused, retrieved the parcel, and handed it back. "Sorry. Are you okay? Here, let me . . . well, if it isn't Cousin Elizabeth!"

Elizabeth gazed down at the vividly pretty face. That face

certainly had no need of makeup applied with a too lavish hand. Between thickly beaded lashes blue eyes sparkled; under a scrap of fur and feathers that did duty as a hat dark curls gleamed. She said uncertainly, "Marilou? Marilou Flanders?"

"The same. You didn't recognize me."

"I haven't seen you for years. The last time I saw you you were a child."

One of the young men, looking bored, pulled at the girl's arm. "Come on, Time's wasting."

"It's *my* time." Marilou's pointed chin lifted and she shook loose from his grasp. "Take off. I'm going to visit with Cousin Elizabeth."

"Will we see you later?"

"If you're lucky." Turning her back on the man, she pointed across the street. "Let's go over to that diner, Elizabeth, and have coffee."

They perched on high stools and while Elizabeth was unloading her parcels on the counter she noticed the pimply faced youth behind it ogling her companion. He leered at Marilou and asked, "What'll you have, honey?"

She gave him a disdainful look. "All I need from you is coffee." She turned to Elizabeth. "So you didn't recognize me. I shouldn't be surprised. I was sent into exile with the holy sisters not long after the famous coal cellar episode."

Recalling Aunt Van's description of that episode, Elizabeth felt herself blushing. Marilou gave a brittle little laugh. "It wasn't as steamy as it may have sounded. All Billy and I were doing were playing doctor. We did take our clothes off but even after I tried to reason with father he believed the worst. To get me off his hands he bundled me off to that convent, probably thinking I'd use the time to contemplate my sins."

"Did you?"

"All it did was whet my appetite to get back to civilization. I've years of being virtually a prisoner to make up for. Years when all my age group were having mad fun. And I fully intend to make up for lost time. I'm going to do father one better."

Elizabeth sighed. "Do you think that wise?"

"Why shouldn't I? The old goat's had one hell of a good time. Women, women everywhere. His latest tootsie is a real 'It' girl, not much older than me. I figure what's sauce for the gander is sauce for the gosling." Marilou asked pertly, "Am I shocking Cousin Elizabeth?"

"I'm shockproof. But what about your mother?"

"What about her?"

"You may be punishing your father but you're punishing Nina too."

"All mother's interested in is brainy Susan. I don't really blame her. I was always daddy's little girl and mother had nothing to say about me."

Elizabeth had a hunch the girl *did* care. The rouged lips were quirked with pain. Carefully she probed, "Now that you're . . . free . . . what do you intend to do?"

"You mean like a profession? Devote my life to important things, like Susan? I'm not brainy and I'm lazy. What I'm doing is having fun, fun, and more fun."

"What does this fun consist of?"

Marilou darted a defiant look at the older woman. "Nightclubs and bathtub gin and dancing and, of course, the most fun thing—men. I suppose here comes the lecture."

Shaking her head, Elizabeth started to gather up her parcels. Marilou threw a quarter in the direction of the counter mand and climbed off the stool. "Wonders will never cease! You're one of the few people who doesn't consider it necessary to lecture this poor sinner."

"I know nothing about having fun. Never had the chance. But I do know all about being lonely. I wonder . . . after the music is over and the dancing done, after the men have vanished—what will your life be like? Nothing lasts forever, not even good looks and good times and youth."

The girl tossed her head. "I knew it was too good to be true. Carry on, let's hear the rest of the lecture."

"I've nothing more to say. It's your life."

"*Elizabeth.*" Aunt Van's voice, shrill with impatience, wrenched Elizabeth back to the present, to the white drawing room and the snow brushing softly against the windows. "*Will* you stop daydreaming? You started to tell me about meeting the Flanders girl and then you just faded away. What did you think about the little devil?"

"Marilou isn't a little devil and I feel sorry for her."

"Sorry for that minx? It's her parents you should feel sorry for."

"Aunt Van, the girl is confused. She's a lost child thrown into a world with no stability, no values. Hitting out blindly, trying to hurt. I'm afraid the one who will be hurt the most is Marilou."

Selecting a macaroon from the cake plate, Aunt Van contentedly munched. "No doubt about Marilou heading for a bad end but I tell you what *I* would do if I were her parent. I'd pack her right back to that convent again."

— 20 —

That evening in the Flanders drawing room a similar remark was made. "I've half a mind to send Marilou back to the convent," Albert told his wife. "She's making the rounds of the speakeasies like a bitch in heat with a pack of dogs after her. I've tried everything I can think of, Nina. I locked her in her room and the little devil shinnied down the drain pipe. I cut off her allowance but that didn't bother her. Too many men ready and willing to pay her way. I threatened to disinherit her and she laughed at me." His wife made a soothing murmur and Albert shot an exasperated look at her. "At least you could pretend to have some interest in your daughter's behavior."

Nina lifted a placid face from her needlework. "*My* daughter? From the moment she was born Marilou has been *your* daughter. You never allowed me to have any say in her rearing. It's too late now for me to intercede."

"And you haven't time to bother. Nina, all you think of is Susan. That girl! Not only taking a law degree with your blessing and that little inheritance from your aunt, but then moving into an apartment with your encouragement. Decent girls stay right at home until they marry."

"Not now, Albert. The mores of society are more permissive than they were even a few years ago."

Jumping from his chair, he strode up and down the Persian carpet, his slender figure showing anger in every line. He raked his fingers through dark curly hair. "That's all I hear. From Susan and Marilou and you. Times have changed. Even Aunt Van keeps singing the same tune. And times haven't changed that much. Every time I go to the club I see friends turning away to hide grins. I know what they're saying. Albert Flanders, bigshot lawyer, who can't even control his own family. Marilou is dragging my name through the mud, Susan is pretending to be a lawyer, and you! You spend half your time down in that storefront office pounding a typewriter. Why? You know Susan can never succeed."

Nina continued to take delicate stitches. "She's doing quite well, Albert."

"With charity cases. With a clientele of the same type of women who once carried placards in suffragette parades. Does she have any men clients?"

"Give her time. That day will come."

"Don't hold your breath." He stopped pacing and glared down at her. "Forget your precious Susan. What are we to do about Marilou? Surely you have some ideas."

"Calm down, dear." Folding her needlework, she stuck it into her basket. When she rose she towered over her husband's slight form. "There's only one solution and you know what it is."

"Marriage?"

"As soon as possible and to someone who lives as far away from New York as you can find. I hardly think matrimony will slow Marilou down for long. Let the scandal be elsewhere."

"But who? I know at least ten men who'd love to marry her but Marilou's having too much fun playing the field. How did we ever have a daughter like her, Nina?"

She touched his rumpled curls and ran an affectionate finger down his cheek. "She's her father's daughter. A female Albert in a more permissive world. Marilou's only sin is she isn't as discreet as you've been."

Catching her hand, he kissed the palm. "How have you ever put up with me?"

"It hasn't been easy but I love you. And I've always known that you, in your own way, love me."

"You're a wonderful woman and I don't deserve you. Why couldn't we have had a daughter just like you?"

"We have, dear. Susan." In the archway she paused and smiled at him. "You have a devious lawyer's mind, Albert. Use it. Get Marilou off your hands even if you have to trick her into marriage."

Slumping down in the chair she'd just vacated, Albert gazed fixedly at the wall.

The answer to Albert's problem was sitting at a table in a speakeasy on West 44th Street called the Busted Flush. He stood six-five in his cowboy boots, weighed in at two hundred and fifty, and was fifty-six years old. He wore a black suit picked out with embroidery and a white Stetson was balanced on the back on his head. He was a Texan, a rancher, and wealthy. His name was Buford Baxter but all his friends and some of his enemies called him Big Bu. The man across the table counted himself lucky to be Big Bu's friend as well as business associate. Big Bu could be gentle as a kitten or as dangerous as a charging bull.

"Must admit, Ed, you've really shown me the town. Great little city but this booze is plumb awful."

His friend grinned tiredly. He was Big Bu's junior by twenty years but the rancher had set an exhausting pace. "Too strong?" he asked.

"Like lemonade." With a thick disdainful finger the Texan flicked the glass away. "I was raised on white lightning and this so-called whiskey is cut with enough water to float a liner. Beyond me how this pack of folks can get high on it. But look at them."

The Busted Flush was crowded with drunks—female drunks, male drunks, young drunks, middle-aged drunks. Their hoots of laughter, shrill voices, and the din from the jazz band rocked the place. Against the wall a couple of hefty bouncers lounged, keeping an eye on the patrons. Big Bu peered across the smoky room. "May not be polite to say this but these females look like something you'd pick up at a bargain basement. Ain't spotted one filly I'd put in my own corral."

Ed took a cautious sip of his own drink. Weak! Old Bu must have a stomach like his own horses. "You still looking for a wife?"

"Been looking for one since Ethel passed on. Man wasn't meant to live alone. Say . . . take a gander at that little girl just came in. One with the two boys. Now, that makes me eat my words."

Ed followed his friend's eyes. The girl was petite, dressed in a tight midnight blue dress, and she had a cap of lustrous curls. She turned her head and he saw the haughty lines of a prominent nose, thickly lashed eyes, a delicate chin. "Forget it. You wouldn't want to sling a rope on that one."

"You know her?"

"Not many people who don't. That's Marilou Flanders. Comes from a fine family—her father's a friend of mine—but she's as wild as they come. She was educated at a convent school but it's anyone's guess how they ever kept her pegged down."

Big Bu was watching the girl intently. Her escorts, one short and fair, the other taller and dark, were arguing about who was going to pull out her chair. They both grabbed the back of it and started to yank. Giving them a disgusted look, the girl circled the table and selected another. "When she's around there's always a fight," Ed said. "Notice the bouncers? As soon as she walked in they came to attention. She drives men wild."

"I can see why. Nicest filly I ever did lay eyes on. Just needs a little gentling."

"Forget her," Ed told him.

The rancher's eyes drifted down the curves of the girl's body. "Know you mean well, Ed, but don't push. Can see she's got the makings of a good woman. Only trouble is she hasn't found a man can handle her. If those lads with her are a sample of the men in her life she's been cheated." Absently, his big hand engulfed the glass and he tossed off the raw liquor as though it *were* lemonade. "Never saw a filly I couldn't break to saddle. Hey, you're right. There's gonna be a fight."

While Big Bu had been admiring the girl her escorts were arguing. The dark boy shrugged, pushed away from the table, and went around to Marilou. He was evidently asking her to dance but she shook her curly head. He grabbed her arm and started to pull her up. In a flash the other boy was around the table. He belted the taller boy and sent him sprawling back, knocking over glasses and ashtrays. The taller boy came up from the floor with his fists flailing and this time the blond went sprawling.

Laughing with delight, Marilou climbed up on the table. While the young men fought she started to shimmy. More people were watching her than the fight. Every curve was gyrating. Ed tore his eyes away. "Where are you going?"

Settling the Stetson firmly on his head, Big Bu grinned. "Gonna lasso me a filly. Thanks for all your trouble, Ed. See you the next time I hit the big city."

He bowlegged his way across the room, his size dwarfing everyone in it. A bouncer moved in on him and Big Bu casually backhanded him. The man's body catapulted away. Reaching the girl's table, Big Bu picked up both struggling boys by the napes of their necks and knocked their heads together. They went limp and he tossed them into a corner. Then he plucked the girl off the table, threw her across a shoulder, and started toward the door. Tiny fists beat impotently on his broad back and she screamed like a scalded cat. The other bouncer made a half-hearted effort to intercept them but when the rancher's free arm lifted he fell back and shrugged.

Leaning back in his chair, Ed bellowed with laughter. His last sight of Marilou Flanders was her small face, scarlet with rage, bobbing over Big Bu's shoulder.

When a maid came bustling into the drawing room Albert tore his eyes from the wall and asked irritably, "What is it, Dora?"

"Miss Marilou, sir. A man's bringing her home."

"So?"

"A giant! He's carrying her like a sack of potatoes, sir."

"Nonsense!"

Dora pointed dramatically at the window. "Look yourself, sir."

Albert looked and his mouth sagged open. At the curb was a

taxi with a staring driver leaning out of the window. Sauntering up the walk was the largest man Albert had ever seen. He wore a white Stetson and cowboy boots and he was in shirtsleeves. Across one shoulder was a struggling bundle wrapped in what looked like the man's coat. Slender legs and strapped sandals thrashed free of the coat. "My God," Albert breathed. "Dora, get Mrs. Flanders." He headed toward the door at a run.

As he flung it wide the man stepped up and asked Albert, "This the right place? This your girl?"

Albert was speechless but he managed to nod. The man patted the bouncing behind and carefully lowered his burden until the sandals touched the carpet. Marilou promptly tore off the coat and threw it at him. Then she kicked him violently in the shins. He caught the coat, draped it over his arm, and patted her curls. "Spirited, ain't you? Better get along upstairs and cry for a spell. Make you feel better."

Marilou showed no signs of weeping. Her face was flushed with rage and the dark blue eyes glistened. "You big ape! Now you're going to get it. Throw him out, papa!"

Papa was staring up at the man. To do that he had to tilt his head back. He finally opened his mouth but from behind him a placid voice said, "Better take the gentleman's advice, Marilou, and go to your room." Nina waited until Marilou took a last kick at the Texan and bolted up the stairs. Then she extended a hand. "I'm Marilou's mother. And you?"

Sweeping off the Stetson he engulfed her hand in his. "Pleased to meetcha, ma'am. Buford Baxter's the name."

"What happened?"

"Little girl got into a dustup at a place called the Busted Flush. No place for a lady. Thought I'd better bring her home." He chuckled. "Her the size of a kitten and she scratched and bit all the way."

Nina turned to her husband. "Aren't you going to offer Mr. Baxter—"

"Friends call me Big Bu, ma'am."

"—Big Bu a drink, Albert?" Her husband glared at her and she said softly, "He went to a lot of trouble to rescue your daughter."

"Very well," Albert said ungraciously. "Come along to my study, Baxter."

"Better call me Big Bu and I'll call you Al. Can't be too formal when we're gonna be related."

Albert's mouth fell open again but he snapped it shut and led the way down the hall with his wife and his unwelcome guest close on his heels. Big Bu looked around the study and selected the biggest chair. "Figure I can squeeze into this one. Have to have my chairs special made. Mighty neighborly of you to offer a drink. Hot work handling that girl of yours." He drained half a glass of Albert's bonded scotch. "Ah, now that's fair likker."

Circling the desk, Albert sank into his chair. "Just what did you mean by that last remark?"

"I don't have much schooling, Al, and I'm a plainspoken man. I won't beat around the bush. I've a hankering to put my brand on your little filly."

"Why you . . . you—" Albert was on his feet, his expression as outraged as his daughter's had been.

"Sit down," his wife ordered. "Hear the man out. He could be the answer to the problem you were mentioning earlier."

"Nina, he's a complete stranger!"

Leaning forward, Big Bu set his glass in front of his host. Albert immediately filled it to the brim. "Ain't denying we ain't friends. But you can find out about me fast. Pick up that phone and ask Ed Vincent about me. He'll give you the lowdown."

"Edward Vincent? I've known him for years. We belong to the same club." Albert raked fingers through curls the same color and texture as Marilou's. "Very well, Mr. Baxter—Big Bu—continue."

"I got a spread north of Laredo and I ain't poor. Wife passed on three years ago and I'm kinda lonely. Ethel was a frail girl and never gave me no young 'uns. Got a big house full of servants. Took a fancy to your girl or I'd never bothered wading in on that fight. Know I'm probably older than you, Al, but some girls hanker after an older man. Figure those city slicker boys can't handle a girl like yours. Lots of gumption but gotta be tamed. Shoulda laid a hairbrush on her little behind when she was a kiddie and—"

"I couldn't agree more," Nina interrupted.

The Texan beamed at her. "Not too late, ma'am. Promise I'll take care of her and treat her right. Make her into a fine

woman. Don't have to decide this minute. Think it over and
check me out. You'll find Big Bu's a man of his word."

"Like Marilou," Nina murmured. "About the only good
thing I can say about my daughter is that she prides herself on
keeping a promise."

Albert was sizing up the Texan as he would a new client.
Money there all right, he thought. Expensive clothes and those
boots looked custom-made. That belt buckle was made of about
half a pound of Mexican silver. Not young or handsome but the
tanned, seamed face inspired confidence. He glanced from the
rancher to his wife and saw the approval in her face. She nodded
at him. "I will check you out but I do believe you are what you
claim. You may be just the man my daughter needs. But it's only
fair to warn you Marilou is a vixen. We haven't been able to
handle her since she was an adolescent. And, of course, my wife
and I can't force Marilou into marriage and there's no possibility
we can get her consent."

Extending his glass, Big Bu waited until it was filled. Then
he chuckled. "More than one way to hogtie a filly. All the way
home Marilou raved about you. Shouted insults and told me her
paw wouldn't wipe his shoes on me. Wouldn't let a man like me
in his door. 'Pears to me if we come in kinda sideways we can
handle her."

Nina's eyes were sparkling with amusement. "Tell us what
you are thinking."

In his slow drawl he told them. As he spoke Albert smiled.
Nina nodded her head several times and when the Texan sat back
and threw down the scotch she laughed. "And I thought Albert
had a devious mind. Big Bu, *you* should be a lawyer."

"Maybe missed my calling, ma'am. Well, Al, what do you
think?"

"I think," Marilou's father told him, "we'll give it a try."

The try was made a week later. Snow swirled around the
house and banked up against the windows. When Big Bu arrived
he was wearing a sheepskin coat and in one hand he clutched a
single scarlet rose. Marilou was waiting in the drawing room, sitting demurely on a sofa, her large eyes glittering with malice.
Shrugging off his coat, the rancher handed it to a maid, scattering
snow over the polished floor. Then he advanced on Marilou and
handed her the flower. "Was going to buy the store out, little

girl, but figured a teeny thing like you should have just one. Suits
you better."

She took a delicate sniff of the rose and gestured to a chair.
"Do sit down, Mr.—I can't remember your name."

"Baxter, but better get used to calling me Big Bu. You all
over your temper at me?"

"You were somewhat forceful but I suppose you meant no
harm." She crossed shapely legs and gazed down at them. "Tell
me, what reception did you get from papa?"

"Felt like an icehouse for a time but your paw thawed
some."

"Why did you ask to see me today?"

"Gotta question to ask, little lady. First I want to fill you in.
I'm older than your maw and paw and can't use long words but
I'm solid. Married up young and Ethel was a good wife while I
was getting a start. But that woman couldn't stand prosperity.
Minute I could afford it I built her this big Spanish house with a
courtyard full of flowers and trees. Even had a fountain put in
and hired a bunch of Mexican girls to look after the place for her.
Figured Ethel would like it. But she pined for the old life, putting
in long hours and working like a horse. Wouldn't buy pretty
clothes, kept on wearing dollar print dresses, sneaking out to the
kitchen trying to do the cooking. Maybe I was wrong but I put
my foot down. Told her, Ethel honey, time for you to sit back
and act like a lady. You done worked too hard all your life. So
she took to sitting by the fountain and just wasted away. Died on
me about three years ago. No sir, that woman couldn't stand
good times. Bet you ain't like that."

"You win the bet," Marilou told him with a sweet smile.

"Ethel didn't give me no children so you won't have stepkid-
dies to bother you. You're gonna like Texas too. Learn to ride
and shoot and have a bunch of babies—"

"*What* in hell are you talking about?"

"Don't cuss. Big Bu's woman don't have a dirty mouth.
What I'm talking about is getting hitched."

Marilou gave him one astounded look and then bellowed
with laughter. She gazed at the man with his seamed face, leather
skin, big yellow teeth, and she howled. He grinned back at her.
"Sure like to hear a girl can give a belly laugh. Like your spirit
too. Well, what about it?"

"A proposal! And you're old enough to be my father."

"Wasting time repeating what I already told you. Better warn you I get what I go after. Now, you speak your piece."

Marilou managed to sober but her eyes still glinted dangerously. What a story this would be to tell to her friends. She said meekly, "I'm honored, Big Bu, but you'll have to speak to papa. I could never marry without his consent."

She had the air of hugging a secret joke but the big man didn't appear to notice. He beamed a wide yellow-toothed smile at her. "You want I should ask your paw?"

"I'd love to hear you."

"If'n he says sure. What then?"

She smothered a grin. "Papa will never consent. You probably don't understand a man like him. He's not actually a snob but he does have firm ideas on his kind of people and on yours. He'd never accept you into his family."

"'What if he does say sure?"

She uncrossed her legs and stretched, the silk of her dress outlining firm young breasts. "Big Bu, I'll make you a promise. If you can get papa's permission I'll marry you whenever you say."

"That's all I want to hear." Turning his head, he bellowed, "Come on in, folks." Promptly Albert and Nina, wreathed in smiles, entered the room. "Marilou just give me her word she'd marry up with me if'n you say yes. Al, what about it?"

"I'd be delighted to give you my daughter's hand in marriage," Albert told him heartily.

Nina went him one better. She kissed the rancher's cheek and told him warmly, "Welcome to our family, son."

Marilou was on her feet. Her pretty face twisted with fury. "You *bastards*. You tricked me. My own parents playing a dirty trick like that. Making me marry an old goat the size of a buffalo. God damn you to—"

Her voice cut off abruptly as Big Bu swept her up in one arm and clapped a hand over her mouth. "Told you not to cuss. You gotta lot to learn." He nuzzled her curls with his lips. "Sound like a cougar bellowing. Never mind, little lady. Get you into that sleeper tonight and you're gonna forget all about them young lads. Got a real man on your hands." Setting her down, he consulted his watch. "If we're gonna get hitched we better make tracks."

She stood docilely beside him, her face chalky. "You'll need a license."

He patted his breast pocket. "Right here. Been carrying it around. Better get your coat. Parson's waiting."

"My clothes," she whispered.

"Maw already packed them. Waiting at the station for us."

Through narrowed eyes Marilou stared first at her mother and then at her father. "I always keep my word and that's what you planned on. Now I've a promise to make to you. You'll never see or hear from me again." Turning her back on them, she took Big Bu's arm. Her head lifted proudly. "Well, what are we waiting for? Let's get hitched."

Contrary to her expectations Marilou not only found life in Texas pleasant but in Big Bu she discovered the most satisfying lover she'd had in her short life. And Texas took to Marilou. His friends and neighbors welcomed her and took her to their hearts.

It was a slow-paced life and few demands were made on the girl. The big Spanish house sprawling among cottonwoods was run quietly and efficiently by a soft-spoken Mexican woman named Cisca. Big Bu presented his bride with a dainty white filly and taught her to ride. In the daytime she rarely wore dresses or makeup but dressed completely in white—jodhpurs, silk shirts, Stetsons. As the cowhands watched the owner's new wife cantering by with pert breasts outlined in silk, round enticing bottom bouncing, black curls clustered under the brim of a Stetson, their eyes widened. Pretty as paint, was their verdict, but got a wandering eye and a hot ass. Better steer clear of that one: with Big Bu's brand on her it'd be plumb suicide to mess around.

Big Bu was aware of the covetous gleams in his men's eyes and just as aware of the predatory calculation in his wife's. He didn't worry. Let them look, no harm in looking.

Roundup time arrived and work speeded up. Big Bu worked as hard as the hands and sometimes was away from home for days. One of his top men broke a leg and Big Bu cussed and looked for another. He hired a fellow named Rusty who had just drifted down from Montana. Rusty was a different breed from the Texans. He was as tall and bronzed but slimmer, and something of a dandy. He shaved regularly and slicked down his hair with brilliantine. He fancied himself a lady's man and had a racy smile and reckless eyes. But he knew his job. Which was why Big Bu took the trouble of warning him instead of firing him outright when he noticed how often those reckless eyes were turning on Marilou.

Leaning against the corral fence, Big Bu watched Rusty rolling a cigarette. He stretched out a hand, took the makings, and deftly constructed one himself. Pasting it to his lower lip he struck a match with his thumbnail. "Doing a good job, Rusty."

"Trying to, boss."

"Treat my men fair, pay good wages."

"I got nuthin' to complain about."

"I have. A word to the wise. Know you're new to these parts, son, but were I you I'd ask about a mite."

Rusty pulled his hat lower over his eyes. "'Bout what?"

"'Bout me, son."

"Can't ride with a man for nearly a month and not know him. Figure I know you purty well."

Big Bu hooked a thumb toward the corral. "That white horse of Mrs. Baxter's is sure a likely filly, ain't she?"

Swinging around, Rusty ran admiring eyes over the filly. "Sure is."

"Know what'd happen if someone stole her? Shoot him dead."

"Wouldn't blame you none, boss. Fair is fair."

Big Bu spat his cigarette to the ground and crushed it under a boot. "Same with anything Big Bu puts his brand on. Ask around, son."

Considering he'd given the younger man fair warning, Big Bu let it go. Rusty didn't need to ask around. He had a hunch his employer would be sheer murder if he was riled. He hung back but he couldn't keep his eyes off Marilou. Those britches, he muttered to himself, looks like they're painted on. And that round ass, enough to drive a man loco. Looka them sweet little titties. And she's giving me the eye. Know she hankers after me same as I do after her.

Rusty was correct. As good a lover as her husband was, Marilou was used to variety. The next time her husband left the ranch she walked past the cowboy, swinging her hips and gazing back with languishing eyes. As though drawn by a magnet he dropped the harness he was mending and followed her up to the house.

Fate was against them. Five miles from the house Big Bu's horse dropped a shoe. Swearing a blue streak he walked back leading the animal. In the barn he hollered for Rusty, got no answer, saw the tangle of harness on the floor, and headed straight for the house. In the courtyard Cisca was standing by the fountain, her hands folded under a starched apron. He lifted shaggy brows and wordlessly she jerked her head.

He took the steps two at a time to the balcony and swung open the door of his bedroom. On the huge custom-made bed Rusty was ramrodding his wife. For a moment he stood in the doorway watching Rusty's bronze body heaving over Marilou. Then he strode to the bed and clamped a hand on the man's shoulder. As Rusty's slick head swung around, Marilou's wide blue eyes stared over that shoulder. Big Bu leveled his gun and blew the top off the cowboy's head. Bits of bone and a gout of blood splashed over Marilou's face. She gave one shriek before her husband's hand clamped over her lips. He swept her up and carried her into the bathroom. He turned on the shower full force and held her under it, watching jets of water washing away her lover's blood. Marilou was hysterical, sobbing and laughing. When she was clean he roughly toweled her and pulled her arms through a dressing gown. Then he carried her to the door, flung it open, and found Cisca waiting on the balcony. Her dark Indian features were impassive.

He thrust the girl into her arms. "Get her into another room and put her to bed. Look after her, Cisca. May be gone a spell."

He clumped down the stairs and into the lounge. Placing his gun on a table he cranked the phone. "Rosie, be a good girl and get me the sheriff . . . Bert, better make tracks out to the ranch . . . just shot me a sidewinder . . . no, this one's got two legs . . . sure, I'll be waiting."

Three weeks later Buford Baxter came to trial. Twelve men, good and true, all ranchers, listened to the evidence and didn't bother leaving the jury box. The foreman leaned forward, received eleven nods, nodded himself, and stood up.

The judge, who frequently played poker with Big Bu, asked, "Gentlemen of the jury, have you reached a verdict?"

"Sure have, y'honor. Not a man in this courtroom wouldn't have done the same as Big Bu. Find a snake in your bed, you shoot it."

"Put it in proper words, Sam."

The Adam's apple in Sam's stringy throat jerked and he said, "Y'honor, we find the defendant not guilty."

Shouts of approval met this statement and Big Bu turned to the sheriff. "Better give me back my gun, Bert."

The sheriff thought uneasily of Marilou Baxter in Cisca's care at the ranch. "Not gonna do something foolish, are you?"

"Gonna do that I'd done it then not now. You ever know me to lay a hand on a woman or child?"

"Always a first time." Bert handed the gun to him. "Don't do nuthin' crazy."

"What I'm aiming to do is sane."

Big Bu ambled to the door through a mass of men pounding his shoulders and shouting congratulations. He returned to the ranch and found his wife crouching on the same bench near the fountain where Ethel had once sat. She turned eyes brilliant with terror on him. He took his gun from the holster, put it on the bench, and sank down beside her. Pulling her unresisting body onto his lap, he patted the lustrous curls. "There, there, little lady, no call to be so scairt. Ain't blaming you overmuch for what happened—"

"You aren't?"

"Always had your own way and you're not used to behaving. Tell you a little story. Few years back I had me the purtiest filly I ever laid eyes on. Really loved that hoss. Smart and full of spunk but she kept on trying me. One day she broke out of the corral and got into the oats. Nigh ate herself to death. Warned her and put her back. Time later she did the same thing. Know what I did?"

Marilou shook her head and stared up at the stern seamed face. He picked up his gun and put the muzzle against her round forehead. He wasn't gentle. The steel ring bit into soft flesh. "I pulled the trigger. Comprehend, compadre?"

"I . . . yes, I understand."

He chuckled. "Welcome your husband home. Give Big Bu a hug and kiss."

She threw her arms around his neck and gave him a hug, a passionate kiss, and, in time, her heart. From that moment she was a model wife and in time a model mother. Eleven years later Big Bu was gored by a Brahma bull and died. He left Marilou the ranch, a great deal of money, and two sons who were a blend of their father's brawn and their mother's beauty.

After the funeral the young widow's first move was to take over the management of the ranch, and she proceeded to run it splendidly. Her second was to have the gun that killed Rusty gold-plated and hung over the fireplace in the lounge. Friends asked why she didn't remarry. Marilou would smile a Mona Lisa smile and tell them, "When Big Bu died I promised myself I would never remarry. What would be the use?" She'd point at the golden gun. "Where would I ever find another Big Bu Baxter?"

She kept her promise and never remarried. The promise she'd made to her parents she kept too. For the remainder of their lives Albert and Nina neither saw nor heard from their younger daughter.

— 21 —

If Georgia Vandercourt had been in her usual form, Marilou Flanders's sudden marriage and hasty departure to Texas would have been blown into a storm of gossip rivaling the recent earthquakes in Tokyo and Yokohama. As it worked out the event passed with scarcely a ripple. Elizabeth explained to her cousin that Aunt Van was obsessed with her daughter's beau. "Honestly, William, you'd think we were having the Prince of Wales for Christmas dinner. Here's Aunt Van's latest guest list. Just who are Mr. and Mrs. Matthew Agrade?"

"He's a partner in the firm of Vincent, Agrade, and Keller.

Stock brokerage. Solid firm. Aunt Van, and I think Albert Flanders, and the Standfords are Agrade's clients but I scarcely know the man." He glanced up at Elizabeth. "Is Aunt Van giving you a bad time?"

"If she isn't on the telephone she's here. Right now Cookie is in an uproar. She and Aggie don't get along and I shudder to think of the kitchen on Christmas day."

"Tell Cookie she *must* get along with Aunt Van's cook. I know Aunt Van can be trying at times but she seldom does anything without a good reason. Humor her, Elizabeth.

Aunt Van was humored but Elizabeth's prediction proved correct. On the great day the kitchen of the Meredith house was a scene of guerrilla warfare, with the maids hired for the dinner backing Aggie and the Meredith staff aiding and abetting Cookie. Elizabeth was forced to leave the entertainment to Alan and William and spend her time on the battlefield trying to arrange an armistice. As a result she had only time enough for a hasty introduction to Charity's fiance. When they were finally at table she examined him with curiosity. Roger Pawder was older than she'd expected, perhaps thirty, and had a build like a champagne bottle, with a long thin neck, sloping shoulders, and a chunky torso. His face narrowed down to a pointed chin and brassy waves marched back from his brow. A chameleon, she thought as she watched and listened, aping in dress, deportment, and speech the Vandercourts' friends. Not for him was Dania Delong's brand of honesty, her refusal to dress or act differently than was her habit. Remembering the dead girl's treatment by these people Elizabeth found herself hoping that Roger Pawder would not find approval. He had two assets—candid eyes beaming honesty, and a beautifully modulated voice that lent authority and importance to the most trivial statement. The other guests regarded him warily and conversationally circled around him like vultures studying a new victim.

"I understand," Horace Standford coldly probed, "that you come from the west."

"Des Moines," Roger told him.

Lifting small eyes from her plate Charity flourished the hand bearing a minuscule diamond. "Next month we're going to be married, Uncle Horace."

"How nice, dear," Lavinia Stokes purred. "Such a *short* engagement."

"Times have changed," Aunt Van said hastily. "Long engagements are a thing of the past."

Alan glanced maliciously from his aunt to Roger. "Just what do you do for a living?"

"At present, nothing. Looking around."

Aunt Van rushed in. "Our Roger thinks he might be interested in stocks and bonds."

"Specialized field," Robert Grant stated. "Have you the background for it? Is your family . . ."

His voice trailed off and Elizabeth wriggled with enjoyment. Get him, she thought, force him into a lie. Roger was too bright for that. Aunt Van's mouth snapped open but he lifted a majestic hand. "I've no background for it, sir. Twenty years ago my mother and father arrived at Ellis Island. They traveled west and my father set up a shop in Des Moines. Not large and far from prosperous. Father's a shoemaker by trade. But those wonderful people wanted me to have a better chance than they ever did and they scrimped and saved to educate me." He paused and then added simply, "I'm proud to be their son."

The wily devil, Elizabeth thought, as she watched expressions changing. Horace nodded approvingly and Robert Grant said heartily, "Well said, my boy."

Matthew Agrade's thin lips relaxed in a slight smile. "After the holidays, Roger, you must drop in and see me. I might be able to give you some pointers."

Aunt Van beamed at the stockbroker and the conversation became general. Knowing these people as she did, Elizabeth knew that Roger was accepted. She resented it and wondered why. Roger treated her as he did the other women—with respect and a charming display of old-fashioned courtesy. Toward his peer group—Alan, Ronnie Grant, Earl Vandercourt—he behaved with bonhomie. With the older men he was easy and respectful but not diffident. A model young man, she thought, and wondered suspiciously if Roger had actually been unaware of Charity's identity when he approached her in the park.

After dinner Nina Flanders helped Elizabeth assist Uncle Herman to the drawing room. They lowered his frail form into his favorite chair. Nina handed him the brass ear trumpet and asked in a low voice, "What do you think of Aunt Van's protégé, Elizabeth?"

"Personable, and I vote him likely to succeed. For some reason I don't like him."

"Most discerning. Neither do I."

Elizabeth continued to perform her duties as hostess but later that evening Doctor John took her into the library for a chat and what he said put Roger Pawder completely from her mind. "I don't want to upset you," John told her gravely. "But I'm concerned about William."

"Is he ill?"

"Have you noticed how much weight he's put on?"

She nodded. Although her cousin's arms and legs remained thin, his body had thickened and the little melon stomach was now a paunch. "His color," she said. "At times he's badly flushed."

"Blood pressure. I examined him last week and it's way up. You must get William on a diet and try to cut him down on alcohol and cigars."

When the guests had left Elizabeth sought her cousin out. William was in the study having a nightcap. He beamed up at her. "A fine day, Elizabeth, you did a wonderful job. Aunt Van was most pleased."

"Doctor John isn't."

"Has he been bothering you with dire predictions? Yes, I can see he has you worried."

"You must go on a diet immediately and cut down on cigars and drinks."

William laughed and rose. "Dear Elizabeth. John is bad enough. Don't you start acting like a mother hen. After all, when grandfather died he was well over ninety."

"And your father wasn't quite sixty-five."

"True, but you must realize I've few pleasures left. Perhaps I do eat a bit too much but I enjoy food. Cigars? Generally not more than two a day. I have a light whiskey before dinner and a drop of brandy after. Hardly enough to cut down on."

"You drink quite a lot of wine. Tonight—"

"Elizabeth." He suddenly hugged her and bent to kiss her

cheek. "What would I do without you? In many ways my life hasn't been a happy one but since you came to this house you've been a bright spot in it. You look after me, worry about me . . . At times I feel as though you're the only person in the world who really cares for me." He released her and turned to leave. Over his shoulder he called, "From now on only one glass of wine with dinner. That's a promise."

Elizabeth stood by the desk looking down at his unfinished drink. She touched her cheek where his lips had pressed. She wondered about her reaction to his embrace. A few years ago she would have flinched away from his touch. She assured herself that she was interested in his well-being only because it was closely connected to her own. Then she admitted the truth. Her hatred of William had first verged into intolerance and now was closer to affection. Did hate, like love, wear out? She shook a baffled head.. Then she went upstairs to her room. She stood over Opie's crib. This was one love that would never wear out. She bent and kissed the baby's warm cheek.

The twenties roared on, making little impact on the household of William Meredith. Silver gray walls cocooned those within, nineteenth century furnishings reflected gracious living, old retainers moved in accustomed orbits. At his office William behaved in much the same fashion his father and grandfather had. Despite Alan's pleading that they come "up to date" his father continued to operate the freight line with caution. Not for him was the madness of overexpansion that was gripping many other businesses.

The only person who might have introduced the clamor of 1927 into the house was Alan but he was at home as little as possible. As Cookie tartly said, he used the house only as a place to hang his clothes and sleep occasionally. The only infringement of the twenties were the disks Alan played on his gramophone. Elizabeth found she liked the music, and as she had during the ragtime era, hung around the upper hall listening to strains of "The Sheik of Araby" "Ain't We Got Fun," and a sentimental waltz, "Three O'Clock in the Morning."

To Elizabeth's relief Alan showed no interest in his son or twin daughters. They were left strictly to Tosh and her. Elizabeth wasn't much interested herself in Alicia or the twins. Alicia continued to be delicate and suffered bouts of bronchitis in the winter months. Her early promise of artistic talent hadn't materialized, although she still painted tiny water colors and did a little sketching. She was a withdrawn girl who had a terror of strangers. She seemed quite content with her cloistered life, escorted to school and to the park, escorted to movies, which she loved, by one of the servants.

The twins more than made up for quiet Alicia. Katie, by herself, might have been easy to handle but Jess was a troublemaker. Katie faithfully fell in with all her sister's malicious tricks and followed her every step. They picked on the weak and helpless. Alicia was terrified of them. She had a horror of worms and frogs. One morning she reached into a drawer for a handkerchief and pulled out a handful of worms. Shortly afterward a frog jumped out of her desk drawer. On both occasions Alicia had hysterics and then nightmares. Then, mysteriously, the sugar and salt canisters in the scullery were switched. Cookie served a dinner with the meat course liberally sprinkled with sugar and the pudding as liberally salted. Cookie didn't have hysterics but she did dissolve in tears.

William threw down his spoon and roared, "Elizabeth, something must be done. This is Jess's doing, isn't it?"

"Jess and Katie's. But they're so sly it's hard to catch them." Elizabeth shrugged. "Katie only obeys her sister and if I push too hard Jess will put the blame on Katie. And Katie is foolish enough to confess."

Katie would have confessed it was entirely her fault. She worshiped her twin. When they were four Jess had swarmed up the maple tree at the end of the garden, faithfully followed by her sister. Agile as a small primate, Jess came safely down but Katie, plump as a partridge and hopelessly clumsy, fell with a thud and was badly bruised. By the time the children were six Tosh conceded defeat. "I'm sorry, Miss Elizabeth, I can't handle them. Katie isn't really a bad child but that Jess! You'll have to get someone younger."

Elizabeth found a young nursemaid and put the twins into her hands. A week after she'd been hired the girl took the twins to the park. She'd been warned how fast and cunning Jess was but relaxed her vigilance while waiting to cross at the entrance near the Plaza. Jess jerked her hand from the maid's and raced across the street. She gained the opposite sidewalk grinning amid a din of horns and shouted curses. Katie, on her heels, wasn't as lucky. The fender of a taxi caught her a glancing blow and she was flung high in the air. At the hospital it was found she'd suffered a concussion and a broken leg. Elizabeth returned from the hospital and fired the new nursemaid. Then she sent Jess up to the attic, stopped in William's room to select a heavy leather belt, and followed the child up the steep stairs.

She drew the girl close to her and looked down into hard cobalt eyes. Jess didn't look like her father but she did remind Elizabeth of Alan. There was a difference. She was much more intelligent. "Katie might have been killed," she told the child.

A thin shoulder moved in a shrug. "Not my fault. I didn't tell her to follow me."

"Katie *always* follows you and you know it. Strip to the waist."

"Why?"

"You know why. You've been raising hell and been smart enough not to be caught. You've terrorized Alicia and harassed the maids and Cookie. You've used Katie and today you nearly killed her. I'm going to belt you and I'm going to warn you. Any more of your sneaky tricks and you get the same. Whether it can be proved or not. Understand?"

Without a word the child removed her blouse and her undershirt. She stood stolidly, not uttering a sound, while Elizabeth soundly beat her. Welts were raised but the child clenched her teeth and endured. "Put your clothes on," Elizabeth said.

The child silently donned her clothes. As she turned to leave she looked up into Elizabeth's eyes. Flat eyes spoke more eloquently than words could have. Like father, like daughter, Elizabeth thought. Now she had two enemies. But she'd accomplished her purpose. From that day Jess's behavior at home left no room for complaint.

Although Elizabeth supervised the welfare of all the children, her consuming interest was still in Opie. As he grew from a baby into a handsome sturdy toddler her love for him also grew. The only dispute she ever had with Tosh was on his account.

Shortly after Opie had been moved from her room into one of his own she stopped, as was her custom, to check on him before she went to bed. When she opened the door she found the room was dark and wondered why the nightlight wasn't on. The boy was terrified of the dark. Feeling her way across the room she switched on a bedlamp. Then her heart lurched. Opie was sitting straight up in bed with his beloved stuffed bear clutched to his chest. His eyes were swollen and red and tears coursed down his round cheeks. "Lizbet!" he wailed and flung himself, bear and all, into her arms.

She held him against her breast. "Lizbet's here and it's all right, darling. The bulb in your light must have burnt out. I'll put in another one."

His head moved violently against her breast. "Tosh did it. Bad Tosh. Said I'm a sissy, scairt of the dark. Said—" He burst into a storm of tears. "Said no more light."

Tenderly, Elizabeth dried his tears. "Stop crying, darling, you're not a sissy. When you're older you won't need the light but I promise you until that time comes that light will burn every night."

"Bad things in the dark, Lizbet, I heard them." Lifting his head, he smiled through his tears. "I knew you'd come and chase them away. You won't let them hurt me, will you?"

"No," she promised. "I'll never let anything hurt you."

"Tosh—"

"I'll speak to Tosh."

As soon as the boy dozed off Elizabeth spoke to Tosh. She was wild with rage. Tosh tried to defend herself. "Miss Elizabeth, it's not my place to say this but I know all about children. You're spoiling that boy. Opie's too big to have a light on all night. Leaving it on is only encouraging him to be a sissy—"

"That is quite enough! Everybody has a fear, adults as well as children. I will not have Opie in the dark night after night, not sleeping properly, terrified. I'm warning you, Tosh, you can handle the other children as you please but never again interfere with my orders about Opie. If you ever do I promise you'll be very sorry."

From that moment Tosh was careful not to interfere between Opie and Elizabeth. The only other person who might have remonstrated with the old maid about the little boy was too busy with her own affairs to notice. Aunt Van seemed as devoted to her son-in-law as Elizabeth was to her boy. The Merediths didn't see much of Aunt Van these days. On one of her fleeting visits she explained this to Elizabeth.

Settling back on the sofa in the Merediths' drawing room, she sipped tea and confided, "I know I'm neglecting dear William but I do seem to have so little time for any of my friends. Only the other day Nina was telling me, Aunt Van, she said, you're making yourself a stranger. But with Charity and her family . . . well, they do take up one's time. And Roger Junior is so clever, the spit of his father. Let me tell you what the little scamp said this morning."

With this Aunt Van went into a monologue about her grandson. Elizabeth didn't bother listening. In almost indecent haste Charity had given birth to three children—two boys and a girl—but the older boy, named for his father, was Aunt Van's pride and joy. She babbled on about Junior as she once had about her younger daughter. The thought spurred Elizabeth into a question. "How is Charity?"

Strangely enough the answer was slow to come. Setting down her cup, Aunt Van finally said, "I was going to say fine but she isn't. Charity's becoming much like Earl and Sophie. She's such a silly girl. Jealous! Really, Cousin Elizabeth, can you imagine her being jealous of her own mother? She insists her husband is fonder of me than he is of her. I keep telling her, Roger is simply thoughtful and courteous.

From the few times in the last years that Elizabeth had seen the Vandercourt family she was inclined to agree with Charity. Roger paid scant attention to his wife but danced attendance on his mother-in-law and showered her with compliments. Feeling it would hardly be tactful to say this she extended the sandwich tray.

Aunt Van waved it away. "Don't tempt me. My diet you know. As Roger says, there's no sense in letting go." She fingered her hair. Not only had it been bobbed and marcelled but now it was a shade remarkably similar to the brassy waves of Roger Pawder's hair. "How do you like my hair?"

"Did Roger suggest it?"

"As a matter of face he did. Buy stylish clothes, Georgie, he told me. He calls me Georgie, you know. Do something with your hair and lose a few pounds. You're a handsome woman, he said, and so I took his advice. So far I've lost twenty pounds."

Aunt Van paused, waiting for a compliment, but Elizabeth was temporarily at a loss. Under Roger's tutelage his mother-in-law had come ferociously up to date. She was clad in a short crepe dress and the fat legs sticking out looked like sausages in flesh-colored casings. The straps of her sandals bit into swollen ankles and a cloche hat mercifully hid most of the brassy hair. Her lips were suspiciously pink and round dots of rouge rode high on her cheekbones. Finally Elizabeth said, "Your hair suits your clothes perfectly, Aunt Van."

"Roger has excellent taste, Elizabeth. You really should have him give you some advice."

"Oh, no."

"He could smarten you up. I see you've finally raised your hem a few inches, but those shoes."

"They're comfortable."

"A woman must sacrifice comfort for appearance. Your hair should be bobbed. Really, Elizabeth, you look much the same as you did before the war. Positively dowdy. Well, I must be off."

"So soon?"

Aunt Van heaved herself to her feet and smoothed down her skirt. "Can't bear sitting here looking at those sandwiches any longer. I'm ravenous but Roger insists I lose weight. Wouldn't do William any harm to diet either. The last time I saw the dear boy he looked dreadfully overweight. Funny color, too. I must hurry. When Roger comes home from the office he likes me there. Always has so much to tell me. He's doing so well with Matthew Agrade's firm. He's a genius with figures, you know. Now, not a word of this, but Roger isn't happy there."

"After all the trouble you went to to get him the position I should think he'd be delighted."

Aunt Van responded with a dark look. "Perhaps I did help him to get the job but Roger is the one who's keeping it, Elizabeth. You mustn't be spiteful. Spinsters get so sour, don't they?"

"Why isn't Roger happy?" Elizabeth asked meekly.

"Because they're such a stodgy bunch. Afraid to take chances. Too cautious to make proper returns on their investors' money." She added mysteriously, "One of these days I may have some good news in that direction. But now I can't say a word. Promised Roger I wouldn't"

On this tantalizing note she took her leave. Elizabeth wondered what Roger Pawder could be up to. Aunt Van had been correct about one thing. The man was a genius at handling *her*. Regardless of his motivations in taking Charity as his wife it was obvious the real target was her mother. And Aunt Van was in control of the Vandercourt family money. Then Elizabeth shrugged. She decided the Vandercourts and Roger Pawder were none of her business. In this she couldn't have been more mistaken.

Three days later Elizabeth received a telephone call that was her business. It was from Lavinia Stokes and when Elizabeth heard her voice she was amazed. For the last few years the Merediths had seen even less of Lavinia than they had of Aunt Van. The woman's voice was so low Elizabeth had to strain to hear her. "Can you talk privately?"

Bertha was just coming out of the drawing room holding a feather duster. Crossing the hall, she went into the library. "Hold on for a minute," she told Lavinia. "I'll take this upstairs."

Recently William had had phones installed in the library, on the landing of the second floor, and in his bedroom. As Elizabeth mounted the stairs she decided to take the call in William's room. What could Lavinia have to say that called for privacy? All pretense about the woman's mental condition had been abandoned. Years before, Lavinia had lost interest in her home for unwed mothers and had unceremoniously booted out the unfortunate women and their keeper. In a burst of generosity she had signed over the deed of the brownstone to her son. Edward had remarried. Cynthia had been petite and an aristocrat. Amanda was a large, raw-boned nurse, the daughter of a couple who ran a delicatessen in the Bronx. After the wedding Doctor John persuaded Edward to bring his bride to the family home. Friends expected Lavinia to fly into a fury but she did worse than that. She refused to acknowledge Amanda's existence. She wasn't rude to the woman, she simply didn't see or hear her. Edward and Amanda and Doctor John tried in vain to break down the barriers erected by Lavinia but it was hopeless.

Finally Doctor John sought out William Meredith. "This time *I'm* looking for advice. Amanda is pregnant and I've no idea how this will affect my wife. It could well send her over the brink."

It was William's opinion that Lavinia had been over the brink for years but he regarded his old friend compassionately. "It might be best if Edward and Amanda moved out. He does own that brownstone in the Village."

"Edward's my partner. It's convenient for him to be at home. Anyway, it *is* his home. But Lavinia . . . I have no idea what will happen when the baby is born. Have you any other suggestions?"

"One. Why don't you take Lavinia away until after the baby's birth? When she sees the child it might break through this obsession with Cynthia."

"It's worth a try. I'll take Lavinia on the Grand Tour."

A month after Edward and Amanda's son was born the grandparents returned. Waiting for them were an apprehensive Edward and his wife with the baby in her arms.

"Your grandson," Edward told his mother. "We've named him for father. John Stuart."

This time Lavinia saw not only the baby but the woman holding him. She raised outraged eyes to her son. "What kind of man are you? Bringing your mistress into my home and showing your bastard to me. What will Cynthia think when she returns from England and finds this whore—"

"Mother!" Edward seized her hand. "Please try and understand. Cynthia's been dead for years. She died on the *Lusitania*. This is my wife and my son. Mother, please."

"Get out! Take this woman and child and get out. I never want to see you again."

"Lavinia," John pleaded.

Lavinia turned her back and walked away. Edward shrugged and patted his father's shoulder. "We'll have to leave, dad. I'll set up practice in the brownstone. But it's time to face the truth. Mother must be put in an institution."

John raised a haggard face. "Why?"

"She'll never get over this delusion and others are suffering. Amanda and I can leave but what about you?"

"Will my suffering be any less because she's locked away? I'll look after your mother."

After her son and his family left Lavinia contentedly returned to her preparations for Cynthia's return and John, who always had been a heavy drinker, retreated into the solace that alcohol offered.

With this in mind, Elizabeth sank onto the side of William's bed and lifted the receiver. "I can talk now."

"Have you seen Lafcadio Norton's latest book?"

"Latest? I saw the one he wrote on his war experiences. It's supposed to be quite successful."

"This one is going to be even more so. It's called *Judith* and it's all about his love affair with William's wife. He's smart and it's written like fiction. All about a penniless young man who falls in love with the young wife of a wealthy man. He didn't situate it in New York and the names are changed but we're all in it. Aunt Van and Nina and Albert and—"

"Am I in it?"

"He calls you Cousin Margaret and he describes you as an old maid so innocent about life you never notice the hero and Judith having an affair. You know what he said about John and me? 'A portly doctor addicted to whiskey who without his wife's money would have been a veterinarian.' And me! 'A vain shallow woman longing to commit adultery but without the guts to do it.' Honestly! We should sue."

Lavinia continued, "In the end of the book the hero comes back and finds Judith has divorced her husband and remarried. Brokenhearted, he goes back to England. I wonder what actually happened to Judith and her daughter. What was the baby's name? Mary?"

"Mariette."

"Norton married a wealthy Englishwoman. Do you suppose Judith and the baby are in England? Could she still be Norton's mistress?"

No, Elizabeth said silently, Judith is long dead and Mariette, now Daisy Huggins, is living on a small farm. Aloud, she said, "I've no idea, Lavinia."

"John asked me to telephone you. He says William is not

well and a shock like this might give him a heart attack. John says William must know nothing about this book. None of us would mention it to him but if someone brought it into your house and William . . . You understand, Elizabeth?"

"Thank you. I'll take steps at once."

Elizabeth hurried downstairs and called the staff into the kitchen. Briggs was the last to arrive and he stood by the table twisting his cap in his hands. "I've a request to make," Elizabeth told them. "There's a new book you may feel like buying. A type of romance. The title is *Judith* and it's written by a Lafcadio Norton. Under no circumstances are any of you to bring this book into this house."

Sally and Cookie and Briggs nodded. Tosh looked bewildered but finally bobbed her head in agreement. Bertha's mouth set into a thin line. "Can't see, miss, how you can order us what we can read or not read. Free country."

"I didn't forbid you to read it, Bertha, only to bring the book here. You must take my word for it that this is important."

"I still don't see where you got any call to tell us what we—"

"That's enough," Cookie snapped. "Miss Elizabeth does have the right. Something happened before you ever came to this house. You do what you're told."

"I'll do it but I still don't like it."

Satisfied, Elizabeth returned to her work convinced that the ghost of Judith and Lafe's vengeance were not going to hurt her cousin. But Judith reached beyond her grave, Lafe reached from England, and William was destroyed.

Lavinia's warning had come in late July of 1928. August arrived with one of the worst heat spells in years. The concrete caverns sizzled and boiled and anyone who possibly could fled the city. Aunt Van and Charity took the young Pawders to their summer home on Long Island and Aunt Van invited the Meredith children to stay with them. Thankfully, Elizabeth packed the twins, Opie, Alicia, and Tosh off with them. At the last moment she decided it might be wise to send Sally to help the old nurse with Jess and Katie. Elizabeth had to take over Sally's work and she found it exhausting. William regarded her with concern. "You'd better go to Aunt Van's too. You look washed out. Alan and I will make out fine."

But Elizabeth was eyeing the ruddy color in her cousin's face with equal concern. "No, I'm staying here with you."

On the eighth day of the month she pulled herself out of bed. Another sleepless, sweltering night, she thought, and enviously pictured the Vandercourts and the children enjoying the breezes from the sound. It was some time before she remembered that this was the fourteenth anniversary of William and Judith's marriage. She wondered whether her cousin was remembering that day too. Practically no work was done in the Meredith house. Elizabeth felt half sick and Cookie was unwell. After a light lunch Elizabeth sent the cook to her room to rest.

"What about dinner?" Cookie asked.

"We'll have soup and cold cuts. Bertha can handle that."

Elizabeth went to the library, plugged in a fan, and tried to write her monthly letter to Nettie Towers. Shortly after two the front door opened and she caught a glimpse of Alan. "You're home early today," she called.

"What a scorcher." He mopped at his damp face. "I'm just in and out. This house is like a furnace."

He continued down the hall and she picked up her pen. A short time later he left the house. Promptly at four William came home. He paused in the doorway. "Tell Cookie not to bother with much dinner, Elizabeth. I'm not hungry."

"Cookie's not feeling well. We're having a light dinner."

"I'm not surprised. I'm not feeling too well either."

Pushing her writing materials away, Elizabeth sat back and closed her eyes. She dozed for a few moments and when she woke her back, pressed against the leather chair, was wet with sweat. She pulled herself up and headed toward the hall. As she did she heard a short sharp scream. Bertha came running up the hall. In one hand was the silver salver piled high with mail, in the other was the paper. "Come quick, miss. Mr. Meredith! He's took bad."

In the study William sprawled across the desk, one arm flung over his head, the other dangling by his side. Elizabeth gently turned his head. His skin was mottled and he was breathing in short harsh jerks.

"An ambulance," she told Bertha. "Then telephone Doctor John. Hurry!"

She lifted the dangling arm into a more comfortable position and then she saw it. Crushed in his fist was a tiny yellow rosebud. She worked it loose and stared down at it, her lips set in a hard line. Judith's favorite flower. Knowing what she would find she shifted William and pulled a book off the blotter. A dust jacket of dark blue. In yellow letters the title, *Judith*, and the author's name. She turned it over. Lafe's smiling face, firm lips clenching a pipe, a powdering of gray in the flaming hair. She opened a drawer and thrust the book and the rose into it.

She stayed by William's side until the ambulance attendants carried in a stretcher, stood over them while they lifted the unconscious man onto it, and insisted on riding in the back of the ambulance with him. At the hospital she took a chair facing the doorway of the waiting room. Doctor John hurried by, glanced into the waiting room, and waved a hand at her. A short time later he retraced his steps to meet another man, this one a gray stooped crane with gold rimmed pince-nez. After they were out of sight she still stared into the hall without seeing it. Twilight darkened into night while Elizabeth's mind roved back through the years she'd spent in her cousin's house. Mainly she thought of the later years when her relationship with William had mellowed into a comfortable existence. William hadn't felt well enough to entertain much and he and Elizabeth spent much of their free time together. Sometimes they read in the drawing room, more often they played chess in the library. More, she mused, as though they were an aging brother and sister or a husband and wife devoid of passion than a wealthy cousin and a poor one. On one of those evenings he watched her move her queen into checkmate and shook his head ruefully. "There are times I'm almost sorry I taught you the game, Elizabeth. You have an affinity for it."

"You were probably banking on my bridge playing." She smiled and stretched. "But I've always disliked bridge and I do like chess." She made a move to rise. "I'll look in on the children and then I'm off to bed."

"No, sit for a while. I've something to tell you. I had an appointment with Albert Flanders this afternoon to draw up a new will. Don't look so alarmed. Doctor John hasn't been giving me bad tidings. It's simply that my will hasn't been revised since shortly after George's death and now I have Alan's children to consider. I'd like to outline the terms to you."

"That's not necessary, William. You've already made a settlement on me."

"I'd still like you to know the terms. You might have a suggestion. Of course Alan will inherit the bulk of the estate, this house, the business. I was tempted to provide for his children but decided to leave that to his discretion. I did leave a few personal effects to Opie and some of their grandmother's jewelry to the twins. The older servants—Cookie and Briggs—have generous pensions and there's also a little something for Sally and Tosh—"

"That was kind."

"Sally has been with us quite a long time. How long exactly?"

"Over fifteen years. She was very young when she came to us. But Tosh hasn't been with us long."

"She's no longer young and with the injuries from the fire might find it difficult to find other employment. And she has been good with the children."

Elizabeth thought her cousin indeed had mellowed. The William of earlier years would have had scant consideration for the aging nurse. "What about Alicia?"

"There're only a few trinkets coming to her in my will. Again I know her brother will provide for her. But I decided to buy two trust funds, one for Alicia, one for you. Alicia's will come into effect when she reaches eighteen, yours will begin next month—"

"But you've already made adequate provision for me."

"A little extra will hardly go amiss. Alan . . . I can't depend on him to give you any assistance and I do want to know you'll be able to live out your life in a measure of comfort. Neither trust is large but there will be a monthly income for you and Alicia." William was picking up the ivory chessmen and carefully returning them to a plush-lined box. "I may be misjudging Alan's attitude to you. In recent years he seems to have steadied down and his work is excellent. Like all modern young people he hungers to expand the business and make what he calls a killing but I think I've convinced him that prudence is the wisest course. With that in mind I signed a power of attorney for him in case I am ill or incapacitated—"

"Doctor John *did* give you reason for this."

"Dear Elizabeth, I never can hide anything from you. Yes,

John is far from cheerful about my health. He insists I retire and I promised him as soon as Alan is able to carry on alone I'd do just that. Now, do you feel the terms of my new will are fair?"

She hesitated and then said slowly, "All except one."

"Yes."

"I feel you're making a mistake in leaving this house to Alan."

"Why?"

"I don't believe he cares for it. Not the way we do."

"As Aunt Van keeps saying, times change. Alan may well not wish to stay on here, but it is traditional in this family that all property goes from father to son."

"What about a grandson?"

"Opie?" A tapered forefinger tapped William's chin. "Hmm, you could be right. The boy might wish to have the family home. Very well, Elizabeth, I'll see Albert tomorrow and on Opie's twenty-first birthday the house will be his. Now, don't look so doleful. As I told John, as long as Cousin Elizabeth is looking after me I'll be fine. You do take good care of me, you know."

Not good enough, Elizabeth thought sadly, as she sat in the waiting room. I watched his diet, I saw he got enough rest, but I couldn't shield him from Judith's ghost. Then her eyes focused and she saw the figure seated opposite her. This one was no ghost. "How is he?" Alan asked.

"I don't know."

"Is he . . . is he still alive?"

"I don't know."

"Heart attack?"

"Stroke."

"Oh God," he moaned. He buried his face in his hands.

She regarded him with icy contempt. Alan was nearly twenty-nine and his youthful good looks had faded. Pleasant plumpness had turned into obesity, the pale blue eyes were pouched, the line of the jaw beginning to sag, the wavy hair receding. "Why did you do it?" she asked.

"A joke, a lousy joke." His voice was muffled. "That book Norton wrote . . . everyone's laughing at it. On the way home I picked up a copy and one of those yellow roses Judith always had

around her. I stuck them on the old man's . . . on father's desk.
He's always been so holier-than-thou. Criticizing my way of life
and making cracks about Dania. I only wanted to take him down
a peg. If I've killed him . . ."

Unable to bear the sight of him, she looked back at the hall.
Her face was white and pinched with strain. Alan's husky voice
continued, "I know you won't believe this but I do have feelings.
I know I was rough on Dania and haven't paid any attention to
her kids but I suffered when George was killed. I went through
hell. I love my father. Father and George . . . they're the only
ones who ever loved *me*." He wrenched his hands away from his
face. "I don't know why I'm spilling my guts. What do you
care?"

"I don't," she said flatly. "All I care is what you did to a sick
man."

They spoke no more. Alan stared at the floor, Elizabeth at
the hall. She saw the doctors first and sprang to her feet. "William?" she asked.

John squeezed her arm. "He's alive. Elizabeth, Alan, this is
Doctor Stevens. He's a specialist and I called him in to look after
William."

Stevens looked from Elizabeth to her cousin. Behind the
pince-nez his eyes looked tired. "Part of Mr. Meredith's left side
is paralyzed. Part of his face and his arm. He can speak only with
difficulty."

"But he will live?" Alan asked.

"I can't give you false hopes. At this moment he's alive but
the danger from a stroke is that often it's the prelude to another,
more severe one. Did Mr. Meredith receive some sort of shock?"

Alan's pouched eyes fixed apprehensively on Elizabeth. She
glanced at him and then said, "Not that I'm aware of, Doctor
Stevens."

"It may be the heat," John Stokes said. "I tried to persuade
William to leave the city until the temperature dropped but he
refused."

Alan took a step forward. "Can we see him?"

John raised his brows and Stevens said, "He's conscious. I
suppose it would do no harm. Only for a few minutes. Doctor
Stokes will take you to him."

They followed John down the sterile white corridor to a sterile white room. As John opened the door Elizabeth noticed his hands were trembling and she caught a smell of whiskey from him. Physician, heal thyself, she thought. A nurse was seated by the bed but when they entered she rose and moved away. Alan went directly to his father's side. Unwilling to be that close to him, she circled the bed and stood on the other side. The mottled color had drained from William's face leaving his skin as waxy white as the pillow his head rested on. The lid on his left eye and his mouth dragged down. His eyes were closed but after a moment they fluttered and the right eye opened normally. The other was slitted.

Alan bent over him. "Father," he whispered.

A gray eye examined Alan's face with no sign of recognition and then swiveled to Elizabeth. His voice was a croak. "Did you . . ."

Instinctively she knew what he meant. The book and rose. "It's taken care of, William."

His hand twitched and again she knew what he wanted. She lifted his hand and held it between hers. His mouth grimaced in something that might have been a smile. "Carry on, Elizabeth," he croaked and his eyes closed.

At a gesture from John Stokes they left the room and shortly afterward the hospital. For the first time Elizabeth got into Alan's car. He turned the long hood uptown and said harshly, "He wouldn't even speak to me." She gazed silently ahead and then he asked, "Why did you do it? Why didn't you tell John and that other doctor about the book?" She merely shrugged and he demanded, "Are you going to tell other people? Perhaps that old gossip, Aunt Van?"

"No."

"I can't believe you're protecting me."

"I lied for your father. He wouldn't want it known that his son had done a despicable thing like that."

Alan gave her a venomous look. "In that case no thanks are in order."

"Gratitude from you is something I neither want nor welcome."

They drove the rest of the way in silence.

— 22 —

The next day shortly after twelve Elizabeth and Alan were back in the waiting room at the hospital. This time Aunt Van, shaking a baffled head, sat between them. "I simply can't believe it. William has been looking poorly, but this! Cousin Elizabeth, you can't have been taking very good care of the boy."

To Elizabeth's surprise Alan snapped, "Get off her back, Aunt Van. This isn't Elizabeth's fault."

"Of course it isn't. I didn't mean to imply . . . When did he have the second stroke?"

"John Stokes phoned after four this morning. We came immediately."

"Did either of you get any sleep?"

Alan shrugged and Elizabeth said in an exhausted voice. "We hadn't been home long when we got the call."

"When did you last eat?"

Alan muttered, "Lunch yesterday, I guess."

"You must keep up your strength." Pulling herself up, Aunt Van smoothed her short dress over bulging hips. "I'll go down to the cafeteria and get something."

Elizabeth fumbled in her handbag and found her cigarette case and lighter. Alan's bloodshot eyes widened. "I didn't know you smoked."

"I've smoked for years."

"I've never seen you. Nothing wrong with it. A lot of women smoke."

"William would have disapproved. I saw no reason to upset him."

"And now it doesn't matter. You think he's dead, don't you?"

"I know no more than you do."

Aunt Van returned with coffee and sandwiches. She wid-

ened her eyes when she saw the cigarette in Elizabeth's hand.
"Really, Cousin Elizabeth!"

"Times change," the younger woman said indifferently.

Elizabeth sipped bitter tepid coffee but pushed the food
away. Time passed and she must have dozed. Then she was
aware that her two companions were on their feet. John Stokes,
looking old and incredibly tired, was entering the room with
Doctor Stevens. The gray crane lifted a thin hand. "Mr. Meredith is alive. For a time I thought we were losing him but he's
rallied."

"How bad is it?" Aunt Van asked.

"He's totally paralyzed. He can't speak."

Clutching the chair for support, Elizabeth pulled herself up.
Aunt Van took her arm. "His mind?" the old maid asked.

Stevens shrugged. "There's no way we can tell."

"Dear Lord," Aunt Van muttered. "A living death."

Stevens removed his pince-nez and polished them. His eyes
looked larger and tireder but they were kind. "I fear that sums
up the situation. When we're certain his condition has stabilized I
suggest Mr. Meredith be moved to a rest home. I'm certain Doctor Stokes can arrange—"

"No!" Tears were running down Alan's plump cheeks. "My
father is coming home."

"A natural reaction but hardly a practical one. Your father
will need professional care, round the clock nursing." The kind
eyes turned toward Elizabeth. "Do you agree with me, Miss
Meredith?"

"I agree with Alan. My cousin loves his home. We'll look
after William."

Aunt Van appealed to John. "How long does he have?"

"Impossible to tell. William might live a few months, perhaps only weeks."

"I've known patients in similar conditions who have lived for
years," Stevens said. "It will be a trying, expensive business
keeping him in a private house. I urge you to think about it before you come to a decision."

"My decision is made." Alan straightened sagging shoulders.
"Expense be damned. My father is coming home. John, will you
help us hire nurses and get things fixed up for him?"

"Of course." Stevens started to protest but John told him, "I've known the Meredith family all my life. They're a stubborn lot. You're wasting your time. To be frank I feel Alan and Elizabeth are right. If William's mind is clear, and it may well be, I know he'd be happier in his own house, among his family." He patted Alan's shoulder. "It's up to you, my boy. You're head of the family now."

Yes, Elizabeth thought dismally, Alan now has his wish. He's in control. Many years before he'd promised her when this moment arrived he'd get rid of her. She wondered how long it would take him to make good on that promise.

By the time they reached the house Elizabeth was so heart-sick and exhausted she thought she would fall into bed and sleep like the dead. But she found she couldn't even doze. She took a warm bath, pulled on a thin dressing gown, and sat in her father's chair staring at his paintings. She could see only William. A living death, Aunt Van had said, and that was his sentence. Unable to move, to speak, perhaps with his mind gone. . . . Grief was replaced by rage. Alan had done this, Alan and that book Lafe had written. Lafe Norton, living on his wife's bounty in England and without a pang of remorse exposing William to sneers and ridicule. William had done nothing to deserve this. If anyone had been the injured party it was he and not Lafe. Lafe had not only stolen William's wife but he was directly responsible for his stroke.

Pulling herself up, she wandered around the room. If there was only some way to reach out and hurt Lafe, upset his wonderful life, and expose *him* to riducule. She stopped in her tracks. There was a way. A rotten thing to do but Lafe Norton deserved it.

From the hidden drawer in the dressing table she took Lafe's last letter to Judith with the clipping of her death. She pulled the letter out and read a few lines aloud. "My fiancée isn't young or even pretty. Anne Louise is five years my senior and has a face like a well-bred horse. But she's a wealthy woman and she adores me."

Lovely, Elizabeth thought, and searched through the drawer for more ammunition. Ah, a recent snapshot of Mariette, now Daisy Huggins. The child had Lafe's features, his thick mane of hair. On the back of the snap she printed Mariette's age and then added, in case there was any doubt, "Daughter of Lafcadio Norton and Judith Meredith." Then she lifted the locket out by the fine gold chain. She took a last look at the two young faces. Too bad about the locket. She'd been saving that for Judith's daughter but it should prove the clincher. She tumbled handkerchiefs out of a cardboard box and packed the four items into it. When the parcel had been neatly wrapped she addressed it to Mrs. Lafcadio Norton. Then she printed in capitals, "Private and Confidential."

Ten days later an ambulance brought William home. By that time everything had been prepared to care for him. The four-poster had been removed from his room and a high hospital bed moved in. All the paraphernalia for an invalid was in place, but Elizabeth had managed to leave some of the old furniture he was accustomed to. The fifteenth-century madonna that William had bought shortly after Judith's death was lowered so he could see it. Two male nurses had been hired. O'Malley, a cheerful Irishman, would take day shift, and night shift would be handled by a stolid Dane named Larsen.

After William's wasted body had been carefully lowered onto the bed, Elizabeth sent O'Malley from the room. Drawing up a chair, she sat down, her eyes fixed on her cousin's face. It looked as though a giant hand had pulled and tugged at his fine features. His mouth sagged open and a thread of saliva dribbled down his chin. Gently she wiped it away. As she touched his chin William's right eye opened.

"You're home," she told him.

For a time that eye remained fixed on her face. Then, slowly, it closed once, twice. Her heart thudded painfully. "Does that mean yes?" Again the eye closed twice. Thank God! His mind *was* clear. "William, would you like to see the children?" The eye closed once. William could be right. This gargoyle face would terrify them. "Everything is fine, William. Miss Patterson tells me Alan is working hard and running the business just as you trained him to. You must forgive him for hurting you. He only meant to play a trick and he's completely shattered. He's downstairs now. Would you like to see him?"

Decisively the eyelid closed once. She patted his hand. It felt like that of a corpse. "It's all right," she soothed. "Everything is all right now."

Alan hadn't waited downstairs. He was in the hall outside his father's door. "I heard you talking to him. Could you tell . . . his mind?"

"Clear, and he can communicate. His eyelid. He blinks twice for yes, once for no."

"Did you ask him if he wants to see me?"

"I did."

"And?"

"I'm sorry."

Tears welled up in the pouched eyes. He really does love his father, she thought. "I'll try to explain," Alan said and opened his father's door. Later he sought her out in the butler's pantry. He shook his head. "He simply looked at me and then closed his eye as though he can't bear the sight of me. Well, I'd better get back to the office. Elizabeth, tonight I want to talk to you."

Yes, she thought, talk to Cousin Elizabeth, tell her she no longer is needed. No longer needed for William, for this house, for the children. Her hands twisted together. *Opie*. How could she bear to be parted from Opie? Without the boy life held no further meaning for her.

While William's room had been converted into one suitable for an invalid Alan had been fixing up a room suitable for the new master of the house. Instead of using the study he'd chosen the library. As Elizabeth entered the spacious room that evening she could see some changes had been made. A filing cabinet had been moved from the study and now stood in a corner flanked rather incongruously by a gramophone and a stack of disks. The refectory table was now behind the desk and bore a tray of decanters and glasses. Three photographs were at one end of it. A large portrait of George looked unsmilingly into space, a recent picture of William with the twins at his side and Opie perching on his knee, and Alicia in profile, a tiny wistful smile lifting the corner of her lips. The desk, which had previously borne only a high polish, was now cluttered with books.

Alan gave his cousin a small smile but didn't rise. He did

close the book in front of him and shoved it aside. "It's always been beyond me why father used that stuffy little study instead of this room."

"Tradition. William's father and grandfather used it too."

"The study's not only small but it's inconvenient. Father had to dash back and forth to use the safe in here." He jerked his head at the oil painting of a high-masted ship under full sail. "Help yourself to a drink and splash some soda in a glass for me. How I wish I could drink. In the last couple of weeks I'd have sold my soul to get sodden."

"There's no answer in the bottom of a glass."

She took a sip of sherry while he upended his glass and drained it. She sensed he was nervous and wondered why. Surely this was his moment of triumph. He said casually, "That butler's pantry is even more cramped than the study. You might as well move your housekeeping stuff into the study."

Elizabeth was even more puzzled. Was he toying with her? She lifted her chin. "Don't play cat and mouse. Get it over with."

"You're thinking of that threat I made years ago." Pouched eyes slid toward her and then away. "I was just a kid at the time."

"You meant every word of it."

"Time for frank talking, eh? Okay, I certainly did. We've never liked each other and we never will, but necessity does make strange bedfellows. When Albert Flanders turned over father's power of attorney he let slip that a financial settlement had been made on you before father's stroke. He clammed up but I take it you can leave here any time you want. Right?"

Two settlements, Elizabeth thought. A cash one when Judith had been turned out of the house and the recent trust fund. She inclined her head and Alan grimaced. "I'm in a weird position. I need you a hell of a lot more than you need me. I'm going to ask you to stay on."

"Why?"

"Because I'm saddled with four kids. The twins are six and Opie's just five. Alicia's thirteen but she's a nervous wreck. They're used to you and I know I can't hire someone to care for them as you do."

"I can't believe your concern is simply because of the children."

"And you'd be right. My main worry is father."

"O'Malley and Larsen seem competent."

"Sure they are but who does he have to comfort him? Oh, for a time his relatives and friends will come with flowers and fruit. But they're too busy with their own affairs to care about a man who can only flicker one eye. Father's made it clear he can't stand the sight of me. You're all he has." Alan bent his head. "I've done enough to him. I can't take that away."

Elizabeth's eyes narrowed. "I'm well aware how you feel about me. I don't believe you're asking me to remain in your house simply to provide comfort for your father."

"All right, I'll lay my cards on the table. Every person connected with this family knows how father depends on your. It would make me look like a heel if I kicked you out when he needs you."

She had a strong feeling he still had cards up his sleeve. She ventured a guess. "And you're not sure how long I'd keep quiet about the reason for William's stroke."

He flushed and the expression in his eyes was venomous but he said evenly, "Can't hide anything from Cousin Elizabeth, can I? You've hit the nail on the head. I don't want you babbling about that book."

"You've often said you care nothing about these people. Why the concern now?"

"Because they're wealthy and influential and I'm in business. Satisfied? Give me your answer. Will you stay on?"

Elizabeth nearly bit her tongue. She'd been about to blurt out an immediate agreement. No, she thought, Alan was counting on that. Instead she frowned and let the silence draw out for moments. Finally she said slowly, "There's always been a lot of work in this house. Now there will be much more. Not only the children but William."

Touching an account book with a fat finger, Alan nodded. "I've checked your salary. Peanuts. What if I double it?"

"Done." She put down her glass and rose.

Their eyes locked, neither trying to mask the animosity. Alan said bluntly, "Nothing's changed between us."

"No," she agreed. "That can never change."

As she went upstairs to look in on William and check on Opie she decided nothing *had* changed. For years she'd been living in a fool's paradise, imagining her days as a poor relative were over. William's stroke and a few words from his son had wiped that security out. She did have enough funds to look after herself but the things that really mattered—this house, the Meredith money, Opie—could be taken from her at Alan's whim. Grimly Elizabeth admitted her hold on the house and on Opie would last only until William's death. And William might die at any time.

Alan's prediction about the reactions of William's friends and relatives proved accurate. For a couple of weeks they rushed in bringing flowers and fruit. But faced with that immobile form and the unnerving stare of one gray eye, their visits became farther and farther apart until, with the exception of Doctor John and Nina Flanders, they ceased.

The burden of companionship for the invalid fell squarely on Elizabeth. She coped, stealing time to sit with him, talk to him, read to him. She disregarded his wishes about the children and brought them one by one to see him. Both Opie and Katie were terrified of the twisted man they couldn't recognize as their grandfather and they fled in tears from the room. Jess's reaction was different. For moments she stood and stared with flat cobalt eyes. Then, so quickly neither O'Malley or Elizabeth could stop her, she darted out a hand and painfully pinched his contorted cheek. "He can't move, can he?" she crowed as they pulled her away. That was the last time she was allowed in the room. Oddly enough it was timid Alicia who accepted and understood her father's condition. She was neither repelled by or frightened of his grotesque face. Her face gentle with compassion, she sat by his bed daily, speaking to him in a low sweet voice, holding up a sketch or a painting she had done so he could see it, knowing instinctively when he tired and needed rest. Alicia proved to be a comfort for William and she was allowed to come and go as she wished.

For a short time Aunt Van dutifully visited her nephew but that soon wore off. On the last day of November when she arrived swathed in a new fur coat and matching cloche Elizabeth assumed she had come to see William.

"No," Aunt Van said, handing her coat to Bertha. "I'm going to sound terrible and perhaps I *am* terrible but I find William quite unnerving. I chatter on and don't even know if he hears me. Like trying to talk to a corpse."

"His mind's clear and there's nothing wrong with his hearing."

Sinking onto the loveseat the older woman looked critically around. She touched the shaggy bronze head of a crysanthemum. "You keep the house well but I swear you never change a thing. Never even move a piece of furniture. By now I'd have thought Alan would have insisted on modern furnishings."

"Alan has no interest in the house. He's seldom here except to sleep." Reaching for the bell pull, Elizabeth asked, "Would you care for tea?"

"Don't bother. I'm still on my diet. Lost a few more pounds." Aunt Van stretched out a leg and complacently examined it. The leg was not quite as heavy as it had been the last time Elizabeth had seen her. "The reason I'm here is to ask you about entertaining."

"If you're thinking of Christmas, I'm afraid not. It's a pity but this is the first year in my memory when we won't be having our party. It wouldn't be fair to William."

"Don't worry about Christmas. Roger—he's so thoughtful, you know—said to me, Georgie, it's time Cousin Elizabeth had a rest from all that work. She has quite enough to do with dear William. So, we're planning on having the party ourselves. You'll be there, of course."

"Alan and the children certainly will be. No sense in spoiling their Christmas. But O'Malley's asked for the day off to spend with his family and I'll have to look after William. I wouldn't think of leaving him anyway. But if you weren't thinking of Christmas what—"

"Just a little get-together. One evening soon. Nothing elaborate. Light refreshment served later in the evening. No drinks offered until after Roger gives his little talk. Roger doesn't touch a drop of spirits, you know. He's not a prude and doesn't mind others drinking but he says alcohol and business don't mix. Clouds the mind." Snapping open her silver mesh purse, she pulled out a folded sheet of paper. "Here's the guest list. The Standfords and Grants. Nina and Albert and Doctor John and

Lavinia. I wish we could just invite Doctor John. Lavinia, poor dear, is so scatterbrained, but I suppose she'll have to come. No doubt John will have some drinks before he arrives. Elizabeth, that man is drinking far too much, but with Lavinia I guess we can't blame him. Enough to try the patience of a saint. And Alan must be there. You tell him I *demand* he be there."

Frowning, Elizabeth stared down at the guest list. "What's this all about, Aunt Van?"

"I can't tell you but it is important."

"I'm sorry, but I don't believe I can do this. Not right now. Not with William—"

"Cousin Elizabeth!" Aunt Van's fleshy lips set. "You're getting too big for your boots and you're forgetting your position in this house. I know you think you're mistress here but you're still only a housekeeper. This is Alan's house and if necessary I'll see him. Do you understand?"

Yes, Elizabeth thought, I do understand. Still a poor relative to be ordered about. Rage flared but she concealed it. One of these days, Aunt Van, she thought wrathfully, one of these days . . . Aloud she said meekly, "When do you want it held?"

"A week Thursday." Heaving herself up, Aunt Van tugged down her corset and adjusted the skimpy skirt. "Telephone everyone immediately and tell them they *must* be here. If any of them try to beg off get in touch with me and I'll talk to them. This is *most* important to dear Roger."

"One question. If William was still in control would he consent to this meeting?"

The other woman considered for a moment and then said slowly, "No. William was . . . is as much a fuddy-duddy as you are. But Alan isn't and I know he'll listen to reason."

As Elizabeth watched the chauffeur helping Aunt Van into her car she wondered uneasily what reasoning Roger Pawder was about to propound. She dutifully telephoned the guests and received assurances they would be there. She didn't want Alan to attend and so she used reverse psychology. "If I were you, Alan, I'd make a point of being home that evening. Aunt Van says to tell you she demands you be."

"Really?" His lip curled. "In that case I'll make a point of not being here. Who the hell does she think she is? Is she bringing the entire family? The last time I saw those brats of Charity's they climbed all over me and smeared jam on a new suit."

"As far as I know only Roger is coming with her."

"Pawder, eh?" Alan smoothed back his thinning hair. "I've been hearing a lot about him lately. Apppears to be a boy wonder on Wall Street. Maybe I'll change my mind."

The evening of the little get-together found Elizabeth and Alan waiting for the guests, but when Aunt Van arrived they were shooed into the drawing room. With her were not only her son-in-law but Roger Junior. Aunt Van was draped in yards of chiffon and enough diamonds to illuminate the room. Roger Senior wore a sober brown suit and a narrow black tie and Junior, except for short pants, was in exactly the same outfit. While Alan and Elizabeth waited Roger and his mother-in-law acted as hosts, greeting the guests and seating them. As Nina Flanders brushed past Elizabeth she lifted an enquiring brow but Elizabeth shook her head.

John Stokes, reeking of whiskey fumes, seated himself near Elizabeth. He glanced around and then said, "Be a good girl and get me a whiskey. Better make it a double."

Roger heard him, turned, and shook a playful finger. "Later, Uncle John. For a time I want clear heads."

"With me you're a bit too late."

Roger merely smiled, hoisted his pant legs, and sat primly down between Junior and his mother-in-law. Elizabeth noted that although Aunt Van had lost some weight her mentor had done exactly the opposite. Roger's tiny head, thin neck, sloping shoulders rested upon a thick torso. Heavy legs strained at the expensive trousers. Placing fat hands squarely on his knees, he beamed around. Elizabeth followed his gaze. Middle-aged people, the women discreetly made up and exquisitely coiffed, sparkling jewels, handmade shoes. Idly she wondered how many millions were represented in that room. She noticed Alan was wearing a derisive smile and he was the first to break the expectant silence. "What is the reason for this occasion?" he asked.

"Youth," Roger sighed. "So impatient."

He spoke as though he had no claim to Alan's age group and Alan's smile broadened. "You're only a couple of years older than I am."

"In years, yes. But I shall not keep you in suspense. First I must make clear that I'm not here through my own wishes but because of this lovely lady at my side." The candid eyes turned to Aunt Van who blushed like a girl. "I'll come directly to the point. I'm no longer with my firm. I've resigned and am about to open my own brokerage office."

Horace Standford cleared his throat. "I'm not sure whether or not that calls for congratulations. I've done business with Vincent, Agrade, and Keller for years. Matthew Agrade's father handled all my father's business. They're a fine firm."

"Granted. I have no complaints about them. Matthew treated me splendidly and I learned a lot from him. But it isn't really my type of firm and it may not be yours. We're all friends and I think, without causing offense, I may speak frankly. All of you, with the exception of Alan, do business with them."

Robert Grant looked as though he *were* taking offense. He said icily, "I agree with Horace. I'm satisfied with Matthew. He's given me good returns on my investments. As a matter of interest, what is *your* type of firm?"

"My type of firm, Robert, is one that understands the present market, one that isn't too timid to make for clients returns they have a right to expect. Again I'm going to take the risk of offending you. I know your portfolios like the back of my hand. Certainly Matthew gives you some return on your investment but you should be making many times as much as you now are. Ten years ago, even five years ago, he was doing his best for you. But he's too cautious, too afraid to step forward and challenge an expanding market. Vincent, Agrade, and Keller do business the same way as their fathers did at the turn of the century. And this, my dear friends, happens to be 1928. In a matter of weeks, 1929. The brokerage house I'm opening is going to be up to date. My clients will receive 1929 returns on their investments."

Looking disgruntled, John Stokes growled, "How about backing that up with figures?"

Aunt Van glared at him but Roger disregarded the remark. He placed a hand on her beefy shoulder. "You've all known Georgie for years. You also know that on the death of her husband Georgie assumed control of his estate and has done a masterful job with it. Will you admit she knows how to handle money?"

There were murmurs of agreement and Albert Flanders nodded his handsome dark head. "We all agree Aunt Van is an astute businesswoman."

"Very well. Georgie, will you tell them about our little transaction?"

"Of course, dear. John, you stop thinking of alcohol and listen closely. Some time ago Roger told me he was dissatisfied with his firm and wanted to start one of his own. I love the boy dearly but I am wary of investments. Three months ago I said to him, Roger, show me. I'll give you ten thousand dollars. Invest it for me and we'll see. So he did. Do you know what happened?" She paused and then said proudly, "In three weeks—mind, just three weeks—he handed me a check for forty thousand dollars. With it he handed me an accounting. I looked it over and said, Roger, you take that money and open your own office. I said, Roger, you're a genius and I'm going to be your first customer—"

"Forty thousand?" Horace blurted.

"Forty. Dear Roger is calling his firm Vandercourt and Pawder. So kind of him because I'm not really a partner but he insisted. The offices are ready and a staff has been hired and I thought—"

"Whoa, Georgie, you're getting carried away." Roger patted her shoulder again. "As I said, this meeting was Georgie's idea. Never get the idea I'm looking for clients. I've hired a clerical staff but all the actual investments I intend to handle personally. To do this I must take on only a select number of clients. A number of clients from my old firm want to transfer to me. But Georgie said—"

"I told Roger, if you're willing to do this for comparative strangers why not for old friends? So I insisted he speak to you."

Aunt Van was beside herself but her listeners, although interested, were attempting to look noncommittal. Nina said crisply, "I don't like to sound like a doubting Thomas but I agree with John. Could you give us facts and figures?"

Snapping open his briefcase, Roger took out a sheaf of typewritten pages and gave them to Junior. The boy hopped down from the sofa and handed them around. Elizabeth accepted one but didn't look at it. She was watching Alan. He fished in a pocket for his reading glasses and looked casually at the sheet. Then a slow flush worked up his throat. "My God," he muttered.

"In three weeks," Horace said in a hushed voice. "I wouldn't have believed it."

"You can easily check my accounting," Roger told him.

John had apparently forgotten his desire for a drink. He thrust his sheet toward Lavinia. "Darling, look at this."

She brushed it away. "You look. Money doesn't interest me."

No reason to, Elizabeth thought bitterly, you've always had so much. She tore her eyes from Alan's excited face and scrutinized the others. Estelle had taken the sheet from her husband and her lacquered head was bent studiously over it. Robert and Grace Grant were talking to each other in whispers. Albert lifted his head and Nina said something to him. She put a hand on his arm and he wrenched away from her. Although the room was quiet, currents seemed to be throbbing through it. Elizabeth's eyes sought Nina and the other woman grimaced.

Roger's beautiful voice resounded. "You have the figures. You're thinking, was this a fluke? I assure you it wasn't. I can't promise the gains will always be this large but they'll be much better than your present ones. I will repeat that I don't need you but perhaps you need me. Because of pressure of time I can't allow you long to think it over but you must have some time. This is a serious step and it must be *your* decision."

"I *can* promise you something," Aunt Van said eagerly. "I give you my word you'll never regret coming in with Roger and me."

Horace raised his distinguished head. "How long do we have?"

Roger's mouth pursed. "At most a week."

"I don't need a week." Alan was on his feet. "My mind is made up and you've got my business. Let's settle it right now. Come to the library, Roger."

"Later, my dear fellow. Any other decisions?"

"I need more time," Horace said, and Robert Grant nodded.

Albert opened his mouth but Nina said, "We'll talk it over."

John looked at his wife but Lavinia was gazing dreamily into space. "I'll let you know tomorrow."

"As you wish," Roger told him genially. "Now, Elizabeth, could we have some refreshments?"

When Bertha wheeled in the tea wagon Elizabeth helped
her. Most of the women took sherry, most of the men asked for
port, Doctor John had a double whiskey and a similar glass, but
this one of cold tea, was given to Alan. Glasses of orange juice
were given to Roger and Junior. Sandwiches were offered but
with the exception of Aunt Van, who after darting a look at her
son-in-law scooped up a watercress sandwich, the tray was waved
away.

Elizabeth expected the conversation to switch to casual
chitchat but it didn't. Questions were fired at Pawder and he
sipped his orange juice and answered them. Observations on
margin, liquidity, futures, dripped from his lips and the other
guests drank in his words as if listening to the Sermon on the
Mount.

Nina, with her hand firmly on Albert's arm, left first. Then
there was a general exodus. An impatient Alan speeded the visitors on their way and, closing the door after the Standfords,
turned eagerly to Roger. "We can talk now. Come with me."

"Still impatient," Roger said avuncularly and followed him
into the library.

When the door closed behind them Elizabeth looked into
the drawing room. Aunt Van was pulling the tea wagon over in
front of her and Junior had curled up and was sleeping on the
couch. Quietly Elizabeth went to the cloakroom and clicked the
lock behind her. Picking up the glass, she pressed it to her ear.
Alan and Roger were talking in low voices and she could only
catch a word here and there. Frowning, she pressed the glass
closer to her ear.

"—goodly sum," Roger said and then in clearer tones, "But
my advice is to raise every dollar you can. What about this house
and the business?"

Elizabeth caught her lower lip between her teeth and bit
down so hard it hurt. "—impossible," Alan was saying. Then the
words "entailed" and "no way I can touch the business."

"Pity." Roger's voice was louder. "Georgie has offered to
sell her jewelry but there I put my foot down. But she has sold
the summer place and mortgaged the town house."

Alan muttered and then said, "That's all I can raise."

"As I said, it is a goodly sum. We'll work with that."

"And you'll double it?"

A deep rich laugh resounded in Elizabeth's ear. "Much more than that, my boy, much more. You'll be amazed."

Elizabeth had heard enough. She crossed the hall to the archway. Aunt Van was pouring herself a glass of sherry. When she glanced up she gave a guilty start and waved at the empty sandwich tray. "Not a word of this to Roger. I'm famished, Elizabeth, half starved."

"I won't be seeing Roger, Aunt Van. I've a headache and I'm off to bed. Alan will see you out."

On the second floor she stopped from force of habit outside her cousin's room. She didn't open the door. She was afraid William might sense her anxiety. No sense in upsetting him. If he discovered what his son was doing with the power of attorney . . .

She looked in on Alicia and the twins, found them sleeping soundly, paused in the nursery to say goodnight to Tosh, and then stepped into Opie's room. He was sleeping on his back, thick brown hair tousled over his brow, a chubby hand clasping a stuffed dog. She straightened the blanket, brushed back his hair, touched a warm moist cheek. Opie, she thought despairingly, your father is down there wagering your birthright on a turn of fortune. Elizabeth no longer coveted the family money for herself. That was for Opie and for him it must be protected. Oliver Pendrell had founded the fortune, his son Peter and William had husbanded it and added to it. Now that idiot Alan was prepared to risk it on the word of a pompous, smug egotist.

The old maid went to bed but not to sleep. She stretched out under the comforter, her eyes fixed on the shadowy ceiling. Alan must be stopped. But how? And Opie, the child who was all things to her, the father she had lost so young, the lovers and husband she'd never had, the children she had never borne . . . the clock struck again and again. After it struck four a completely exhausted Elizabeth finally fell into a troubled sleep.

By ten o'clock that morning she was seated in Albert Flanders's reception area watching his large, plain secretary industriously typing. The large head lifted and the woman smiled. "Mr. Flanders should be free shortly, Miss Meredith."

Elizabeth nodded. She felt horrible. Her throat was raspy and she thought she might be running a temperature. This was

the first time she'd been in Albert's office and she tried to interest herself in her surroundings. The reception area was reassuringly welcoming, producing an atmosphere of solid affluence,
tradition, and professional rectitude. White painted walls were
hung with eighteenth-century prints and the room smelt of furniture polish. There was a circular table with a carved pedestal,
several mahogany chairs surrounded it, and gazing down was an
oil painting of the founder of the firm. He was a large man, be-
whiskered, and he displayed a seal on his watchchain between a
huge thumb and an equally huge forefinger. His expression was
forbidding. Albert's grandfather, Elizabeth thought, looking
about twice the dapper man's size and with none of his grandson's beauty. The curly hair, prominent nose, and fabulous blue
eyes must come from the distaff side of the family.

The door of the inner office swung open and amid the rich
odors of cigar smoke and brandy fumes Albert ushered his visitor
out. The man looked much at home. He loomed head and shoulders over the lawyer and wore a fur-collared overcoat and a jaunty homberg. Shaking Albert's hand, he majestically left.

Albert gave Elizabeth a wide smile. "Cousin Elizabeth.
What a surprise. What's the problem? Going to sue someone?"

Elizabeth didn't return the smile and Albert told his secretary, "Hold all calls, Miss Handry. Elizabeth, do come in."

The inner office was even richer and more reassuring than
the reception area. The mantel was of Italian marble, the walls
were mellow paneling, a Monet hung on the wall over an enormous, leather-topped desk. Albert rounded the desk to perch on
an equally enormous leather chair. Elizabeth wondered idly if his
small feet touched the Turkish carpet.

Albert must have sensed her thought. He made a sweeping
gesture. "My grandfather's, every stick of it. Built to accommodate him and neither father nor I ever dared change a thing.
Afraid the old devil would come back and haunt us. Only change
I've made is to move his portrait out of the reception area.
Couldn't stand those eyes." He sighed heavily. "Grandfather
would turn over in his grave if he knew there won't be a Flanders
to take over for me."

Elizabeth was gazing at a couple of leather-framed photographs on his desk. One was of plain Nina flanked by her two

pretty daughters and the other was of two small boys, one looking only a few months old. "Perhaps Marilou will relent and one
of her sons will take over the firm."

"Not a chance. Marilou hasn't softened one bit. I'm afraid
the last we saw of our daughter was when she got on that train
with Big Bu. She hasn't even sent a Christmas card. Her husband
is a decent chap. He sent this picture of the boys and writes every
month to let us know how Marilou and his sons are. No, I'm
afraid I'm the last of the line."

"There is Susan."

Disdainfully he waved that remark away. "Now, what do
you wish? A will? William did see to it that you have a nice little
nest egg."

"Advice."

"Ask away."

"Does Alan have the legal right to make decisions about
William's money? William *is* still alive."

"But incapable of handling business affairs. With the exception of the shipping line and the house, yes, Alan can do as he
wishes. Why are you concerned?"

"I'm certain he's investing every cent of the family money
with Roger Pawder."

"Is that so terrible?"

"That money is the rightful inheritance of Opie. And the
twins and Alicia, of course. Alan's playing Russian roulette with
their futures."

"Come now, Elizabeth, Alan is merely transferring his investments to another firm. William dealt with brokers as old-
fashioned and nervous of risks as Matthew Agrade. Young Roger
is a go-getter and knows what he's talking about." Leaning forward, Albert folded his delicate hands and said slowly, "I can see
you're worried. Let me reassure you. Many people much older
and wiser than Alan are doing the same thing. Both Horace and
Robert Grant telephoned this morning. They're going over to
Roger's new firm. So is John Stokes—"

"Nina didn't seem impressed."

He smiled indulgently. "You sound exactly like Nina.
Women shouldn't trouble their pretty heads with business.
You're simply not fitted for it. Horace and Robert both said

they'd had problems with their wives over their decisions. John didn't. Lavinia was sensible and signed the papers with no fuss."

"Lavinia is *not* sensible and you know it. She's a mental case and as long as she can continue fantasizing about a dead girl and knitting for a child that was never born she—"

"Calm down. You know Aunt Van as well as I do. She may look ridiculous but she has a mind like a man's. A wonderful businesswoman. I value her opinion so highly that I'm throwing everything I have in with Roger. Selling our summer home, and I'm going to raise money on our house in town. That should answer your questions. Alan is doing exactly the right thing. My advice is to go home and have a nice rest or, better still, go shopping and buy a new hat."

Elizabeth didn't take his advice. She went directly to his daughter. She'd taken a taxi to Albert's office but she decided to walk to Susan's. It was a mistake. Icy wind swirled through the streets, tugging at her felt hat, reaching chill fingers through her thin raincoat. Before she'd covered two blocks snowflakes drifted down, adding to her misery. By the time she reached her destination her oxfords and lisle stockings were soaked. The door of a delicatessen swung open and the odor of cooked meat, spices, and dill swirled out. Elizabeth hadn't bothered with breakfast but the smells didn't make her hungry. They made her feel sicker.

Stamping snow from her shoes, she opened the door and stepped into Susan's office. It was a far cry from her father's. The floor was covered with cheap linoleum, a tiny Christmas tree sat in front of the window, four wooden chairs were lined against the wall, and Nina Flanders, wearing a woolen skirt and a heavy sweater, sat behind a table that looked as though it belonged in a kitchen. She rose from behind the typewriter. "You look like a drowned kitten. Elizabeth. Give me that hat and coat."

Handing her the wet garments, Elizabeth sank onto a chair and wriggled chilly toes in damp shoes. "You should have worn a heavy coat and galoshes," Nina scolded.

"I didn't think."

"Did you come to see Susan or me?"

"You . . . Susan . . . someone." Elizabeth burst into tears and searched blindly for a hankie. She felt a crisp square pushed into her hand and buried her face in Nina's shoulder.

Without asking questions, Nina opened the bottom drawer of a filing cabinet and pulled out a square brown bottle. "The sun isn't over the yardarm but I think a drink is in order. Brandy pilfered from Albert's private stock. For emergencies or celebrations. Not that there's been much cause for celebration so far."

Elizabeth scrubbed at her eyes and sipped. Nina continued. "Not an impressive office, is it? Nothing like Albert's."

"I've just come from him."

"Oh? Well, if you need legal advice you came to the right place. Susan is twice the lawyer her father is. She's extremely quick. Feeling a bit better? Good. Ah, here Susan is now."

Susan, dressed in a smart black suit with a flood of snowy lace at the throat, was ushering out two clients. Not only did her office differ from her father's but so did her clientele. The man was in working clothes and wore patched boots. The woman's shoddy coat was frayed at the hem. Both spoke in thick mid-European accents. The man shook Susan's hand, not once, but twice. As the door closed behind them Susan smiled at Elizabeth and gestured at the inner office. Elizabeth and Nina, still holding the bottle, followed her. The private office wasn't much better furnished than the reception area. A cheap pine bookcase was filled with legal tomes and an electric heater beamed with warmth.

Nina pulled back a chair. "Take this one, Elizabeth, the other has a weak leg. We have an attic full of furniture at home but Albert became pettish and refused to let us use it so this stuff was picked up at secondhand stores. Well, at least we have this brandy." She poured a generous amount of her husband's brandy into two glasses and raised her brows at Elizabeth. When the other woman shook her head, she handed a glass to her daughter. "Indulge yourself, Susan, this is an occasion."

Susan's eyes, as lovely as her father's, searched Elizabeth's haggard face, lingered on the swollen eyes. "But not a celebration."

"See? I told you she was quick. Definitely not a celebration. Elizabeth's just come from your father."

"Let me guess," Susan said. "Alan's decided to throw in with Roger Pawder's up-to-date firm."

"And there's no way to block him. Your father told me that."

"Alan has oodles of company," Nina told her. "I was up half the night trying to persuade Albert to steer clear of that young man. When he refused I tried to get his promise he'd hazard only a percentage of his money but not only is he going in whole hog but he's borrowing money on our home and selling the summer place."

"He told me that. He said the Standfords, the Grants, and Doctor John are in too." Elizabeth looked at Susan. The young woman was a beauty—she looked much like her younger sister and her father but there was a difference. Marilou and Albert had expressions of arrogance, Susan looked compassionate. "Tell me, am I being hysterical?"

"Have you reason to think Aunt Van's wonder kid is crooked?" Susan asked.

"No. I think it's worse than that. I believe he's honest and sincere and convinced he can do what he claims. I think the danger from him comes from the fact he's so conceited he can see no other viewpoint but his own."

"I agree," Nina said. "That's what I tried to tell Albert. Good intentions do pave the way to hell."

Elizabeth swung almost angrily on Nina. "What's wrong with people? None of you have ever known hunger or want. You have so much and have had for generations. The Flanderses and Merediths and Stokeses have lovely homes, clothes, cars, servants. So do the Standfords and Grants. Why do they need more?"

"Greed. Good old-fashioned greed. Visions of sugarplums and of doubling or even tripling their money are dancing through their heads."

"It just isn't the wealthy." Susan bent over the desk. "It's everyone. Working people are selling their houses, cashing in their Liberty bonds. It's like gold fever. This country seems to be in the grip of a madness, a mass hysteria. That couple who just left. They've scrimped and saved for years and have a little fund set aside to educate their sons. They asked my advice about speculating. I told them to get their money into government bonds and keep it there. If I'm right they'll thank me. If not . . . probably come around and tear my hair out. You haven't asked advice but I'd give you the same. If you have any extra cash get it in bonds."

"I already have. Tell me, how do you think this will end?"

Susan shrugged an elegant shoulder. "I haven't a crystal ball and I'm a lawyer, not an economist. I can only guess. There's a possibility father and Alan and Aunt Van are right. I have no doubt money will flow in for a time. If Pawder is a financial genius he may sell out at the right moment. If not . . ." She frowned and added, "My hunch is that this is a house of cards and sooner or later it's going to come crashing down." More lightly she said, "That's only one person's opinion and I could be wrong. Now, how about letting me buy lunch? There's a deli up the street that does lovely hot pastrami."

"Thank you, no. I'd better get home." Elizabeth rose and the room whirled around her.

Nina's strong hand clasped her arm and eased her back into the chair. "You're not only upset, Elizabeth, you're sick."

"I didn't sleep well last night and I might have a touch of grippe."

"I'll take you home and call Doctor John."

"No . . . just a cab. I'll go straight to bed."

Nina wouldn't let her put her damp coat back on. She bundled her in her own heavy wool one and Susan insisted on tying a wool scarf around her head. Both women took her out to the cab. As Susan helped her into it, she asked, "Did father give you any pointers?"

"He told me to go out and buy a new hat."

Nina and her daughter hooted with laughter. Nina sputtered, "That's exactly what he told Susan when she entered law school."

"Buy a little hat to put on your empty little head, little girl," Susan giggled. "Leave the mental work to men. That's father. Take care, Elizabeth. If you want to talk, remember mother and I are here."

Despite the warm coat she shivered all the way home. When she entered the house her teeth were chattering. Bertha looked alarmed and Elizabeth told her, "You and Cookie will have to cope. I'm going straight to bed."

"Shall I call Doctor Stokes?"

"No. I just want to rest."

"I'll bring you tea and a hot water bottle."

"Do that," Elizabeth said. As she pulled herself up the staircase she silently admitted that neither tea nor warmth were going to help her sickness.

— 23 —

In Manhattan 1929 arrived amid scenes of hectic gaiety. Hotels, ballrooms, speakeasies were crowded with celebrants. At midnight Times Square was jammed with screaming, singing people. Champagne flowed in fountains and the infant year was toasted as one of prosperity and good fortune.

As the year moved into spring and then into summer the predictions seemed to be coming true. Speculation fever continued unabated. Fortunes were made and money flowed as lavishly as the champagne. Even Elizabeth's fears receded and she began to think that Susan and Nina Flanders and she had been wrong and the rest of their friends right. It truly seemed like a time for rejoicing. Alan gained more weight, wore a smug expression, grew a mustache, bought a new car, established a mistress in an expensive apartment. When she took the housekeeping records to the library for his approval he brushed them aside.

"Spend all you like," he told her jovially. "Money is no object."

Deciding he was asking to be robbed blind, she did just that. She padded the accounts and tucked the difference between her figures and the actual running expenses into a metal box she kept under her bed. She dubbed it Opie's Box.

Alan Meredith wasn't the only one to glow with good fortune. Estelle Standford draped her lacquered beauty in rubies, Grace Grant went her one better with emeralds, Doctor John imported bonded whiskey from Canada, Albert Flanders managed to get a sixteen-year-old beauty pregnant and bought off her parents, Aunt Van continued to lose weight and had a designer come from Paris to fashion her new wardrobe. Elizabeth watched enviously but left her savings in government bonds.

In August the Standfords and Grants set sail for a European tour and a bon voyage party was held in their staterooms. Crowded back in a corner and largely ignored, Elizabeth wondered why she had bothered coming. Doctor John and Albert appeared without their ladies. The good doctor had a token glass of champagne and then proceeded to demolish a bottle of whiskey. Albert was busily ogling a young niece of Estelle's. At the height of the party Aunt Van and her son-in-law appeared bearing flowers and still more champagne. Aunt Van's hair was freshly dyed and she was wearing one of her new outfits. As the woman simpered up at Roger, Elizabeth thought she looked decidedly like a thin pig. Everyone clustered around Roger like bees around a particularly succulent flower. Even Doctor John deserted the whiskey and Albert the girl to hang on the man's every sonorous word. Roger accepted the homage with stately grace.

The good times continued to flow and in early September when Elizabeth seated herself opposite Alan at the breakfast table he was humming as he helped himself to grilled kidneys, sausages, bacon, and scrambled eggs. He darted a glance at his cousin's meager breakfast. "Why the long face? Oh, I suppose it's Opie. You miss the little chap, don't you?"

"He seems too young to go to boarding school. I still think day school would have been better. And it's so far away."

"Not that far. Only in Tennessee. You know it was father's wish."

Elizabeth nodded. Before his stroke William had decided on the academy. The school was a fine one, expensive. But she longed for her boy.

Alan poured more coffee and told her, "Good news yesterday from Roger. I'm making money hand over fist. Still think I made a mistake?"

"I never said you did."

"You didn't have to. That aura of disapproval of yours speaks louder than words." Leaning back, he carefully wiped his fledgling mustache. "Father still knows nothing about it, does he?"

"I see no reason to upset him."

"He always figured George was smarter than me. Wait until I tell him his black sheep now has gleaming white wool. Maybe tonight I'll take the figures up and explain them. I'll bet after that he'll be glad to have me come in and see him."

"Do you think it wise? It's still so speculative and your father's very conservative. You wouldn't want to endanger his health."

"You could be right." Alan pushed back his chair. "Tell you what, I'll make a bargain with you. I won't say a word to father until I sell out and I'll give him—what do the French call it?"

"Fait accompli." Elizabeth crumbled her toast. "You're thinking of getting out of the market?"

"Considering it. When we saw the Standfords and Grants off I was thinking I'd like to do the Grand Tour myself. Maybe next year. Perhaps buy more freighters and expand the company. On New Year's Eve I'm going to tell Roger to sell." He stretched and said happily, "I've a feeling 1930 is going to be one hell of a fine year."

I hope it is, Elizabeth thought, I hope the good times will roll on. But she was glad Alan was going to get out of the market. Opie's future, she told herself, looked like a bright one.

Through the remainder of the crisp September days and into October Alan's ego and waistline continued to swell. His tailor had to let out his suits to accommodate a growing paunch, and he took to smoking cigars. On October twenty-fourth he returned home shortly after lunch time. Taking one look at his face, Elizabeth asked, "What's wrong?"

"I'm not sure. Some sort of dip in the market. I'd better get in touch with Roger."

It took him over two hours. When he came out of the library he looked in better spirits. "Roger assures me it's a tempest in a teapot. Seems there were unusually large sales of Kennecott and General Motors stock and some sellers' panic this morning. But Thomas Lamont—"

"Who is he? Do we know him?" Elizabeth asked anxiously.

"I do, slightly. He's with J. P. Morgan and Company. Anyway, Lamont met with some of the leading bankers and they raised an emergency fund that steadied the market."

"Don't you think it might be a good idea to sell out now?"

"*Women*. If it were left to you we *would* have a panic. Don't look so ghastly. Roger says everything is hunky-dory and will stay that way if we keep our heads. Too late to bother going back to the office. I'm off and don't wait dinner for me." He winked. "Going to celebrate."

With his mistress, she thought, probably at a speakeasy. Still disturbed, she telephoned Susan Flanders. "Yes, I know all about it," Susan told her. "But I can't tell you any more than Alan has. Father's been in a tizzy but Pawder calmed him down. He's advising his clients to hold steady."

"What if everyone doesn't hold steady? What if most people try and sell?"

"In that case," Susan told her bleakly, "you'd better start praying."

Through the next five days multitudes of prayers may have wafted toward heaven but neither they nor the efforts of the bankers and Thomas W. Lamont could stem the tide of doubt and fear that pervaded the market. The dams were breached and by Tuesday, October twenty-ninth, panic had taken hold and stocks dropped forty dollars, fifty dollars, even sixty dollars a share. On that day, afterward known as Black Tuesday, the bottom dropped out of the stock market.

On that Tuesday Elizabeth woke at seven, regarded the dim light seeping through yellow silk, and decided it was going to be another overcast gloomy day. Time to call Opie, she throught drowsily, and then realized with a pang that Opie no longer was in his room but at the academy in Tennessee. Sighing, she pushed back the comforter.

By the time she reached the dining room she found Alan had made an early start and had already left. She had a solitary breakfast, sipping coffee and eating ham and eggs while glancing through the business reports in the morning paper. The news didn't seem good but she shrugged. There was nothing she could do and Alan certainly hadn't appeared to be worried.

She went through her customary routine of getting the twins and Alicia ready and dispatching them in the care of Briggs to their schools. The remainder of the morning she devoted to menus and accounts in the study. Later she recalled how ordinary it had been, no premonitions of disaster troubling the Meredith house.

In the late afternoon she was in the butler's pantry arranging a centerpiece of mauve and yellow asters when the door flew open and Alan stepped into the room. She glanced up and flowers fell from her suddenly nerveless hands. His face was the color of putty and his hair stood on end as though he'd been running his fingers through it.

"Has Roger called?" he asked.

"No. Is something wrong?"

"You might say that. The market's crashed." She grasped at the table for support and he said irritably, "Don't throw a fit. Roger's a smart man and probably managed to salvage most of our money. But it's been one hell of a day. Horace and Robert phoned twice from Rome and Doctor John's called at least half dozen times, to say nothing of Albert. They've driven me crazy. How in hell do they think *I* know anything?"

"Roger?"

"We've all tried to get him but no luck. His secretary says he was in his office this morning but she hasn't seen or heard from him since."

"Aunt Van?"

"Tried her twice. Both times Sophie answered. Most of the servants have the day off and Aunt Van's shopping. Sophie hadn't seen Roger since breakfast time. I'd better phone around and see if I can locate him. Don't bother with dinner for me but have Cookie make some coffee."

When Elizabeth took the tray to the library he smashed the receiver of the telephone down and swore. "No answer from the Vandercourt house. I tried his office again and Roger's secretary told me the same thing as before. No sign of him."

"Surely if Roger had bad news he would have been in touch by now."

"Right. He's probably up to his ears." He shoved the tray aside and picked up the phone. "I better try his club and a couple of restaurants he goes to."

Elizabeth heard the children in the hall and left the room. She ate with them or at least she pushed her food around while they ate. She thought she'd managed to hide her anxiety but as usual Jess was sharp. Pushing dark bangs off her brow, the child asked, "Something wrong?"

"Not a thing. You go on upstairs and amuse yourselves. Don't forget to do your homework. Alicia, why don't you sit with your father for a while?"

Alicia nodded her flaxen head and obeyed. Katie followed her upstairs but Jess lingered. "Aren't we going to the park?"

"Too chilly. Run along."

"Something *is* wrong," Jess said with relish.

Little monster, Elizabeth thought wrathfully, nothing could be hidden from that brat. She returned to the library and found Alan slumped in his chair, his face buried in his hands. The telephone shrilled and he grabbed it. "Hello . . . Aunt Van? . . . where the devil have you been? . . . any sign of Roger? . . . I see . . . Yes, I'm sure it's all right . . . Yes, I'm trying to keep cool . . . she's right here." He handed the phone to Elizabeth. "For you."

Aunt Van spoke in a hoarse whisper. "Come over here right now. For God's sake don't bring Alan."

"What—"

"Now. Right now." The line went dead.

She said goodbye to a humming line and carefully hung up. Alan was watching her eagerly. "What does the old girl want?"

"Some sort of domestic crisis," she lied.

"That makes me feel better. If Aunt Van's in a stew about a domestic crisis it looks as though she's right and Roger will pull us out of this. Tell her to have him call the minute she hears from him."

Elizabeth pulled on a coat and hat and located her purse. When the Buick William had bought shortly before his stroke drew up to the Vandercourt house Aunt Van was standing on the steps. Without waiting for Briggs to open the door, Elizabeth sprang out and hurried to meet her. Aunt Van was bundled up in a brocade robe and her dyed hair was twisted around curlers. Her face was the same color Alan's had been earlier.

She tugged Elizabeth into the hall and shut the door. Although lights were blazing in all the rooms, the house was quiet. As quiet, Elizabeth thought, as the grave.

Aunt Van was trembling. "It's Roger. He came home a while ago and I was getting dressed to go to the theater and we had a talk and then he went upstairs and closed himself into the library. I can't get him to open the door. He's locked it."

"Charity. Have her talk to him."

"I asked her. She said he's more my husband than hers and I could handle it. Then she went up to the children. Elizabeth, there was a sound."

"What kind of sound?"

"Sharp." With shaking beringed hands, Aunt Van fingered a curler. Sparks flew from the diamonds. "Probably a backfire from a car."

From behind them came a throaty chuckle. Elizabeth jumped and spun around. Sophie was standing in the doorway to the drawing room. She was wearing a pink flannel wrapper and wisps of graying hair fell untidily around her face. Behind thick lenses her weak eyes peered gleefully at her mother. "Backfire? You know as well as I do that father kept his pearl-handled revolver in the desk in the library."

Elizabeth's heart thudded painfully. "We need a man. Where's Earl?"

Stepping aside, Sophie waved an expressive hand. Earl was sprawling on Aunt Van's cherished sofa, his head thrown back, spectacles sitting crookedly on his nose, his mouth gaping open. "Dead drunk," his sister said, "and I don't blame him. Recently Earl and Charity and I received a small inheritance from one of father's cousins and Roger and dear mother tried to force us to invest. Charity and I wouldn't but Earl was badgered into it. He never could hold out against mother. Today he lost every cent."

Aunt Van drew herself up. "I'm glad your father never lived to see this. His three children . . . one drunk, another calling her mother names and shutting herself away. And you, Sophie, I swear you're enjoying yourself."

"I am, mother. And I wish father had lived too. At least he wouldn't have lost the money he worked so hard for. But with the life he had with you, maybe he's better off dead."

"Shut your mouth!" Aunt Van swung on Elizabeth. "Don't just stand there. Do something."

"We'd better call the police."

"No! The scandal. Maybe Roger dropped off to sleep."

Sophie sniggered. "He's sleeping, all right."

"I told you to shut up. Elizabeth?"

"Is your chauffeur here?"

"Of course he is. He was going to drive me to the theater. Henry's down in his room. Why do you want him?"

"Aunt Van, we must get into that room. Roger could be wounded . . . bleeding. Sophie, go get Henry."

Still sniggering, Sophie headed toward the kitchen. As she moved past Elizabeth the spinster's nose crinkled. A pungent odor surrounded Sophie. Elizabeth raised her brows and Aunt Van grunted, "Sloan's Liniment. I swear she bathes in that stuff."

Elizabeth tried to catch the older woman's eye but Aunt Van was looking anywhere but at her. "That talk you had with Roger. What did he tell you?"

"I'm ruined!" Aunt Van tugged at a curler, this time hard enough to yank it out. "*All* of us are *ruined*. Horace and Robert and John and Albert and Alan. Elizabeth, I'll *never* live this down. They'll blame *me*."

With good reason, Elizabeth thought; you're the one who got them into this. She heard a door open and then Henry trotted up the hall. He was smoothing down his hair and the top buttons of his tunic were undone. "Come upstairs," Elizabeth told him and led the way. Henry followed, with Aunt Van and Sophie trailing. As they went down the hall a door creaked open a few inches and Elizabeth caught a glimpse of Charity's flabby face. Then the door slammed.

Aunt Van pointed at another door and Elizabeth banged her fist against the panel and called, "Roger. It's Elizabeth Meredith. Please open the door."

Only mocking silence greeted her words. She had a dreadful feeling of déjà vu. She remembered standing in another hall, before another locked door, remembered Judith's lifeless body sprawled on a bloodsoaked blanket. She could smell the odor of flowery perfume from Aunt Van, the stench of liniment from Sophie's scrawny body, tobacco and beer fumes from Henry. She could hear them breathing. She could feel her nails biting into the flesh of her palms. She lifted her chin and told the chauffeur, "Break it down."

Henry glanced at his mistress, received a nod, and backed up. Lifting a sturdy boot, he kicked the door just below the knob. Wood splintered and the door swung open. The chauffeur peered into the room and hastily sketched a cross over his breast. "Saints preserve me."

Elizabeth stepped into the room and smelled the odor of blood and something more unpleasant. She heard Aunt Van's moan and, unbelievably, Sophie's chuckle. In the chair behind the desk Roger sprawled. One dangling hand clutched a pearl-handled revolver. Mercifully the desk lamp left his face in shadow, but behind him the pale wallpaper was spattered with dark stains and wisps of brassy hair.

"Put the barrel right in his mouth," Henry said hoarsely. "Musta blew the back of his head right off."

"We can see that," Elizabeth told him crisply. "You telephone for the police. No, not that one. Use the one downstairs." She pulled the door closed behind her. Turning her head, she stared at Aunt Van. "You knew he'd shot himself. Why did you call *me*?"

"I must take these curlers out," the other woman said vaguely and turned her back.

Grabbing her arm, Elizabeth wrenched her around. "Answer me!"

"How dare you!" Aunt Van managed to look and sound affronted.

"Why?"

"Because I simply can't face Alan and the others. You'll have to tell them. Tell them that creature ruined me too. Tell them he's to blame, not me."

Elizabeth's mouth snapped open but it was Sophie who said rather sadly, "No, Roger wasn't to blame. He was only a . . . an instrument. If you hadn't sponsored him none of the others would have trusted him. You're the one to blame."

"Well, regardless of that, I *refuse* to be blamed. And I wash my hands of him. The police can get in touch with his parents. They can have his body."

Elizabeth stared at the woman's implacable expression.

"You can't do that. Roger was Charity's husband, the father of your grandchildren. You can't treat him like a piece of garbage."

"A piece of garbage? Elizabeth, you've described him perfectly. I'll tell the police to get that piece of garbage out of my house. Now, I simply must fix my hair. I can't be seen like this." She turned and marched down the hall. Over her shoulder she called, "Elizabeth, you tell the others. Mind you tell them I've lost everything too."

Wordlessly, Elizabeth turned to Sophie. Sophie's untidy head nodded. "Elizabeth, you've finally seen the real Georgia Vandercourt. Not the amusing, befuddled, gossipy matriarch she pretends to be but a stony-hearted, unforgiving bitch."

"She won't even bury him. She was so fond of him and now . . ."

"Roger is no more use to her. Like her decor. When she tires of it she throws it aside and calls in a decorator." Hunching thin shoulders, Sophie said gleefully, "But decorators are expensive. No more of them for mother. Elizabeth, the day I've been waiting for is here. Ever since she killed Judith—"

"Your mother was not responsible for Judith's death."

"—ever since she killed Judith I've been waiting. Mother dear is going to pay. How she's going to pay!"

Sophie was as appalling as her mother. Her eyes were moist with unholy joy and triumph. Aunt Van had said she was unbalanced. Elizabeth decided Aunt Van could be right.

Hours later a weary and depressed Elizabeth returned to the Meredith house. Alan heard her key in the door and ran into the hall. He looked ghastly. "I still haven't heard from Roger. Is he at home?"

"Yes."

"I'll go right over and talk to him."

"You'd better take a medium with you."

"What . . . what do you mean?"

"He's dead." Pulling off her hat, she rubbed her aching head. "Shot himself."

"Oh, my God." Alan sagged against the wall. "Then it's all over. I'm wiped out. Poor . . . I've never been poor."

Taking one disgusted look at his crumpled face, Elizabeth edged around him. "I'll have to get in touch with the others. Let them know."

He pawed at her arm. "Elizabeth . . . what's it like to be poor?"

She picked up the telephone. "You'll soon know," she told him grimly.

PART III
Family Money

Lifting the pot off the burner, Elizabeth gingerly set it on the kitchen table and reached for a ladle. As she filled tart shells she gave thanks that Cookie had been able to prepare the mincemeat before the latest bout with rheumatism had struck. With the wrist of the hand holding the ladle she brushed back a strand of hair that had fallen over her brow. She seemed to have no time for herself, not even a few moments to pin her hair properly. Perhaps she should have it bobbed, although where the money for that would come from she had no idea.

She glanced at the calendar. November eighth, 1931. Over two years since the day when the Merediths' fortune and so many others had been wiped out. Two years of worry, anguish, and unrelenting work. She was so tired she could hardly stand and she shouldn't really have bothered with baking but the children deserved a few treats. God knew they didn't get many. She worked on, roughened hands moving over the pastry shells. Finally she sank onto a chair, wanting a cup of coffee but without the energy to walk to the stove to get the pot. She'd rest a few moments and then she must start dinner. She could heat up the remains of the lamb stew, and yesterday Cookie had baked bread. In the fridge was a rice pudding for dessert. None of them were fond of rice pudding but it was cheap.

Supporting her head with both hands, she sighed. She tried to think of something cheerful. Opie was doing well in school and she should be thankful she'd been able to keep him there. But there was a turkey to buy for Chistmas and the children must have a few presents. They hadn't had a decent Christmas since

'28. She should really look on the bright side. They were better off than many families were. At least they still had a roof over their heads.

That's what she had told Alan on that bleak January day in 1930, a bleak January after a bleak Christmas, a festive season that had come and gone with no rejoicing, without the usual parties and celebration. Elizabeth waited for her cousin to broach the subject but Alan was shattered. Losing patience, she gathered up the account books and her notes and marched into the library.

"We have to talk," she told him.

He shot a gloomy look at the books and muttered, "Nothing to talk about. We're wiped out."

"Not quite. We still have a home and an income from the business."

"Not much and going to be less. In case you haven't noticed, the whole country's in a slump and it's going to get worse. Not much business and running costs are eating up the profits. Sure we have a roof over our heads, but the business can't support this house."

"We have to cut expenses."

"I don't know where to start. If I could just unload this white elephant of a house—"

"That's impossible and you know it."

"Okay, genius, tell me how to do it."

She flipped open a book. "With a little money from the company and the income from the trust fund William set up for me—"

"Hey." He straightened and his expression brightened. "Alicia has one too."

"When she's eighteen. That's not for three years."

"Right. Do you mean you'd be willing to throw your money in to keep us going?"

"I have no choice. To survive, both of us must work at this." She pushed the book across the desk. "These are the present expenses."

His pouched eyes flickered down the items and widened. "Whew."

She watched him. His hair had given up the struggle and he, like his father, had only a fringe left around a shiny pate. He'd

lost weight and his jacket hung loosely but his face was still fleshy
and jowls drooped along his jaw. How she loathed him! Carefully
masking her feeling, she asked, "Well?"

"This tuition for Opie. We could take him out of the academy."

"The tuition has already been paid for this year. And Opie's
staying in that school. That is your father's wish."

"Father. I never thought . . . does he know about the
crash?"

"Yes."

"So you wouldn't tell him when I was making money but as
soon as I fall on my ass you babble. Still Cousin Elizabeth. Can't
wait to make me look rotten."

"It wasn't like that at all. One of the servants might have
talked about the crash in William's hearing. The shock . . . it
could have killed him."

"I suppose so. How did he take it?"

"He's still alive."

"If you could call it that." Alan glanced back at the figures.
"Where *do* we cut? The cars?"

"You'll give yours up?"

"Of course not. I was thinking of the Buick."

"We need it. To take the children back and forth from
school. Cheaper than cabs."

"Who'll drive it? We can't afford a chauffeur."

"Briggs will."

"But—"

"I'll get back to that." Leaning over the desk, she touched a
line. "We'll have to take the twins out of private school and put
them in public school. Not Alicia. She's used to her school and
her teachers. If we try to move her she'll be so overwrought it
will cost as much in doctor's bills."

"And it won't bother the twins?"

"Nothing bothers Jess," the old maid said drily. "And Katie
will go anywhere Jess does. That's the first cut. The second is
that our standard of living must be cut. Food for instance.
Hashes and stews and that sort of thing. Simple desserts. No
more flowers from the florist. In the rooms we don't use we'll cut
the heat off. Some of the servants must go. I've already told Sally

and Bertha we can't keep them on. One of William's nurses—"

"No," Alan moaned. "Father must be looked after properly."

"He will be. O'Malley's cheerful and jolly but he isn't as competent a nurse as Larsen is. O'Malley goes and Larsen has agreed to work longer hours for less pay. He'll take the day shift—"

"What hours?"

"Six in the morning until eight in the evening. Night shift will have to be taken by Tosh and me. Mainly me because Tosh is not strong. I can't run up and down stairs all night so I'll have to move into the room next to William—"

"Judith's room," Alan broke in hotly. "My mother's room. The mistress's room. You've always wanted it. There's no way I can stop you but I hate the idea of you winning."

"It's not much of a victory," she told him tartly. "Mistress of a family and a house on the verge of collapse. Now, the servants. We'll keep Briggs and Tosh and Cookie on—"

"What do you suggest we pay them with?"

"I've spoken to them. All of them are too old to find another job and besides this is the only home they have. They've agreed to remain for their board and room."

Getting up abruptly, he splashed soda in a glass and poured sherry in another. Handing the sherry to Elizabeth, he lifted his glass in an ironic salute. "To Cousin Elizabeth, miracle worker. Going to keep two children in private schools and six adults on practically nothing. Going to keep this huge house running with three doddering old servants and a male nurse. Going to be upstairs maid and downstairs maid and night nurse for an invalid. Going to bloody well kill herself."

"At least I'll die trying." Elizabeth gathered up the books. "It could be worse. Aunt Van—"

"Don't mention that bitch's name! And never let her into this house again. That's an order."

"Yes, sir!" Turning smartly, Elizabeth stalked out of the library.

A few days later she received a telephone call from Aunt Van. The older woman said hesitantly, "I was thinking of coming over to see you, Elizabeth."

"I'm sorry, but . . ."

"You don't want to see me."

"I'd like to see you but, as you once pointed out, I'm not mistress here. Only the housekeeper."

"Don't be bitter. Please, not now. It's Alan, isn't it? Don't bother answering. Everyone *hates* me. Blames me for what happened. I knew they would."

Elizabeth felt a stirring of pity. Aunt Van sounded crushed. "Alan's young. Not mature enough to make allowances. I'm sure the older people feel differently."

"Then why haven't I seen any of them? Except for Nina Flanders not one of them has even bothered phoning."

"They're busy trying to pick up the pieces. Both Horace and Robert Grant lost their businesses and their houses."

Aunt Van drew her breath in sharply. "That bad? Where are they?"

"Doctor John and Lavinia lost their house too. Edward and Amanda took them in and they're living in that brownstone in the Village. Doctor John was planning to help Edward with his practice but Lavinia has gone catatonic from shock and he has to nurse her."

"Estelle and Horace?"

"Their son-in-law Antonio has rented a store in the Bronx and started an Italian restaurant. Antonio cooks and Maud works as waitress. They live in some rooms over it and Estelle takes care of the children."

"Horace?"

"Sits and broods."

"Oh God. Maybe you shouldn't tell me anything else."

"You'd better know, Aunt Van. Robert and Grace Grant are living in a small apartment with Ronnie and his wife and two children. Ronnie is trying to sell vacuum cleaners and his wife has a job at a five and ten. Grace and Robert look after the apartment and the children and—"

"Don't say another word!"

"There is some good news. We've had to make cuts but we're coping and the Flanderses are doing well. They lost their house, of course, and Albert and Nina moved into Susan's apartment. Albert broke down and took Susan in as a partner. In fact she's handling the law practice. Albert has taken up golf and is obsessed with it."

Aunt Van gave a weak chuckle. "At least he can't afford his fancy women anymore. Marilou's husband is supposed to be wealthy. Isn't he helping them?"

"Buford Baxter was gored by a bull a month ago and died. Marilou wouldn't give Nina or Albert the time of day."

"She always was a minx."

The line hummed and Elizabeth thought the older woman might be crying. She asked gently, "Aunt Van, how are you making out?"

"Charity left. Right after Roger's death she packed up and took the children to Florida. Said at least they wouldn't freeze there. Sophie . . . Sophie's taken everything out of my hands. Made me sell my jewelry and most of the furniture. She's paid off some of the mortgage on this house. With Earl's pay and that bit of money Sophie inherited they manage to keep us going." Lowering her voice, Aunt Van whispered, "I'd swear that girl's happy to see me ruined. Never consults me about a thing. Just goes ahead and does what she wants. Know what she's up to now? She's turning my beautiful house into a *rooming* house. Putting in hotplates and renting rooms to Lord knows what kind of riffraff."

"I'm sure she'll arrange it so you and Earl are comfortable."

"All we'll have left is the drawing room, the study, and the kitchen. Sophie's making the drawing room into a bedroom for us and fixing up the study for Earl. Imagine it, Elizabeth. People running up and down the stairs, drinking and carousing and cooking and . . . oh, I can hardly bear it. Sophie fired all the servants, even my Aggie, and sold the cars. She's doing the cooking and you should see the meals. All I had for dinner last night were two boiled potatoes, three sausages, and a spoonful of peas. My legs are bothering me something awful and she won't even call a doctor. Elizabeth, *what* am I to do?"

"Aunt Van, I know it's hard. It's hard for all of us. But I'm certain Sophie is doing her best. What does Earl say?"

There was no doubt Aunt Van was crying. She sobbed, "He . . . he won't even speak to me. Looks through me as if I'm invisible."

How the mighty have fallen, Elizabeth thought. She tried to soothe the distraught woman. "I'll phone Edward Stokes and have him look at your legs."

"I'd rather have John. He's always looked after me."

"John has his hands full looking after Lavinia. Edward has been taking care of William and he's a marvelous doctor. After you've seen him you'll feel better."

That afternoon when Edward came to examine William Elizabeth made good on her promise. The following evening the doctor telephoned her. "Aunt Van is fairly well, Elizabeth. She has varicose veins in both legs and they're painful but I gave her some medication that will help. Now, don't worry about her. At least Sophie is keeping them afloat. I'll try and check in occasionally."

"How old is Aunt Van, Edward?"

He chuckled. "Aunt Van's age has always been a carefully guarded secret. My guess is that she's a few years older than William, which would place her in the early seventies, but with her constitution she may be good for another twenty years."

As she replaced the receiver Elizabeth made a resolution. For propriety's sake, she simply must get over and see Aunt Van. She didn't. The Meredith house and the work in it took up every minute of the day and each evening she set the alarm to check on William during the night. Nearly two years dragged by and Elizabeth became thinner and tireder.

Now, in the warm kitchen filled with the rich scent of mincemeat, Elizabeth admitted Alan had been right. She was slowly killing herself. I'm nearly fifty-four, she thought, and working harder than I ever have in my life. My savings are diminishing and I may not be able to pay Opie's tuition next year. What am I to do?

Alan found her there, her elbows braced on the table, her face buried in her hands. He looked down at her untidy hair, then at the ranks of tarts. "Baking goodies, eh? Cookie sick again?"

"I had to send her to bed after lunch. Her rheumatism again," Elizabeth said dully.

"So now the maid of all work is cook. Come to think of it, you look a little like a kitchen slavey."

Bitter tears prickled at Elizabeth's eyes. "Don't."

"Be of good cheer. This year Christmas is arriving early. Behold your Santa Claus."

She lifted her head and her words came out as an accusation. "That's a new suit."

"And shoes, shirt, and tie." Flicking out his tie, he inspected it. "Sulka. Like it?"

"We haven't even been able to buy gifts for the children."

"I promise the kids will have a gala Christmas. No more sad tunes for us. Forget 'Brother Can You Spare a Dime.'" He did a few foxtrot steps, singing gaily, "Happy days are here again."

She watched with amazement. Gone was the sulky depressed man she'd faced for two years and in his place was this jubilant Alan. "Are you drunk?"

He did two more steps and then stopped. "You know better than that. If I'd been imbibing I'd be coming out in spots and panting like a dog. I'm drunk on happiness. And old Santa has gifts for Cousin Elizabeth." He pantomimed lifting a heavy pack from his back and lowering it. "What have we for the miracle worker? Ah, several miracles. An upstairs maid, a downstairs maid, another nurse for father. And right down at the bottom of the bag is . . . yes, a kitchen maid to assist Cookie so you won't have to slave out here anymore."

"You *are* drunk."

"Ye of little faith. Tomorrow, Elizabeth, you start hiring. Be sure you get a good nurse for father." He sobered and said in an entirely different tone, "In a short while I'll be repaying every cent you've spent on this house. I've hated being in your debt."

She pulled herself to her feet. "You are serious. Where is the money coming from?"

"It's really none of your business but I'll tell you. You and father always thought I was a failure. Well, all by himself little Alan has snagged a contract for shipping to Barbados. And that contract is going to put me on easy street. Don't wait dinner for me. Time to celebrate. I'm going to have a steak three inches thick with all the trimmings. Tell Cookie no more meatloaf or hash. From now on only chewing meat is served at my table." He stared at Elizabeth. "You look like a ragamuffin. For Christ sake have something done to your hair and buy some decent clothes."

Elizabeth watched the green baize door swing to. Easy street, she thought, a new contract. Then, without warning, she started to cry. Not bitter tears this time, but warm and comforting as they dripped down her cheeks.

Within weeks prosperity had returned to the Meredith house. Elizabeth wasn't able to find Bertha but she managed to track Sally down. The maid hadn't been able to locate a new position and she was only too willing to return to her old job. She suggested Elizabeth give her younger sister a job as downstairs maid and it was agreed that Irene would be taken on trial. With Cookie's approval a plump girl named Rose was installed as kitchen maid. Elizabeth interviewed dozens of applicants for night nurse for the invalid and from them selected a short husky Italian with soulful eyes and a flashing smile. Mario took over the night shift with William and for the first time in years Elizabeth was able to sleep peacefully.

When the house was running smoothly, Elizabeth made an appointment with a hairdresser and finally had her hair bobbed. As the long dark tresses drifted to the floor she proudly noted there wasn't a strand of gray among them. She then went shopping and selected three dresses, some underclothes, and new shoes. As she walked along the streets she tried to blind herself to the results of the Depression. It was impossible. The brightly decorated stores, the displays of toys and luxury merchandise only mocked the breadlines, the derelicts lined up outside soup kitchens. Many of the beggars were crippled and wearing remnants of uniforms. On a windswept corner she paused to buy hot chestnuts from an elderly man who reminded her a bit of William. His shabby suit had once been well cut. What had he been, she wondered, a banker, a businessman?

Opie came home to a marvelous holiday season with gaily wrapped presents under a glittering tree, a table groaning with food, tickets to *Hansel and Gretel* and the *Nutcracker Suite*, skating in Central Park. Elizabeth accompanied the children but all she really saw was Opie's happy face. She watched him skating, his sturdy body bent into the wind, a striped muffler flowing out behind him, and she glowed with love and pride. Her boy, taller than he'd been in the fall, his face beginning to lose its baby roundness and giving promise of the stark planes of the Meredith bone structure. Such a handsome child, she thought, and he's mine. It isn't necessary to carry a child for nine months and experience birth to be a child's mother.

Opie was waving and shouting. "Watch me, Lizbet!"

She watched him do a figure eight. Lizbet, the name he'd called her from the moment he'd started to talk. As good a name as mother.

The months passed and Alan continued to provide a lifestyle much like the one they'd had before the crash. Elizabeth, usually alert and suspicious, didn't question the source of his income. Not until early March. She was having lunch with Susan and Nina Flanders at their favorite delicatessan. Nina smiled across the table. "You're looking better, Elizabeth. That hair style is becoming and I do believe you've gained some weight."

"I owe it all to Alan and that contract he arranged."

Susan put down her sandwich and her dark brows raised. "Contract?"

"I don't know the details but it has something to do with Barbados." Elizabeth laughed. "Whatever he's done has put servants back in the house and taken a load off my shoulders."

"Odd," Susan murmured.

"What do you mean?"

"Shipping lines much larger than his are going under. Either Alan has talents I never suspected or he's incredibly lucky."

He must be lucky, Elizabeth thought, and shrugged off the young lawyer's words. A few days later they returned to her. Flipping through her desk calendar she noticed that Miss Patterson, once William's secretary and now his son's, was having a birthday the following day. Elizabeth reached for the phone.

"I'm sorry," Miss Patterson said, "Mr. Alan isn't in the office at present."

"I wasn't phoning Alan. I wanted to wish you a happy birthday. How is your mother?"

Generally Miss Patterson was eager to chat but this time she was close to curt. "Fine," she said. Then she asked, "How is your family making out?"

"Much better since Alan got that new contract. It's been a life saver."

There was a pause and then the other old maid asked, "Mr. William? Is he well enough to have visitors?"

"He'd love to see you but you must be careful not to say anything that would upset him. We try to keep him as reassured as we can. No shocks, you know. When would you like to come?"

The line hummed and then Miss Patterson said rapidly, "Maybe I better not."

There was something wrong. Elizabeth was frowning but she kept her voice light and unconcerned. "We must celebrate your birthday. Let's have dinner tomorrow night. At the Plaza. My treat. Do come."

"The Plaza?" Promptly the secretary took the bait. "I'd love to. I'll arrange for mother to be looked after and meet you there at seven."

Elizabeth was there before seven. She watched her rounding a palm and decided Miss Patterson was looking extremely prosperous. She was wearing English tweeds and looped around her shoulders were a fine pair of red foxes. For a time they chatted, speaking of the weather, the state of Mrs. Patterson's health, the terrible economic situation. They ordered and the secretary looked up from her salad plate. Abruptly she said, "I don't know what to do, Miss Meredith. I thought of going to Mr. William but I don't dare." She fingered her fox. "Do you like my furs?"

"They're beautiful. New?"

"Mr. Alan gave them to me at Christmas time. He said they were a present but I know why he did it. They're a bribe to keep my mouth shut."

Elizabeth's eyes widened but she decided against pressing the other woman for information. Instead she extracted an oyster from the half shell and waited. Miss Patterson put down her fork and started to talk, leaning across the table, her voice a husky whisper. "He's sold out the firm—"

"He can't!"

"He has. Given up the leases on the warehouses, sold the equipment, sold all the freighters to concerns in Central America and Greece. All that's left is the office and he's fired all the staff but Norma—she's the receptionist—and me. And our time is up at the end of the month. I've been at my wits' end. It's wrong but what can I do? I can't tell Mr. William. It might kill him. Miss Meredith, I'm not worried about myself. I was going to quit soon anyway. Mother and I will be all right. She has a little income and the house is ours and I've saved . . . but what about you and the children and Mr. William?"

"The contract?"

"There is no contract."

Elizabeth stared at the other woman's thin worried face. "How did Alan do it? He isn't allowed to touch the business."

"He forged his father's signature, that's how he did it. He's a criminal."

Yes, Elizabeth thought, that he's always been. A scheming, cunning, dishonest . . . so that's why they were on easy street. Alan was spending the proceeds of the family business. Miss Patterson was talking and she hadn't heard a word.

"—so I said to Norma, are you certain? And she said she was and . . ."

"Certain about what?"

"You didn't hear me. Poor dear, I don't wonder you're upset. I said Norma was at one of those speakeasies a couple of weeks ago and she swore she saw Mr. Alan at a table with some flashy women and men."

"That's not unusual."

"But Norma said they looked like gangsters. She recognized one of the men. Said he looks and talks like a gentleman but he's been pointed out to her and he owns the place." Miss Patterson's high forehead wrinkled in thought. "She mentioned his name. Len, maybe. I think his last name starts with . . . was it K?"

Elizabeth slipped back in time to a sunny afternoon. Dania was painting her nails a brilliant red. Her head was bent and platinum hair fell over her cheeks. She too was whispering as though fearing to be overheard. Bad company, Dania had said, Alan's keeping bad company. Then Elizabeth remembered, "Carelli," she said slowly, "Leo the Lion Carelli."

"That's it. How on earth do you know?"

"Does it matter?"

"No. What matters is I'd rather you didn't let on to Mr. Alan about what I've said. He's hinted . . . he said I'd better be quiet or else. And if he's friends with crooks . . . well, you can't tell what they'll do."

"He'll never know from me. I promise." Elizabeth patted her hand. "Now, enjoy your dinner."

Having unburdened her soul, Miss Patterson ate with a hearty appetite while Elizabeth pushed her food around. Not until she was back in the mistress's room at the Meredith house was she able to think coherently. Sinking into her father's chair, she gazed around the room as though she'd never seen it before. Two years ago when she'd moved into it she'd made few changes. It was much as it had been when she'd first seen it. She had discarded the chaise longue and brought down Judith's dressing table and her own black and scarlet lacquer desk. On the wall at the foot of the bed she'd hung her three paintings and a young Elizabeth gazed happily back at her. It had taken so long to get to this room, so many heartaches and sacrifices, and nobody, certainly not that disgusting Alan, was going to dispossess her. Opie was hers, this room was hers, this house was going to be hers.

Having come to this decision she coolly went over the facts. She didn't believe even Alan would kill the goose whose eggs might be tiny but still were made of gold. No, Alan wasn't spending the proceeds of his thievery. Some connection between him and gangsters. He'd known this Carelli for years. What else had Dania said about the man? Carelli's father was a crime tsar on the East Side. They owned speakeasies. The one Dania had worked at—the Dead End—had been theirs.

What was her next move? Certainly she could expose Alan's crime but what benefit would it be to have him jailed? None. He was more valuable free. She must form a plan to find out what had happened to the residue of the family money. She'd start by paying more attention to him, to how he was acting, what he was doing. Yes, Elizabeth thought, I'll watch him closely.

At first there didn't seem to be anything to be learned from watching him. He'd returned to his pre-Depression life—leaving for work in the morning, arriving home to check through his mail and have a glass of milk in the library, going upstairs and changing for dinner and the evening out. Elizabeth began to look through her cousin's mail. Bills—heaps of bills. Bills from his

tailor and for the sporty robin's egg blue roadster he'd just
bought. Bills from an apartment house, doubtless for a new mistress. More bills from Saks and Bloomingdales . . . his woman
again.

Then, one Friday evening, she got her first clue. This was
the evening Alan always remained at home and Elizabeth had
got into the habit of spending it in either the study or her bedroom. She decided she'd change that habit and took a magazine
to the drawing room. The doorbell shrilled about nine and she
jumped up and answered it. A boy in a messenger's uniform
handed her a manila envelope and held out the book to be
signed. She had no idea Alan was right behind her until she
turned. He ripped the envelope from her hand. "That's for me."

"I know, I was just going to bring it in to you. Something
important?"

"Nothing to bother your head about." He tossed the envelope up and caught it. "More dull business details."

"You sound like Albert Flanders. Women should stick to
housekeeping and buying new hats."

"How right he is." Laughing, Alan disappeared into the library.

Elizabeth went slowly up the stairs. Friday evening, she
thought, was Irene's night off. Also the only night of the week
fun-loving Alan stayed at home. Next Friday . . .

The following week found her crouched in the shadows at
the bend of the staircase, peering down into the hall. Promptly at
nine the messenger boy arrived again. She waited until the library door thudded closed and then tiptoed down to the
cloakroom. Holding the glass to her ear, she sighed with exas-
peration. All she could hear was a voice bellowing a love song
from the speaker of his new radio. The next week she was in
luck. This time Alan didn't have the radio on and she could hear
every sound in the library. A rustle of paper, a chuckle, another
sound she couldn't immediately identify. A muted thud and then
a metallic click. Ah, he'd swung back the oil painting and was
opening the safe. She waited for it to close but it didn't. Then a
series of sounds and finally his voice, giving a telephone number.
She pressed the glass so tightly to her ear that it was painful but
she was rewarded.

Alan's voice—jovial. "Yes, it just arrived. Thanks a million
. . . business must be booming. . . . No, no problems. Only that
old maid cousin I was telling you about. She's a snoop but I
guarantee she hasn't a clue. . . . Certainly I've covered my
tracks. . . . What's that? . . . Look, Leo, I hate to hear you say
that. I enjoy seeing you. . . . You could be right. Might be smart
not to be seen in public together. . . . By the way, I must thank
you again for that introduction. Gloria's a peach, everything you
claimed. Can't figure out why you passed her on. How you can
go for that mousy librarian I don't know. . . . Look, Leo, I'm
sorry. Didn't mean to overstep the line. . . . Sure, it's your business." A forced laugh. "A silent partner should be silent. Say,
that's a good one. . . . No, I'm not a fool. Never write a thing
down. Hello . . . hello." The sound of the receiver being
smashed back on its bracket. "Bastard didn't even say goodbye!"
    Silence for several moments and then another sound. Rus-
tling. Scratching? Ah, Elizabeth had it. Her lips curved in a
smile. From the time he'd been a child, Alan had committed everything that happened to him to his diary. He'd lied to his friend
Leo. He *was* writing the details down. Moving silently she left
the cloakroom and tiptoed up the stairs. So . . . a manila envelope delivered the only night of the week a maid wouldn't be
answering the door . . . Leo Carelli . . . silent partner . . . diary.
It was risky but she must search the library.
    After breakfast the next day she went to Alan's sanctum and
shut the door. She proceeded to go through the contents of his
desk. The drawers were untidy. Ledgers crammed the lower
drawers, bills were thrown willy-nilly in the two upper ones. The
shallow drawer across the top was a mass of writing paper, pens,
bottles of ink, a broken cigar case, two flasks. No diary and no
manila envelope.
    She was staring down at the contents of this drawer when the
door creaked open and a tousled head was stuck around it.
Damn! She looked up at the small figure in a nightgown and
quilted robe. She'd forgotten all about Jess and her cold. "What
are you doing down here? You're supposed to be in bed."
    "I'm hungry."
    "Tosh took your breakfast up."
    "I'm bored," the child whined. "Nothing to do."

Pushing the drawer in, Elizabeth got up. "You get right back to bed. Doctor Edward said you were to stay in bed today."

Jess's flat cobalt eyes roamed around the room. Then they settled on Elizabeth. "What are you doing in here? Daddy doesn't allow anyone in this room."

"That doesn't apply to adults. Only children." Elizabeth rounded the desk. "Off you go."

Jess retreated and ran up the stairs. Halfway up she paused and hung over the banister. Her bangs fell forward over her eyes and her nose was reddened from her cold but there was something about her that was far from childlike. A snake, Elizabeth thought, coiled to strike. The girl spoke in a husky whisper. "You're gonna get it. I'm gonna tell daddy."

Biting her lip, Elizabeth looked after her. Forgetting the child was at home had been a bad mistake. If it had been Alicia or Katie she wouldn't worry but Jess . . . yes, she would be pleased to tell her father Cousin Elizabeth had been rummaging through his desk. The old maid shrugged. Nothing she could do about that. She rang for Briggs and told him to bring the car around. There *was* something she could do.

— 25 —

The back editions of *The New York Times* smelled musty and Elizabeth's nose wrinkled. Morgue wasn't a bad name for this room. Disregarding the smell and the uncomfortable stool she perched on, she bent over the papers. She'd started in the early twenties and worked up to date but a glance at her notebook suggested her work had been far from productive. Births, deaths, marriages of the Carellis had been faithfully reported but there was nothing to learn of their personal life.

Tapping her fingers impatiently, she wondered who would be able to give her details that might help. Then her hand stilled. There was a man . . . a member of William's club who was connected with the paper. She closed her eyes. Short, heavy, a florid face. He'd come to dinner a couple of times a number of years ago. Bates . . . Henry Bates. An editor or something of that sort. If he was still employed by the *Times* . . . Returning to the lobby, she appealed to the receptionist. In a short time she was seated in an untidy cubicle opposite her quarry. Bates had put on weight and his stomach flowed over his belt. The flesh on his face looked loose and his nose was a strawberry red. A heavy drinker, Elizabeth thought, and showing the effects.

Lacing his hands over the bulging stomach, he gave her a genial smile. "Must admit this is a surprise, Elizabeth. Haven't seen you for . . . it must be six years. How's William?"

"Much the same. It's only a matter of time."

"Sad. I'd prefer to be dead, myself. But you didn't come here to discuss William. What's on your mind?"

"The Carelli family."

She expected him to show surprise but he didn't. He simply nodded. "I can make an educated guess about what your interest is in that bunch of gangsters."

"You can?"

"I'm a newsman, Elizabeth, and I've seen young Alan with Leo Carelli a number of times. Must admit I've never cared for the boy but because of William I figured I'd better put a flea in his ear." He rubbed an ear and winked at her. "Wouldn't repeat to a lady what Alan told me to do with my advice. But if you have any influence with your cousin better tell him to steer clear of Leo the Lion."

"He probably won't listen to me either, Henry, but I feel I should know more about the Carellis."

"Exactly what do you want to know?"

"The background. Anything you can tell me."

"Okay, here goes. Pietro Carelli founded the American branch of the family. Arrived at Ellis Island around the turn of the century with his wife and three older kids. Pietro wasn't your usual humble immigrant. They came from Sicily and he had a little money, an incredible amount of toughness, and one heck of a lot of savvy. He found work on the docks but didn't stick with manual labor. Within months he was running a loan shark business and from there he branched into other crime. It was the Volstead Act that really set Carelli up. Prohibition played right into his hands. He already had an organized band of cutthroats and in no time flat got into the rum-running business. Pietro really found the streets paved with gold. He started a bunch of speakeasies and ran girls and gambling as well."

"His children?"

"Five. Four daughters and one son. Leo the Lion, the apple of the old man's eye. Pietro was a peasant and was well aware of it but he hungered for his son to be a gentleman. Had Leo educated and I must admit the man has all the trappings of a gentleman. Just surface polish. Leo proved that when his father died about four years ago and he stepped into control. He's even more venomous than Pietro, and that's saying something."

Elizabeth glanced down at her notebook. "Leo is married and has children."

"Two, a boy and a girl. Leo's a devoted family man and cherishes his mother and his sisters and their families. Keeps them entirely separate from his business. His wife, Angelina, is a beautiful woman and was convent-reared. His daughter is also going to a convent school. But don't let this loving family man bit fool you. Most of the mobsters act the same." Bates waved a hand at a grimy window. "That's a jungle out there and Leo's nickname fits. He's king of the beasts. Anything else you'd like to know?"

"Is he . . . would you call him a man of honor?"

"Leo the Lion?" Bates hooted with laughter. "A mobster, probably a murderer—honorable? Come on, Elizabeth."

"Would he keep his word?"

Bates sobered and his brow furrowed. "He's a staunch Catholic. Yeah, I suppose he might. Depends."

She rose and thanked him. He took her hand and looked earnestly into her eyes. "Wouldn't do any harm to warn young Alan off but, Elizabeth, don't figure on making an appeal to Carelli. Keep clear. That guy's pure murder."

She thanked him again and in the elevator glanced at her watch. She'd missed lunch and it was too late to go home for dinner. There was no way she wanted to face Alan anyway. She stopped at an automat and had a cup of coffee and a dry ham sandwich. While she ate she ran over her notes. Leo and Alan were partners. Leo was sending a weekly payoff to the Meredith house. Alan was in deep but if he was straight with the gangster he might be all right. But Alan was a fool and as dishonest as they come. Maybe he would cross Carelli and that would be the end of him. A delicious thought, Elizabeth conceded, but that would be the end of the family money as well.

When she got home she was relieved to find that Alan was already off for his evening on the town. She passed Jess in the hall and saw a flash of unholy glee in the cobalt eyes. When she was summoned to the library the following afternoon she wasn't surprised.

Alan glanced up and grunted, "Shut that door."

She wasn't invited to sit but she took the chair opposite him. He didn't beat around the bush. "I hear you were rummaging through my desk. Snooping again, eh?"

"I was out of envelopes. I had some correspondence to finish and I looked to see if you—"

"Bullshit." Picking up a letter opener shaped like a dagger, he tapped it on the blotter. "Same old Elizabeth. Never changes. Think I'm dumb enough to leave anything important where you could find it?"

"I was looking for envelopes."

"Sure and there're snowballs in hell too. Forget it." Savagely, Alan dug the point of the dagger into the blotter. He glanced up at Elizabeth and with great deliberation moved it and cut deeply into the gleaming mahogany.

"Don't!"

"Thought that would get to you. You know, cuz, I can do what I like in this house. If I feel like it I can burn every stick of this old crap."

"This house and the contents belong to Opie."

"When he's twenty-one. Right now it's mine." He flung down the letter opener and said explosively, "I went to see

Edward Stokes today. Asked about father's condition. Edward
tells me he explained to *you* months ago that father is failing. His
heart is shot and his blood pressure dangerous. Edward tells me
he only weighs about ninety pounds. You never said a damn
word about it to me."

"What was the use?"

"It makes a difference. To me and to you. Better start looking for someplace to go. When father goes, so do you."

"The house will still need looking after and so will the children."

Leaning his heavy body back, Alan smiled like a cat full of
cream. "That's where you're wrong. All father's friends figure
you're Saint Elizabeth. Devoting your life to this family. What a
bunch of bull. All you're devoted to is this damned mausoleum
of a house. You think it's a temple or a shrine or something. You
even wangled it so father left it to Opie, not me. God, how I hate
this place!"

He paused and waited for a response but Elizabeth was silent. Then he jerked open a drawer and threw a bundle of money
across the desk. "Now we're even, cuz. I don't owe you one red
cent. Count it. Every dollar you spent on the house and kids is
there. Plus interest and full wages for the last two years." Tip-
ping his chair back, Alan stretched luxuriously. Elizabeth picked
up the money and made a move to rise. He waved her back. "I'm
not through yet. Want to tell you my plans. As soon as father is
gone I'm getting out of this house. Found a dream of a penthouse
on Park Avenue."

Elizabeth wrenched her eyes from the deep gash he'd put in
the desk and her eyes wandered past her cousin to the ranks of
books behind glass doors, to the marble of the fireplace, the gracious vault of the ceiling. Alan had pulled out a tiny gold instrument and was clipping a cigar. He lit it, puffed out an aromatic
cloud of smoke, and said, "This house will be rented—"

"You can't!"

"I can't sell but I sure as hell can break it up into a rooming
house. Like Sophie has with the Vandercourt place. I was thinking of selling this old junk but then I figured it'd bother you more
if I just leave it here. Picture it, cuz, drunks upchucking and
grinding butts into your precious oriental rugs. Leaving glass

rings and cigarette burns all over your beloved furniture. Sticking
hotplates on cherry bureaus and—"

"It's *sacrilege*."

"Hey, I like that word. Sacrilege. The holy of holies. Like to
stay on as janitor and watch it?"

"I hope," Elizabeth said evenly, "you burn in hell."

He smoothed his mustache and leered. "There's more. This
dump is one of your weak spots but you've got another. Opie.
My son. For too long you've acted as if Opie was your own. I'll
stick the twins and Alicia in boarding schools. Wouldn't want
them to cramp my style. Going to have lots of female company in
my penthouse. But Opie's my son and going to be a man. I'm
taking him out of school and going to raise him like his old man.
When he's old enough I'll see he gets pros to break him into sex.
He's not going to be another William or George or Oliver Pendrell. He's going to be street smart. Like father, like son. . . ."

Elizabeth could no longer hide her horror. "Please, Alan,
not the boy. Leave him in school. Throw me out, rent the house,
do what you want. I'll go quietly but don't . . . for God's sake
don't corrupt your own son."

"That's the ticket. Beg, get down on your knees. Jesus, how
I love this. Won't do you any good. I've been waiting for you
since you came here. But I couldn't get at you. For a while father
handled you all right but he got soft. You had him eating out of
your hand. Kept Alicia a near invalid just in case I got disinherited and she was the heir. Undermined me too. But you've
wasted your time. Now, get the hell out of my sight and as soon
as father is gone get the hell out of this house and my life."

Elizabeth played her last card. "After William's stroke when
you asked me to stay on you said your main reason for doing it
was fear that I'd talk about the dirty trick of yours that caused his
illness. Alan, I can still talk. I can tell everyone we know about
the book and the rose and also about your plans for Opie.

Throwing back his head, he bellowed with laughter. "Take
an ad in the paper! Shout it from the top of the Empire State
Building!" He sobered and said with deliberation, "The people
who might care are no longer wealthy and influential. In fact
they're paupers. Alan is in the driver's seat now and I don't give
one damn about any of that bunch."

"But why did you keep me on here after the crash? They were paupers then."

"Smarten up, cuz, you know why. I needed you for unpaid help and I needed your money to keep this place going. God, you've no idea how tough it was to be decent to you! But I'll never need you again. Take my advice and get the hell out of this room before I throw you right out of the house."

Later Elizabeth had no memory of reaching her room. One moment she was in the library, the next standing in the middle of her own bedroom. She thought she might have lurched into the Boston fern on the landing, felt the dry fronds brushing against her like delicate, human fingers, but she was never sure whether this had actually happened or she had imagined it. She took a decanter from her drink tray and splashed a little brandy into a glass. A few drops spattered on the carpet and she got down on her knees to wipe them up. She had a vision of another, uncaring hand dropping the cut crystal glass, of gleaming splinters and liquid cascading across the muted colors of the carpet. She gazed around the beautiful room and saw it mutilated and scarred. A storm of angry, frightened weeping shook her entire body and she could hardly haul herself up. She collapsed across the bed seeing Alan's triumphant face and knew in that instant that she could kill him, could drive that dagger of his deep into his body as he had driven it into her grandfather's desk. Sanity prevailed. If she did that Opie would be left unprotected without guardian or support. He'd be put into an orphanage. Her boy, her handsome decent boy . . . there must be some other way.

Pulling herself up she went to the bathroom, turned on the cold water tap, and splashed moisture across her swollen eyes, bathed the back of her neck. She combed her hair, not looking at her own reflection but at the mirrored image of tile and old glass and marble. This mirror had reflected her grandmother's face, her aunt's, Judith's. She'd hoped some day it would reflect the face of Opie's bride. She knew what she had to do, and reached for the glass knob of the door leading to the adjoining room. Her fingers trembled. It will kill him, she told herself. Then she straightened her shoulders and lifted her chin. William was going to die soon anyway. Edward had told her it couldn't be much longer. Let him live, she prayed to a deity she didn't even believe in, let him live long enough to save Opie. She opened the door and walked into the master's bedroom.

The only light in the room came from the one beside Mario's chair. His dark head was bent over a movie magazine and as he rose Elizabeth caught a glimpse of a pretty face and a fall of white-blond hair. Harlow, she thought, every man's dream. She waved toward the high bed. "Is Mr. Meredith sleeping?"

"I believe he is, Miss Meredith."

"I'll sit with him for a time. Take a break and have coffee or go for a walk."

"How long do I have?"

"An hour or so. I'll ring."

He promptly dropped the magazine and left. Sinking into a chair by the bed, Elizabeth switched on a shaded lamp. William's wasted body hardly mounded the bedclothes. Childlike, she thought, her eyes searching the contorted face. His skin was waxen and he looked as though he were dead. Anxiously she touched a wrist, the skin chill against her own. She felt the flicker of a pulse and his eye opened. She thought of expressions about eyes—the window of the soul, eyes laughing or angry or sad. But the eye alone expressed no emotion. It was the flesh around the eyes, the play of expressions across the face that lent that illusion. William's eye merely reflected light. But that eye wandered over her ravaged face, her swollen eyes, and she could sense his concern.

"I need help," she said. "First I must tell you some things that will . . . I'm going to hurt you. I shouldn't worry you but . . ."

She paused, as though waiting for a response, and the eye steadily regarded her. Then she told him everything. She told him about Aunt Van and Roger Pawder and the crash. She outlined the two years that had followed the crash and then the seeming miracle when Alan had brought back prosperity to the house. She told him about Miss Patterson and the discovery that his son had forged his name and sold off the business assets. At that point the eyelid flickered and fell. Please, she prayed, don't let him die. She dropped her gaze to her hands twisting together in her lap and when she raised her eyes she gave a sigh of relief. The eye was open, willing her to continue.

"I found where the money has gone, William. Alan has invested with a gangster, he's this man's silent partner. Alan's receiving money every week and I think it's quite a lot. Do you . . . shall I continue?" The eyelid flickered, once, twice. "I've just come from the library. Alan has told me his plans when you're . . . when you are no longer with us. He'll force me to leave and he's going to turn this house into a rooming house with a janitor to look after it. But that isn't the worst. Alan is going to take Opie out of the academy and have the boy with him in the penthouse. Opie will be surrounded by gangsters and their women, by evil men and prostitutes. He's going to debauch his own son. William, this can't happen!"

The answer came immediately. *No.* She received a silent question, tinged with bitter mockery. How can a man who can't even move a finger help? What can *I* do? "Do you remember Alan's diaries? He still keeps one and I have a hunch he commits all his thoughts and actions to it. If I can get my hands on it I may be able to find the answer. Find some way to stop him. He keeps the diary in the safe. William, will you give me the combination?"

Again an immediate answer. Yes. She pulled out her notebook. "A three-figure combination?" No. "Four?" Yes. "I'll start counting. When I reach the right figure tell me."

It took time. Finally she read it back to him. "Fifty-four . . . left to thirteen . . . right to twenty-nine . . . left to thirty-six."

William told her it was correct. Then, from the expressionless eye one tear trickled down his twisted face. Gently she wiped it off. She took his hand. "Rest," she told him. "I'll stop him. This house and the children will be safe. I give you my word. William, it's all right now."

She rang for Mario and glanced at her lapel watch. Nine minutes after ten. That should give her about four hours before Alan came home. If he came back early . . . Pushing that thought from her mind she hurried downstairs. All the servants but Rose had gone to their quarters. The kitchen maid was puttering around and Elizabeth admired the pies she had just made and urged her toward the back staircase. Then she went to the library and clicked the door lock behind her. It took two tries to open the safe. Its interior was as tidy as the desk was cluttered. Piles of banknotes, separated into denominations, were lined up on the top shelf. On the lower was only a leather-covered book. It bore a resemblance to Lafe's *Judith*. Dark blue with tiny gold letters spelling out "Five Year Diary" and Alan's initials.

Switching on the desk lamp, she positioned the diary directly over the ugly gash in the mahogany and flipped the book open. It began in 1929. Names sprang up at her, Aunt Van, Pawder, her own. She thumbed through 1930 but found nothing of interest. Alan's comments reeked of self pity. Awful food, having to rely on the "old crabapple" for help. No ready cash to purchase feminine company. The first six months of 1931 was much the same. Then in July she found an entry she read intently.

"Met Leo Carelli tonight at the Gold Gorgon. Hadn't seen him for ages and it was wonderful to talk to him. Leo made quite a fuss over me and offered to stand drinks on the house. I told him I still preferred my private stock and pulled the old tea flask out. Wouldn't want him to think I'm a sissy. He asked how I was making out in the hard times and I told him the truth. Lousy. Broke and having to depend on an old maid cousin I hate to keep me and the house going. Leo said it's a shame for a fellow like me to have the shorts and hinted he might be able to put a good thing my way. Have no idea what he had in mind."

In August Elizabeth picked up the thread. Alan had dropped into another speakeasy and again had met the gangster he admired. This time Carelli had been direct. "Leo said if I could raise some cash he'd invest it for me and money would flow in like water. I told him he sounded exactly like the spiel that bastard Pawder gave us and he laughed and told me he didn't deal with the stock exchange. Leo said this was a chance he wouldn't offer to anyone but me and I believe him. He's always envied me because I'm a Meredith and once said he'd give everything he has if he could have been born into my family. I listened to him and thanked him and then had to tell him the truth. Pawder and Aunt Van cleaned me out. Leo said not entirely, I still have the house and the shipping line. When I told him they're both tied up so I can't touch them he shrugged and said tough luck but a bright boy like you should be able to figure something. Told me if I do come up with anything to get in touch. Jesus! Wish there was a way."

The early days of September were filled with soul searching. How abused poor Alan was, what a lousy deal he'd had. Then on the fifteenth Alan's tune changed. His writing, ordinarily small and cramped, was larger and ragged. "Why didn't I think of it before? I can't sell father's precious business outright but I sure as hell can get rid of it piecemeal. I know it's forgery and risky but the only person who could prosecute is father and he can't do one damn thing. By the time anyone finds out he'll be dead and it will be my property anyway. Carelli is right. If you can't run with the hare you should team up with the hounds. Heard that the shipping magnate, Coropopolous, is at the Waldorf. Think I'll contact him tomorrow."

The next entry was jubilant. "Eleven at night and I'm bushed. What a day! Talked that slimy Greek into buying a bunch of freighters. He told me he knows a guy in Panama who may be willing to take the rest of them. Came to terms and I drove a hard bargain. Got to keep this quiet. Must find a way to shut Miss Patterson's mouth. Can't have her babbling away. Miss Patterson's scared of me anyway and I'll use a bribe. As Leo says, everyone has a price."

The details of his perfidy flowed onto the page. He noted down every cent from the proceeds of his thievery. When he arrived at the total Elizabeth's brows lifted in surprise. No doubt about it. Alan *had* driven hard bargains.

By the first of October he was able to report progress. "I met with Leo tonight and we're now silent partners. He'll start paying off on my share in a couple of weeks. Boy, am I going to make a splash! Going to buy new clothes and get a roadster. Going to find myself a tootsie, something long and blond and lovely. Going to make up for these shitty years. Another thing I'm going to do is pay off the crabapple. I hate to waste the money on her but if I don't she'll talk and people will figure I'm a heel. The sight of that bitch turns my stomach! As soon as father passes away I'm getting rid of her for good. Been paying attention to Miss Patterson. She hasn't said a word about the sales but I've got to keep her quiet until father is gone. Saw her drooling over an ad showing fur pieces today. Think I'll buy her something nice. It'll cost but what the hell, it's insurance. I'll also hint delicately that dames with big mouths can get hurt. She's a gutless dried up old maid and there's no way she'll carry tales to the crabapple. Boy, but I feel on top of the world!"

You never did understand people, Elizabeth told her cousin silently. Miss Patterson took your bribe and listened to your threats and talked anyway. From there on Alan wrote about his nightlife, much of it spent with his hero Leo and the gangster's second in command, a man he called Sal. Alan boasted about their trust in him, how they talked openly about their business. Reading between the lines, Elizabeth sensed that Alan did a lot of eavesdropping while pretending to be drunk. She couldn't picture the shrewd Carelli confiding details about "hits" and "payoffs" and "shakedowns" to Alan Meredith. But Alan had confided all these secrets to his dear diary.

She continued to take notes and as she worked her lips twisted in a grim smile. In January of 1932 Alan wrote, "Went to a swell party with Leo last night. The women were knockouts! Leo's a great guy but I don't like that Sal. Know he doesn't like me either but what the hell, Leo's the one who runs the show. The only question Leo has ever asked is if I put anything down in writing. Told him *no*. Asked him if he figured I was dumb. What Leo doesn't know won't hurt him. Pretended I'd passed out last night and heard Leo and Sal and another of the boys talking about Finn McCaul. Seems he tried to give Leo's old man a hard time but Pietro handled him. Sal says this McCaul is trying to muscle in on the Carelli protection racket but Leo laughed and called McCaul "a Hiberian Mustache Pete." Leo sure has a way of talking. Sal pulled a long face and said McCaul might not be a brain but his kid brother Benjy is plenty smart. Leo told him maybe so but Benjy isn't boss, Finn is. Sal said to watch out, those McCauls hate his guts. Leo said a lot of people do and laughed again."

Elizabeth wrote Finn and Benjy McCaul. Then *she* laughed. At the end of the entry Alan had carefully jotted down the name and address of the candy store where the rival gangsters had their headquarters. A stickler for details is our Alan, Elizabeth thought.

Near the end of January Alan bubbled with joy. "Gloria!

What a girl. She makes every woman I've ever known look like a dog. I can't get over my luck. And I owe it all to Leo. Came marching into the Busted Flush last night surrounded by his bodyguards with two luscious babes on his arm and handed Gloria over to me like offering a stick of chewing gum. If you want her, she's yours, he told me. Want her! Little Alan is a tit man and Gloria has the biggest tits I ever did see. Rest of her matches them. Got hair like Harlow's, that white color. Thought it came from a bottle but when I got her peeled down found it was real. How the guys will drool when I take her out on the town. Rented a classy apartment for her and told her to buy anything her little heart desires. Gloria's expensive but she's worth it."

Two days later he told his diary more. "Found out why Leo passed luscious Gloria on. He's certainly a puzzling man. Reminds me of Albert Flanders but just the opposite. Albert married a wife who's a dog, has an office staff just as plain, and when he had maids picked girls whose faces could stop a clock but his girlfriends were always beauts. Leo's the dead opposite. Went to dinner at his home the other night and what a bevy of honeys he has around him there. His house is littered with crucifixes and pictures of saints but his maids look like they came out of a chorus line. What builds. His wife Angelina—Leo calls her Angel—is a bit plump but still a knockout and his little daughter looks just like Angel. When he goes to the clubs Leo's always surrounded by beauties so I figured he liked his women good-looking. But I happened to hear Sal and a guy called Bronco talking about Leo. Seems he only has those women for window dressing. Get this. Leo's crazy in love with a *librarian*. No kidding. Bronco called her Joy Harrison and I went down to the library where she works and checked her out. No harm in knowing a few things. When I saw her I almost fell over. Dowdy clothes, hair pulled back from her face, glasses, build like a plank. No tits or ass. Asked around and found she's well educated and supposed to be brainy. Her family had a lot of money before the crush but her mother died years ago and her old man had a heart attack when he lost his money, and died. Can't understand Leo. All the knockouts he could have and he goes for this lemon. Tried to kid him a little about her and he nearly bit my head off. Got to watch that. Leo could be a bad enemy."

Elizabeth scribbled more notes and read on. "I'm still curious about Leo and that librarian. Found out she lives in a little house in Queens and Leo visits her there every Wednesday night at eight sharp. Damn fool doesn't take his bodyguard with him, only uses Bronco to drive him there. Of course it's a deep dark secret. Nobody but Sal and Bronco know about her—except me. Can't help wondering what Finn McCaul would pay to find out about Joy Harrison. If he ever did know Leo would be a sitting duck." He added pettishly, "Sometimes Leo can be a pain in the ass. Says we can't be seen in public together again. Gets my goat because people really look up to you when you're with Leo the Lion. He keeps harping at me too. Tells me to keep my mouth shut about our deal. Think that bastard Sal is working on him about me. Leo should worry. No one knows, not even glorious Gloria. Only one who knows is you, dear diary."

"And me," Elizabeth said aloud and jotted down the address of the Harrison woman. She closed the blue leather book and replaced it exactly as Alan had left it in the safe. Swinging shut the door, she spun the combination and pulled the oil painting down in place. Taking a glance at her watch she turned out the lights and hurried to the kitchen. Then she took time to stretch her stiff back.

She patted the pocket where her notebook was and opened the fridge. She was suddenly famished. For two days she'd barely nibbled. She sliced cold chicken and roast beef and piled it on a plate, then added a whole wheat bun and a chunk of Camembert. On a tray she arranged a linen napkin, a dish of sweet pickles, and reached for the milk. As milk foamed into a large tumbler she heard the front door open. Alan. She'd cut that rather fine. A moment later the baize door swung open and Alan grinned and pointed at the tray. "Up late tonight? The condemned woman is eating a hearty meal, eh? Make the most of it, cuz, you won't be dipping your snout into my trough much longer."

"You picked an apt simile. Somehow I always associate you with swine and sties."

"Pretty lippy but then you've got nothing to lose now." He

nodded his head and his jowls trembled. "You can't hurt my feelings. I got the world by the tail."

"Best to proceed with caution. That could be similar to taking a tiger by the tail." She slid the dish of cold meat onto the tray. "When your outlined your master plan you didn't mention the servants."

He was pouring a glass of milk. Without turning, he said, "No reason to. The house goes, you go, those relics go. No way I'm taking them with me. Going to have maids who look like something."

Like they should be in a chorus line, Elizabeth thought. "Cookie and Briggs have been serving your family since before you were born."

"And getting well paid for it."

"Neither of them have savings. Cookie has been supporting a widowed sister and her family. Briggs—"

"You're breaking my heart!"

"Alan, your father provided for Cookie and Briggs in his will. He left something for Sally and Tosh too."

"So? That will was made when there was still something to leave. Part of nothing is nothing and that's what they'll get." He swung around. A border of milk edged his mustache. "Tell you what. Seeing you're so concerned about those old biddies you can break the news to them. Tell them they're being thrown out on their ears."

Elizabeth's hands tightened convulsively around the tray. "Don't you have a shred of pity?"

Tossing the rest of the milk down, he slammed the glass on the drainboard. "In this world you look after number one. I don't give a damn if they have to beg on the streets. Lots of people doing that now." He laughed and called over his shoulder, "See beggars all the time when I drive by in my new car."

Elizabeth stood by the table, her elbow pressing against the bulge of the notebook in her pocket. That remark about Joy Harrison and the interest Finn McCaul would have in that love affair. Seeds of treachery? Yes, if Alan believed it was to his advantage he'd betray Carelli as callously as he had the old servants.

She went to her room but before she ate she put the notebook into the secret drawer in Judith's dressing table. She went

immediately to sleep but she wasn't allowed to rest long. Throwing on a robe, she opened the door and saw Mario's powerful
figure silhouetted against the hall light. She knew what had happened. "William?"

"I'm sorry. He died a few minutes ago. I've phoned for Doctor Stokes."

"Have you told his son?"

"I came directly to you."

"Tell him now."

Elizabeth went to her cousin. All the lights in the room were
blazing but they wouldn't bother him now. Death had been kind.
The contorted lines in his face had relaxed and he looked as he
once had. Both eyes were open, staring sightlessly at the
madonna. Had William identified that serene dark face with his
young wife's? She'd never know. Had he died still loving his Judith, still loving his younger son? She'd never know that either.
William's secrets would go to the grave with him.

Tenderly, she closed the staring eyes. I killed you, she told
his shade, as surely as though I'd garroted you, I killed you. But
I'll make it count. No matter what I must do I'll see that the
Meredith children and the Meredith house are safe.

— 26 —

Despite the Depression, floral offerings flooded into
the funeral home. Alan ordered a blanket of pink and white carnations to cover his father's coffin and the room where it sat was
crowded with sprays, cushions, crosses, and wicker baskets of
blooms.

The cars that followed the hearse to the cemetery were as
numerous. On one side of the grave the family were lined up
with the servants behind them. Across the fragrant blanket of

carnations were the Flanderses, John and Edward Stokes, the Standfords, and the Grants. The old guard, Elizabeth thought, missing many of their numbers. There was no sign of the Vandercourt family or of Uncle Herman. During the brief burial service Alan and Alicia wept steadily, Katie looked bewildered, and Jess simply blank. Opie was beside her. She stole a look at him and saw that although his features were composed he was nibbling at his lower lip. She could hear Cookie's sniffles, and sobs from some of the other servants. Behind the heavy veil Elizabeth's eyes were dry. She was numb with grief, far beyond the relief of tears.

Only the old guard returned to the house. Refreshments were served and many of the mourners heaped their plates. Doctor John ignored the food and helped himself so liberally to William's aged scotch that after his third trip to the drink table his son had to guide him to the leather sofa in the library. Edward lifted his father's legs and removed his shoes while Elizabeth tucked an afghan around his heavy boddy. "It's mother," Edward told her. "Finally father had to agree to have her put away."

"A private rest home?"

"We can't afford that. No, we had to commit her to a state institution." The younger doctor sadly regarded his father's bloated face. "It's hurting him but he couldn't look after her anymore. Amanda tried to help but she has her hands full with that big house and Johnny."

"He's going to miss Lavinia."

"He's devoted to her. Why I don't know. She never really cared about him or about me. I've always thought that fixation with Cynthia was only another way to punish us. She made father's life a living hell but . . . he still loves her."

As they returned to the drawing room Elizabeth mused on the strange ways of love. The mourners now seemed to have had their fill of food and were conversing. It was a drastic change from the group of people who had gathered to listen to Roger Pawder. No more flashing jewels, Parisian gowns, or glossy furs. Except for the Flanderses they were uniformly shabby. Robert Grant's suit looked as though it had come from a rummage sale and Horace's shoes needed resoling. Elizabeth noticed that while Grace Grant had put on weight Estelle had done just the opposite. Without the becoming clothes, the expensive facials and hair care, Estelle's lacquered beauty had lost the battle with the years. She was now a lean aging woman with a bitter expression and a spiteful mouth. Aunt Van's mantle seemed to have fallen on her scrawny shoulders and she was in full cry. "—And did you notice Arnold's godparents? Hanging well back so they wouldn't have to speak to us. I'll bet they were the first ones out of the cemetery. And their clothes! They must have worn the oldest ones they have."

Albert Flanders grinned. "Probably expecting to have the bite put on them for a loan."

"You can't really blame them," Nina said placidly. "If they handed out money to everyone who needs it they'd be in trouble too."

"That's what they said when I went to them about Arnold," Estelle raged. "I buried my pride and asked for help to keep him in that home. I told them, you *are* his godparents and if he's put in a public place God alone knows how he'll be treated."

"They turned you down?" Grace asked.

"Cold. Oh, they think they're so clever not to have lost their money in the crash. They boast that Matthew Agrade didn't lose a penny of their money."

Susan was lighting a cigarette. Through a cloud of smoke her eyes glinted. "You must admit they did use good judgement, Estelle."

"Much better than ours." Estelle turned waspishly on her husband. "If you'd only listened to me. I told you and told you—"

"It's over," Horace told her wearily. "No use going over it again. Let's drop it."

Grace passed a pudgy hand over her eyes. "Funny. Everything we always took for granted gone . . . all gone. If I wanted a gown or a fur or a bracelet, I'd just sign for it. If I wanted to go out I'd ring for the chauffeur." She forced a laugh. "I never knew what it was to travel by bus or subway. I simply can't get used to crowds and being pushed and shoved around."

"A pickpocket took my wallet the other day," Robert said

drearily. "Little good it did him. All he got was a dollar bill and an outdated license. No car left anyway."

Stirring her coffee, Nina said brightly, "At least we all have a place to live and enough to eat. Have you any idea of the number of homeless children walking the street now?"

"And the unemployed," Susan said. "At last report there are over thirteen million—"

"And I'm one of them," Horace broke in. He held up his shoes, displaying holes in the soles. "Worn through my shoes walking the pavements looking for work but, as they say, you can't buy a job."

"Antonio is doing quite well with his reataurant," Nina said. "Perhaps you could help him."

"I'd rather jump out a window than be busboy in an Italian restaurant," Horace blurted.

"We never ask you for a thing," his wife told him. "And all you do is sit around while we work. Maud and Antonio just wear themselves out and so do I." Estelle held up reddened hands. Elizabeth had a fleeting memory of those hands—soft and white and manicured, flashing with jewels. "I never worked in my life and now I have to take care of the flat and the children. You wouldn't *believe* that place. Three children and four adults crowded into those pokey rooms. It's over the restaurant and no matter how I air it it stinks of garlic and oil." She paused and her mouth worked convulsively. "And we owe it all to Aunt Van and her dreadful son-in-law."

"Aunt Van is hardly having an easy time herself," Edward pointed out.

"*Good.* I hope she starves. When I heard about Earl and the scandal I just laughed and laughed. Serves her right."

Alan lifted his head and for the first time seemed to take some interest. "What's this about Earl?"

"You haven't heard?" Robert Grant chuckled. "I suppose the bank is trying to keep it quiet because his father, a fine chap, was once its president. Harry Alcott told me about it. He was shocked. Seems Earl, some time ago, embezzled a sizable amount of money and took off. He made a good job of dropping out of sight. I could hardly believe it. Didn't think the boy had the gumption. Earl's always been so quiet but I guess it's the quiet ones who have to be watched."

"Good for him!" Alan exclaimed.

Susan's beautiful eyes fastened on him. "You admire Earl for stealing?"

"Sure. If you can't run with the hares the only course is to run with the hounds. I hope they never find him."

Nina was frowning. "Do you mean to tell me Aunt Van is alone in that house with Sophie?"

"Hardly alone," Grace said. "I hear the place is crowded with roomers. I wouldn't know, of course, there's no way I'd speak to a Vandercourt."

"That's not what I meant." Nina turned to Edward Stokes. "Elizabeth said you were dropping by to see Aunt Van occasionally."

"Once in a while. She seems fine. Lost more weight but with her legs that's on the side of the angels. Sophie told me she's watching her mother's diet."

"When did you see Aunt Van last?"

"Not for some time. Sophie said she'd telephone if Aunt Van needed me. It must have been . . . Earl was still at home when I last saw her."

"Then it must be months. Edward, I really think you should drop in."

Estelle's narrow face hardened. "You're making too much of this, Nina. That horrible woman is the reason we're all ruined. We trusted her. Of course, *you* seem to be doing very well."

Albert swung on Estelle. "We do have a law practice, my dear."

"I understand you're not working at it. Taken up golf."

"Semiretired. Susan, with Nina's help, handles the work. Little girl seems quite competent and, much to my surprise, my clientele has accepted her." Albert stretched his small frame and added expansively, "Grandfather would be pleased to know a Flanders is carrying on."

His daughter smiled at Estelle. "If you're looking for someone really prosperous, what about Alan?"

The woman swung on Alan. "*Two* cars. And I notice you

still have a full staff of servants. Just how are you doing it?"

"Luck. Managed to snag a contract that keeps us going."

Susan's dark brows lifted. "Really? Must be quite a contract. I hear you're painting the town red."

Alan's swollen eyes glared at her. "For such a little girl you've got a big mouth."

"For such a little man you've got a big vacuum right between your ears. That's a new suit, isn't it?"

"So what? You don't look like a scarecrow yourself and I hear your new apartment is in the high rent district."

"I work for what I get."

"You're saying I don't?"

"You said it, I didn't."

"Susan! Alan!" Nina said sharply. "Have you forgotten why we're here?"

They've all forgotten why they're here, Elizabeth thought sadly. For them William had ceased to exist when he had his stroke. But Susan looked abashed and Alan hung his head.

"Poor dear William," Estelle said gently and then rushed on. "I went to visit Uncle Herman this week."

"How is he making out financially?" Robert asked.

"Still has the first nickel he got his sticky hands on. Well off."

Robert nudged his wife. "Perhaps you should drop in and see the dear old fellow, Grace."

Susan winked at her mother and Estelle snapped, "Waste of time. Uncle Herman is bedridden and senile—"

"He can't last much longer," Grace said thoughtfully. "Heavens, he must be close to a hundred."

"Ninety-three. But don't expect any provision in his will. Some female relative with the face of a gorgon has descended on him and taken charge. I had to practically fight my way past her to get to Uncle Herman and then he didn't even recognize me. I know she's got him to sign a will in her favor." Estelle looked indignantly around. "Where was she when the rest of us were looking after Uncle Herman, carting him around because he was too stingy to have a car, shouting down that ear trumpet—" Breaking off, she started to sob.

Heaving a heavy sigh, Horace pulled himself up. "We'd better get home."

"On the subway," his wife sobbed.

Alan helped Estelle up. "Not today. I'll drive you in my car and Briggs can take Grace and Robert. Albert, you still have a car?"

"As a matter of fact, my boy, two. I still have the Packard and Susan and Nina have a roadster."

Despite her tears, Estelle was able to take a last shot. "Nice to be *some* people."

Alan helped Edward take the old doctor down to the car. The younger men were almost carrying him. Thankfully, Elizabeth closed the door and returned to the drawing room. Irene was gathering up the plates and piling them on the tea wagon. As soon as the room was tidy, Elizabeth switched off most of the lamps and helped herself to a stiff scotch and water. She sank on her favorite chair in a shadowed corner. Later the front door opened and Alan wandered in. He stood in front of a window, his hands clasped behind him. She didn't think he was aware of her until he spoke. "Not one of them cares a damn about father. Chance for a free meal and some gab."

"He's been dead for them for years. Since his stroke."

"Notice the kids? Alicia was the only one who cried. The twins and Opie . . . not a tear."

"Alicia is the only one old enough to remember William as he once was."

"And you? Do you care? Did father really mean anything to you?"

Elizabeth's head was aching. She massaged her temples. Too exhausted and sad to pretend, she said softly, "When I first came to this house I hated everyone in it. You probably don't remember—"

"I remember. You were wearing a shiny serge suit and a frumpy hat. So, you hated the Merediths. Your father's death?"

"And his life. If Uncle Peter or William had helped even a little it would have been different. My father wouldn't have gasped his life out in an alley. But in time I learned more about the Merediths. William and your grandfather were true Victorians. They wouldn't have dreamed of going against Oliver Pendrell's wishes. He didn't want my father or me helped, and so we weren't. But regardless of William's narrow views he was a man of honor, of decency. First I started to tolerate him, later I became fond of him. By the time he died I . . . I loved him."

"As you love Opie. He too is a true Meredith."

"With something extra added. Courage and compassion and humor. Even at nine—"

"And now you're going to lose this paragon." Alan swung around. The lamp at his elbow threw a ring of light upward across his face, pitilessly exposing the swollen eyes, the weak mouth, the sagging jowls. "How soon can you clear out, cuz?"

"When do you want me to go?"

"How about a week?"

"Judith gave me a month."

"Judith?" He grinned. "So little roundheels got your number finally. What happened?"

"She left. I stayed."

His eyes narrowed. "You trying to scare me? Let me tell you, cuz, little Alan doesn't believe in the boogie man and doesn't scare easy. You had the goods on Judith but what can you do to me?"

Elizabeth's dark eyes bleakly regarded her cousin. William had loved this man. For his sake she made one last appeal. "Alan, please reconsider. Do anything else you want but please leave Opie in the academy."

"In a few years you won't recognize your paragon. I'm going to show Opie how to be a man about town. Break him in young." He waved a hand. "Where do you suppose the tenant of this room will put his hotplate and cooking stuff? Over there might be a good place for it."

Elizabeth brooded over the spot he was indicating. Her eyes traced the lines of the Adam mantel, the graceful sweep of chair backs and legs, the luster of fine old wood. She rose and moved stiffly toward the archway. Alan called jovially after her, "One week, cuz, and I'll bet I'm one Meredith you still hate."

"I *never* hated you. That isn't a strong enough word. I loathed you."

"And still do."

"You lose your bet, Alan. I no longer have any feeling for you."

It was the truth.

In the morning Elizabeth was up early to see Opie off. It was an overcast day with the promise of rain in the air so she threw a cardigan over her shoulders as they went through the hall. Briggs was patiently waiting by the car. Elizabeth gazed down at the boy by her side. How handsome he looked in his school uniform. She resisted the impulse to smooth his unruly hair back. Opie no longer welcomed demonstrations of affection. At the foot of the steps the boy stopped and looked up at the house. "This isn't a bad place, is it?" His voice was casual but his expression was similar to Elizabeth's when she looked at their home—proud and loving. "Dad says I'm growing up."

"You are. Soon you'll be taller than I am."

"Lizbet, what was my mother like?"

"She was pretty and high-spirited and generous. She gave me Polly and the flapper doll you played with when you were very small. She was a marvelous dancer."

"Dad says she was a tramp who worked in nightclubs."

Elizabeth's lips tightened. The boy was still carefully looking at the house. "I knew your mother, Opie, and she was *not* a tramp. Certainly she worked in a nightclub but she was my friend and I valued her. Dania was gay and pretty and like a butterfly. Like butterflies she died young."

The boy's dark eyes, so much like her own, moved from the house to Elizabeth. "Dad says I must start acting like a man. He told me we won't be living in this house anymore. He says you . . . you are leaving us. Funny, when I'm away I dream of this house. I run up the steps and the door opens and you're always waiting. My mother left me. Are you going to leave me too?"

There was fear and hurt in his eyes. She forced herself not to touch him. "Your father was joking."

"You think so?" He bit at his lower lip and then blurted, "I don't want to live anywhere but here. And I don't want you to go, Lizbet."

"I give you my word I'll be here. Waiting."

"Good!" The adult manner vanished and he twisted his cap

in his hands, a flush working up smooth olive cheeks. "Another thing, Lizbet. The boys are kidding me about Briggs always taking me back. They say he's my nursemaid and I'm a baby. Their parents send them by train."

"We can't have that. I'll make another promise. This is the last time Briggs will take you. You can travel by train."

"I *knew* you'd understand." He flung his arms around her, remembered his age, and extended a hand. "Until June, Lizbet."

Gravely she shook his hand. "Until June." A few drops of rain spattered down and she said, "Off you go."

His face split into a wide grin. "April showers bring the flowers—"

"—that bloom in May. Into that car, young man."

Still smiling, he climbed into the passenger seat. Briggs closed the door and said gruffly, "What did Mr. Alan mean by that, miss? About moving outta here?"

"Probably his idea of a joke. Pay no attention."

Big hands twisted his own cap. "I've been here a long time. Me and Cookie. She come the month before I did."

She noticed his eyes were still red-rimmed from William's funeral. She also noticed the fringe of hair under the bald dome was no longer carrot red. It was now iron gray. Impulsively she squeezed his arm. "After you deliver Opie I have a job for you. Get a couple of men and move that hospital furniture out of Mr. William's room. We'll set it up like it was before his illness."

His face brightened. "I guess Mr. Alan will be moving in there now."

"Perhaps. But in time it will be Opie's. He owns the house, you know."

Briggs seldom smiled but this time he did, a wide smile of relief. "Clean forgot about that. Yeah, his dad musta been kidding."

As the car started Opie rolled down the window and waved all the way to the corner. When she could no longer see it she turned back to the house, her eyes caressing the silver gray lines. It was raining harder and moisture ran down her face but as she ran up the steps she was singing. "It isn't raining rain, you know, it's raining violets."

Irene was dusting the hall. "Someone's pretty happy this morning, miss."

"It's a wonderful day, Irene."

"It's raining, miss."

"Still a wonderful day. I have some work to do. I'll be in the study and don't disturb me unless it's important."

"Some accounts to do, miss?"

"A long overdue account." Elizabeth shut the study door and smiled impishly at Oliver Pendrell's stony face. "When I move into the library," she told him, "I'm going to miss that stare of yours. Come to think of it, I'll take you along."

Taking a notebook out of her cardigan pocket, she put it down on the desk. She slid open a drawer and pulled out recent purchases from the five and dime. A pad of notepaper and matching envelopes. Bending intently over the desk she started to print. In a way she looked like a child carefully drawing a first alphabet.

The McCaul headquarters behind the Mott Candy Store in the Bronx was squalid. For security reasons the window was barred and the door leading to the alley had been reinforced. A naked light bulb spilled light over an old rolltop desk, a spittoon sat on the floor, a few wooden chairs were ranged around. The one concession to comfort was the huge upholstered chair that cradled the elder McCaul's powerful body. Finn liked the room but his younger brother didn't. As Benjy shut the door to the store behind him he said, "What a dump this is!"

"Still bellyaching, little brother?" Finn reached a beefy hand and spilled whiskey into a water glass. "Every time you come in here you wrinkle your nose like you smell limburger cheese. Let me tell you this is heaven compared to that tenement in Jersey I took you outta. What brings you here so early?"

Benjy held out an envelope. "This."

"Have to wait. Gotta strip a hunk off that Larry. Give him a yell."

The younger brother opened the door and stood aside while a big man sidled in. Larry was the size of Finn but after one glance at his boss's face he seemed to shrink. "What's this I hear about Schultz giving you the finger?" Finn bellowed. "He gets away with it and every merchant on that block is gonna hold out on us."

While Finn glowered Larry went into halting explanations. Finn's face was close to the color of his flaming hair and his brutal face matched his brutal body. Piggish eyes glinted balefully. Benjy had the same coloring as his brother but to Finn's broadsword he was a rapier. Thin and quick and cunning. A disdainful smile hovered around Benjy's lips as Larry stuttered, "Honest to God, boss, I dinna know what to do. I told the bugger he had to come through and he kept saying no, I don't want any protection from anybody but you guys."

"Listen good, creep. You haven't been with us long but you know how we operate. First sign someone's holding out and we bust up his joint. That don't work, we bust him up. You get down there and tell that sausage maker you're gonna put him through his own meat grinder. Mess up his crummy store and then use a baseball bat on him. You come back empty-handed and I use a bat on you. Got me?"

Larry backed out of the room and Finn shot a look at his brother. "Suppose you'd handle that different."

"No finesse."

"What in hell you talking about?"

Benjy examined his nails. "Schultz has a pretty wife and a couple of kids."

"So?"

"A hint about acid in that pretty face and over his kids and he'd fall in line. No sense in breaking up good property. No profit in that."

A hint of admiration flashed across Finn's coarse features. "Pretty smart college boy, ain't you? Tell you what, little brother, you get to be boss and you can use that . . . whatcha call it? Finass? For now we'll do it my way. Now, what do you want?"

Benjy threw the envelope down. "Addressed to both of us. That's why I opened it."

"So?"

"It could be dynamite."

Thick fingers fumbled a single sheet out. He read the block

letters aloud. "The Lion has a girlfriend he visits every Wednesday at eight P.M. Nobody with him but a driver. 1121 Reed Street, Queens." Throwing back his head, Finn roared with derisive laughter. "What a bunch of baloney! And you haul this shit in to me."

"Look, Finn, I did some checking. A girl named Joy Harrison lives at that address. She works in a library—"

"Cut it out, kid. I'm gonna die laughing. Look, someone's trying to pull our leg. Leo Carelli has a flock of cuties working at his clubs he can take his pick of. Shit, he never goes anywhere without a bunch of soldiers around him and that house of his is like a fort. Can you see him sneaking off with just a driver to meet some moldy dame who works in a library?"

"Leo's well educated, Finn. Certainly he can take his pick of show-girls but did you ever try talking to one?"

"And ain't you hoity-toity, little brother. You don't talk to dames, you screw them."

"Maybe you do but I've a feeling Leo might go for an intelligent woman. Think of it, Finn. If this is the straight bill of goods we'd have him cold."

His brother poured more whiskey and tossed it down. More than anything he'd like to rub Carelli out. Not only for his territory but for a personal reason. When he'd bullied and muscled his way out of that tenement in Newark he'd brought his two young brothers with him. His favorite had not been Benjy but Curly. Curly was a feisty kid and had been knifed to death by one of Carelli's boys in a fight over a woman. On the boy's nineteenth birthday he had died. Carelli refused to give the killer up. All he said was, "It was a fair fight. Your brother lost." Finally Finn had got his hands on the killer and cut him to ribbons but he'd never got to Carelli.

Finn looked up at his brother's thin excited face. Have to do something about this kid. Smart as a whip and ambitious as hell. Hot to step into big brother's shoes. Better take him down a peg. "Okay," Finn said slowly. "I think it's a wild goose chase but you go ahead. Handle it yourself."

Benjy beamed and was prepared to be generous. "Any suggestions?"

"Sure, don't use any of that finass on this one. Get a couple

of cars of boys over there with tommy guns. If the Lion don't
show send them into the house. Rough up the dame and find out
what she knows. Bust up the house. Teach a lesson to whatever
loony wrote this here letter."

"Right!" Importantly, Benjy marched triumphantly out of
the room.

His brother was wearing a wide satisfied grin. Shredding up
the letter, he dropped it into the spittoon like a handful of con-
fetti.

The Carelli headquarters were wholly different from the
room behind the candy store. The building overlooking the East
River belonged to Leo and he used the top floor for his offices.
In his private office the floor was covered with fine Persian rugs,
the walls glowed with old masters, and his desk had once belonged to a Borgia. On its polished top rested a collection of
antique jade. As Carelli stretched out a hand for the envelope his
lieutenant was extending, gold glinted in snowy cuffs.

"Trouble?"

"Could be, Mr. C."

Slender fingers deftly extracted the single sheet. "Cheap envelope and paper. Block printing. Clever. Handwriting or even a
typewriter isn't hard to trace. Hmm . . . interesting, Sal."

"More'n interesting. Told you that society boy was gonna be
trouble."

"Let's not hang him yet." Carelli read aloud. "McCaul has
been tipped about Wednesday and Joy. Meredith ratted."

"I warned you about Meredith. Always hanging around with
his big ears flapping but, no, you had to do business with him.
Kept saying he's an aristocrat. Far as I'm concerned Meredith's
another name for rat."

Carelli's eyes flickered and Sal fell abruptly silent. "Not so
fast. We could have a troublemaker on our hands. Reason it out.
Alan gets a very good living from his investment. If the McCauls
gunned me down how could that possibly be of benefit to him?"

"Maybe Meredith figures he'd get a bigger share from
them."

Carelli's lips moved in a wintry smile. "Then he doesn't

know the dear Irish lads. His share would be a hole in the back
of his head." The smile vanished. "Please explain how anyone
but you and Bronco know about Miss Harrison."

"Haven't a clue, Mr. C." Sal spread his hands. "But Meredith does know about the lady, don't he?"

"Yes, Alan did mention her. He tried to be funny and palsy
but I thought I'd put him in his place." His eyes locked with Sal
and the bigger man moved uneasily. Anyone looking into those
eyes would know where Leo got his nickname. They were large
and golden and flecked with green, the cold ferocious eyes of a
lion.

"Only time the lady was ever mentioned when Meredith was
around was . . . yeah, he was passed out cold."

"Alan couldn't have been as drunk as you thought." Carelli
sighed. "Very well, we're forced to take this seriously. The first
thing to do is to take Miss Harrison to a place of safety. That
lodge in Connecticut. The caretaker and his wife will look after
her. I want a couple of reliable boys to stand guard and—"

"The lady ain't gonna like it, Mr. C."

No, Carelli thought, Joy won't like it. Picking up a delicate
figure of a girl, he ran a finger over the carved jade. This piece
reminded him of Joy. She was a marvelous woman. Not pretty
but with a fine sensitive proud nature and a wonderfully percep-
tive mind. From the beginning she'd warned him. Don't give me
gifts, Joy had said, don't try to buy me. I'm not for sale. If your
business ever touches me, Leo, we're through. But you love me,
he'd protested. I love *you*, she said, but I hate your business. I've
tried to make excuses, say you followed your father, but it's . . .
ugly. You deal in murder and violence and crime. Don't ever let
it touch me, Leo.

Putting down the jade girl, Carelli said slowly, "I'll take
Miss Harrison to the lodge. You'll have to look after this." He
glanced at his desk calendar. "That's tomorrow night."

"You wanta couple of cars out there?"

"No." Templing his fingers, Carelli rested his pointed chin
on them. "One man. An observer. To see but not to be seen."

Sal snapped his fingers. "The Shadow. He's like a ghost,
Mr. C."

"Fine."

"And Meredith?"

"We'll see."

Opening a drawer, Carelli carefully slid the letter into it.

On Wednesday night Carelli waited in his office, posted by a wide window, watching the reflection of lights on the river. He saw a ship slowly churning its way toward the sea but what he was thinking of was Joy's slim erect figure as she got out of the car and gazed at the lodge. His eyes traced the pure proud lines of her nose and chin. "You don't mind, do you, darling?" he asked. "It will only be for a couple of days."

"It appears I have no choice, Leo. Are you going to leave those . . . those men here?"

"For your protection."

"Strange. Before I met you I had no need for protection." She lifted her chin, brushed by him without a glance, and disappeared into the lodge.

The tiny clock on the mantel was chiming midnight when the door opened. Carelli continued to watch the ship. "Well?"

"The Shadow just reported, Mr. C.," Sal told him. "McCaul's soldiers, led by brother Benjy, were there in force. Two carloads of them. Cars parked a few blocks away. They spread out around Miss Harrison's house and the Shadow counted four tommy guns. If you'd turned up they'd have cut you to pieces."

"You don't have to stress the obvious. What took the Shadow so long to report?"

"They hung around waiting until after ten. Then they broke in the back door and they used axes on the house."

Carelli's hands clenched into fists. Joy. Her cosy little house furnished with what she'd managed to salvage from the family home. Candlelight dinners in front of an open fire, firelight and lamplight glinting on mahogany and maple furniture, on needle-point and tapestry, on her slim hands tenderly handling Spode and Dresden. "Can it be repaired?" he asked in a thin tight voice.

"After those bastards left the Shadow went in. They made a clean sweep. Chopped the furniture to pieces, broke everything in the china cabinets. Mr. C., I'm sorry but look at it this way. If Miss Harrison had been there . . ."

"Yes. I am indebted to whoever sent that warning. I owe her life and mine to that person." Swinging away from the window, the lion eyes hungrily sought the tiny jade girl. McCaul's hoodlums had destroyed his relationship with Joy as brutally as they had her beloved possessions. Goodbye, Joy. Farewell, my love.

Sal stepped closer, his tall bulk towering over Carelli. "Meredith?"

"Ah, yes, Alan Meredith." Carelli slid into a chair and fingered his chin.

"We can cut him to ribbons slowly. Very slowly, Mr. C."

"A warming idea and one we can't afford. Alan is a member of the Meredith family. He's not a hoodlum."

"You got the police in your pocket."

"If we use violence against members of our own profession, certainly But a hit against a Social Register type . . . no, they wouldn't stand still for that."

"You gonna let that rat get away with it?"

"Certainly not. But it must look like an accident. What pier did he use for that shipping line?"

Sal demonstrated one of the reasons he was second in command. With no hesitation he said, "Nineteen."

"And the watchman?"

"Old guy named Tilton."

"He can be bought?"

"Tilton's straight."

"Every man has a price. Any family?"

"A daughter. Her legs are paralyzed and she's in a wheelchair. Tilton's crazy about the kid."

"Slip him some money and a warning about his daughter's continued good health."

Smiling grimly, Sal nodded. "How do you want us to handle it?"

Carelli told him. As he reached for a cigarette lighter his hand touched the jade girl. "I'll set Meredith up for you, Sal. I want him to know he's going to die. Don't hurry it."

"I won't. This I'm gonna enjoy."

That Friday night the envelope didn't arrive by messenger. Instead Alan received a telephone call from Carelli. As Alan shrugged a lightweight topcoat over his new suit he noticed Elizabeth in the drawing room, her smooth head bent over a book. She didn't speak but she did lift her head and their eyes met. For some reason her expression chilled him. Damn old crabapple, he thought, it will be a pleasure to see the back of her when she leaves.

Traffic was heavy and he was late when he turned the blue roadster onto the pier. Old Tilton came out of the watchman's shack, his cap pushed back on his head, yawning and scratching his ribs. Sleeping on the job again, Alan thought, but what the hell, nothing much left to guard. He rolled down the window and the old man stuck his head in. "Thought I recognized that sports car, Mr. Meredith. Haven't seen you for some time."

"Company waiting?"

"Come in an hour ago. Drive right in."

Alan handed him a folded five-dollar bill. "How's your memory?"

"Hell of a thing to get old." Tilton's face split in a wide grin. "Can't even remember what I had for breakfast this morning."

Alan grinned and rolled the car through the gateway. Tilton morosely regarded the red taillights. Still time to call the cops. And if he did those hoods would hurt Janie. They'd meant what they said. He shrugged. Never liked that cocky Meredith anyway. Nothing like his father had been. What was that trinket Janie had on her dressing table? Bronze monkeys. Yeah, see no evil, hear no evil, speak no evil. Tilton went into the shack and shut the door.

Pulling the roadster up beside a black car, Alan killed the motor and jumped out. The door of the car opened and Sal unfolded his long length. "You're late," he grunted.

"Traffic." Eagerly Alan crawled into the back seat beside another man. His head was turned away but he wore the white fedora and white silk scarf that were Leo's trademarks. Sharp dresser. "Hey, Leo. Great to see you." The head turned and Alan looked into Bronco's small eyes. "What's going on? Where's Leo?"

"Couldn't make it." Sal crowded in from the other side.

"Celebrating his wife's birthday at the Dead End. A lot of lead-ing citizens are there too."

"Leo will expect me to drop in." Alan smiled. "You going to take me there?"

"Not exactly."

"In that case hand over the money. Leo hinted there was going to be a bonus this time."

"There is. Leo was thinking of you. Wants you to toast his wife's birthday right here."

A puzzled Alan eyed the tall bottle Sal was holding out. "Nice of him but no thanks. Always drink my own stock."

"Got a flask on you, eh?" Sal's hands slid deftly over Alan's chest. "Must have forgot to pick up your booze. This whiskey Mr. C. sent is the best, right in from Canada. Vintage stock like you drink. Here, have a belt."

"I said no, and keep your damn hands off me."

Another pair of hands were on him. Bronco wrenched his head back while Sal jammed the bottle neck against his mouth. "Open wide. Wouldn't want to break those pearly teeth of yours."

Alan opened his mouth to protest and liquor cascaded from the bottle. He swallowed some and spit the rest all over Sal. Sputtering, he tried to shake the man off. "Have you gone crazy? When Leo hears about this you'll be pushing up daisies!"

"Wrong, rat." Sal forced the bottle neck into Alan's mouth. "Mr. C. will give Bronco and me that bonus he was hinting at. Cheers."

The whiskey hit Alan's stomach and it churned like liquid fire. God, he thought, this stuff is going to kill me. He gulped air. "Cut it out. I can't drink."

"Sure you can. Drink from your pretty flask all the time. Drink and hang your ears out. Flapped your big mouth and tried to have the boss and his lady cut down by McCaul—"

"I never—" More whiskey poured down his throat. It was hitting him hard. His head was swimming and Sal's rough fea-tures blurred.

"Got a story to tell you," Sal said jovially. "Soon as you're tanked up we're gonna tap that bald head of yours and lower you into the water. Gonna snag your coat on a piling and watch you drown. Wish we could cut your balls off but Mr. C. says no. Big shot like you gotta die nice. Have another drink and think about cold water, rat."

Alan tried to spit out the liquor but Bronco grabbed his jaw and squeezed his mouth shut. He swallowed and the world tilted around him. What was happening? What were they talking about? Ratting on Leo and Joy to McCaul? Then his nice safe luxurious world exploded around him. They were going to kill him. He was going to *die* in the sewage-choked waters off the pier. *Who* had done this to him? At that moment he knew. He knew who and why but not how. He saw her face in the lamplight, her eyes boring into his. Alan Meredith opened his mouth and screamed, "Elizabeth! Cousin Elizabeth!"

Sal seized the opportunity to drain more whiskey into the gaping mouth. Across the sagging body, Bronco asked, "What's he yelling about?"

"He's not only a rat," Sal said indifferently, "but he's a crazy rat. Okay, let's finish it."

The police arrived while Elizabeth was having luncheon. She left the dining table and hurried down the hall. The plainclothes man and a uniformed officer were stationed by the marble topped table. The uniform was peering into the drawing room. When the other man saw Elizabeth he removed his hat and nudged his companion. The officer whipped off his cap. The plainclothes man flipped open a wallet and she had a glimpse of a metal shield. "Lieutenant Harkness, Twenty-third Precinct. This is Sergeant Murphy."

"Elizabeth Meredith." She glanced at the hovering maid and said sharply, "That will be all, Irene."

Murphy pulled bemused eyes from the drawing room and watched the flutter of ribbons on Irene's cap as she stalked down the hall. Harkness was steadily regarding Elizabeth. "Mr. Alan Meredith live here, ma'am?"

"Yes. But he isn't here now, Lieutenant. Mr. Meredith didn't come home last night."

"That happen often, ma'am?"

"Once in a while. What do you want him for?"

"I'm not looking for him. I'd like to speak to his next of kin."

"His father died recently and there's only his young sister and his children and an aged aunt. I'm his cousin. Perhaps I can help you." Too cold and precise, Elizabeth thought. She managed to sound alarmed. "Is something wrong?"

"Yes, ma'am. Better brace yourself. I have bad news. Mr. Meredith has been in an accident."

"Car?"

"No, he—"

"How bad?"

Harkness studied the lining of his hat. "Bad as it can be. He's dead, ma'am."

Don't overact, Elizabeth warned herself. She contented herself by putting her finger tips on the marble top and leaning slightly. "Take me to him," she ordered.

"We'll need identification. Sure you don't want to call someone else to do it? A friend, maybe."

"No." She straightened. "I'll do what is . . . what is necessary."

They tried to be gentle. As the morgue attendant pulled back the sheet she felt Harkness's hand on her arm but she pulled away. It wasn't as bad as she'd imagined. She found the stench of disinfectant more disturbing than the rigid figure on the slab. She waited for some emotional reaction but a dead Alan affected her no more than if she had looked down at a squashed cockroach. "This," she said evenly, "is my cousin, Alan Peter Meredith."

Reaching past her, Harkness twitched up the sheet. "Over here, ma'am. In that office."

He gallantly seated her and then perched on another chair, his fedora balanced on one knee. "Mr. Meredith drowned off the pier where the family operated the shipping line before it was sold and—"

"Sold? I don't understand."

She probably doesn't, Harkness thought. Meredith had done it very quietly. He flipped a notebook open. "The watchman,

name of Adam Tilton, told us the freighters and the other assets
were sold late last year—"

"They couldn't have been, Lieutenant. They were the property of William Meredith and he died only a short time ago."

Yeah, Harkness thought, that he knew too. Alan Meredith
had been crooked as a snake. He lifted his eyes and met the dark
one regarding him. Elizabeth Meredith might be getting on but
she was a fine-looking woman. Better looking than her cousin
had been. "Does it really matter now, ma'am?"

She sighed. "I suppose not. The business came to Alan in his
father's will. I suppose he merely . . . anticipated a bit."

Nice way to put it. Helluva lot better than saying her cousin
was a lousy crook. "That's the way we see it. Can't prosecute a
dead man. I figure this gives Mr. Meredith a good reason for
taking his own life. A combination of a guilty conscience and
spending the money on high living."

"No." The smooth dark head shook. "Alan was *not* the type
to commit suicide.

Harkness consulted his notes again. "Tilton says Mr. Meredith turned up at Pier 19 at ten last night. He was alone and
when he rolled down his window Tilton says he smelled like a
distillery. Dead drunk, could hardly drive. Tilton says he tried to
persuade Mr. Meredith from going out on the pier in that condition and was told to mind his bloody business—"

"That does sound like Alan."

Darting her a keen look the detective thought, no love lost
between the cousins. He continued, "The watchman went back
into his shack and says he had coffee and listened to the radio.
My guess is he was sneaking a nap. He has an invalid daughter he
has to look after all day. About four this morning he realized Mr.
Meredith hadn't driven back out and he went looking. Found the
roadster door open and a bottle of whiskey, nearly drained, on
the front seat. Tilton hunted for Mr. Meredith and when he
couldn't find him, called us. Mr. Meredith's topcoat was caught
on a piling and we located his body fast."

"I still can't believe this, Lieutenant. My cousin was an excellent swimmer. Drunk or not I can't believe . . . those bruises.
On the side of his head."

"Looks as though he struck his head on a piling when he went over."

"It must have been accidental."

"Could have been. He might have got dizzy and fallen. But that's up to the coroner's inquest."

Elizabeth stood up and pulled her gloves on. She refused their offer of a ride home and Murphy flagged a cab for her. He looked after it with as bemused an expression as he had worn in the Meredith house. "Some dame. And what a house. Never seen anything like it except in movies. Did you get a load of that cute little maid in the cap and apron? But that Meredith woman is sure cool. Didn't even flinch when she saw the body."

"Breeding," the lieutenant told him. "Hell of a lot of class. The kind of lady who wouldn't show a flicker if you hacked her leg off."

"Yeah, I suppose. Hey, you know Meredith had been playing footsie with Leo the Lion Carelli? Figure there could be a tie-up with his death?"

Harkness's eyes became cold and forbidding. "Better let sleeping dogs lie."

"Sure thing. Guess it'll be called a nice clean suicide."

"More likely a nice clean accident. I don't think anyone's going to be eager to pin a suicide label onto a Meredith. Well, let's get back to work and earn an honest buck."

Murphy hid a cynical grin. Easier to earn a dishonest one as Harkness well knew. He shrugged. Disturb sleeping dogs and curiosity could kill a cat named Murphy.

— 27 —

When Elizabeth got home she wasted no time. Without bothering to remove her coat she went directly to the library and emptied the safe. The money and diary she hid under her coat and took them up to her room. She counted the money and smiled. Over two thousand dollars. The diary went into the secret drawer with the notebook, the money into Opie's Box. She secured the metal hasp with a new padlock and hid the box in the wardrobe, pushed back behind some hatboxes. Only then did she remove her hat and coat and tidy her hair.

She knew the staff would be waiting for her report and she found all of them in the kitchen. Cookie and Tosh had places of honor in rocking chairs near the window. Briggs, clasping a steaming mug, hovered near Cookie and at the long table Rose was icing a cake with Sally and Irene watching her. As Elizabeth stepped into the kitchen apprehensive faces turned toward her. "Mr. Alan has had an accident. He's dead."

Sally sniffed. "Good riddance to bad rubbish."

"It's not wise to speak ill of the dead," Tosh chided.

Cookie was more charitable than Sally. She started to cry. "I remember when Mr. Alan was born, how proud Miss Ruth and Mr. William were on him. Such a bonny baby. Not red and wrinkled but pink and white like a rose."

"Some rose." The ribbons on Sally's pert cap flew as she turned to the cook. "Come off it! You didn't like the skunk any better than I did."

Elizabeth agreed silently with the maid but Sally was becoming much too big for her britches. Time to bring a halt to that. "Are you planning on taking a new job, Sally?"

"No, miss. Can't find a job now for love or money."

Briggs nodded his gray head. "Amen to that."

"In that case you'd better watch your mouth, my girl. One more outbreak like that and you will be discharged."

Sally flushed scarlet and hung her head. Briggs muttered, "Not my place to question, miss, but how you gonna run that business now that both men are gone?"

"Very simple, Briggs. I'm not. Prior to his death Mr. Alan disposed of the shipping line."

Irene had been eyeing her chastened sister. She said pertly, "Then you're probably going to have to fire most of us anyway, miss."

"You really are Sally's sister, aren't you? What I said to her goes for you too." Elizabeth lifted her chin. "You will all be kept on. Let me worry about your wages. You worry about earning them."

Their relief was almost tangible. Cookie wiped at streaming eyes with a corner of her apron. "Miss Elizabeth, when will you tell the children?"

"I'll tell the girls as soon as they come home."

Tosh shook a worried head. "Alicia is going to be terribly upset, miss."

"I'm aware of that. Have you any of that sedative Doctor Edward prescribed for her?"

"Yes, miss. You want me to—"

"Exactly. Before I tell her. In a hot drink."

"Opie?" Briggs asked.

Cookie let out a wail. "He's too young for all this. Only a baby and losing his grandfather and his father so close together."

"He'll have to be here for his father's funeral," Elizabeth said crisply. "And Opie is no longer a baby. He's a Meredith and he'll be fine. Tosh, you and Sally help Cookie up to her room. Use the lift. Rose, you'll be in charge of dinner."

"Will you want a full meal, Miss Elizabeth?"

"Yes. Life must go on and we must keep up our strength. Follow the prepared menu and don't overcook the beef. Briggs, when you pick the children up don't give them a hint of this. Now, all of you get busy and earn those wages you're worried about."

They got busy and so did Elizabeth. On her way down the

hall she paused in the study to unhook her grandfather's painting and carry it to the library. Taking down the oil that concealed the safe, she hung Oliver Pendrell in its place. Standing back, she grinned at it. "Proper place for you. Guarding an empty safe."

Then she tapped her chin and decided what she would move. The radio could stay but the victrola would go to the attic. The account books on the defunct business would go too. The rest of the room would stay as it was. She touched the scar on the desk top. This would be refinished. She eyed the curtains with disapproval. Showing signs of wear. They'd have to be replaced. She sat down behind the desk and pulled the telephone over. When she had Susan Flanders on the line she told her the news. She had expected the girl's reaction to Alan's death to be similar to Sally's but Susan sounded shocked. "I'll not pretend Alan was one of my favorite people, Elizabeth, but we grew up together. I can't really see him committing suicide."

"That's exactly what I told the police." Elizabeth went into details about the sale of the freighters.

"So that's where the sudden prosperity came from. I wonder how much he spent on wine and women and so on?"

"I thought you might tell me that."

"Oh? No, you're mistaken. Alan was one of the few clients father still handles. Alan firmly believed women have the same amount of intelligence as a louse. Father's not in the office today. In fact he seldom does come in." There was a pause and then Susan said, "He's probably teeing off right about now. I'll leave a message at the club and have him call you. Elizabeth, can mother and I help? We could phone around and spread the news."

"I'd be grateful. You phone the others and I'll phone Aunt Van."

She rang off and asked for the Vandercourt number. It rang three times before she heard Sophie's breathless voice. "Elizabeth? What do you want?" Neither her words nor tone was gracious. Briefly, Elizabeth told her about Alan's death.

"What's that supposed to mean to us? We haven't seen hide nor hair of him since the crash."

"I thought Aunt Van should know."

"Don't expect us at the funeral."

"You didn't come to William's either."

"Mother dear didn't want to."

The receiver at the other end crashed down and Elizabeth rubbed at her ear. She fought off a sense of unease. No matter how Aunt Van felt about Alan she couldn't see the woman not attending William's funeral. Perhaps Aunt Van had no desire to see the people she'd help ruin. She shrugged and phoned Opie's school. Remembering her promise, she instructed the headmaster to send Opie home by train.

She was about to phone the mortician who had handled William's funeral when she heard the children's voices in the hall. She shepherded them up to the nursery and found Tosh stirring a pan of cocoa on a hotplate. Tosh was the only one who still slept in the large room but it still looked like a place for tiny children. Dolls were ranged along the shelves and a teddy bear missing an ear sprawled in a tiny rocking chair. Behind the children's backs Tosh carefully measured the sedative into Alicia's cup. Why they all thought of Alicia as a child, Elizabeth didn't know. She'd grown into a young lady and was petite with fine bones and pastel coloring. Seventeen, Elizabeth thought, next year she must arrange a small coming out party for the girl. She must also encourage Alicia to seek friends of her own age. With some animation in that pale face the girl would be quite pretty. A husband . . . with an effort Elizabeth jerked her thoughts back to the present. As gently as she could she broke the news of Alan's death to his sister and his daughters.

Elizabeth was watching Alicia but the strongest reaction didn't come from that direction. To her surpise it was Jess who broke into tears and launched herself like a small catapult at Elizabeth. Hard fists pummeled at her and Jess screamed, "You killed him! You killed my daddy!"

Later Elizabeth rubbed at her bruised shoulder and made a mental note that Jess had an uncanny awareness. In the future that child must be closely watched.

In the morning Elizabeth took a cab to Fifth Avenue. Choosing an expensive hairdresser, she paid many times as much as usual for a set and a manicure. Then she strolled into Saks and selected a narrow black skirt, a beautiful black cashmere sweater, and stylish pumps. On her way through the fur department she paused to caress the sleeve of a honey mink. Almost instantly a saleswoman popped up at her side. "Madam has superb taste," she breathed. "This coat is really divine. Do try it on."

Elizabeth slipped it on. Honey mink framed her face, cascaded richly from her shoulders. She pirouetted in front of the mirror, thinking of other mink coats. Judith's and Aunt Van's and Estelle's. The closest she'd ever got to mink was hanging up other women's coats.

The saleswoman was properly enthusiastic. "Madam has such a divine build. So many ladies are much too short and plump to carry fur to the best advantage. But madam looks simply . . . simply—"

"Divine? I'll take it but I won't need it until fall. Will you have it stored?"

"Of course." Then delicately, "Madam perhaps has an account?"

"No, I'll write a check," Elizabeth said and did.

"An account is so convenient, madam."

"Divinely so." Elizabeth thought briefly of Grace Grant and her words about signing for dresses and coats and bracelets on an account. Why not? "I believe a little later I will open an account."

Having disposed of the important errands Elizabeth took a cab to the undertaking firm. Mr. Pierce, who had profitably buried William, welcomed her with muted but genuine delight. "Tragic." He rubbed white gloved hands together. "The father and now the son. Cut down in the flower of their lives." Droplets of moisture beaded his hairline and his upper lip. He steered Elizabeth into the showroom and toward the line of expensive coffins. "Something similar to the elder Mr. Meredith's, dear lady?" A white glove licked out and whisked a grain of dust from a lid. "This one is most tasteful. Hand-rubbed oak, and observe the handles. Silver."

"I'm afraid not." Elizabeth managed a small sad smile. "Times are hard."

"They are, dear lady." A long sigh and then he touched another coffin. "Mahogany. Not quite as handsome as oak but . . ."

Elizabeth slipped away and crossed the room. "This one will do."

Looking disappointed, he scurried to her side. "Pine. Our cheapest model. Adequate but without the lasting quality of oak or mahogany." Lowering his voice, he warned, "It will *rot*."

So will Alan, Elizabeth told him silently. Aloud she assured him it would do.

He regarded the coffin critically. "Perhaps with a floral blanket similar to the one the dear departed ordered for his father. I could take care of that for you, dear lady."

Probably gets a cut from the florist, she thought. "Hard times," she reminded him. "The family will send a spray."

When she left him clutching Lieutenant Harkness's phone number, the little man appeared to be close to tears. Tough, Elizabeth thought, but one cannot afford both mink and an oak coffin on the same day.

After an extravagant and delicious luncheon at the Waldorf she jauntily made her way home. She spent the afternoon removing Alan's effects from the library and bringing in her own. From a cardboard box she took household account books, photographs, and the pen set the Merediths had presented on her graduation from Miss Penelope's Academy for Young Ladies. She ranged her photographs beside the ones already on the refectory table. She had a recent portrait of Alicia, another of the twins, an excellent one of William, and two of Opie in his school uniform. She hesitated and then propped a snapshot of Daisy Huggins against her half-sister's photograph.

When she had finished she paused in the doorway to survey her rightful domain. For an instant she saw the shadowy form of Alan behind the desk. Then it was gone. I really must replace those curtains, Elizabeth thought, but it will have to wait. After the funeral . . .

— 28 —

Alan Meredith's funeral seemed to be a continuation of his father's. The same minister mouthed the same words, the same mourners faced the family over the grave, even a similar misty spring rain dewed the lid of the coffin.

There were some differences. Instead of a weeping Alan at Elizabeth's side he now rested, beyond tears, in the cheap pine box at her feet. The floral offerings were not as numerous or as lavish. Nevertheless those flowers attracted more glances than had the ones at William's burial service. Even during the prayer astounded looks were directed at a towering horseshoe of red and white roses. Before the church service Mr. Pierce, impeccably garbed and sweating profusely, had appealed to Elizabeth. "Look at that, dear lady. There's no card and I think a terrible blunder has been made."

She stepped closer to the huge horseshoe. Across it a gilded ribbon bore in script the words, "Better Luck on Your Next Venture." Elizabeth turned away, her shoulders shaking with helpless laughter. Leo the Lion must have a sense of humor, certainly a touch macabre, but genuine.

Mr. Pierce mistook her agitation for sobs and patted her shoulder. "There, there, dear lady, I'll have it removed. No doubt a joke. In bad taste, of course, but a frightfully expensive one."

She managed to control herself. "No, leave it with the other offerings. I'm sure Alan would have wanted it that way. You could cut off the ribbon though."

The ribbon had been removed and the horseshoe positioned at the foot of the coffin. As Elizabeth stole a look at the profusion of roses she struggled to conceal her mirth. It was definitely suitable. All gangsters' funerals were supposed to have something similar.

The minister finally finished his long and rambling address, soil was sprinkled on the coffin lid, and the mourners filed past the family. Miss Patterson, wearing her red foxes and a faintly satisfied smile, touched Elizabeth's hand and said piously, "The Lord giveth and He taketh away." Lowering her voice, she added, "In this case He showed excellent judgment."

The feeling of déjà vu extended to the gathering at the Meredith house. The same people heaped their plates, selected the same seats they'd used after William's service, Doctor John drank scotch and had to be guided to the sofa in the library by his patient son. The conversation was different. Instead of working through their personal tales of woe they were avidly discussing the dear departed. By now Alan's sale of his father's property was common knowledge.

Horace Standford summed the situation up. "I suppose, to be charitable, we must look at it in the best possible light. Alan wasn't actually stealing. The company *was* willed to him by William."

"At the time he sold the assets they certainly weren't his," Albert Flanders snapped. "If I'd had any idea what the young scoundrel—" He broke off abruptly, apparently having recalled they had just buried the young scoundrel.

Grace Grant helped herself generously to cold cuts and Stilton. "I can't help wondering where all that money went. There *was* nothing left, was there?"

"Not even in the safe. All Alan left were debts. Not a penny for his children or his sister or—"

"*Father.*" Susan's eyes were blazing. "Professional ethics! You simply can't give details about a client's business."

"Not applicable, my dear Portia. We're all family here." Albert brushed her away with a wave of a shapely hand. "Alan managed to spend every last dollar of his ill-gotten gains. Thank God the debts can't be charged against this house or its contents. William was foresighted enough to protect these."

"Poor Elizabeth," Estelle murmured as though the old maid wasn't in the room. "How will she cope with this huge house and these orphaned children?"

"Adequately," Elizabeth said crisply.

Reminded of Elizabeth's presence, Estelle turned her head

in that direction. "Will you try to stay on here?"

"Yes."

"I suppose," Grace said brightly, "you could turn it into a rooming house like Sophie has the Vandercourt house."

"I doubt William would have approved of that."

"But the work," Estelle protested. "With no servants."

"The staff will be kept on." No longer was Elizabeth ignored. Every eye in the room was fastened on her.

"And the cars?" Robert Grant probed.

"We'll have William's Buick. The roadster has already been taken away. Alan neglected to pay for it." Elizabeth had to fight to control her expression. She could read their minds.

Horace asked aloud the question all were asking silently. "*How* will you do it?"

Susan's eyes were blazing again but it was Nina who said placidly, "I believe that is Elizabeth's business, Horace."

"Nonsense. As Albert said we're all family here. Concerned about the welfare of Cousin Elizabeth."

Elizabeth said something she'd been longing to say for years. "I'm not your cousin. In fact, I'm not related to any of you."

"Of course you are," Grace assured her. "We're all related to the Vandercourts."

"I'm certainly not. Aunt Van was William's aunt by marriage."

Glances were exchanged. Patronizing glances. The poor old thing was upset by the recent deaths. Best to humor her. Horace soothed her. "We've always thought of you as Cousin Elizabeth and admire your devotion to the family. We're not prying, simply interested."

"*I* would call it prying," Nina said sharply. "Elizabeth has always been a wonderful manager. I'm certain she neither welcomes nor needs your advice."

Horace gave up on Elizabeth and turned to Albert. "Do you know how she'll manage, old chap?"

"Well, Elizabeth does have a little trust fund William—"

"*Father,*" Susan said again.

"Be quiet. Yes, Horace, and there's a small income for Alicia that she will soon be receiving. Perhaps with both—"

"I'm not one to mince words," Estelle told them quite unnecessarily. "And I ran a house similar to this one for years.
There's no possible way to keep it going and employ a staff on
two small incomes." She shot a nasty look at Nina. "As for Elizabeth being a manager, wonderful or otherwise, I'm inclined to
doubt that. You must remember her background. Leon Meredith
was a wastrel. He lived in poverty and died that way. Where he
found the money to drink himself to death I don't know. He
must have stolen the bread from his family's mouths and—"

"Shut your vicious mouth!" Elizabeth was on her feet, her
voice a whiplash. She stared at the circle of shocked faces and
thought, this is the first time you've dared speak to them like
this. Still time to play the part of a poor relative, bend your head,
be meek. Her chin jerked up. Too many years of snubs and insults. Too many years of bowing her head. She used one of
Alan's favorite expressions. What the hell did it matter? No
longer was *she* the poor relative, *they* were. She continued frig-
idly, "You've maligned my father for years. Before his death and
after. He was a fine man, sensitive and kind. His one downfall
was in having a selfish brutal father who disinherited him because
he wasn't a businessman. His other downfall was in being born
into *your* world. You wouldn't recognize talent if you fell over it.
I won't stand for it further. The next person who says a word
against Leon Meredith is going to be thrown out of this house."

The Standfords and Grants were as dumbfounded as though
a piece of furniture had leaped up and assaulted them. But Edward was nodding approval, Nina was making a clapping motion,
and Susan's face beamed unholy joy. Again, Elizabeth could
read the thoughts of the Standfords and Grants. Cousin Elizabeth seemed very sure of herself. She was going to keep the
house going, keep a full staff of servants, run a car, educate the
children. Ergo, Cousin Elizabeth was no longer poor. Perhaps
before William's death he had turned money over to her, perhaps
she had received funds from another source. But they scented
money and if they behaved maybe some of it would rub off on
them.

The fastest on his mental feet proved to be Horace. Antonio
was hoping to build an addition to the restaurant. Perhaps with

Elizabeth's help . . . he cleared his throat. "Please be seated, Elizabeth. You were quite right to speak harshly to us. I must apologize for my wife. Estelle speaks thoughtlessly but she really means no harm. I was about to chide her myself when you broke in. You see, I've always thought highly of Leon. We attended the same school and though I was much younger I always looked up to him. Regarded him with hero worship. Yes, I can honestly say I was your father's friend." He turned commanding eyes on his wife.

Estelle hastened to back her husband up. "I am *so* sorry, Cousin Elizabeth. Of course, I have nothing against dear Leon." She couldn't resist showing her claws again. "I'll tell you who spread gossip about your father. It was that dreadful Aunt Van. She poisoned our minds against Leon. We shouldn't have listened to her then any more than when she involved us with that awful Roger Pawder. Do say you forgive me."

Elizabeth hadn't and didn't say it. Wait until autumn when dear vicious Estelle sees my mink, she thought, she'll be trying to lick my hand. She said abruptly, "I suggest we change the subject."

They hastened to comply. Having exhausted the weather, Franklin Roosevelt's chances of being elected to the highest office in the country, the Lindbergh kidnaping, and a few other topics, they took decorous leave of Elizabeth. Horace briefly debated about mentioning his son-in-law's project, Robert Grant considered speaking to Elizabeth about her thoughts on a change of job for his son Ronnie who certainly wasn't cut out to sell vacuum cleaners. Both men wisely decided this was neither the time nor place but made mental notes to approach her at a later date. Finally the door was closed behind them and while Albert was helping Edward Stokes steer Doctor John to the car, Nina and her daughter lingered.

"Don't let me keep you," Elizabeth told them. "Albert will be waiting."

"He brought his own car," Nina said. "As usual he's making a beeline for his club."

Susan was wearing a wicked grin. "I wanted to congratulate you on the way you told them off. Good for you! I nearly yelled bravo."

"It was a long time coming," Nina said. "I've no idea why you didn't break years ago."

Elizabeth gave them a warm smile. "As you know, Nina, I was in no position to speak my mind. Poor relatives must guard their mouths."

"And now you are."

"Do *you* want to know where the money is coming from?" Susan cried, "Yes!"

Her mother looked searchingly at Elizabeth, shook her head, took her daughter's arm, and said, "Elizabeth, I have no desire to know."

When Susan and her mother were seated in the spacious living room overlooking the East River sipping nicely chilled martinis the young lawyer voiced her curiosity. "Why did you cut Elizabeth off like that? Just when she was about to tell all."

"She wasn't about to tell anything."

"Well, I *would* like to know."

"No, you wouldn't." Spearing an olive, Nina nibbled at it. "As you grow older and wiser you'll find there are some things best left alone."

"You make our spinster friend sound positively Machiavellian."

"I've always considered she is."

"Expound, oh old and wise one."

"You're supposed to be sharp, Susan. Consider the facts."

"Which are?"

Nina turned to look down at the river. Her voice was muffled as she said, "Years ago William told me his wife Judith had finally come to her senses and they were going to get rid of Elizabeth. Buy her off with a little dressmaking business. A short time later the storm of scandal about Judith and her lover broke. She and her child were thrown out of the Meredith house. Whatever happened to Judith and Mariette I don't know but I've always thought Elizabeth does."

"And Elizabeth?"

"She remained, but in a much stronger position. Lending an air of respectability to William and the children."

"And you think our meek little spinster . . ."

"As your generation would say I think Elizabeth blew the

whistle on the lovers. I have never believed that she was ignorant of that flaming affair. In fact, I've a hunch she encouraged it."

"I don't blame her. She was struggling to survive."

"And succeeded admirably."

"Any other evidence?"

"A couple of weeks ago when I was shopping I met Alan. He persuaded me to lunch with him. I could never bear the boy but I couldn't get out of it. He told me something rather interesting."

"A drink is in order." Susan refilled their glasses. "Continue your presentation, counselor."

"In strictest confidence Alan told me he was 'going to boot Elizabeth's ass out of his house.' He was planning on turning that lovely place into a rooming house. He had plans for Opie. He boasted about taking the boy out of the academy and 'teaching his son to be a man.' "

"Merciful God. Similar to handing the child over to the Marquis de Sade."

"Exactly. And Opie is the apple of Cousin Elizabeth's eye."

Susan was running fingers through her cap of curls. "Is there more?"

"Yes." Her mother hesitated. "I want your word you'll never repeat this."

"Cross my heart and hope to die."

"That's what Alan did. He went down to that pier and died."

"Mother, he was tight as a tick. Probably fell in. Alan was always guzzling whiskey."

"Did you ever see him buy a drink?"

"He was a snob. Boasted he only drank his own stock. From a silver flask, of course."

"Which was filled with cold tea. No, don't interrupt. A number of years ago I picked up Alan's glass by mistake and took a sip. It was filled with tea. I asked William about it and he told me that while his son was fighting a gallant war in the wilds of Kansas the army doctors found Alan was severely allergic to alcohol. Alan was ashamed of this and pretended to drink and even acted drunk on occasion. William made me promise not to tell anyone and I never have until now."

"Then he couldn't have . . . Mother, he *was* murdered. Are you saying Elizabeth filled him with alcohol and threw him off that pier?"

"Hardly. But you have the rest of the evidence in your hands."

"I've no idea what you mean."

"Susan, you were the one who mentioned Alan was running with a strange crowd."

"He was. Chumming with gangsters and their molls. He seemed to admire them. I saw him twice with Leo Carelli. . . . You're implying that Elizabeth arranged for gangsters to execute Alan Meredith."

"I am. I've no idea how and I don't want to know." Nina held out her glass. "I seldom go beyond two martinis but I think I could use another. The evidence is presented. Judith Meredith threatened Elizabeth. She disappeared. Alan Meredith threatened Elizabeth. He was murdered. The verdict, your honor?"

Picking up the martini pitcher, Susan tried to smile. It wasn't successful. "The first thing I should do is cut you off booze. What you have is a pile of circumstantial evidence. But I must admit you've made my flesh crawl. However, Alan's allergy can be checked out. As responsible citizens I suppose our duty is to tell all to the police."

"I vote we don't."

"Your reason?"

"Actually two." Nina stared down into the silvery liquid in her glass. "Elizabeth's had an unbelievably rotten life. A member of a family and treated for years as an underpaid servant. I can remember a time when I don't think she got enough to eat and what she did get she could hardly chew. Her teeth were in terrible condition and she must have suffered agonies with them."

"So, fondness and admiration for the defendant. The other reason?"

"Consider what would have happened to Opie if his father *had* lived."

"I've already considered. I second the motion for silence." Susan's brow knit. "Have you any hunch about the source of her sudden prosperity?"

"No, and I don't want to even guess." Nina added grimly, unwittingly using an expression of Lieutenant Harkness's, "In this case I think it wise to let sleeping dogs lie."

— 29 —

The period following Alan's funeral were the happiest days of Elizabeth's life. She indulged herself by keeping Opie home for a week and only after he'd been sent back to the academy did she turn her energies to putting her house in order. The entire house received a thorough cleaning and she hired a seamstress to make up curtains and bedspreads. An elderly and talented craftsman was called in to refinish the desk in the library and another workman soundproofed the wall in the library. After he had finished she turned up the radio full volume and tried the glass on the cloakroom wall. No matter how she strained she couldn't hear a thing.

In the evenings she pored over travel brochures. In August Opie would be nine and she was planning a birthday surprise. They would do some traveling and she made notes on Germany, Switzerland, England. She made plans for the twins. For the summer they would be sent to camp and in the fall enrolled in a boarding school in northern Vermont. She wasn't taking a chance on having Jess and her ungodly intuition around too much. Elizabeth considered Alicia's future. On impulse she arranged a party for classmates from the girl's school. Initially Alicia was terrified of acting as hostess but when the time came she not only came through with flying colors but enjoyed it. At the end of the evening, flushed and charming in a new gown, she gratefully hugged and kissed the old maid. Yes, Elizabeth thought, with time and patience Alicia could be coaxed out of her shell.

So delighted was Elizabeth in her new role as head of the family that she thought nothing could increase her feeling of well-being. Shortly after Alicia's party something did happen that gave her great satisfaction. She was working on account books in the library when a tap sounded on the door and Irene opened it. "A gentleman to see you, Miss Elizabeth. Shall I—"

"No need to stand on formality." A man pushed past the maid and added genially, "Miss Meredith and I are old friends. Aren't we, Elizabeth?"

Elizabeth blinked. It appeared she'd been wrong in Atlantic City when she thought they'd never meet again. The man in English tweeds and a turtleneck sweater was Lafcadio Norton. She struggled for composure and found it. "That will be all, Irene. Lafe, this is a surprise!"

Crossing the room with long strides, he held out a hand. She hesitated and then gingerly held out her own. He lifted it to his lips gallantly and brushed the back of it. "Do sit down, Lafe. I had no idea you were in New York. A visit?"

"No. Actually I came back over a year—"

"And you've never even phoned."

"I didn't know whether I should or not, Elizabeth. But when I heard of William's death and then his son's I had to see you and offer my sympathy."

You also, she told him silently, knew you wouldn't be welcome in this house. She regarded him warily, wondering why he had come. The years didn't seem to have changed him much. There were lines around his eyes and mouth, the flaming hair was duller and graying at the temples, but he still seemed larger and more vital than any man she'd ever met. "And how does your wife like the city?"

"Anne Louise isn't with me." He sank into the chair opposite and gave her a rueful smile. "We were divorced shortly after you sent that charming package to her."

"How sad."

He leaned forward, staring directly into her eyes. "*Why* did you do it?"

"You bear some responsibility for William's stroke. Because of your heartless book about Judith he lived for a number of years in hell. He was totally paralyzed and couldn't make a sound. Now, it's my turn to ask why *you* did it."

His eyes fell away from hers. "Writers can't be held responsible for their material. You use what you can. And if you wanted revenge you may rest assured you got it. Anne Louise was appalled at what she called my cruelty—my treatment of Judith and the child. I think what hurt her most was that I'd had her convinced I loved her and not her money. I do have a way with women, Elizabeth." Lafe shook his head. "*Horse-faced and rich.* First she threw me out, then she divorced me. She also told every soul we knew about Judith's suicide. By the time Anne Louise was finished I was persona non grata in London." He said abruptly, "I could use a drink."

Swiveling her chair around, Elizabeth picked up a decanter. "Scotch? Yes. As I recall, no ice and no water."

He took a long swallow and regarded the glass approvingly. "Fine stuff. Anyway, to make a long story short I came back here. At first I wasn't worried. Both my books had done well and I had some money of my own. I also figured I'd be writing more books. So I lived as I was accustomed to—extremely well. The only trouble is I can no longer write. I don't know what happened. Perhaps it's writer's block, maybe I only had two books in me . . . I don't know." He finished his drink and handed the glass to Elizabeth. As she bent over the decanter she permitted herself a smile but when she turned back to Lafe her expression was noncommittal. "It's been hell for me, Elizabeth. I'm stony broke and I'm living in a lousy tenement—"

"Did you try for a job on a newspaper?"

"Every one in the city. No dice. They're interested in younger men."

"What do you want from me? A loan?"

"No." He glanced around the room, his eyes lingering on the bookshelves. "I take it you're the head of the family now."

"I'm the only adult Meredith left."

"I noticed the car outside and Briggs fussing around it. For someone who wanted so little from life you seem to have landed very soft. This house, servants, and you're looking prosperous yourself. The Depression doesn't seem to have changed anything here."

"We get by. Lafe, I'd appreciate it if you'd get to the point. What do you want?"

He smiled, that charming smile she remembered so well. "I want you."

"You certainly had no interest in me years ago."

"Years ago I was a blind stupid fool so infatuated with Judith I chose the wrong woman. Neither Judith nor Anne Louise was right for me. I see that now and I hope it's not too late. You loved me once, I know you did. and I—no, I'll tell the truth. I don't love you but I admire and respect you and in time I know I will love you." His eyes flickered over her face and he continued earnestly, "My dear, neither of us is young anymore. Let's not waste the years we have left. You need a man to help you raise the children, someone to lean on, someone to help you . . .

He spoke on and his voice and handsome face were having a hypnotic effect on Elizabeth. She found she was picturing life with Lafe, his arms around her, his lips pressed against hers. She fought loose of his spell and asked icily, "And just what do *you* need?"

"You, my darling, only you."

"No." She got to her feet. "What Lafcadio Norton needs is another meal ticket. You mention children and yet you haven't even asked where your own daughter is." Circling the desk, she looked down at him. He'd crossed his legs and there was a large hole in one sock. His shoes were scruffy and cracked. The tweeds were well cut but shabby. Desperation time, she told herself, time to have a try at the spinster who seemed so prosperous. And she'd nearly fallen for it. "You speak of love, Lafe, and yet you love only yourself. You ruined Judith's life and William's. No doubt you ruined Anne Louise's. But you're not going to ruin mine." She crossed the room and flung open the door. "Get out of my house. Go back to your tenement. That's where you belong."

Pulling himself up he walked toward her, not with long lithe strides but slowly, as though he'd suddenly aged. "You owe me; you broke my marriage up," he whined. "How about that loan you mentioned? Even a few bucks. Please, for old time's sake."

She stared at him with disgust and then she went back to the desk, yanked open a drawer, and snatched up a handful of household money. She thrust it at him. "Here. Don't ever come back. You won't be admitted." She called down the hall, "Irene, will you show this . . . this gentleman out."

Elizabeth didn't wait to watch Lafe ushered out. Closing the door, she returned to the desk. So this was the man she'd yearned to spend her life with. What a lucky escape she'd had. She wondered what the future held for him. He certainly did have a way with women; for a moment he'd almost swayed *her*. Perhaps he'd find another woman, plain and lonely and rich, to support him. Maybe he would write another book. Maybe . . . it really made no difference to her what happened to him. She'd evened her personal score with Lafe Norton. Closing all thought of him from her mind, she flipped open a ledger.

On the eighth of May Elizabeth received a telephone call. She hurried into the hospital where William had once been a patient and into the waiting room where she'd sat with Alan and Aunt Van. In chairs near the door Nina and Susan Flanders huddled with Albert, resplendent in a tweed cap and jacket and checkered plus fours, hovering over them. As he seated Elizabeth he managed a surreptitious glance at his watch. "I can't do anything here," he told the three women. "It's sad. In fact, it's horrible but . . ."

Nina didn't look up. "You might as well go along to your game."

"All in the line of duty. That's where valuable business contacts are made. More deals are made on the golf course . . ." He added, rather pathetically, "I can't help."

"Nobody can," Susan told him flatly. "Go along, father."

Elizabeth waited until the dapper little man obeyed and then she asked, "How did you find out?"

"Aggie phoned the office," Nina said. "She was upset. She'd baked one of Aunt Van's favorite cakes—"

"Seed cake."

"Yes. When she took it around Sophie did her best to keep Aggie out of the house but the old cook pushed past her. She demanded to see Aunt Van but Sophie said her mother wasn't feeling well and was resting. Aggie shoved by her and took the cake to the kitchen. She said the smell there was . . . anyway, she was ordered out of the house and she phoned me."

Nina's voice wavered and stopped and Susan continued, "We got in touch with Edward Stokes and arranged to meet him at the Vandercourt house. Sophie tried to keep us out but Edward told her not to be silly and shoved her aside. We stood in the hall and . . ."

As Susan spoke on, Elizabeth closed her eyes. She could see Edward and Susan and Nina facing a flushed and abusive woman. Edward tried the door to the drawing room and found it locked. "I rented it," Sophie sputtered. "After Earl left we didn't need it but we did need the money."

"Where is your mother?" the doctor demanded.

"None of your business! What right have you to push your way in? Sneaking and prying into *my* business."

Edward strode down the hall with Susan and Nina at his heels and Sophie ranting behind them. He swung open the door to what had once been a study. It was now used as a bedroom. A flannel wrapper was thrown across the single bed and the room reeked of liniment. Against a wall a long sofa was jammed.

Nina pointed at the sofa. "Aunt Van's beloved sofa. She never would be parted from it."

The doctor swung on Sophie. "Take me to your mother. Right now."

The woman pushed back her straggling hair and managed a conciliatory smile. "She's resting, Edward. Please don't bother her. You know I take good care of her. There's no need to worry."

Still staring at the sofa, Nina touched Edward's arm. "The kitchen."

They went to the kitchen.

Opening her eyes, Elizabeth regarded the two other women. It wasn't only their expressions that were alarming. Their bodies were slack with exhaustion and horror. "You found Aunt Van?"

"In the butler's pantry that opens off the kitchen." Nina tried to straighten her sagging shoulders. "She was huddled on a cot, filthy, bruised, she's lost most of her hair. Under the cot was a chamber pot full of . . . the stench was overpowering. On the floor was a bowl with some caked stuff in the bottom—"

"Dog food," Susan broke in. "For months all Aunt Van had

to eat was dog food." Her voice rose, ragged with hysteria. "Sophie starved her and beat her and subjected her to absolute degradation. Edward started to examine Aunt Van and Sophie jumped on him and clawed and shouted she wasn't through, that her mother hadn't suffered enough. Mother and I had to pull her off. She's mad, stark raving *mad.*"

"Sophie seemed so strong," Nina muttered. "It took the three of us to get her on the floor and tie her hands and feet with dish towels. Edward got his bag and gave Sophie a shot and the ambulance came and took Sophie and Aunt Van . . . oh God, Elizabeth, Aunt Van's dying."

With shaking hands Elizabeth was trying to light a cigarette. She finally managed it and took a puff. The taste turned her stomach and she crushed it out. "There's no hope?"

Susan's glossy cap of curls shook. "None."

There was nothing to say. Elizabeth brooded over the grotesque pictures their words had conjured up. She saw pampered, vain, self-indulgent Aunt Van at the mercy of a madwoman. Kept prisoner in a pantry, fed dog food, beaten and reviled. She asked, "Sophie?"

Susan didn't look up. "She'll be committed. The last time I saw her she was in a straitjacket. For years she must have been insane and no one guessed."

Aunt Van did, Elizabeth thought guiltily, and she told me. But I brushed it aside as more of Aunt Van's endless prattling. Time dragged by and finally she looked up and saw Edward. He wore a white coat and above it his face, so similar to his father's was chalky. "She's conscious now," he told her. "You'd better see her." He brushed a hand over his eyes. "Be careful what you say. Something merciful has happened. I told her who I was and she said I must be joking, said I'm too old and stout to be that young man."

"Her memory?" Elizabeth asked.

"As far as I can tell she thinks it's about nineteen fourteen. These later years have been wiped out. She's only holding on by a thread. Let her die in 'fourteen."

They went to her. A nurse was taking her pulse but she stepped back and allowed the other women to cluster around her high bed. Elizabeth didn't recognize the face on the pillow. A few colorless hairs straggled around a face like a wizened apple. In that face the eyes looked large. Aunt Van gazed from Elizabeth to Nina and then fastened on Susan. "Who's this young woman? She looks like Albert. A relative of his?"

"Yes," Nina said gently. "A visitor. Why don't you wait outside, dear?" Taking the hint, Susan quietly left.

"Do be seated," Aunt Van said hospitably. "You're my first visitors. So nice of you to come and see me. The young man who was joking about being Doctor John's son says I've been ill."

"You have," Nina said. "Quite ill."

Aunt Van's eyelids fluttered and she asked plaintively, "Why isn't Doctor John looking after me?"

Elizabeth's and Nina's eyes met and then the old maid murmured, "He's traveling, Aunt Van. With Lavinia, you know."

"I seem to be out of touch. And I'm so tired I'm not thinking clearly. But tell me, how're William and Judith? And the boys, of course."

"Fine . . . we're all fine, Aunt Van. Perhaps you should rest."

Aunt Van's voice was now very weak. "I will, Cousin Elizabeth. Mark my words, people will be flooding in here tomorrow. I'd like to see Charity right now. Such an imp for her age. Only fourteen and wanting her hair up and her hems let down." A claw of a hand twitched against the white spread. "It will be good to go home. Aggie will be cooking and . . . she's not as good a cook as Cookie but . . . did I tell you I'm going to have my drawing room done over?"

Tears were cascading down Nina's cheeks and it was Elizabeth who whispered, "Sleep, Aunt Van. Soon you'll be going home."

The eyes in the wasted face fixed on Elizabeth but they no longer saw her. Aunt Van had gone home. The nurse bent over the bed and Edward followed Nina and Elizabeth into the hall. Susan hurried to take her mother's arm. "The sin of omission," Nina sobbed. "Not caring enough to even take an hour and go to see her. If I had—"

"How do you think I feel?" Edward asked brusquely. "For God's sake I'm supposed to be a doctor."

Elizabeth opened her mouth but it was Susan who said

crisply, "I'm going to be blunt. The three of you have massive cases of guilt. It is tragic and disgusting but—"

Elizabeth did speak. "If I'd—"

"*If.* If Aunt Van had been kinder to her family. If she hadn't ruined Sophie's only chance to marry and hadn't treated her like a drudge. If she hadn't browbeat Earl and forced him into a profession he hated. If she hadn't taken Charity's husband and made him her own. If Aunt Van had been different she wouldn't have suffered and died like this. But she wasn't." Susan squeezed her mother's arm. "All of you buck up. It's done, it's finished. At least Aunt Van died happy. Now, I'm going to buy you a drink."

Edward managed a wan smile. "You're damn good medicine, young Susan. But I have to bow out. I must get home to Amanda and the boy."

"You listen to Amanda. She makes good sense. Mother, Elizabeth, you come with me. I'm not taking no for an answer."

She took them back to the apartment and mixed drinks. "No sherry for you tonight. Down this."

Elizabeth had no idea what was in the tall glass but whatever Susan had concocted warmed her to her toes. A little color seeped back into Nina's face and she said, "We'll have to arrange her funeral. There's no one else."

Elizabeth nodded. "I have a coffin in mind. Oak with silver handles."

"So we atone, too little and too late."

"Sophie said something odd," Susan said. "When we were struggling with her she shrieked that her mother deserved to suffer because she'd killed Judith."

Her mother nodded. "That's right. I'd forgotten. Elizabeth, do you know anything about Judith? Is she dead?"

"She died years ago. I never said anything because of William. I suppose that no longer matters. I'll tell you about her death."

She told them not only about Judith's death but about her life. The only details she omitted were her own plotting for the girl's downfall and the use she had made of the daisy hatpin in the cottage in Atlantic City.

The other two women listened intently and when Elizabeth

had finished Nina sighed heavily. "All these years she's been buried under another name not far from the Meredith plot. What a
tragic end for a lovely girl. What happened to Mariette?"

"Her name has been changed to Daisy Huggins. She's fifteen
and lives on a farm near Albany. William was going to put her
into an orphanage, but I persuaded him to place her with the
family of one of our maids. Do you remember Gerda?"

Nina thought for a moment and then said, "A stern sort of
girl. Religious."

"Her husband is even sterner and fanatically religious but
Joshua Huggins is not unkind. I've visited Daisy twice a year and
although her childhood hasn't been ideal she's been well fed and
well looked after. Much better than it would have been in an
orphanage."

Nina extended her glass and it was refilled. "I suppose William provided for the child's support?"

"Until he had his stroke he did. After that I took care of
her." Elizabeth smiled. "I could hardly ask Alan for the money."

Susan snorted. "I can imagine what he'd have told you.
What's Daisy like? Does she look like either of her parents?"

"Actually like both of them. She has her father's height—
Daisy's taller than I am—and she has her mother's wonderful
skin and violet eyes. Among the Hugginses she looks like a pea-
cock in a henhouse. Spectacular! A mass of red gold hair and
she's so . . . so vital. I'm planning on bringing her home soon.
Daisy certainly isn't a Meredith but she is Alicia's half-sister and
her place is with us."

"What about the scandal?" Susan asked.

"Like yesterday's newspapers. Dead and gone. What was a
scandal then is no longer of interest."

"I agree and we'll be looking forward to meeting Daisy Huggins," Nina said. "By the way, Elizabeth, seeing this is con-
fession hour I have something to confess. I'm still puzzled about
Alan's death."

Elizabeth was lighting a cigarette. Without looking up she
sensed something behind the casual words. She felt a strong feeling of tension from her companions. Nina, she thought, who always saw so much and said so little. Could she know about Alan

and alcohol? Could William have confided in her? Elizabeth came to an instant decision. "I think Alan was murdered," she said abruptly.

There were no outcries, no exclamations. She had been right. They *did* know. Susan asked softly, "What makes you think that?"

"It was a closely guarded secret but Alan couldn't stand alcohol. He found out about his allergy when he was in the army."

Nina leaned forward. "Why didn't you tell the police?"

Elizabeth gazed into the other woman's shrewd eyes. "Alan was mixed up with gangsters. Had been for years. Before Dania left him she told me about it. Lately he was spending money like water. On himself and on his women. Maybe he was getting short of money and tried to get some from those hoodlums. Alan was a coward and a liar but he was cunning."

Susan's dark brows lifted. "You think he was shaking down *gangsters*? For that he'd have to be either mad or suicidal or both."

"Look at the facts. I never met Adam Tilton but William often mentioned him. He said the watchman was honest. Yet Tilton lied about Alan being drunk and he also must have lied about him being alone on that pier. So . . . Tilton must have been frightened into lying. Who would have the power to do that? Gangsters!"

"*Why* didn't you tell all this to the police?" Nina repeated.

"I've heard some of the police are being paid off by gangsters—"

"How right you are." Susan laughed. "The joke around City Hall is that the city payroll for our boys in blue is smaller than the one from racketeers."

"For all I knew the lieutenant handling Alan's case had been bought. Look at my position. I've four children in my care and soon will have a fifth. Women and children are vulnerable. I didn't care. Alan was dead. Nothing could bring him back."

"If he was that much of a fool, who'd want to?" Susan asked.

Draining her glass, Nina set it down. "So that's what happened to Judith and Alan."

Elizabeth said sadly, "That massive case of guilt you were

talking about, Susan, I have three. Judith, Alan, Aunt Van. I didn't check up on Aunt Van and show Lafe's letter to Sophie. I didn't tell the police about Alan. I didn't—"

"Allow me to blow your guilt away." Susan leaned over and squeezed Elizabeth's arm. "Alan's no loss. He lived like a weasel and he died like one. Judith? The young lovers may have been charming and great looking but remember this—while Lafe was casting Judith aside for a wealthy wife his love was busily casting him aside for William's wealth and position. Some romance. As for Aunt Van . . . Sophie had good reason to hate her mother anyway. Would Lafe's letter have made that much difference? Sophie was mad."

Elizabeth got to her feet, smiled down at the girl, and touched her glossy curls. "You know something. Edward was quite correct. You *are* good medicine."

"My daughter, the lawyer." Nina chuckled. "Phone tomorrow, Elizabeth, and we'll make arrangements with Mr. Pierce."

Elizabeth's smile vanished. "There won't be many mourners at Aunt Van's funeral."

"She may be luckier than some. Only the people who care will be there."

Late that evening, after a weary Albert had returned from his club and gone to bed, Susan found her mother in the kitchen making coffee. Leaning against the doorjamb, the girl smiled triumphantly. "So, your circumstantial evidence against the defendant has been shot to smithereens. Not only did Elizabeth explain away all your evidence plausibly but she volunteered the information."

Measuring coffee into the percolater, her mother set it on a burner. "I believe the definition of plausible is seeming to be probable but open to doubt."

"I'm not inexperienced and I'd say every word she said was the truth."

"What about the words she didn't say."

Throwing back her head, Susan hooted with laughter. "You really are the devil's advocate, aren't you? Be a sport, mother, and admit Elizabeth is actually what she appears to be—a nice, middle-aged, maiden lady doing her best to raise a batch of orphans. She's not a villain—she's more of a martyr. She's dug into her own pocket to raise a child who has no claim on her."

Her mother opened a cupboard and took down a couple of mugs. "Where does the martyr's sudden wealth come from?"

"What an imagination you have." Susan thoughtfully spooned sugar into her mug. "Okay, I'll let *my* imagination run wild too. Elizabeth is craftily shaking down a big bad gangster for lots of dough."

Nina nearly dropped the milk bottle. "You don't believe *that*, do you?"

"Careful! Of course I don't. Elizabeth is no more suicidal than Alan was. Possibly years ago William made some sort of settlement on her. Maybe she's been lucky with the horses. Maybe she has a still in the basement. It's none of our business anyway. Is it?"

"No," her mother agreed. "It's none of our business."

— 30 —

There were few mourners at the church service and even fewer followed Aunt Van's hearse to the cemetery. Besides Elizabeth, the Flanderses, and John and Edward Stokes, there were only the old cook Aggie and, supporting her, Cookie and Briggs. Aggie's grief became increasingly vocal and tender-hearted Cookie, who detested both Aunt Van and Aggie, burst into a sympathetic accompaniment. Beneath the cooks' howling the words of the minister were drowned out. As no reception had been planned the mourners shook hands, exchanged a few words, and went their separate ways. Nina and Susan bore off a weeping Aggie, and Briggs drove Elizabeth and Cookie home.

In the hall Elizabeth took off the black felt hat with the heavy veil she'd worn to three funerals, and handed it to Irene.

"Put it in that box for the church rummage sale."

"It's a nice hat, miss. Bit of ribbon and some flowers and it would sure look good on my mom."

"By all means give it to her. Irene, tell the staff I want to speak to them this afternoon about two. I'm planning a treat for this evening. A movie and dinner afterwards for all of you and the children."

"That's sure nice of you, miss. I've been wanting to go to *I Am a Fugitive from a Chain Gang.* Paul Muni's in it and I'm crazy about him."

"No. That's too adult for the children and would give Alicia nightmares. Opie likes westerns and Alicia and the twins like musicals. We can decide later. Now, I have some work to finish in the library. Under no circumstances are you to interrupt me."

"Another overdue account to settle, miss?"

The old maid smiled slightly. "Irene, this one is current."

Locking the library door behind her, Elizabeth glanced at the telephone and the black instrument seemed to taunt her. Butterfly wings were brushing against the walls of her stomach and as she stretched her hand out she noticed her fingers were trembling. Yes, she admitted, I'm frightened. Anyone with any sense would be frightened of this next move in the deadly game of chess that had begun when she had mailed those two envelopes. But she could delay no further. After she'd paid her share of Aunt Van's funeral only a small amount of banknotes was left in Opie's Box. She needed money and she needed it soon.

Taking a deep breath she reached for the telephone and gave the operator the number she'd memorized from her cousin's diary. A gruff male voice answered, repeating the number. "I would like to speak with Leo Carelli."

"Who's talking?"

"Elizabeth Meredith."

"Whatta want?"

"That is between Mr. Carelli and me." The line hummed and Elizabeth said hastily, "At least give him a message. Tell Mr. Carelli it's a matter of life and death." The line went dead and Elizabeth hung up the phone. Could that have been the gentlemanly gangster? No. The voice was too coarse, too uneducated.

Restlessly, she wandered around the room, willing her eyes away from the hands on the mantel clock. She switched on the radio, heard a raucous voice singing *Mammy*, and turned it off. She brushed a grain of dust from the glass on Opie's photograph and straightened a gilt frame. In her stomach the butterflies grew even more active and when the telephone pealed she jumped. She let it ring four times before she reached for it.

This voice, although cultured, was as terse as the first. "Whose life or death?"

"Yours, Mr. Carelli."

"Where?"

"My home. The address is—"

"I know the address. When?"

"Seven tonight."

"I'll be there."

Replacing the telephone, Carelli swung his chair around and gazed down at the river. He was aware of Sal's silent displeasure. After moments, Sal growled, "I don't like it one little bit."

"I'm vastly intrigued. What could Miss Meredith possibly want with me?"

"No good. Probably wants to finish the job that ratty nephew of hers started."

"Cousin, Sal. Miss Meredith's Alan's second cousin."

"I don't give a damn if she was his mother." Moving around where he could see Carelli's face, Sal glowered down at him. "Mr. C., you really going to that house?"

"I am. I can hardly envision a maiden lady in her fifties waiting with a gun."

"She could hide an army of McCaul's soldiers in that place. I'm putting my foot down. You walk in there tonight with lotsa protection or . . ."

"Or what?" Carelli's golden eyes flickered over his lieutenant's face. Then his thin lips curled into a brief smile. "You *were* right about Alan. So . . . call out the troops, Sal."

It looks like an invasion, Elizabeth thought wildly, as she watched three black cars drawing up. From her post by a drawing-room window she could see the doors of two of them opening

and men moving into the shadows and circling around toward the
alley. There was no sign of life from the one in the middle. Leo
the Lion's, she decided, and fought down an insane desire to
laugh. What would William think of gangsters surrounding their
house, of a man called the king of the beasts waiting to see if all
was clear?

She shivered and retreated to the hall. In the gilded mirror
her reflection stared back at her. The expression on that face was
composed and gave no hint of butterfly wings, now more like the
leathery wings of a bat, trying to break through her stomach lining. What a day it had been! First the funeral, then getting the
servants and children out of the house, and racing upstairs to
dress. For the first time in her memory she hadn't known what to
wear. She pulled on her mulberry crepe and then tore it off. She
selected a new summer dress with caped sleeves and tried it. In
both dresses she felt . . . feminine and vulnerable. In desperation
she donned her new purchases from Saks. The black skirt and
sweater made her look taller and slimmer. Against cashmere William's pearls glimmered richly. She shot another look at her reflection in the hall mirror and thought hysterically, I should have
bought a bulletproof vest. Suicidal, Susan had said, anyone who
is mad enough to threaten a gangster is suicidal.

The doorbell shrilled and Elizabeth counted ten before she
reached for it. When she swung it open the bats' wings were
abruptly drowned out by the terrible thudding of her heart. Two
huge men towered over her. Both wore fedoras pulled down over
brutal faces. Both wore overcoats, the one on the right in blue,
the other in a bilious shade of green. The men's right hands were
stuck into patch pockets. The bulges in the pockets were much
too large for just hands. Guns. They were pointing guns at *her.*

Which one was Carelli? Which brute was the man she must
deal with?

Blue Coat stepped one way, Green Coat the other. A man
in a black overcoat, a white fedora, and a white silk scarf moved
up between them. The cultured voice she'd heard earlier said,
"Miss Meredith, I presume?"

"Please come in, Mr. Carelli."

He came in with his two burly guards at his heels. They
didn't stay with him. Blue Coat moved into the drawing room,

Green Coat strode into the library. As Elizabeth watched incredulously they reappeared, Green circling her to go down the hall, Blue heading toward the staircase. "What . . ."

"A necessary precaution," Carelli told her smoothly. "They have orders to check out the premises."

"There's no one in this house but me. The servants and the children are out for the evening. I give you my word."

From the shadow of the hat brim, he regarded her. Then he said, "I'm inclined to take your word." He raised his voice. "Moxie, Pete. Back."

Like well-trained dogs they fell back and stationed themselves on either side of their master. Carelli was taller than Elizabeth but between the two men he looked like a stripling. "Where would you like to talk, Miss Meredith?"

"In the library." Her eyes brushed Green Coat. "I'd hoped . . . I'd rather speak with you in private."

Again she was conscious of shadowed eyes fixed on her face. "Very well." The white hat jerked. "Out."

Blue Coat protested. "Boss, Sal said not to let you outta sight!"

The hat jerked again and the men left. Carelli closed the door and removed his hat and scarf. He shrugged out of his topcoat. Under it he wore a conservative dark suit. "You must forgive my men's behavior, Miss Meredith. They're accustomed to dealing with a rough element."

As Elizabeth hung his clothes neatly on brass hooks she decided that as far as danger was concerned she'd pick the two hoodlums over their master. Carelli was a shock. She'd braced herself for a man looking like Mario with dark eyes and hair and a swarthy skin. Carelli was as fair as Alicia, with smooth blond hair and a delicate skin. He had a high color and a charming smile but those *eyes*. Neither the smile nor the charm reached icy golden eyes.

In the library she tried to steer Carelli toward the chair she'd positioned in front of the desk. She'd feel better with the width of the desk between them. Instead he wandered around the room as she watched the decisive, graceful movements of his slender body. He paused in front of her grandfather's painting. "Oliver

Pendrell, founder of the American branch of the Meredith clan. The youngest son of a baronet."

"An impoverished baronet."

"Granted but still a peer of the realm. And he certainly rectified that. Married the heiress to a shipping line and established the Meredith Lafroux Company."

"You know a great deal about my family."

"A hobby of mine. Tracing distinguished lines. Ah, and are these charming children all Merediths?"

"All but that one." Elizabeth pointed at the snapshot of Daisy Huggins. The plaited hair, loose cotton dress, and clumsy boots couldn't hide the girl's fresh young beauty. "Daisy is Alicia's half sister and will also be living here. This is Alicia, Alan's young sister, and these are his twin daughters. Jess and Katie are eleven. The boy in the uniform is their brother. Also an Oliver Pendrell but we call him Opie."

"Interesting." He picked up the twins' picture. "One harmless little dumpling and one far from harmless." He pointed to Jess. "If I were you, Miss Meredith, I'd watch this one."

"You're most discerning but tell me your reason."

"My wife's young brother had eyes like hers. Flat, hard. And he . . . but I'm forgetting why I'm here. Would you explain this matter of my life and my death."

"Please be seated." Again she tried to steer him toward the desk but he moved away and sank down on the sofa. "Would you care for refreshment?"

"Dry sherry, if you have it." He ran an appreciative hand over the leather arm. "This is a wonderful room. You're fortunate to live in a house like this one."

She busied herself with a decanter. "You like antiques?"

"I must. I buy enough of them. But buying someone else's past isn't the same as inheriting it. Knowing your ancestors used these chairs, that desk, handled those books."

Handing him the glass, she sank down in the chair opposite him. Between them was a small cherry table. Not as reassuring as the desk would have been but it must serve. He sipped his sherry and smiled. "Excellent. At a guess I'd say older than I am."

"William laid this sherry down a couple of years before

Alan's birth. I believe my cousin was a friend of yours."

"Hardly a friend. An acquaintance. He married a girl who worked in one of my clubs but of course you know that. Has Alan some bearing on this meeting?"

"He's the sole reason for it. Alan died penniless. While I'm explaining my reason for calling you I would like you to consider my position. I have five young people to raise and to educate and I have this house, which you appear to admire, to run."

"A grievous position, Miss Meredith. Perhaps I can help. Would you consider selling this house?"

"As you well know that is impossible. This house is the property of Alan's son."

Golden eyes enviously regarded the room. "Perhaps you should rent it. I'd be willing to offer—"

"*No.*" She softened her refusal. "I can't picture the children being raised anywhere but right here."

"In that case all I can offer is my condolences on your cousin's recent death."

Elizabeth's lips twitched in a tiny smile. "Let's just wish him better luck on his next venture."

Not a flicker of emotion passed across the man's sensitive features. "*How* may I help?"

Her move. One of the final moves in this desperate game of chess. Don't underestimate your opponent, she warned herself, under that attractive exterior is a ruthless man. If Carelli ever even suspects you were the one to put his Joy in jeopardy . . . She said slowly, "I have attended three funerals in less than a month. William's, Alan's, and their aunt's. I am physically and emotionally exhausted. So, Mr. Carelli, we won't fence. I was the one who wrote you that letter of warning. To prove it I'll describe it. Five-and-ten stationery. Block printing. McCaul has been tipped about Wednesday and Joy. Meredith ratted."

"I am in your debt. You saved my life and also the life of someone dear to me. Why?"

"I couldn't afford to allow you to die."

He extended a slim gold case and when she took a gold-tipped cigarette he lit it with a matching lighter. "I hardly think Alan would have confided in you. I gathered he thought less than highly of you."

"The feeling was mutual." She rose and tapped her knuckles on the paneling between two bookcases. "A cloakroom is next to this room. If you hold a water glass on this spot you can eavesdrop on what is said in here. When I heard what Alan was planning with the McCauls I alerted you. For that I paid a price. Alan was no loss but his support for this house was. You had my cousin murdered, Mr. Carelli."

"The inquest called his death accidental."

"But the coroner didn't know Alan never drank. He couldn't. Alcohol would have killed him. No, don't interrupt. I know what you're going to say. His flask, his frequent appearances of drunkenness. Acting, Mr. Carelli. Alan was an excellent actor. But this weakness of his is in army records and I've written a letter to refer the proper authorities to these records. It also recounts his partnership with you."

Light flared in his amazing eyes. "You overheard that too. Miss Meredith, I'm afraid word of mouth doesn't carry much weight. Now that Alan is dead it will be impossible to prove a link between us."

"The evidence I have is written. A young friend aptly described my cousin the other evening. She called Alan a weasel. He was a cheat and a coward and a liar. He lied to you. He wrote everything down. Vanity, I suppose, thinking everything he felt or saw or heard was of interest. Though, in this case, I imagine his diary would be of great interest in certain quarters."

"I presume the diary is in a safe place."

"Both the diary and the letter are in good hands. In the event of my death or harm befalling any member of my family the package will be handed over to the F.B.I."

He smiled. "Not the city police?"

Her lips relaxed and she smiled back at him. "Hardly. The diary recounts the names of the police officers on your payroll. In fact, the lieutenant in charge of Alan's case is mentioned twice. Incidentally, don't think this package is with any of my friends. I'm well aware of how powerful you are and I wouldn't endanger a person I'm fond of."

His fair brows rose. "Is this . . . this evidence in New York?"

"That question I won't answer."

He finished his sherry and Elizabeth refilled his glass. As she tipped the decanter she noticed her hand was now as steady as a rock. After a time Carelli said slowly, "I rather think you're bluffing, Miss Meredith. I don't doubt you overheard various things but I don't believe this damning diary exists."

"I'm prepared to prove it does." The old maid went to the desk and extracted several sheets of notepaper from a drawer. "Before I disposed of the diary I copied down some entries that will have interest for you." She spread the pages out on the cherry table. "Here we have the list of the police officers you control. It itemizes the amount you pay them and how and when. Alan was thorough. This is an account of the brutal killing— Alan calls it bumping off—of one of your rivals. Peter Funicelli. It names the men in your employ who tortured him and then shot him in the back of the head." She tapped another sheet. "This is the most horrifying of all. A murder you did yourself. Earlier you mentioned your wife's young brother. Name—Charles Ziffona. Nickname—Chuck. Eighteen years old. Because he was family you did the job yourself. You took him to a wrecker's yard in Jersey and slid an icepick into his left ear. His body was jammed into the trunk of a derelict car and you put an ebony rosary in his hand."

There was still no emotion in the man's face. He merely nodded. "You're wondering how I could do this to a boy so dear to my wife. It was to spare her pain. Angel's a devout woman and if she'd ever known . . . Chuck was a child molester. He attacked two little girls, one three and the other five. Both children were hurt badly. I warned him. His third victim was my daughter. I interfered in time to save her but I knew Chuck had to die. Angel would have suffered more knowing what her brother was than she did when he died. She thinks the boy was killed by Finn McCaul."

Elizabeth slid back into the depths of the leather chair. "At the end of this account Alan added that he wondered how your wife would react if she knew her husband had killed her brother."

"He really was slimy, wasn't he?"

"You picked a poor silent partner."

"He was a Meredith. I thought he was honorable."

"Alan bore the name but he wasn't a true Meredith." Gathering the sheets up, she went to the hearth and touched a match to them. They flamed up briefly and then charred into ashes. "Still think I'm bluffing, Mr Carelli?"

"The diary exists and it *is* damning. Now I suppose we get to the amount you're going to blackmail me for."

"I *am* a Meredith and I don't blackmail. All I want is what rightfully belongs to me. You have in your keeping the residue of the family money."

"You will want it returned?"

"Not at present. According to Alan he was receiving some of the interest on his investment. The rest built the capital up. I'd like to be your partner on the same terms."

He gave her an amazed look and broke into laughter. It sounded as though he were genuinely amused. "How nicely you put it. You make me sound like your stockbroker. Very well, same terms. A weekly payment. How long do you intend to leave your capital with me?"

"A year. Perhaps two. Until it is large enough to warrant investment in blue-chip stocks."

"By that time it will be a small fortune. Crime does pay."

"I fully intend to make it into a large fortune. One point does worry me."

"And that is?"

"When the money is returned to me will there be . . . I'm not quite certain how to phrase this."

His mouth twitched with amusement. "I take your meaning. You're wondering if the funds can be traced back to unsavory sources, if awkward questions will be asked. No, my dear Miss Meredith, nothing of that sort will happen. I employ a staff of lawyers and accountants to avoid difficulties like that." He again extended his gold cigarette case. "There is a point that worries me too. Should you die a natural death or in an accident exactly what happens to the diary? Suppose you are killed in a car crash or by falling down the stairs?"

"I've made no provision for accidents. Not after Alan's so-called accident. They're too easy to arrange. If I die, no matter how, the diary and letter go directly to the F.B.I."

"That seems unfair. It would appear I am the one at risk."

"I run equal risk. In the event of your death what would happen to the family money?"

"Again I take your point. It seems we will have an active interest in each other's well-being, Miss Meredith." Crushing out his cigarette, he rose. "Our business is concluded. If you wish to speak with me ring the same number you did today and leave a message. Say 'Silent needs active' and I'll be in touch." He waved toward the wall. "If I were you I'd have something done about that weak point. Someone might eavesdrop on you."

"That has already been attended to."

"I should have known." In the hall he adjusted the silk scarf in precise folds. "Only two more things. One remark, one question. Having met you I think I would have returned your money without the diary. You remind me of someone who is dear to me. She doesn't look like you but the way you move and speak, the way you lift your chin brings her to mind."

His librarian, Elizabeth thought, Joy Harrison. "The question, Mr. Carelli?"

"You're a lady and obviously live a sheltered life. Do you have a clear idea where the profit from your investment will come from? It comes from prostitution, gambling, extortion, illegal sales of both alcohol and drugs, and—"

"Murder."

"Precisely. Does this disturb your conscience?"

Elizabeth glanced into the mirror. Expensive clothes, perfect pearls, professionally styled hair, and smooth, well cared for skin. Nicely fitting dentures. She looked younger and more attractive than when she had entered this house twenty-one years ago. She smiled. "Nearly all my life I have been a poor relative. If I'd been born into the wealthy side of the family I might have developed much differently. I might have been a nicer person. But early I learned two facts. A poor relative must live by her wits and can't afford the luxury of a conscience. Rather like you. You too must live by your wits and a conscience would only be a drawback. We are not dissimilar, Mr. Carelli."

He threw back his head and roared with laughter. "An interesting corollary, Miss Meredith, and one that has never occurred to me. Poor relatives and gangsters! I have a feeling we're going to be excellent partners." He held out a hand and with no hesitation Elizabeth took it. He squeezed her hand gently and released it. Still chuckling he opened the door. On the steps his guards were posted. Blue Coat stepped in front of him and Green Coat fell in behind. Men were moving out of the shadows, returning to the cars. The invasion was over.

Shutting the door, Elizabeth snapped the lock and braced her back against the panel. The butterflies no longer fluttered, her heart was beating normally, but a sensation of lassitude was overwhelming her. For several days she had eaten practically nothing; for a number of nights she hadn't slept. She didn't think she could force food down but this night she would sleep.

Forcing herself away from the door, she gathered up the sherry glasses and the ashtray full of gold-topped butts. Taking them to the kitchen, she washed them and emptied the ashtray. Then she moved heavily down the hall, pausing to switch the lights on in the dining room. She touched the heavy chair at the head of the table. When Opie was old enough to be head of the family he would sit here. In the meantime it was hers. She wandered into the drawing room and turned off the lamps. When she returned to the library Oliver Pendrell's glacial eyes leaped out at her. "So, you disapprove of the man who sat on your sofa tonight," she whispered. "Desperate times call for desperate measures. I'll bet you used a few yourself."

She gently touched William's pictured face. "I kept my promise. This house and the family are safe." She turned off a light and the only remaining lamp shone on the row of photographs on the refectory table. Elizabeth took a long look at Jess. "The Lion was quite correct. You'll bear watching. Any trouble will come from you." Her eyes sought Opie and lovingly dwelt on the face under the peaked cap. "My darling, I won. I'll watch you grow and in time marry. I'll be at your wedding and if I live as long as Grandfather did I'll see your children. They'll be my grandchildren as you're my son. No harm will come to you." In his uniform the boy stood as straight and as proud as a young soldier. Involuntarily she glanced at the other picture of a young soldier. By a trick of light it looked as though George's gaze was sad.

War, Elizabeth thought, war had taken this boy from William. Suddenly she shivered. Could war take her beloved boy, reach cold, bloodstained fingers into this house? *No.* George Meredith had given his life in a war to end all wars. Opie was safe.

Turning off the lamp, she went into the hall. She'd leave lights on here for the children and the servants. An untouched newspaper sat on the marble-topped table. She glanced at the front page. Another article about that man in Germany. The silly little man with the dangling lock of hair and the toothbrush mustache. She must have noticed it earlier. This must be the reason for the fanciful thoughts about war and Opie. Ridiculous! Adolf Hitler was a joke, a foolish little man who bore a marked resemblance to Charlie Chaplin.

Smiling and wrapped in an aura of supreme confidence, Cousin Elizabeth slowly mounted the staircase of the house she had made her own.